HIS MOUTH SEEMED TO BURN AGAINST HER FLESH...

He said nothing, only lifted her in his arms and carried her to the bed. One oil lamp cast a soft glow on the rose draperies.

"No, no, no," said Katie, trying to push him away. "I cannot do this . . . I must not . . ."

"The body of a girl, the heart of a lioness, the spirit of a winged bird. I have longed for you," he whispered. "I have longed for such a time that now I burn intensely. Do not deny me, my songbird."

She moaned a little, pushing at his strong shoulders. He rose like a mountain above her. She was a small person at the foot of the mountain. Her mind was dazed, confused, as he went on caressing her. Something was burning inside her, a softening heat, a tremulous longing. . . .

The
Court
of the
Flowering Peach

Janette Radcliffe

A DELL BOOK

Published by
Dell Publishing Co., Inc.
1 Dag Hammarskjold Plaza
New York, New York 10017

Dell ® TM 681510, Dell Publishing Co., Inc.

ISBN: 0-440-11497-7

Printed in the United States of America

First printing—September 1981

*The
Court
of the
Flowering
Peach*

Katherine Adair gazed down at the drawing page, scarcely seeing the delicate trailing vines she had been sketching. Her slim hand rested on the polished dark mahogany table, the white muslin sleeve with the embroidered band of peach blossoms pushed back to her elbow.

"My word, Katie, what a deal of noise there is, to be sure." Her father's gentle brown eyes gazed into space as he frowned slightly.

Their wing of the London town house of the China merchant Mr. Douglas Llewellyn overlooked back streets, and sounds of carriages and gaiety rarely reached them. The large library, the study, and their private rooms were muffled as though to shut them off from the merry world that surged around them.

"It's the wedding, Father." Katie lifted her head also and listened to the shrieks of laughter, the music of violins and pianoforte, the crash of a bottle on the cobblestones outside.

"Ah—the wedding." Owen Adair's thin, scholarly face shadowed. He stood to pace to the door, peer out, then return. His steps were noiseless on the fine red and brown Persian carpet. He was fifty-five, but looked older; his dark hair had grayed; his skin was pale. He had worked hard for many years for his revered patron, Douglas Llewellyn, and the Llewellyns had been good to him. They had given him a home and work—a refuge—since the death of his wife. And Matilda Llewellyn had raised Katie as her own daughter, almost.

Nonetheless, there was always the barrier. Mr. Adair was a clerk; Katie, his only child. The schoolmaster from Cornwall, near Llewellyn Hall, close to the border of Wales, had followed devotedly his hobby of Chinese language, culture, customs, silk fabrics. Mr. Llewellyn, discovering Adair's passion for the Orient, had employed him as a clerk to assist in his work.

Mr. Adair had proved invaluable. He could translate the letters to and from the Oriental markets in Canton and Macao. He could keep the elaborate complex books and manage to arrange the accounts so they were comprehensible. And he and his daughter had such artistic ability that Mr. Llewellyn had employed both of them in recent years to draw patterns pleasing to the English taste, for the silk makers of China to follow in making up silks for them.

Katie had learned Mandarin along with her French and German studies. When only twelve years of age, she was allowed to assist her father with the books. And her creative talent, her father admitted, was far superior to his. She had learned of Chinese customs and ways from him, studied nightly more books and papers. And at eighteen, she knew as much about the business of the China trade as her father and nearly as much as his patron.

A tap at the opened door to the main hall startled them both. Mr. Adair turned to greet Mrs. Matilda Llewellyn as she rustled in, splendid in a gown of purple tussore silk, a gray and purple plumed turban on her graying head. Katie stood also, respectfully.

Mrs. Llewellyn's face was weary. She was rouged, but that did not conceal the tired lines, the unhappiness in her fine dark eyes.

"Katie, my dear, you may come now and survey the wedding party from the gallery. The maids have gathered. Mrs. Garrison will afterward serve you some punch and wedding cake."

Katie hesitated. She had no desire to survey the radiant, triumphant bride. Her heart ached for Rupert—how unhappy he must be, best man for his brother when he longed to be the bridegroom.

Mr. Adair held a chair for the matron. She sank into it with a heavy sigh. "I should not remain. How peaceful it is here, my dear Mr. Adair. Would the wedding were over! I must soon begin to train my new daughter in her duties." Her mouth set firmly. "She cannot gad about forever. Her mother has sadly indulged the girl."

Katie and her father exchanged a swift glance. Selina Bedingfield had led many suitors a merry dance. The beautiful girl had burst on the London season last spring as a magnificent jewel, as one admirer phrased it. She had settled on Rupert Llewellyn, newly returned from the Napoleonic Wars, romantic, ramrod-straight in his blue and crimson uniform—and so wealthy! Rupert had fallen desperately in love with the sparkling blond girl with eyes like violets.

But the violet eyes then discovered his elder brother, Terence—rake, Corinthian, much more fun than serious Rupert. And Terence was on the outer fringes of the friends of the prince regent. Terence had usurped Rupert's position as favorite within a month.

Mrs. Llewellyn sighed again and said absently, "She does not act as a lady should. I blame her foolish mother. However—" She struggled out of the chair, wincing as her swollen feet held her splendid bulk once more. "I shall train her. I *shall* train her. Come, Katie. Would that Selina had your sweet, docile disposition!"

Katie followed silently in the wake of her patroness, like a small tugboat in the wake of a fine three-masted schooner. Mrs. Llewellyn went upstairs and downstairs, as the hall wandered this way and that, up a couple of stairs, and down, in the old-fashioned manner, and she panted as they arrived in the musicians' gallery overlooking the great hall.

"There, now, dear, enjoy yourself! Are they not splendid?" she added proudly, gazing down into the hall.

The beautiful bride in a magnificent gown of white taffeta and a jacket of white ermine, her veil flung back, was the center of attention. She had reluctantly consented to the January wedding in 1816 as Terence did not want to wait. Terence had laughed at her objections and gaily promised to remain in London for the honeymoon and the London season to follow. He knew his bride. She had no wish to retire modestly to the country, as was the custom. She adored London, she declared, and the season was just about to begin. Why should they miss such fun? Besides, she detested the country . . . in the winter, she hastened to add, under Mrs. Llewellyn's steely gaze.

The housekeeper, Mrs. Frances Garrison, rustled up to them, extra-fine in her black silk.

"Katie may remain for half an hour, and see that she has cake and punch," said Mrs. Llewellyn, with a friendly nod at the respectful maids, gathered along the railing, smart in their black and white uniforms.

She went down the stairs, clinging to the banister, and soon joined the crowd milling about the great hall and the two huge opened drawing rooms.

Mrs. Garrison gestured to two maids to give Katie room at the railing, and they parted to make way for her. She was one of them, yet not really. She belonged nowhere, she thought, gazing down into the rooms below. The music was louder here, she realized as she caught a glimpse of the musicians in the east drawing room and of Terence, splendid in crimson velvet, his silk shirt ruffled, his laughter loud. He was dancing with one of the bridesmaids, one in beautiful yellow silk.

Katie's gaze wandered over the crowd, searching, searching. Then she saw him. Rupert, in his dark blue velvet, his face sober, his head erect, his back straight. How gallant he looked, how fine and handsome, his dark head with its curly locks that no amount of pomade would keep down. His deep blue Celtic eyes, how direct and honest they were. She liked Rupert ever so much better than Terence, who was a tease and an idler. She had no liking for idlers, especially when they made dear Mr. Llewellyn work so much harder. He had tried so to teach Terence the business.

Rupert glanced up toward the gallery. Katie shrank back, but the crush of maids prevented her from moving far. Then she lost sight of him again. Her eyes caught Mrs. Bedingfield, a creature to marvel at, plump and blond and laughing, in her deep red velvet gown that was held about her with long purple sashes. Her mink cape rivaled her daughter's ermine, both gifts of Terence.

Mrs. Bedingfield looked triumphant. The marriage of her only daughter, and to such a very wealthy man! A friend of the prince regent's, as near the top of the trees as a modestly wealthy widow could expect to get. And Selina, glowing and happy, so beautiful in her bridal gown . . .

Katie turned away, smiled politely at the maids who made way for her. She moved toward the stairs to the upper floor. Mrs. Garrison moved with her, saying quietly, "Katie, there is cake and some fruit punch in the kitchen—"

Katie shook her head blindly. She had no heart for merrymaking. Mrs. Garrison put her hand on Katie's arm for a moment, then let her go. She was a kindly woman and saw much of what went on in the household.

Katie moved up the stairs to the next floor and paused to wipe quickly at her eyes with a tiny lace handkerchief. Then a voice behind her made her start violently.

"Katie? Why have you not come to the reception?"

It was Rupert, taking the steps two at a time. He came to her in the long hall that led to her wing of the house. She tried to smile at him; her heart ached so for his grief. His face was pale, but he had a set smile on it, and his shoulders were well back.

"I was not invited, Rupert, you know this."

He frowned. "Mother?"

She nodded.

He sighed. "She has a singular sense of propriety. You are practically one of the family."

"No, I am an employee, a clerk," she said gently. "Do not trouble yourself, Rupert. I understand."

He looked down at her. He was so tall, so fine, gazing down at her from his superior height of about six feet to her five feet three. "Well, miss, we can have a dance at least." He said it with his quick charming smile, that unexpected mischievous grin that had taken her heart when she first met him. So serious usually, then that boyish grin and the gentleness and comprehension that were like his father's.

"Oh, Rupert, thank you, but your mother—"

"She is not up here," he said, and put his arm out to her. She set her hand on it, and solemnly, to the more faint sounds of the music, they danced as though in a set.

She forgot her simple muslin gown, her feeling of being lonely and out of place. She forgot everything but that Rupert, the man she had adored since her girlhood, was dancing with her, holding her hand high as they turned to the music, smiling down at her as they bowed to each other.

The music ended. He bowed a final time; she curtsied deeply, then rose.

"You will have something to drink, Miss Adair?" he asked with mock seriousness.

"Law, sir, it would go to my poor head," she simpered.

He laughed softly. "What's in the bowls down there surely would! Selina insisted on adding bottles of good champagne to the fruit punch—I hate those mixtures. I like things straight and uncomplicated," said Rupert, his face shadowing. But he had said her name naturally. Perhaps he would get over her in time. He had had three months to accustom himself to the fact that Selina was marrying his brother.

Katie smiled and shook her head at him. He reached out and gently touched her head. "What have you done to your hair?" he asked. "Where are the long braids?"

She had not worn long braids since she had turned eighteen this past April. But he had not noticed until today!

"Oh, I decided to put up my hair in a chignon," she said. "It keeps my hair out of my face and is more— neat." Also more demure, more like a maid, she thought bitterly.

"It makes you look older," he said thoughtfully. "More of Mother's ideas?"

Katie looked uncomfortable. It had been Mrs. Llewellyn's suggestion, and her maid had put it up that way first at the suggestion of her patron. However, she could not criticize his mother to Rupert.

"Well, I must go back to that—party," he said. He bowed again to her, solemnly, then went down the stairs, taking them two at a time in his high boots. She gazed after him until he had disappeared around a bend in the stairway, and then she returned to her wing.

She found her father absorbed in sketching, and she seated herself once more on the high stool before the mahogany table. They worked in silence, in a quiet communication of the heart and mind. Her father understood her, and she was grateful for that.

The following afternoon they were working again on the sketching when a tap came at the now-closed door to the main hall. Katie had no wish to catch a glimpse of the newlyweds who had the rooms directly below theirs, a floor of their own and newly decorated drawing room, bedrooms, dining room. Selina had insisted on it. If she could not "yet" have a house of her own, she would have separate apartments, she had said coldly. It had caused quite a commotion in the Llewellyn house and much whispering among the servants, who figured that "Madame will be coming and going at all hours and not wanting her in-laws to know."

Mrs. Bedingfield remained in the smart flat which Terence had had newly furnished for her. She would continue to entertain as she had in the past.

Mr. Adair went to the door, and in came Mr. Llewellyn and Rupert. Mr. Adair bowed to them, and Katie stood up automatically.

"Do not let us disturb you, my dear," said the older Mr. Llewellyn to Katie, and gave her a pat on the shoulder as he peered to see what she was working on. "Charming, charming! A nightingale in the wisteria—quite lovely!"

She glowed at his praise and thanked him. Then she sat down again, intercepting a kindly smile from Rupert. Rupert looked as though he had not slept much. The party had gone on well past midnighht the night before.

"Mr. Adair, I have another pupil for you," said Mr. Llewellyn, putting his hand now on Rupert's shoulder. The father and son were much of a height and had the same fine features, the noble nose and firm chin. The older man's hair had grayed, but in his wine velvet morning gown and well-folded neckerchief of white lawn, he looked the equal of any Corinthian,

thought Katie, proudly. And Rupert—in his dark blue
suit and modest white shirt with only one ruffle at the
throat, he looked splendid as he always did.

"Indeed, sir, I shall be proud to assist Mr. Rupert as
well as I can," said Mr. Adair, eyeing the young man
keenly.

"Good, good. I want him first taught the books;
show him how they work. Next week I want him to
come with me to the warehouses. You will accompany
us and help me explain how matters go. You know I
shall be sending our *China Princess* off to Canton this
March. I want Rupert to learn as well as Terence—"
Mr. Llewellyn gave a slight frown on saying the name
of his elder son, and there was a thoughtful pause.
Then he continued. "Well, well, Rupert will be a good
pupil and well suited. He knows the good of discipline and is accustomed to hard work."

"You have resigned your commission, Mr. Rupert?"
asked Mr. Adair.

"Aye. The army has little need of so many majors
now that old Boney is finally put away for good," said
Rupert. "I have resigned, and it has been accepted. I
must get to work and help Father as well as I can.
There is much to learn; I know this from the way you
and Father work so hard, Mr. Adair."

Mr. Llewellyn clapped his shoulder again; his face
glowed. "Ah, it is splendid work, and most interesting,
my son! The China trade! I myself sailed twice to
China and was reluctant to leave! If I had not had so
many responsibilities at this end, I should go again,
instead of leaving all the adventuring to my super-
cargoes! I have been thinking of sending Terence on the
next voyage."

There was a short silence. All were staring at him.

Rupert finally cleared his throat. "Terence, sir? You would send him? But he has just—just married—"

"It will be a pleasant and unusual jaunt for Selina," said Mr. Llewellyn with a firmness about his mouth that boded ill for any who contradicted him.

Katie thought: Selina! On a sea voyage! And trying to housekeep in Macao! She dared not look up again from her sketching as the men continued to converse. Presently Mr. Douglas Llewellyn left them, and Mr. Adair proceeded to show Rupert some of the books and correspondence.

The next weeks Rupert worked closely with them. He worked long hours, apparently accustomed to such. Terence, however, made a more reluctant pupil. He had been trained for some years but made many excuses to escape from performing duties at the warehouse, counting out trade goods and listening to his father's lectures on the Orient, and he fretted when Mr. Adair's long, complicated explanations of the Chinese and their ways kept him from his adored bride.

Selina came several times to the apartments of the Adairs, asking coldly for Terence, tapping her daintily shod foot angrily when she had to sit and wait for him. Several times she got up and left them and went out in her carriage with only her maid, a dour soul named Milbank, to accompany her.

Milbank was an older woman, with an ugly face and black hair slicked back in a bun; she wore the darkest of gray and black. But she adored her beautiful young mistress. She was a skilled hairdresser, able to tease Selina's blond locks into the latest fashions and even to invent more daring ones. She was a fine dressmaker, skilled with her needle in embroidery and lace. In short, Selina had found a gem and kept her for herself no matter how much her mother protested she needed Milbank with her.

It was not long before Katie began to hear rumors about Selina. She rose late and went out calling in the afternoons while Terence went to the warehouse. And she insisted on accepting every invitation for an evening of pleasure at the home of friends or at assembly rooms, returning in the wee hours of the morning. As a result, Terence himself would be late to Mr. Adair's rooms and missed many an explanation and much work. Selina continued to go out, whether or not her new husband accompanied her.

She was very popular with the gentlemen, though much less so with the ladies, and few came calling on her. She seemed to prefer it that way. One of the older maids whispered to Katie that an elegant viscount was enamored of Selina, as well as a rich young wastrel named Mr. Prestwick and another Corinthian close to the prince.

"But she is married, and so recently!" whispered Katie, shocked. She knew she should not encourage the maid, but she was fascinated.

The maid just shrugged. "All I know is when the day comes that that madame is mistress in this house, I'll be leaving! I've had a pleasant offer or two, and nothing could persuade me to remain here under that—that—well, I'll go! Mrs. Llewellyn has been a-trying to get the young Mrs. Llewellyn to learn the ways of the household, but she doesn't stay around enough to learn much, I'll tell you! And Mrs. Garrison, good soul that she is, was shaking her head the other day at the waste of fine foods and wines. Sending up trays at all hours, to have them come back half-eaten, bottles smashed. Fine parties they have in the apartments!!"

Though her rooms were muffled with thick carpets and fine tapestries, Katie still heard sounds. The apartments below theirs were filled with laughter, music, loud voices, and late-at-night quarreling and loud yelling. And Terence frequently had a sullen expression when he arrived in the morning for his schooling in Chinese ways.

On a bright February day, however, there was an unexpected treat. Mr. Douglas Llewellyn announced he was taking all of them, Katie included, to the wharves. The ship's captain had arrived and had been hired; the crew was being chosen, and now the final counts on the merchandise were going forward.

They all went down to the wharves in one large barouche, driven by a coachman and escorted by two footmen as outriders. Katie, in a warm rose woolen gown, with a cloak to match, was glowing with excitement. She had gone to the wharves infrequently, and it was always thrilling. The scents of the spices and the cedarwood, the smell of the saltwater, the sight of the fine sailing ships, even though their sails were not spread—all moved her to dreams. If only she had been born a boy! She could have gone a-sailing to the Orient also!

"Well, Katie, my dear," said the older man kindly, "your cheeks are pink today, and your brown eyes sparkle! You like the ships, eh?"

"Oh, yes, sir! It is most kind of you to invite me!" Her hands were clasped tight in her beaver muff, a gift of her employer on her eighteenth birthday. The matching hat sat neatly on her hair, fastened up in a demure manner.

"You are growing up a fine young lady. Mr. Adair is most proud of his daughter," said Mr. Llewellyn. He patted her arm. "Well, today we shall see that you do not work so much. Rupert, you will show her around the ship. Terence will accompany me to go over the store lists with Captain Potter."

Rupert said, "Yes, sir, gladly," and smiled kindly at Katie.

Terence made a little face. His eyes were bloodshot, and he kept yawning behind his gloved hand. More late nights, thought Katie. He would never learn this way. She wondered if his father had thought further about sending him to China.

They reached the wharves, and Rupert took Katie on his arm like a grand lady to show her over the huge ship. They climbed up the gangplank, and a sailor stared at her admiringly as Rupert began to explain what everything was.

"But you must have been on a ship before, Katie."

"Oh, years ago," she said quickly. She wanted him to linger, to hear the sound of his deep, clear voice as he talked to her.

He showed her the captain's quarters, and she admired the way the little cupboards fitted so well and the tables were fastened to the walls. He took her around to see where the ballast lay and explained how the stores of furs and machine goods would be set.

"On the return voyage the crates of porcelain will serve as both ballast and goods. On top of them will lie the silk crates, well above the waterline, so they will not spoil. And tucked about everywhere will be trunks of other materials, the carved ivory, jade, and, of course, the chests of tea. That must be very high, so it will not get wet in the fiercest of storms."

She nodded. She knew they earned much from the teas. Britain had taken to the China teas, and they commanded high prices. The silks were much desired, but there was such a high tarriff on silk products from other lands that Mr. Llewellyn sighed and often said he wondered why he continued the silk trade.

Much of the China silk came in raw form, to be finished in Britain. These were most welcome—huge bolts of raw creamy white silk, to be patterned in the English looms. Yet the Orientals did such magnificent work in silk weaving that Katie thought it far superior to British-made. She longed to travel one day to China to see the silk looms. However, even Mr. Llewellyn had not seen those. Foreigners were not allowed to wander about China at will; they were confined to Canton, and only to the factories (the display places and private apartments of ther merchants) on the waterfront on the Pearl River.

Rupert escorted her from the ship, and they went to join the other men, working on the accounts. Katie was then introduced to the captain Mr. Llewellyn had hired for this journey. Captain Abraham Potter was a red-haired man in his mid-forties, single, brusque, competent. His sea blue eyes saw much, thought Katie. She admired his uniform of blue with the gold braid on it. He talked little, listened much, and absorbed all quickly.

"You'll hire a supercargo for the goods, Mr. Llewellyn?" he asked.

"Aye, I will. But not yet," said Mr. Llewellyn thoughtfully. "I am forming a notion about that."

"As you will, sir. I'd like to be a-sailing by the end of March and get a lead on the voyage. The Cape can be a demon of a place at the wrong times," said the captain, nodding his red head wisely.

"March will suit me well. Now as for the sailors' grub, you'll get them the best. Well-fed and cared-for men will obey you willingly, eh?" said Mr. Llewellyn.

"My feelings exactly, sir. Couldn't say it better myself. Well-fed, well-treated men will respond to orders in the bad times as well as the good."

"I have always found it so," said Rupert quietly. "If one's men know one does his best always, and will treat his men as men, he need not fear the worst of battles."

Captain Porter nodded and stuck his pipe back into his mouth. Terence was yawning but finally said indifferently, "I don't see that it all matters so much. They receive their money at the end of the voyage and go spend it all. What matter how much or how little?"

"I do not seem to have taught you well, my son," said Mr. Douglas Llewellyn with displeasure. "Now, how does the count match on the beef and the rum?"

They went over the figures on that also as Katie waited quietly. She liked to gaze about the huge warehouse, to try to identify the different smells. Boxes of tea were being unloaded. And shelves held trays of other spices, camphor, cinnamon, pepper, coriander, delicious to sniff. Katie wandered farther, sniffing and looking and absorbing all the sights of the warehouse.

Rupert came looking for her presently, to find her standing fascinated where men unloaded crates of porcelain. One older man was opening the crates with great care and taking out samples of painted and glazed porcelain vases, dishes, bowls, strange octagon-shaped dishes, salt and pepper sets, chocolate pots, and tiny cups.

"Come, Katie, I will not lose you here." He laughed and tucked her gloved hand under his arm. She thrilled to the warm touch of his body under her hand. "Do you find this all fascinating, eh? Would you own some of those pieces?"

"Someday I shall," she murmured. She would save the money she was given, and instead of buying a gown, she thought she would wander about the shops and buy a vase such as the one she saw being removed from the case. She gazed at it longingly; it was beautiful, of a white glaze, with a flowered design in rose-pink and cream-colored flowers.

"Of course you shall," said Rupert comfortably, and drew her out into the cold sunshine to hand her into the barouche. "You have good taste, Katie; you shall have fine possessions one day."

Katie smiled back, glowing at his praise, yet thinking that in her silent apartments she would never have much money to indulge her tastes in beautiful objects.

Still, she could buy little pieces from time to time and treasure them. She might buy a small piece of green jade, carved as only the Chinese could carve it. And a lovely flowered vase, in which in the summer-time she would place a few flowers. One did not have to be wealthy to own and enjoy a few of the treasures of the earth. Her father had taught her that.

"The best treasures are of the mind, Katie, dear. I want your mind to be richly furnished with the most beautiful sights and sounds and the finest of reading. Those are the true treasures, those that are stored up where it counts." And he had tapped his high forehead. "And after that are the rich works of men's best minds and hands. Look at this piece of jade—" And he would hole up a piece of Mr. Llewellyn's jade, which he generously allowed them to set in cases in their rooms, and he would talk to her about the properties of jade and how the pieces were carved.

She was silent in the evening, as she and her father ate in their small dining room. She could hear the sounds below them, in Selina and Terence's apartments. They must be having another party. Music thumped, while the shrill voices penetrated even upstairs. Her father raised his eyebrows.

"Terence will be sleepy and inattentive again tomorrow," said Mr. Adair, fingering a fine orange before peeling it, as though he loved the texture and scent of it. "I would have him as well drilled in obedience and control as Rupert. However, Rupert has the advantage of being eight years an officer of His Majesty's army. He knows the value of schooling and training that a man must learn before he can do and teach."

"They are quite different men, Father," said Katie, eating her orange with satisfaction. "How juicy this is —and how kind of Mrs. Llewellyn to share their Christmas fruit! Rupert, you know, has a stern discipline. He always had, even as a boy. And in having control of himself, he can control others. Terence— well—he always loved his fun."

"Aye. There is much difference," said Mr. Adair. "I wonder—" But he hesitated, then stopped speech.

After dinner they retreated to their books. Katie

was reading a popular novel, a little guiltily, but her father only smiled.

"You have worked hard this week, Katie. Enjoy your little amusements; tomorrow will bring more work to us."

So he read his Chinese work on silk weaving, and she read her novel, in contented silence.

2

Trouble finally erupted in the Llewellyn house. The maids were whispering, flushed with excitement. Katie, absorbed in her work, was finally aware of it.

Selina had been flirting with a young man, a Mr. Prestwick. He and Terence had been drinking, and young Mr. Prestwick had made some rash remarks about Selina. Terence had challenged him to a duel!

The prince regent had forbidden dueling. He had seen it lead to the murder, as he called it, of some of his fine young friends. Any man caught dueling was due for a stern lecture from the prince. And any man who wounded or killled in a duel might be sent abroad into exile for a year or more.

More whispers, more turmoil. Even Mr. Adair became aware that something was amiss as Terence came no more to be tutored. Rupert looked strained and absentminded, clearly troubled, coming regularly to work, but taking twice as long about his sums and his Chinese translations.

Then the tragedy. The duel took place on a foggy morning in mid-February, scarcely a month after Terence's happy wedding day. And young Mr. Prestwick lay dead in the woods where they had fought with dueling pistols.

Mrs. Llewellyn wept. Katie caught a glimpse of Selina, and she looked as excited and triumphant as she had done on her wedding day. Was she so pleased, then, with the attention, at the cost of a man's life? Katie felt such contempt and anger that she did not trust herself to remain in the other girl's presence. She excused herself in the hallway, where they had both come in from the snow and wet outdoors, and went quickly to her rooms.

All became involved in the tragedy. When the prince regent sent for Terence, they held their breaths. Would the noble prince be very angry? What would he say?

"Perhaps he will send us to Paris for a year," said Selina, and the maids quoted her with contempt and laughter.

"She cares nothing for that poor Mr. Prestwick! And him an only son, and his father threatening to hang Mr. Terence! Poor Mr. Llewellyn! His elder son, and in such a trouble!" Whisper, whisper, speculations, and rumors.

Came an afternoon, and one of the maids came to the Adair apartments. She bobbed a curtsy to them, her eyes wide and sparkling with excitement.

'Sure, and Mr. Llewellyn says, can you come at once to his study, Mr. Adair and Miss Katie?" she said breathlessly, her Irish accent coming strongly to the fore.

"Of course. You say—he wishes Miss Katie to come?" Owen Adair roused himself from his studies and ran his hands through his thinning gray hair.

"Yes, if you please, sir. You and Miss Katie, to come at once to his study, sir."

"Yes, yes. Dear me. I wonder why he wishes us both, Katie." And Mr. Adair exchanged his morning robe for a short coat of blue wool. Katie put on a pelisse of rose wool over her woolen dress as it was chilly in the drafty halls.

She was shaking with apprehension. Why in the world would she and her father be called to Mr. Llewellyn's study? Unless—perhaps they were withdrawing to the country! Her heart gave a great leap. Oh, if they could only return to beautiful, peaceful, remote Llewellyn Hall! Set in the heart of green countryside, it was near enough to the sea to hear the pounding of the waves. Her favorite walks lay on the cliffs, looking out to sea and the port where the fishing ships came into harbor. Perhaps the prince had told Terence he and the family must exile themselves to the country for a time! That, for Katie, would be no hardship—except that the *China Princess* must be loaded and sent off to the Orient within the month.

They descended to the next floor and into the other wing to enter Mr. Llewellyn's vast study. The walls were lined with shelves, some containing books, some beautiful treasures of china porcelain, jade, ivory, and carved wood. Mr. Llewellyn sat behind his desk, his face haggard, his hands flat on the shining surface of the cedarwood.

The entire family was gathered. The men rose when Katie and her father entered. Rupert showed her to a chair with a kindly smile for her. But his troubled face showed his disturbance over the situation.

Terence flung himself back into the armchair, where he sat sullenly beside his bride. And Selina— Katie dared a look at that beautiful creamy white face, the artful fall of blond curls, the gown of violet taffeta, the cape of mink around her shoulders. Her face was animated; her eyes sparkled.

Mrs. Matilda Llewellyn sat heavily in an armchair

near her husband's desk. Her plump face was crumpled in grief, while her gaze continually sought the face of Terence, her elder. Rupert retired to the background, not sitting, but leaning against a wall near the crimson-draped window.

"Kindly seat yourself at my side, Mr. Adair," said Mr. Llewellyn, courteously indicating the heavy carved chair near his own. Mr. Adair bowed slightly and sat down, face alert to his part in the matter.

Selina couldn't contain herself. She burst out, "I do not see why your chief clerk should be involved in this matter! It is a family one, after all!"

Katie's look returned to Mr. Douglas Llewellyn, surprising a curious satisfaction in his attractive dark blue eyes.

There was anger also, and his cheeks were flushed. "You shall soon see, Selina, what all is about. I wish first to appraise Mr. Adair and Miss Katie as to the matter."

Selina sent a glance toward Katie, and there was spite in those beautiful violet eyes. Katie was startled. She had thought the lovely woman was not even aware of her.

"Katie and Mr. Adair," said a deep voice from behind her where Rupert stood at the window, "are practically a part of the family and have been for many years. I do not know what we would have done without their efficient and brilliant assistance in the China trade. And their presence in our household is most welcome, for their quiet modesty and ever-willing spirits are an asset to our family."

"Thank you, Mr. Rupert," said Owen Adair, rather flushed at the generous praise. "You are always most kind."

"Well said, Rupert." His father nodded. Mrs. Llewellyn sat silent, her plump hands twisted, her face troubled, as though all this to-do about the Adairs did not take her mind from other matters. "Yes, yes, I do not know what we would have done without the magnificent help of Owen Adair and his daughter. And they are much involved in what is to come. We have less than a month to plan the future of the next two years."

That did catch all attention. Mr. Llewellyn was crisp and decided, and his tone stern.

"As Terence has informed me, and a note from the prince regent has confirmed it, the prince has sent Terence into exile for at least one year," he continued slowly. "He is most angry and upset at the dueling and the death of Mr. Prestwick, God rest his soul."

"It need not be a hardship!" cried Selina. "We can go to Paris—it shall be great fun, I promise you, Terence!" And her hand caught that of her husband and gave it a squeeze.

The big hand remained passive in hers; he gave her an ironic look. Katie caught it. He knew something she did not, she decided, and he was not too pleased with his bride just now.

"No. I have decided," said Mr. Douglas Llewellyn deliberately, "that I cannot do without Terence's aid in the next year. Besides, he needs to learn the business as my elder son and chief heir. What better way than to go to China?"

The words fell into silence. Selina grew pale, and she jerked her hand from Terence's. She stared, pouted, then caught her breath. But her father-in-law did not allow her time for speech.

"The *China Princess* must sail within the month," he

said heavily. "She is being loaded now down at the docks near Dover. She already has on board the trade goods. She is taking on sailors, food, and so on. Terence, you are required to leave London. I wish you and Selina to proceed with all due speed to the coast with your trunks and cases—not too many, the ship will not carry too much. You may take four small trunks and one large trunk of household goods."

Katie sat stiffly. Selina—to go to China! She wanted to laugh at the sight of Selina's outraged face and yet sigh with envy. How she herself longed to go on such a journey! And Selina would consider it a prison sentence!

Mr. Llewellyn began to speak of other plans. "Mr. Adair, I should like you to consult with my wife and Mrs. Garrison as to the household goods they should take with them. Katie, will you assist in the packing of their trunks and advise them as to the hot climate and the muslins and such? Rupert, you will attend me at the warehouse and assist me in the final tallies."

Rupert was murmuring, "Yes, Father," when Terence burst out.

"Father! Am I to have no say in the matter? The prince did not send me into exile in the Orient! I see no need to go so far! What if something should happen in the family—I could not return quickly—what if—"

"I do not anticipate anything happening. I am comparatively young and healthy," said his father dryly. "And your mother enjoys splendid health, I am happy to say. No, you will be of service to the family and learn much of the business if you do as I command. You will go as supercargo to the hong at Canton and carry out my commissions. You should understand the works by this time. I have taught you for many years now."

Terence was flushed and angry. "I have not learned as much as I should have, as you well know, Father! I need more training, I do not speak Chinese—"

"There is no need for that. A linguist will be assigned to you at Macao. I have told you over and over of that matter. You will dock at Macao. Captain Potter will get you there safely, God willing. Selina will set up housekeeping there. Contacts will be made with a linguist and a go-between for you and the hong merchant at Canton. I have always dealt with Houqua, and no doubt he will again assist you in the dealings."

"And what will I do?" exclaimed Selina. "I will die on the voyage, I know it! And when we get to—what is it—Macao! What would I do? Sit in my rooms and weep for home?" Tears came into her beautiful violet eyes. Terence caught her hands, but she pulled them away, and after reaching for her handkerchief, she dabbed her eyes.

"No, you will be quite busy," said Mr. Llewellyn, his voice crisp. "You must manage a household in Macao and entertain the foreign visitors there, being a fine hostess for your husband. In his absence at Canton, you will manage by yourself—"

"Absence—in Canton! Whatever do you mean? You think Terance would desert me, his bride?" cried Selina, genuinely scandalized.

"He must. Foreign women are not permitted in Canton. He has to go with his male assistants to sell our woolens and iron objects, the copper utensils, and so on. In turn, he will buy and pay for silks, porcelains, ivory, whatever he can persuade them to sell to us. I hope you will use good judgment, Terence! I wish you knew more of the values of jade, ivory, silks. They may cheat you and sell you inferior goods. However, it is too late to try to train you in so much." And he gave a heavy sigh.

"Inferior goods! They had better not try to pass off inferior stuff on me!" cried Terence, outraged. He sat up straight, glaring at his father. "I know quite a deal about porcelains and the like! They shall not pass off inferior stuff—"

"Good, good, I am glad to hear it," his father rejoined calmly. "Selina, you will aid your husband, receive the goods as he sends them to you, store them in dry places—"

Selina drew herself up haughtily, and her lovely face had turned ugly with rage. "I—am—not—a—clerk!" she cried. "You will think again, Father! I have no intention of making a—a servant of myself!"

There was a short silence. Mr. Llewellyn eyed her dispassionately, his dislike of her showing briefly, then blotted out by a blander look. "I believe, when you arrive, you will adapt yourself to such duties, my dear, to assist your husband, who will be working very hard. It is from such journeys, you realize, that we obtain our wealth. The very fur you wear was obtained in trade with the Russians and the Chinese in the Orient. Many of the objects you daily use, as your dining service, come from the Orient. And the fact that you married my son, and are now a wealthy wife, is due to the trade I am in, and that I am successful at it!"

It was a strong rebuke, delivered in a forceful voice. Selina stared, then collapsed into weeping.

Mr. Llewellyn nodded to Mr. Adair and to Katie, indicating they might leave the room. They escaped gladly as Selina's voice rose in wailing. "I cannot do it. I will not do it. I was not raised like this. I will hate every minute—you cannot do this. I was gently raised—I will go to my mother—"

But no weeping by Selina, no pretty looks, no coaxing, no protests from her gallant husband, would sway Mr. Llewellyn. He was quietly, furiously angry at his new daughter-in-law. She had caused all this trouble by her flirting, her outrageous encouragement of other men even after her marriage to his son. She was responsible for another man's death. She had caused his son to duel, to receive a dreadful reputation, to incur the wrath of the prince regent himself!

Selina and Terence were bundled off in haste to the docks at Dover. They went to live aboard the *China Princess,* as the Dover Inn rooms did not please them. Katie thought secretly that they might not have left so soon, but her employer wanted to be rid of them and get them on their way as soon as possible. Terence set to work and did his share of the tasks that he and the captain had to carry out—they had received almost daily reports from him.

Katie assisted Mrs. Garrison in furnishing the trunks and sending them on. Selina had insisted on taking almost a dozen smaller trunks of her dresses, furs, jewels, little caring about sheets, blankets, pots and pans, and everyday silver.

Owen Adair was much distressed by the whole event. He felt close to Douglas Llewellyn, and indeed, he often received the confidences of the gruff businessman. They went out daily to the warehouse and prepared to send the *China Princess* on its way. Katie was working hard; her father worked even harder, rising early and retiring late, preparing the accounts and tallies, pushing himself to finish sketches and lists of directions for Terence.

Mr. Adair returned late one afternoon, soaking wet. It had been raining hard on that late February day, a cold, soaking rain, and he had walked some distance from one warehouse to the docks office and back again. Ignoring his wetness, he had continued to work and then got soaked again walking to the carriage where the coachman waited. There was an area around the wharves where the carriages were not allowed to wait. Mr. Adair had been too distracted, and was also too modest, to send a workman in his place to ask the carriage to come closer.

He coughed violently in the night. Katie heard him, arose, and went to him. He was in such distress that she added more blankets. After a small hesitation she rang the bell for the night maid. An older maid appeared, sleepy-eyed, but alert at once as she saw Mr. Adair's condition.

"Oh, Miss Katie, he should have the doctor!"

"I cannot send for him tonight." Katie hesitated. "Would not a pot of hot tea help? And some herbal medication for his chest?"

The maid agreed and ran back and forth for the remainder of the night with hot poultices, medicines, and hot tea. In the morning Mrs. Matilda Llewellyn came to study Mr. Adair's face, and she sent at once for her own doctor.

Mr. Llewellyn came up also later in the morning after the doctor had been. By this time Mr. Adair was quite weak from coughing, and his forehead was very hot. He tried to get up anyway.

"I am ashamed to be still abed," he said weakly. "So much—work—to be done—ashamed—"

"Indeed, my friend," said Mr. Douglas Llewellyn kindly, "I should be very angry if you arose. You must rest and be over this soon."

Mr. Adair did not improve. He soon slipped into a feverish delirium and rambled on about the work, his long-deceased wife, about Cornwall and the sea. He seemed to dream that he was drowning and would sit up and wave his arms wildly, trying to swim away from the cliffs.

Katie would soothe him, bring more hot tea, more medicines. She was up with him much of the nights and through the day. A maid always sat with her, on Mrs. Llewellyn's instructions. Indeed, the whole household was much concerned and helpful, for all liked the kindly Mr. Adair, who was no trouble at all and so fine a man and scholar.

At first the doctor came daily, then twice a day, morning and evening. He held the man's frail hand, felt the pulse, and shook his head, his lips pursing.

He murmured to Mr. Llewellyn. Katie tried to hear what they said. But they said little to her beyond encouraging her to get more sleep.

She could not sleep; she could eat little; she was so anxious. Her father had been ill before, but he had always responded to tea and medicine and recovered. Now he was so frail; his fine mind seemed to have wandered away. He did not know her many a time.

Then one night, as she and the maid went to tend his coughing, they found him sitting up, the covers half flung off and dragging on the floor. "So hot," he muttered. "So—very—hot—summer has been long—"

Katie covered him up, and the maid brought the pot of hot tea. He could not drink—he seemed to choke on it—and he fell back on the pillows.

"Oh, dear Father, pray drink of this," Katie coaxed him, holding the cup to his still lips. "It will help your poor chest—"

The maid bent over with her anxiously. Her father half smiled at Katie dreamily, then closed his eyes. The coughing had ceased.

"Oh, he is breathing much more easily," exclaimed Katie. The hoarse, hard breathing had ceased. He lay still and looked peaceful, with the slight smile on his lips.

The older woman bent to him also and touched his face, and his hand. Then she drew Katie back from her father.

"He's gone, Miss Katie," she said quietly.

"Gone?"

"Yes, my dear. Gone. Dead, he is. To his final rest, God have mercy on him and us all." The Irish maid crossed herself and then saw Katie's dazed, incredulous face.

Forgetting her station, the Irishwoman drew Katie into her arms.

"He is at peace, dear Miss Katie. He's at peace. You can weep for us here on earth, but he is in heaven now, dear man."

Katie felt herself being rocked back and forth in the hearty arms of the Irish maid, but she felt nothing. She could not believe it. Death had come so quickly, stealing in to snatch her father from her and leaving with him.

She could not cry. Mrs. Llewellyn was wakened and

came to her and was very kind. She ordered another maid to sleep with Katie, but Katie could not sleep. She lay awake beside the snoring girl and stared into the darkness. This could not have happened. It was a nightmare. In the morning she would waken, and her father would be better, smiling at her and telling a little joke, as he often did.

Morning came, another dark, rainy day. The heavens had opened up and wept for Mr. Adair, said one of the maids. The men from the funeral parlor came and took him away and returned him in a casket, to lie in the front drawing room for a short time.

He was buried within two days in the Llewellyn plot in a nearby churchyard. Katie wanted to object as she knew her father had meant to be laid beside his wife in the small Cornish town where they had lived. But she had not the heart to argue or make a fuss; her spirit was weighted by her sense of aloneness.

Katie overheard Mrs. Llewellyn murmur to her husband. "Oh, what in the world will become of the dear girl? What about Katie? She is but eighteen and alone in the world."

"She has us," her husband responded.

But I don't, thought Katie. I have no one. No one. No one. There is no one left to whom I belong in the whole world. It was a desolation beyond grief. Her sorrow for her father now extended to herself, and she felt terribly ashamed that she could be so selfish as to worry more about herself than her father.

Her father was in heaven, where there was no hunger, pain, or need. But she was on earth, where there was all of them, and more. Whatever would become of her?

Fortunately there was still work to be done. Numbly Katie followed the Llewellyns' directions. Rupert came daily to work at the high desk where her father had worked, tallying the accounts. Katie worked opposite him at the huge mahogany table, finishing up several sketches which must go with the ship. Mrs. Garrison was still counting linens, adding up pots and pans, packing the 'trunks to go with Selina and Terence.

The newlyweds, in disgrace, had not come to Mr. Adair's funeral. Mr. Llewellyn had sent them a terse note, and Terence had responded with a perfunctory note to Katie, stating, "I am so grieved at your sad loss."

She thought he did not care a whit. He had resented taking lessons from her father, had sneered at him behind his back, and had teased Katie mercilessly since she was a child. Only Rupert had always been kind, unfailingly kind.

A tear trickled down her cheek. She blotted it quickly before it could fall on her drawing. But another tear came, and another. In her desolation she could not work. It all seemed so futile.

She did not see Rupert rise from his desk and come to her side. The first she knew he was there was when his arms went about her and he drew her head back to his chest.

"Dear Katie, how sorry I am!" he murmured in his deep voice. She shivered, and he held her closer, stroking back her hair softly with his big capable hand.

Katie shut her eyes tightly. The warmth and strength of his arms comforted her, but also released in her the grief she felt, the agony of loss, the terror of the years ahead of her without the dear shelter of her father.

She wept and sobbed into Rupert's big handkerchief as he rocked her back and forth and whispered soothing words of comfort.

"Go ahead and cry, Katie. You have not wept, and that is not good. You must weep and mourn and then begin to live again. Dear Katie, how fortunate you are to have had such a good fine man as a father. Such a wonderful person he was; he left a splendid impression on us all, which lives after him."

"Oh, Rupert." She sobbed. "I am so sorry to give way like this. But indeed, I cannot help it—oh, dear Father, dear Father, I cannot believe he is gone. I wake in the night and think I hear him calling me—"

He murmured once more and stroked her hair soothingly again and again.

Mr. Douglas Llewellyn came in and saw them so. Katie mopped her eyes once more, and saw him, and tried to straighten from Rupert's gentle embrace. Mr. Llewellyn smiled at her lovingly and shook his head, his eyes seeming curiously speculative.

"Do not mind me, Katie. Go ahead and cry. Matilda and I have worried that you did not cry. I shall send for some tea for us all, and then we shall work later. Work is a blessing, for in it we can lose ourselves, and at the same time we can add to our good works in this world, eh?"

She thought of work. Oh, how dreadful if she did not have work, if the Llewellyns should turn her out or try to find some other place for her to live! Would she become a maid? She was suited for nothing but the work that she did, but would they keep her on without her father?

"Oh, sir, I do love the work," she said hurriedly, wiping her face again with the very wet handkerchief. "You know—that I would work very hard for you—not so well as Father. But one day I will have much more experience. I will do anything—"

'Nonsense, Katie, do not fret so!" Rupert said sternly, still stroking her forehead. "You know you shall remain here with us forever! How would we manage without you, eh?" he coaxed. "No one makes such fine patterns as you; no one can translate Chinese characters now but you. Tell her, Father, we cannot do without her!"

Mrs. Llewellyn came in then, and the conversation was changed. But Katie noticed that Mr. Llewellyn had said nothing! Yet he *had* looked at her queerly and strangely. Was he making plans for her? And should she dislike the plans as much as Selina had? He was a strong, dominating man and accustomed to having his way. What, if anything, did he have in mind?

She thought nothing about marriage. She was not in a position to meet eligible young men; she had met no men of her rank. And what was her rank? That of the clergy, schoolmasters, and shopkeepers?

Her deep worry about her future added considerably to her agony over the loss of her father. Nightly her pillow was soaked. She slept alone now in the empty apartment. Trays of food had been sent to her, and she ate alone, in silence, without the affectionate speech of her father, without his presence.

The rooms had been quiet before, but pleasantly so.

Now they were quiet with the emptiness of her being alone, terribly alone, and terrified that each new day might be her last in these familiar rooms. Then what would she do?

"Oh, Father, oh, Father," she whispered over her sketches when she was alone during the day. "Oh, Father—" And she would try to forget and work harder, hoping to prove her worth and ensure their keeping her on.

She could scarcely eat and sleep for the terror of the future. Rupert saw and worried about her and tried to reassure her with his clumsy masculine words.

"Come, now, you are a good soldier, Katie," he chaffed her one day. "You will take the loss and come up again to fight on. I know your kind; you will not falter in the battle of life."

She tried to smile, weakly. He had been born to wealth, though it was true he also worked hard for it. And he had been a good officer and an honorable member of society. But he did not know what it was to wonder how a woman would manage in the world, with no relatives, no close friends to turn to.

She checked the figures he brought to her and talked more calmly to him. And all the time she worried and worried.

The *China Princess* would be off soon, and the work would slacken as she had little to do with the daily accounts. Rupert could take them over. Or more likely, Mr. Llewellyn would promote one of his underclerks to Mr. Adair's position, and Katie would not be needed any longer. Of course, she might help with the translation of Chinese if they did not find a man to do that work.

She pressed her fist to her mouth. Rupert patted her back impersonally.

"Good girl," he said, and she could have laughed with hysteria. He had no idea how she felt about him, how she adored him, how she would miss him when she left the household. He had no conception of the grief she felt over her father, who had protected her, taught her all she knew, shared her narrow and sheltered life, and given her work to do. He could not possibly comprehend how terrified she felt, how she shook and trembled in bed at night in the empty apartments, wondering what would happen to her. I am a coward, she thought, I have no courage at all. The future looms before me like some dread monster.

3

"Marriage!" said Rupert blankly, rubbing his face. "But—marriage, Father!"

"I know, my son. It is very soon and must be done quickly," said Douglas Llewellyn thoughtfully. "Poor Katie must have a secure feeling and a sure home. How do you think she feels? Her only relative in the world—dead! And she a delicate female of sensitive feelings. You have always been fond of Katie, and she is fond of you. You two are much alike, gently bred, with similar interests and a strong sense of duty and responsibility. Yes, I think you will deal well together."

Rupert shook his head, as though shaking off a fantasy. "I had not dreamed to marry—you know, Father, how I felt about Selina," he said with quiet dignity. "You were good enough to comfort me when she turned from me—to Terence—"

"I am only sorry she did not turn to some man in another family," said his father grimly. "She is a frivolous piece of goods, badly raised, with no sense of shame. You are well rid of her—"

"Father!" Rupert sprang to his feet, his face whitening. "Selina is a good fine girl of good breeding, and beautiful—how can you speak so of her? I love her, I adore her as a goddess far above us human mortals—"

"I have read enough of Roman and Greek goddesses, such as Juno, Minerva, Venus, to know they do incite human men to violence and murder," said his father, very dryly indeed. "I presume it is of such goddesses that you speak?"

"No, Father! Do not jest about this! She is a fine woman, a bit spoiled by her mother, I do admit—"

"I am glad you can see that, at least. But we speak of Katie. Selina is settled, I hope, with Terence, whereas Katie is not settled—she lies awake nights worrying about her future. The dear girl would not be turned out by me." And his tone gentled. "She is a good girl, a good obedient lady, with a fine knowledge of many matters which will aid us in our trade. That is my point at last, Rupert. Katie needs security. And we do need her knowledge of China and the Orient trade, her skill with languages, all she has learned from my dear friend Owen Adair." And he gave a deep sigh.

Rupert sat down slowly in the armchair once more. "You are serious about this, Father." He shook his head incredulously. "You wish me to marry Katie Adair? Oh, I like the girl well enough; she is like a little sister to me. But—marriage? Must it be marriage? Cannot you assure her future without dragging me into it?"

"No," said his father flatly. He seemed to study his fine large hands as they were pressed to the cedarwood of his desk. "I think this is the answer, and I wish her in the family. She will make a fine wife, good, obedient, charming, intelligent. And she will be useful to us."

"I cannot love any but Selina. After her, other females seem drab, gloomy, indifferent. I have no wish to marry, Father."

"Just so. You are ripe to fall into the hands of another Selina," said his father, who then went on quickly before Rupert could protest. "My dear son, you have been in bloody and difficult situations for many years. You are weary of all that and prime to settle down with a fine woman. I pray of you, be guided by me. Katie will make a splendid wife for you; she will give you sons, guide your household, assist you in your work, and take a deep interest in it. You could not have a better wife than Katie Adair!"

Rupert let himself be persuaded. Indeed, he had felt so gloomy and depressed for the past months that he cared little what happened to him. In losing Selina, he had felt he lost all he wanted in the world except the good of his parents. He could not forgive Terence for cutting him out, his own brother! And then laughing cruelly about it to Rupert. "What, did you think she would settle for a fine flashy major in the army when she can have a son and heir, with all the fortunes and homes that go with me? What can you offer such a queen, a beauty?"

The words stung. Selina had been gentle with him, pressing his hand, allowing him to kiss her cheek when he went to see her. But she had been firm in her resolution to marry Terence. He could not understand the matter.

Reluctantly Rupert went up to the Adair apartments. He found Katie working on a sketch at the tall mahogany desk. She seemed thin and drawn, her face pale and older than usual. She glanced up and smiled at him, a ghastly shadow of her usual cheerful composure.

"Ah, Katie, what are you working on?" He went over to her and put his hand on her narrow shoulder.

"Ah, that is splendid," he said kindly, scarcely seeing the sketch of butterflies flitting over a border of columbine.

"Thank you, Rupert. Does your father need me?"

"Not now. And Mother has the packing well in hand." He felt something inside him flinch as he said it. Packing—for Selina to go to China, where she had no wish to go, weeping over it bitterly, poor darling! And out of his sight and longing for two years!

"Then do you wish me to work on something for you?" Her large, soft brown eyes were anxious and eager for his approval.

The dear child, he thought. His heart softened. She was a good girl, as his father said. Always so willing to help, so hardworking. What fun had she had in life? Nothing, he thought. Her biggest treat was to be allowed to go to the warehouse! If he married her, he must try to see that she went to dances—Dances! The last time he had been dancing was with Selina—their waltz at the Prestwick home—and then the disaster the following week.

He forgot his mission for the moment; his heart contracted with grief. Selina—gone from him! Her light laughter like bells, her beautiful creamy pale face, her violet eyes, which danced so with pleasure, her soft hands clinging to his . . .

Katie had bent again to her sketching, drawing with steady hand, intent on her work. She wore a drab brown wool gown, and over it a black shawl to keep her warm against the chill of the apartment. Such dark colors, signs of her mourning—

He stiffened with resolution. He had always tried hard to do his duty, and his father had told him what his duty was now.

"Katie, I would speak with you," he said.

"Yes, Rupert?"

He took her hands and lifted her down from the tall stool. They went over to a blue silk sofa and sat down together. Her dark eyes were questioning. He kept hold of her hands and tried to think only of her. He must from now on think only of Katie and his duties to the family and work.

"Katie, my dear, you know I have always been fond of you," he began firmly.

The eyes widened. She flushed, then went pale again. Her hands shook in his. "You have always been—most kind," she whispered.

"Now that your dear father, whom we all loved and admired, is gone from us, you are alone in the world. My father is most concerned about your future, and so—so am I." He cleared his throat.

"If—if you and your father—have any use—for me—I would work—very hard and long for you both," said Katie, her slim form shaking. He saw the tremors running through her slight body and felt sorry for her. How thin she was, now that she slept little and ate less.

"I know you would, Katie. You need someone to look after you. Father and I—agree—that is, I mean, I think you should marry me," he blurted out.

"Marry?" she whispered.

"Yes." He could not look straight into the honest brown eyes and say it. He glanced over her shoulder at the white jade Buddha which squatted on a shelf behind her shoulder in the bookcase against the wall. He said to the Buddha, "You see, you are very necessary to us all—to me. You know so much of the work, and the many years you and your father—that is—you are dear to—all of us. Your security, your peace of mind, your welfare are of importance to me. Would you, dear Katie, consider marriage to me?"

For a moment he hoped with all his heart that she would say no, she had given her heart to another. But he knew also there was no other. She went out little and met no one. Why had his mother permitted this situation? She should have looked out for Katie, taken her out, even encouraged her to entertain, and join in the family outings— But no, Katie had always worked.

There was a little silence. Katie was gazing at him anxiously. He finally looked into her face and was shocked at her pallor.

"Katie, my dear, will you not answer me?"

"Oh, Rupert—" She paused and licked her pale lips. They were well shaped, he saw, softly bowed and full, as though she had more passion in her than he had dreamed. Her grave face was a sweet oval, and the large brown eyes were beautiful. Indeed, looking closely at her, he thought she was prettier than he had recalled. He squeezed her hands encouragingly.

"Yes, my dear Katie?"

"I cannot believe that you want—that you wish to—" She hesitated. "I mean, lately you have loved—"

"*She* is beyond my reach. I must forget her," he said gravely, matching her honesty. "But I think we two shall deal well together, Katie. I have always liked and admired you. You have an excellent mind and good training. Father said—I mean, he and I both think highly of your mind and your adherence to duty always."

Another hesitation. He wondered what she was thinking.

"And you, Rupert, is this what you wish?" she asked. There was a solemn note to her voice.

He responded to it and nodded. "Yes, Katie, this is what I want. You shall be a fine wife to me, and I shall try to be what you wish in a husband. Shall you say yes to me?"

His gaze was drawn to her pale sweet mouth, her soft full underlip and well-shaped upper lip. When she nodded and whispered, "Yes, Rupert, I thank you," he bent and pressed his mouth to hers.

She started violently and stiffened, and he put his arms about her firmly and drew her to him. He kissed her again and felt her mouth quiver.

He drew back. "There. We are engaged then!"

She attempted a smile. "We can be engaged—for a time, Rupert. If you decide you don't want—I mean, if we wish to call it off, there will be much time to consider—"

But Mr. Douglas Llewellyn gave them no time. To his wife's dismay and shock, he ordered the wedding in a week. Rupert was present when his mother was presented with the order. "Yes, a week, Matilda. No such fussing and wild parties as with Terence. That was enough for us all! And Mr. Adair so recently dead—"

"But to marry Katie! Our Rupert!" protested Matilda Llewellyn. She put her handkerchief to her eyes. "Douglas, you go too fast! Rupert is but lately—"

Rupert interrupted hastily; he wanted to have no such reminders. "Katie is a fine lady, and I—I like her immensely. She shall suit me well, Mother."

In spite of her protests, and Katie's weaker ones, the

marriage was arranged for a week later. Katie was to wear a new gown of pale peach silk with lace over-dress of white. There was little time to sew more clothing for her, but her new father-in-law seemed strangely intent that her wardrobe should be increased heavily, and at once. To his wife's surprise, he himself went to the dressmaker's with them.

He ordered piles of muslin gowns for Katie, in white, peach, pink, rose, blue, all her favorite colors. He ordered slippers to match, silk pelisses, bordered with velvet. He ordered a fine mink jacket and another in white ermine. He went on and on, until Katie cried out.

"Indeed, dear Father-to-be, this is too much! Summer will not be here for a time—indeed, it is scarce March—all this can wait—I do not need so much—"

But he persisted, and perhaps his wife guessed his intentions, for she fell in with it all. Katie stood for fittings for the entire week before her wedding.

The wedding was a quiet one, held in the main drawing room of the Llewellyn town house. Only a few guests were present. Mr. Llewellyn gave Katie away; the minister brought his wife as a witness; a few of the clerks were present, along with a next-door neighbor with two daughters who were about Katie's age. All seemed bewildered to sit there and watch young Katie Adair, daughter of Llewellyn's chief clerk, married to fine young Rupert Llewellyn in a blue velvet suit and sapphires.

The wedding feast was nothing like that of Selina and Terence. A fine meal was present on the table set for twenty, and they all ate and drank and toasted the bride and groom. But there was no orchestra to play, no dancing, no merrymaking, no stream of beautiful bridesmaids in colors of the rainbow.

Rupert had dreaded his wedding night. He was beginning to recover from the daze he had been in the past week and to realize what he had done. He had married a young girl he had known since childhood, a young girl not out of her teens, a frightened pale girl, who looked at him out of big brown eyes, terrified out of her wits.

They stood in her apartments, where he was to live for a time. Mrs. Llewellyn said she would have them redecorated as they wished, whatever color he wanted. He had replied that the present furnishings suited him well. He scarcely saw them.

Katie, in her pretty gown with the muff of white ermine and the violets pinned to them, looked as strange as he felt. She just stood there, helplessly, looking about the room.

"My dear Katie," he was suddenly inspired to say, "I think you are more weary than you know. Would you wish to go to your own bed alone? I am not going to make heavy demands on you so soon. I think you have endured enough emotions—"

She nodded, and tears sprang to her eyes. She attempted a smile. "You are—so good, Rupert," she managed to say.

He felt guilty. It was his feelings he had been pleasing, not hers. He had no wish to make love to her; he felt no passion, no rising desire for this pale child. Only compassion—

"Go to bed, then, my dear," he said gently. "There is still work to do in the morning, I am sorry for it. But

Father said we must go to it now and get the *China Princess* ready for sailing in two more weeks."

"Yes, there is work to be done," said Katie wearily, and went off to her bedroom and shut the door.

Rupert had to ring for a maid to make Owen Adair's bed up for him. He flinched from the open curiosity on her Irish face; all the household would know by morning that he had not slept with his bride.

He went to bed to lie awake and silently curse himself that he had so readily fallen in with his father's plans. He had felt so numb, so indifferent to life for months. What did it matter? Yet—yet he had a feeling that his father was twisting his life about to suit himself.

He rose early and began to work on the accounts. Work—yes, work, hard work, was the only cure for his misery. At least he could forget for a time the sullen misery of his existence.

Katie came out soon after he began work. She had dressed in the dark blue gown she often wore for work, with a black shawl around her shoulders. Her pallor was such that he guessed she had not slept either.

Breakfast was brought to them. They felt better after drinking the hot China tea. They consulted each other about the accounts; she had three sketches to finish, to be sent with the ship. She set to work while he went down to speak with his father, ignoring the servants' raised eyebrows.

His father invited them to luncheon with him. "Katie must become accustomed to the fact that she is indeed one of the family now," he said pleasantly.

Katie came down for lunch, still in the dark clothes. Mrs. Llewellyn gazed at her with vague disapproval.

"Katie, my dear, you should begin to wear your new clothes. Your father has gone to much trouble to improve your wardrobe," she rebuked her gently.

She had not approved of the wedding and had fought strongly against it. Katie was not of their class; Rupert would find someone splendid later on when he was "over" Selina. It was too hurried; she could not reconcile herself to the event. But when her husband insisted and closed the subject, she had resigned herself. After all, Katie was young, and willing, and a sweet child. She could be trained.

"Yes, Mother," said Katie meekly, in such a low voice they could scarcely hear her. She ate little and blushed when spoken to. Rupert was in a quiet depression. Katie would *not* do. All society would laugh at him for having married such a dull child. What mockery! She was like a drab sparrow, flitting away when called to, with her thin body jerking at a touch of his.

Mr. Llewellyn kept the conversation going, but he seemed to have much on his mind. At the end of the luncheon, as Katie toyed with a piece of orange and Rupert tried to enjoy his chocolate puffs, Mr. Llewellyn said, "I should like all of you to come to my study for coffee."

They came with him. Mrs. Llewellyn sank into an armchair. Her hands still fiddled much, and she seemed tired and older, thought her son. Terence's duel and his exile had affected his mother very much. She had lost her brightness.

"Now," said Douglas Llewellyn, setting to the desk. A maid in starched white had brought in a tray of coffee and set it before Katie to pour out for them.

The girl was conscientiously pouring out the hot coffee into beautiful white and gold-rimmed porcelain cups from China.

Everyone waited for what the head of the household would say. Rupert carried cups about, then settled with his cup near the desk. Katie leaned back and sipped at the coffee.

"I have been considering carefully this matter of sending Terence to China," said Douglas Llewellyn.

Rupert started violently. So that was it! Terence was to be brought home, and Rupert and Katie sent in his place! Oh, sly Father, clever Father, the father who adored his elder son no matter what he did! He choked on his coffee.

"He must leave the country," continued his father. "However, I have not been as strict with him as I should have been. He does not know enough of the Chinese customs, of trading and the business."

Katie was gazing at her new father-in-law, her face expressionless, her eyes wide and brown and blank. What she was thinking Rupert could not guess. His own thoughts were bitter as gall.

"So I have decided to send you, Rupert, and Katie along with Terence and Selina," said Douglas Llewellyn.

Then they all did gasp. He allowed no time for questions, however, proceeding to speak rapidly.

"Katie knows the language; Katie knows the books, the silk market, and designing. Rupert, you have always been fond of the porcelains and have learned much about them. The merchants will not be able to cheat you easily on them; you will pay a decent price, no more. Between you two, you can manage to choose the jade, the ivory. Rupert, defer to Katie regarding the silks. Katie, you will advise Rupert and Terence as wisely as you may, regarding all the purchases.

"Rupert, I will trust you to work well with Terence. You have quarreled bitterly over his marriage; you have lived apart for many years. Yet you are brothers and fond of each other. It is to your advantage to work well together. Terence is in charge; he is the elder. But I shall write to him and urge him to defer to your judgment and especially to Katie's."

"You are sending them both—both my sons?" It was a poignant cry from Mrs. Llewellyn, and she began to weep. Rupert went to comfort her, giving his father a hard look which the older man understood but avoided.

"Yes, yes, it must be, Matilda," he said wearily. "Terence has much to learn. Selina knows little about housekeeping, Katie must advise her about that. Also, Katie, my dear, I wish you to be in charge of the warehouse in Macao and the loading of the ship—you understand how it must be done, and the men will be gone to Canton for part of the time. It will require tact on your part, but I shall make it clear to Captain Potter that you know much about these matters."

She swallowed and seemed at a loss. Then she said obediently, "Yes—Father. I will do as you command."

"Good girl! I will depend on you," he said cheerily. Rupert straightened. His father was taking it for granted that all would do as he commanded.

"Father, I wish to say—"

"Later, later, my lad!" his father said as though he were a boy, and not twenty-six years of age and with eight years of experience as an officer in the army. "There is much to be done. You have but two weeks to pack your clothes and household goods, finish loading the ship, and be off to China!"

"So that was why you were in such a hurry to have clothes made for Katie!" said Matilda Llewellyn indignantly, giving a final wipe to her eyes and nose. "Really, Douglas, do you think them all pawns, to be moved about at your will?"

"Permit me to do what I think best!" he told her stiffly, outraged. "I trust you will do all that you may to assist us in this family venture, Matilda!"

When he spoke so, everyone jumped to do his will. A good-natured man, he could be enraged and stormy on occasion, and no one wished to be in the way of his wrath when it did rise.

Rupert, working furiously the next two weeks, sometimes wondered why it was. Why did everyone jump to his father's time? Katie was working like crazy, packing, sketching, running about in a daze. She packed his gear also; he had no time for it. She saw to his new lawn shirts, the light cottons for the tropical climate they would endure in Canton and Macao, the sheets and other linens, pots and pans.

"Of course, Selina has much," said Matilda Llewellyn as Katie and Mrs. Garrison counted silver and pans.

"We shall live with her and Terence?" cried Katie, aroused from her pallor and weariness to outrage.

"Yes, my dear, of course," said Mr. Llewellyn, avoiding her incredulous stare. "The houses there are large and airy, and you shall have one for the four of you."

"Oh, my God!" cried Rupert. "What will you do to us, Father?"

"I trust you will all manage quite well," said Llewellyn blandly. "Selina and Katie will keep things running in Macao. You and Terence will spend most of your time in Canton, bargaining for the goods. I hope all will be settled from September to January or February. Then you can start for home again."

"Oh, my God," moaned Rupert again, and Katie muttered under her breath.

"I do not think it will do," said Matilda Llewellyn simply, her hands to her head. "I cannot think it will do!"

"It must."

And that was his final word on the subject. Letters had flown back and forth between the town house and the *China Princess,* and Terence and Selina were apprised of the situation. Terence had sent some forceful words on the subject, furiously angry. "Why cannot you send Rupert and his little Katie to China without us? My wife and I are quite prepared to go to Paris instead!"

"No doubt," wrote his father in reply, showing the answer to Rupert in some satisfaction. "But if you wish to remain my son and heir, you will do as I tell you to do! I am displeased enough with you both. Do not make me do anything so final as to disinherit you!"

Rupert did not expect a tender welcome when he and Katie arrived at Dover and the *China Princess* a fortnight after their wedding. He and his bride in name only arrived at night, weary and silent in the big barouche. Some of their goods rode with them, bumping their legs. Others followed in another two carriages. Captain Abraham Potter met them as they came up the gangway.

"Ah, here ye are. Well, we can sail in another two days then," he said in satisfaction, eyeing the weary train curiously.

Terence came sullenly from his cabin. "Well, I hope you are satisfied," he said disagreeably. "You'll do as I tell you, Rupert, and you also, Katie! I am in charge, I'll have you know."

They stood in the large crimson and mahogany-trimmed drawing room of the fine vessel. Selina was lounging in a large chair, radiant in violet silk and her mink jacket.

"They will probably try to take charge, Terence," she said disagreeably. "You know what your father said. Katie knows about silks, Rupert knows about porcelains, be advised of them!"

"Father said we are to work together," said Rupert stiffly. "Now, if we might go to our cabins—"

"Cabins? You have one together," said Terence. "Or are you not truly wed? Little Katie Adair, did you truly snatch a husband off the top of the trees?" He was sneering at her, and Rupert grew enraged. He knew the blows were meant for himself mainly.

"I pray you will not quarrel," said Katie, a tremor in her voice. "We have a long voyage together and long periods of work in Macao and Canton. We must work in harmony—"

"Oh, now, the little clerk is telling us what to do!" cried Selina. "Are you going to be obedient to her, Terence? Oh, what a mess you made when you dueled with that dreadful man! But you did not need to obey your father! The prince only said you must leave England for a year! Not go around the world!"

Katie again said unexpectedly, "I wonder at you,

Selina. It is entirely your fault, the duel and now this exile. Cannot you be ashamed and willing to make it easier for all of us? If you will all work in harmony—"

"Be quiet!" Rupert turned on his new wife. Captain Potter watched them all, his mouth tight. "Katie, be silent! How dare you reprimand Selina? She has been the victim in this! Ordered to go off to China, her delicate health, her bright spirit. Forced into exile because Terence could not control his vile temper!"

"Oh, you do understand!" said Selina. She jumped up, hurried to Rupert, and put both hands on his arms. She smiled up at him, alluringly, radiantly, as she had in the past that now seemed to live only in his bitter memories. "Oh, Rupert," she said softly. "You understand my nature. You comprehend me. If only I had married you—"

Terence was brightly flushed of face, partly from drink, which Rupert could smell on his breath, partly from rage. He snatched Selina's hands from Rupert. "Let him alone! How can you say such filthy things? Selina, you are my wife, and you had best remember that! You chose between us; you love me; you told me so often enough! Get to our cabin at once!"

"Don't order her about in such a tone!" Rupert was half-mad with rage and regret. His little beautiful love! How frightened she was of Terence, to fall back gasping and hold her slim hands over her heart! "You are a bully and a brute; your rakish ways have sickened her! Yes, she should have married me! I have been an officer and a gentleman; I know how a lady should be treated! You order her to go into exile with you; you could have protected her—"

"Please—all of you!" Katie was quite white, but she dared touch Rupert's arm. He shook her off. "We must not quarrel among ourselves. Please, it is late—do let us find our cabins and obtain some rest. There is much to do before we sail—"

"Aye, little lady, much to do," said Captain Potter's heavy voice. "Won't help to fuss and quarrel and lose our sleep, will it? Mr. Rupert, I'll show you and your lady to your cabin. Mr. Terence, you best have some coffee and cool yourself down. It'll be a long voyage—"

As Rupert half turned, Terence sprang at him, snarling. The two men were at once engaged in exchanging blows. Terence struck Rupert on the head. Rupert, in better condition, struck him back instantly, blows falling on Terence's head and chest. He had his brother down and on the carpet and was pounding at him, half-crazy with rage and fury.

Selina was screaming at them. "Hit him, Rupert; he has hit me often enough! You are a big bully, Terence! There, hit him again—" She was jumping up and down with rage, cheering Rupert on. His heart swelled for her; she did love him, she must love him! She had made a frightful mistake, falling for Terence and his charming, deceitful ways.

"Now that will be enough!" Captain Potter's voice rose over the turmoil as Rupert banged away at his brother, and Terence yelled at him, and Selina screamed at them both. "Mrs. Katie, you tell your husband he must take you to your cabin."

"Come, Rupert," said Katie, pulling at his arm. "You have hit him enough! He is bleeding all over the carpet—"

Rupert staggered to his feet. She was right. Terence was bleeding profusely from his nose, swearing as the blood flowed copiously all over his white ruffled shirt and over the carpet. Selina was weeping, her hands over her face, her form shaking. Captain Potter rang for a sailor, who came to bring water and cloths.

"Now, Mr. Rupert, I'll show you to your cabin," said the captain grimly. He pushed Rupert in the back, toward the door.

Rupert almost struck the big man, but something in the cool look the red-haired man gave him quieted him. Sullenly he followed Katie into the mahogany-lined hallway.

Rupert paused at a cabin door as the captain started past. "This is ours?"

He peered inside the opened door, at the large lavishly furnished cabin, the two large beds, curtains at the windows, the trunks half-opened and spilling their contents.

"No, Mr. Rupert, that is the main cabin and is occupied by Mr. Terence and Mrs. Selina," said the captain.

Rupert's mouth compressed. He followed Katie's slim back and high-held bonnet down the corridor, to the end. The captain flung open the door, and they walked into a much smaller cabin, where trunks had been brought in, still tightly strapped. The bunks had been made up, narrow bunks much smaller than the grand beds in the main cabin.

"A wee bit smaller," said the captain, with a half smile. "But Mr. Terence has first choice, him being first supercargo appointed by your father, Mr. Rupert. You'll do well to remember your brother is in charge of the cargo. And I am in charge of this ship!" With that profound remark he left them and closed the door gently after himself.

4

Katie was stinging with anger and humiliation. Must Rupert show so clearly his love for Selina? No wonder Terence was in a jealous rage! And Selina was worse, encouraging them to come to blows! She must derive some satisfaction in her bitter state that she had foolishly married Terence while loving Rupert. She could have married Rupert; why had she not?

Her head whirled. She was so weary her head ached. And there stood trunks to be unpacked, nightclothes to be taken out, and then the long voyage before them.

A sailor appeared with a tray of hot tea and some cheese and bread. He left the tray, went to the trunks, and kindly unfastened the two small ones that Katie indicated.

While Rupert sullenly drank tea, Katie removed the top layer of clothes, the nightshirts and her nightdress, robes, for the ship was cold and drafty, and a shirt for Rupert in the morning. When she returned to sit down at the small table and drink her tea, it was cool.

"Well, we might as well turn in," said Rupert gloomily. "I must say, Katie, you did not improve our situation! I will not endure being told what to do! And in the morning I shall inform Captain Potter that he is not in charge of me!"

Katie did not know what possessed her. Jealousy,

perhaps, hurt and anger at Rupert's obvious love for Selina.

"But Captain Potter is in charge of us all, Rupert," she said definitely. "He is captain of the *China Princess*, and as captain he has final say in all matters."

Rupert stared at her, his face becoming even more red. "Katie!" he said ominously. "You are my wife! I wish you would not continue to contradict me."

"As an officer," she went on, unable to stop talking, for sheer nerves, "you must understand that only one man can be in charge. Would you really prefer that Terence should tell the captain when to sail, when to raise and lower the sails, when to put into shore? We should be in a sad state then, for Terence knows nothing of such matters."

"Why, why should Terence be in charge?" yelled Rupert in a fuss, and banged his fist on the table, so the tin plates rattled and the china cups jumped. "I know much more than he does about the trade—"

"But your father put Terence above you, and he is the elder son and heir," said Katie.

This truth did put Rupert into a temper. "Oh, go to bed!" he snarled, and flung himself about the room, leaving her no privacy to remove her clothes in peace.

Katie managed to keep her back turned to him. She slid off her dark blue traveling dress and took off her boots and hose. Her pantaloons and underdress came next, and the nightdress was slid over her head, to conceal her body as she removed the last garments against her skin. He was drinking deeply from the whiskey bottle as she slid into the narrow bunk next to the cabin wall.

She shut her eyes resolutely as he banged down the bottle and took his nightshirt in hand. She heard the rustle of his shirt as he removed it, and he muttered as he stumbled about the cabin. He blew out the candle at last and came over to her. She went stiff.

He lifted the covers and came into the narrow bunk with her. It was so close that even though she pushed herself to the far side, the wall prevented her from moving farther.

"Rupert," she gasped. "There is another bunk for you—"

"Oh, but you are my little wife," he said, and his breath was thick with the drink. He breathed in her face, and she quailed. Was this the nice, gentle Rupert she knew?

He put his arms about her. She struggled instinctively and struck out at him with her fist. "Let me go!" she gasped.

"Why should I? You agreed to marry me! You were eager to marry me! As my wife you should be a good obedient girl!"

At his insulting, disagreeable tone she went stiff. She still struck out at him, frightened, until he caught her hand and wrenched her arm and put it above her head.

His head bent; his hot mouth sought her lips. He kissed her into silence, though she tried to cry out to stop him.

His body was naked! She had not realized that until he pulled up the hem of her nightdress and put his warm body against her cold one. The heat of him alarmed her; the closeness frightened her. She had never touched a man before. Mrs. Llewellyn and Mrs. Garrison had talked to her, gently, about marriage, but the reality was alarming.

In the small, close, chilled cabin her thin body

shook as Rupert lay over her and kissed her lips, her throat, her small young breasts. His hands seemed to be everywhere, stroking her upper body. Then one hand moved to her slim thighs and went over them. The intimate touch outraged her. No one but herself had ever touched her there.

"Don't, Rupert," she panted. "Do not do that! Oh—please—why must you be so horrid?" Her voice rose to a scream as he parted her legs and put one large leg between her thighs.

"Why are you crying?" he sneered, his voice blurred. "This is what you wanted, isn't it? You agreed to the marriage, even though you knew—you knew—" He stopped as his lips found her mouth again and drank hungrily from it.

They fought in the narrow bed. She struggled with all her terrified strength to push him from her. But when she had pushed him from her throat and breasts, he only pushed harder at her thighs. He was kissing her arms, her waist, moving about, thrashing with her in the thin bunk.

He had her against the wall, penned in with his larger body and agile strength. He held her there, firmly, and pressed to her. She tried to scream; he put his hand quickly over her mouth.

"Be quiet! Do you want the whole ship to hear you?" he snarled in her ear.

Then she realized that the thin walls would indeed reveal what they were doing. She burned with shame, and in her sudden silence he took her.

The pain shot through her. She was young, unprepared, never having even cuddled and kissed with a man before. She had no idea what she should do, how she should feel, and he had not troubled to help her.

The hurt of his entry into her unprepared body was indeed the worst physical pain she had ever known. She writhed in horror and tried to pull from him. He would not have it; he pushed further into her.

"Oh, my God," she moaned against his stern hand on her mouth. "Oh—my—God—oh, it hurts—oh, Rupert, don't—you hurt me—you hurt—"

Tears were flowing down her thin cheeks. She felt as if their struggling had gone on for hours. She felt a sudden flow of wetness on her thighs, then, pressing inside her, a gush of warmth and wetness. Rupert sighed deeply, his body relaxed, and his hand came from her mouth. For a long moment he lay on her, resting. Then he made himself sit up.

"There. It is done," he said flatly, his voice dragging. "Get some sleep, Katie."

Sleep? She felt a hysterical laugh bubble in her throat. She lay half-naked, chilled, frightened, in pain, and he told her to sleep.

Rupert got up and lit the candle. Then he came back to her and gazed down at her. She tried to shield herself by pulling at the sheet. Gently he held her hand from it.

"You're bleeding, Katie. I'll get a cloth and water."

"Bleeding?" she gasped, and sat up abruptly to stare down at her thighs. Dark blood stained her thighs. "Oh, am I injured? Oh, it does hurt—"

Rupert's mouth compressed. He soaked a towel in water and came back to her. To her further intense shame, he washed her thighs for her in cool water, then dried them. For a man to do this—and stare at her so—She could have died of embarrassment. Her head was lowered; her long braids swung over her shoulders.

When he had finished, he pushed her back against the pillows, drew her nightdress down to her ankles, and pulled the sheet and blanket over her body. She huddled into it, her eyes wide and terrified in her white face.

He touched her hair. "That's all, Katie. I'll sleep in the other bed tonight. But don't think you can get out of your duties as wife," he said harshly. "You married me; you'll take the consequences! We all have to face our duties, you know!"

And with that he blew out the candle again and lay down in the other bunk.

In the darkness she wept silently.

The next morning Katie wakened late. Rupert had dressed and gone out. Her trunk lay opened and waiting; the duties before her waited. They would sail in two days.

A sailor brought her tea and some food. She ate mechanically. The tea was hot and stronger than she liked, but it was hearty. She unpacked their trunks of goods they would need for the voyage, stowing her undergarments and his neatly in the drawers of the built-in cupboards. Her dresses and his suits and shirts were hung in the cunning closet which shut with a sliding door. She hung up two of her fur-lined cloaks, then took the thick plaid one and swung it around her shoulders before going up on deck.

Selina was hysterical the night before the dawn sailing. She left their dinner and wine and ran to her cabin. Terence flung down his napkin and followed her. They could hear her weeping and crying out, "I want to go home! I will die in this horrible ship, I know!"

Terence's voice was low and soothing; they could not hear his words. But they could hear her clearly, blaming him for it all: the duel, the exile, his insistence that she should accompany him, all.

Captain Potter was red and finally excused himself with relief to go up on deck. Katie and Rupert sat in silence. She was weary and thought he was also.

They had both worked hard to help the ship prepare to leave. She had tallied goods; the final crates had been loaded; Rupert had helped onshore in the warehouse until it was emptied and everything on board.

Dawn came soon, and Katie washed, dressed, and went up on deck, to say a final silent good-bye to the English shore. She would not see it again for a long time, she thought, and she watched as the ship pulled out slowly from the wharf, and the sails were raised. Other ships gave a hoot of mournful sound to bid them farewell. Rupert came to stand at her side as the orders were given. "Hoist the foremast, steady as she goes, 'ware the side—"

She was surprised when Rupert put his arm about her shoulders, hugging her cloak to her with his own warm body. "Well, this is farewell to old England, Katie," he said.

"Yes—farewell—and hello to adventure," she said bravely.

He squeezed her quickly. "Good girl, Katie. That's the spirit," he said warmly, the most pleasantly he had spoken to her for two days. "We could have a jolly time of it. Let's do, shall we? It will be a long voyage, six months until we reach Canton. Let's be friends, all right, Katie?"

She smiled shyly up at him and nodded in relief. She hated to be at odds with Rupert—she still cared for him, no matter what he did. She understood his bitterness, though she did not like it. He had been taking out his anger on her.

Captain Potter did not join them for meals until they were well on their way. Selina finally emerged from her cabin, at Milbank's insistence. The middle-aged maid in funereal black could do more with Selina than her husband or anyone else. She had urged her mistress to wash and dress, had done her hair beautifully in long shining curls, and now Selina was prepared to face the world again.

It was a relief to them all, especially Terence. He was sick of her crying and her accusations. Never very patient, thought Katie, he had met his match in someone who could outshout him in a temper and outlast him in sulks. And when she put her handkerchief to her eyes and sobbed, everyone wanted to do all in his or her power to stop her grief. She was so pretty, so charming when she was in good mood.

The *China Princess* soon left English waters. It was amazing how rapidly it flew along with its tall sails catching the winds, hurling them south along the coast of France. They would catch glimpses from day to day of a distant blue shore. The war with France was finally over. They need not fear the ships of France, coming out from hidden harbors to give battle with blazing cannon.

The captain knew his way as he had made this journey a dozen times. And around the coast of Africa and up to the Indian Ocean he would be traveling paths he had navigated at least six times. It was reassuring to travel with a man like Captain Potter—a man of adventurous spirit, calm competence, his men well in hand.

He and Rupert arranged for the half a dozen best sailor-marksmen to be further trained, and Rupert had that in charge. When Selina asked why, she was evaded.

Katie asked the captain why. He studied her face, then told her bluntly, "Pirates, ma'am. Pirates. No matter how peaceful our England is with her neighbors at this time, there be always pirates. First, in the coast near the tip of Portugal and across to North Africa. Them be the Barbary pirates. You'll have heard of them."

"Oh, yes," she said, concealing her shudders. "They are dreadful, uncouth men! No sense of honor."

"Beg pardon, ma'am. That ain't the way of it," the captain blandly corrrected her. "The Barbary pirates, they think they're doing this, attacking our ships, as a patriotic gesture for their country. To them, we are the barbarians!"

She absorbed that thoughtfully. The captain talked little, but when he did, she felt he had much to teach. And she had ever been eager to learn of the world, its manners and customs, its strange ways, its beauties, and even its uglinesses. Only thus could she begin to understand people.

"So they do bloodthirsty deeds for the sake of their country?" Katie finally asked.

"Aye, Mrs. Katie. Even as our good Englishmen fought the French at Waterloo!"

When she had taken that in, he told her further of the pirates of the South China Sea, a different breed altogether. "Most Chinese are law-abiding and obedient to their elders and their officials, most unnaturally. so. They run about and it's 'yes, sir, no, sir, right away, sir,' with them. But their pirates, they are outlaws, outside the law, and a more wicked lot you'll never behold. Murder for a few coins and a bit of jade, they will."

She shuddered, and he quickly changed the subject.

Katie enjoyed the days, they were so lovely. And Rupert was kinder to her. He came to her bunk several times in the next weeks and months and was much gentler with her. He would kiss her and hold her for a time, until she was ready for the rise of his passions, and even her own timid responses pleased him.

In the silence of the night, with only the quiet sounds of the ship and the sea lapping about them, he would kiss lightly her wide mouth and her soft throat and fondle her breasts and thighs. He liked to hold her naked body against his and rub slowly against her. It began to thrill her, this sensuous movement up and down, up and down. His hand would stroke her back, he would draw her closer, and his breathing would quicken.

Then—then he would come over her and spread her legs. Katie knew by now he liked her to put her hands on his body, to stroke his back and chest, and to kiss his throat. While she did this he would bring their two bodies together slowly, slowly, almost teasingly so, building up her emotions and causing her own desires to rise. When they kissed, she would open her mouth, and his tongue would thrust inside. Sometimes he nibbled on her lower lip, teasingly, until her tongue pressed against his.

It was terribly exciting once the pain was gone. One

night they lay together for a long time, and he went to sleep on her breasts and thighs. She had to wiggle about to get him off her—he was so heavy—and he slept against her for several hours, keeping her warm and snug between his body and the wall.

He was kinder to her before Terence and Selina also. In fact, as the voyage progressed, things became easier for them all. Terence had time to woo Selina as she liked. They strolled the deck on moonlit nights, and laughed and kissed frankly, and retired early.

Rupert spent more time with Katie. They talked about what they would do in Macao and read over his father's written instructions, which were set out in much detail. "We will need to hire many Chinese. You can help me, Katie," said Rupert thoughtfully. "We will consult together about the house. Of course, Selina must have a say in it—"

"Of course," said Katie obediently. She only hoped that Selina would take some interest in the house and in instructing the servants. Katie would have much to do with the silks and jade, the porcelains and teas.

Days they often spent on deck, leaning over the railing. A school of fish brought them running, until that became old stuff. But when a school of porpoises came to play about the ship like big friendly dogs, Katie was so fascinated she hung on the railing all the day and could scarcely tear herself away for meals or to sit in the shade. How fascinating they were, those giant animals. A sailor told her that they could be very friendly and swim alongside a man in the ocean near a beach. "I've swum from a beach and found meself in the middle of half a dozen of them, and not a fear in the world, missus," he told her, as he scrubbed busily on the well-polished deck. "They'll play about you, nose you, not a bite do they take. It's just play-ing, and they're a-saying they's friendly."

Rupert came up then, to listen and question him about the sea creatures. He shared his lore willingly and gave them a shy smile when he had to move to another part of the deck.

Down they went along the African coast. Now the shores were the deep green of the jungle, outlined with golden sand beaches. They had stopped at Lis-bon Harbor to take on fresh water and more firewood for the cookstoves. The captain avoided these harbors and had sailors on guard all night.

"Slavers all about here," he said. "The blacks on-shore know it. To them, we're all wicked men, like the slavery men. They'll come swarming about the ship if we don't guard, and come aboard with their sharp knives. I've known them attack a small vessel and kill all aboard. If we should have to go ashore, I'd take a large party with me, you may believe it."

They did have to take on fresh water down around the west coast of Africa. Rupert and Terence went ashore with the first mate while Captain Potter kept a sharp eye out. Five sailors went with them, all well armed, and another five carried water casks. The first lieutenant was experienced in these parts and found the stream where they had obtained fresh water be-fore. Rupert was fascinated by how the man smelled the water, tasted it, waited, and looked about sharply.

"What do you look for, sir?" asked Rupert.

"Animals and birds and their signs," said the man, and pointed to some tracks in the mud near the stream. "See there? Lion made that. And other smaller cats there. And some antelope, I know their signs. And the birds has been here. Yep, it's all right to get water. The signs are fresh."

"What does that mean?" Terence frowned. He disliked asking for information from his inferiors. But in this case they knew so much more than he did, and he knew he must learn the ways of the country. And his idle brain had benefited from the work he had been doing; he was more alert and interested in the project. It could be much more exciting, a voyage like this, than a dozen balls, he had finally told Selina at dinner one evening. To this point of view she had spiritedly objected.

"That the water is not poisoned, Mr. Terence. If it was, they wouldn't come to it. And we would see bodies of small animals and birds about. Ain't any." And he directed the water casks to be filled.

As they returned to the ship, Rupert suddenly turned back. He had had a funny feeling down his back, like the times in war when he had sensed an enemy about, probably beyond the campfires or in the trees. This time he glanced about as though idly studying the mountains beyond them. And watching, turning suddenly and then back to the trail, then around again, he spotted a black man watching them.

He moved to the lieutenant. "Someone watching us," he murmured.

The man nodded, not gazing around. "Aye, Mr. Rupert. There be half a dozen of them in them trees. But they'll not bother us now. They been watching for an hour."

Rupert was annoyed with himself that he had not seen them before. He glanced about, catching another look of two men standing still as trees among the tall, massive, thick-leaved trees and brush. They were black as coal, shiny of face, of tall, sturdy build, with long bows and arrows in their hands. Even as he watched, they seemed to melt into the trees and were gone in a blink of his eye.

He was thoughtful as he returned to the ship. He told the captain of the matter, and the red-haired man nodded. "Aye, they watch. They rarely attack, although some will. Afraid of us, and afraid we will linger to capture some of them. We'll be on our way, right smart. Too bad them fellows need to live in fear."

"You are a man of humanity," said Rupert slowly. "Some captains would think of the high profits from such cargo."

"Aye, they would," said Captain Potter. "But I'll not take a man's freedom from him, less he is a villain."

On they sailed down the coast. They came to the Cape of Good Hope and hung on the railing there to eye the oddly shaped houses of the Dutch settlers on the black continent. Then they were sailing east and north, up the coast, past black villages, fields of tobacco, wide mouths of swift-running rivers. They docked several times to take on water, with Captain Potter giving directions about where to stop.

And one day the sailors returning from the water mission brought with them a small monkey with a little black face. Katie exclaimed with delight and asked to hold him. She took him in her hands, and he chattered to her as though talking, waving his little paws and giving her a sober look from his wrinkled little features.

He was small and brown, with a tiny black face and a long tail that curled over her arm. Even Selina overcame her fear of strange things and came to touch his head and paw timidly.

"What an odd creature to be sure!" she exclaimed. "What London would say should I carry such a bit around with me!"

"You would be a sensation," said Katie, smiling. "I wonder if the little animal would last to be carried home again?"

The sailor took him back to his own bunk, where he was kept as a pet through the voyage. The sailor sometimes came up after dinner and let the ladies pet his little friend.

The ship sailed between a broad island and the coast of Africa. The island was Madagascar, said the captain, and he and Rupert went ashore with several men, to bargain for spices. They sailed north again, this time to Zanzibar for more spices. The kegs of the fine sharp cinnamon, nutmeg, and camphor and the casks of precious oils were excellent cargo; they took up little room and would command a fine price in London. If they had room and space on the ship on the voyage home, they would buy more and take them along. For now, a smaller amount would do, and they might use the items for trade in Canton.

Terence and Rupert had begun to talk and plan. Katie and Selina sat in on the sessions, Selina showing more interest to Katie's great concealed relief. She asked about Macao and the society there of Britishers, French, Portuguese and seemed satisfied there would be an exotic circle of people in the midst of which she herself would shine, as Terence assured her.

Katie quietly schooled the men in jade and porcelain and silks. They took well to her little speeches, following their father's stern instructions. She explained how to look for quality objects. Fortunately both had grown up in the midst of good jade and fine porcelains of their father's choosing, and that made it easier for her to instruct them on how to choose the best. She would be in Macao, and though the men might come down sometimes from Canton, the instant decisions had to be theirs. She was not allowed, as a female, to go to Canton. No foreign women were permitted in the hongs of Canton, in the warehouses there, the factories, as they were called. A factor was an agent, and they called the warehouses factories, where goods were piled up as they were purchased, before being put on small junks and carried twelve miles downriver where the *China Princess* would be at the wharf of Whampoa.

The captain sat in with them on some sessions, explaining patiently how matters were carried on in Canton. "For it's their country, you see, and they have their little ways. All have to go to one merchant, his own hong merchant, and bargain with him. And before you get to him, you'll have to pay cumshaw—that is, gifts—to the chief Chinese customs inspector at Whampoa. He is responsible for you, and if you come to grief, he protects you as much as he is able. He likes watches, clocks, musical boxes. Your father put in a deal of that sort of stuff for cumshaw. All the Chinese like watches, and they can't get enough of them."

They listened, questioned, exclaimed. He knew his business, and what he said was much as their father had instructed them and had written down for them. They began to look forward eagerly to their arrival.

But first there was the Indian Ocean to cross. It was hot, humid, almost unbearably so. The ladies put on their lightest muslins and carried parasols and still sought the cooler interior of the parlor cabin to pant and fan themselves. Katie listened to Selina's wails of dismay with more sympathy, for she herself felt miserable in the wet heat.

They came to the Spice Islands and moved into port there to trade off a few goods for their precious black pepper. The *China Princess* took on six kegs of it and paid for more to be held for their return.

Captain Potter returned from ashore at evening with a look of satisfaction. He told Rupert and Terence and the ladies, "There's another British ship in port, and two French, and an American. I've been talking to their captains. We decided to proceed together to Macao. Safety in numbers. So, Mr. Terence, sir, if you'd go ashore with me tonight, we'll make final agreement with your permission, sir."

"Why do we have to go together?" asked Terence.

"Pirates in the South China Sea," said the captain patiently. "They been bad lately, I'm told. Swarming all about. With all of us shipping together and looking armed, with my two cannon poking their snouts out the sides and armed men aboard carrying rifles, I think we'll get through. They won't dare touch us."

"Must we go with French ships?" asked Rupert, his face shadowed. He had so lately been in battle against them.

"Aye, Mr. Rupert," said the captain, with a kindly look to him. "The wars are forgotten this side of the world. We're all Europeans and Americans, too, this part of the foreign world. You'll see tomorrow, when a Frenchman is coming aboard to bring some wines and we'll give him a gift in return. He'll be nice as can be, and all battles forgotten."

And so it proved. A French contingent came to visit; they all went to visit the American ship and were amazed at the smart appearance of their former colonials. The British were friendly in spite of being tied to the rival British East India Company. As the captain had said, in this strange Orient, they were bound in friendship and similar backgrounds. They had a friendly two days in port, with much visiting back and forth, and Rupert was surprised to find how well he liked one young Frenchman who was the supercargo on his ship.

Katie got along well with them all. After being shy at first, she began by translating for beautiful Selina, who was the belle of the party, the prettiest by far. Several wives were aboard, but they were mostly middle-aged, plump, and reddened by the sea winds. Katie and Selina received most of the attention.

Katie could speak French, German, and also Chinese, and the men were amazed by her. Rupert put his arm around her when they had attended dances and looked critically at any man who asked his wife to dance. He was proud of his young wife, who had seemed to blossom almost unexpectedly these months. She could shine even in the presence of Selina, who this particular evening was glorious in a gown of green and blue shimmering silk and a gauze overdress. His Katie looked well in rose silk, and he felt more contented than he had at the beginning of the voyage. Selina was beyond him, but he had a fine wife himself.

After the bad beginning of their first night, for which he blamed his state of intoxication and bitterness, they had dealt well together even in bed. He had been surprised and pleased at Katie's quickness to learn about caresses and lovemaking. She might be young and shy, but in the darkness of the cabin, in the narrow bed, she had proved a willing pupil. Her slim young form could quiver with passion, and he enjoyed her lithe body immensely.

Yes, it was becoming bearable, he thought. The life which had seemed so bitter had eased, and he could laugh and squeeze his wife's slim waist and nod graciously to allow his French friend to guide Katie in the intricacies of a new dance called the waltz, somewhat scandalous yet in England. They danced well together, and Selina clamored to learn the dance also.

It was a gay bright party, which ended well after midnight. Sailors came to escort them home again, to their own *China Princess,* along the dark wharves. The lights of their ship looked good to them, and Katie said, "Home again. I wonder when we will arrive in Macao . . . and what we will find there."

"Friends, more friends, Katie," said Rupert, and kissed her cheek on the well-lit deck in front of the grinning sailors.

5

During the next several days, as they traveled north-east toward Canton and Macao, they were immensely glad of the company of other ships. Pirates were sighted daily. Usually they hung about just near the horizon and surveyed them with long spyglasses.

However, on two occasions large pirate junks, longer than the *China Princess,* came up boldly almost within firing range and studied them. Captain Potter had sent the ladies below out of sight.

Rupert quietly asked why.

The captain said grimly, "Because some of them go crazy with sight of white women. And such pretty ones as we are carrying!" He shook his red head. "No, best keep them out of sight. We'll show our arms boldly as well."

The other ships in their small group were showing their cannon, and men with rifles trotted on deck and stood at the ready. The two huge junks, with their two large sails each, studied them, then veered off about sunset.

Armed guards remained on deck all through the night. Morning showed an empty sea, but Captain Potter remained on the alert. Either he or his first mate constantly scanned the sea with the long spyglass.

Rupert was immensely thankful when the *China*

Princess pulled up at one of the wharves of Macao Harbor and sank anchor. Two small sampans approached, looking official with scarlet banners and a canopy to shelter the chief man from the sunshine. Captain Potter piped them aboard.

Rupert and Terence met them, dressed smartly in their finest clothes of silk, and paid them deference. The chief mandarin welcomed them briskly, and they went to the main cabin to receive him with tea and the cumshaw, discreetly given as "gifts."

The two ladies were there. The mandarin eyed them with blank face, received their curtsies as his due, and ignored them. However, when Katie began to translate for him, he did look surprised. He was hesitant about speaking directly to her.

Rupert said slowly and distinctly, "This is my wife, Mrs. Llewellyn, who is very well educated in Chinese ways and language. Her honorable father, who has now died, trained her in the many ways of the Chinese. Her father and she admire much the excellent silks, the porcelains, the wisdom, and the beautiful arts of the Chinese. Making this her study, she contributes much to our trade with your magnificent country."

Terence looked as if he would like to insert a joke or a sneer, but Captain Potter gave him a stern look, and he subsided, saying nothing.

The mandarin bowed slightly, disdainfully, to Katie, but his black eyes showed his curiosity. "It is forbidden to teach any foreigner the Chinese language, madam. However, since you already know it, that may be well."

Katie bowed her head in the splendid rose bonnet with lute strings and answered his words with her most careful Mandarin accent. "I shall endeavor to be of aid to my husband and to his trading company. It will be a great pleasure and an honor to assist in purchasing the beautiful objects of the Chinese to carry home. My country much admires the jade, the silk, the ivory, the porcelains, all the beautiful treasures which the Chinese people make with such skill."

He nodded to her but still spoke in his careful English. "An interpreter will be hired and assigned to you. That will be his duty, madam. You wish to hire a house and servants for the ladies in Macao?" He turned to Rupert.

Terence interrupted rudely. "I wish a fine palacial house, with many rooms. My wife must be kept in comfort. It is barbaric that she cannot come with us to Canton—"

The mandarin's face showed his disapproval at these words. His voice became stiff and formal. "I regret many houses are not available for your choice. One house is for hire. I will show it to you. If it does not suit you, then I regret you must return home with disappointment."

Captain Potter intervened. "We understand, of course, that no ladies are permitted in Canton, sir," he said very respectfully, giving Terence a stern warning look. "Whatever house you have found for my employers will be gratefully accepted. We know you are an honorable and intelligent man, with many connections of consequence. Therefore, whatever you have found will be splendid, we know."

The mandarin did not show any gratification. He bowed his shaved head with the single long pigtail that trailed down his back from his brilliant scarlet silk hat. He accepted the compliments as his due.

Rupert hurried to add, "We are most grateful for your assistance. We will be directed by you. This is the first journey of my brother and of me, though my honorable father has made two such journeys in his youth. He has often spoken longingly of his wish to return to beautiful waters of Canton."

Terence then remained silent, while Captain Potter and Rupert, by deferring to the mandarin, asking his advice, and accepting all he said, placated the man. He would meet them the next morning, he said, and escort them to the house he had chosen for them. He would hire servants for them, a linguist to accompany them to Canton, a pilot to take their ship up to the wharf at Whampoa, and so on. A hong merchant in Canton would accept their goods and help them purchase what they wished.

Then Rupert firmly introduced another subject. "My wife, Mrs. Katie Llewellyn," he said, "is a most skilled artist in the designs of silk. Would it be possible for her to be in contact with silk merchants, in order to suggest designs that we wish to have made, to take back to England with us? She knows the English markets and has some sketches to show you." He nodded to Katie.

Katie opened the folder before her, a large flat cardboard folder of her best designs. Silently she moved the folder to Rupert, who bowed to the mandarin and laid the folder on the table before him.

The mandarin moved stiffly, his face a little troubled, as though this were something beyond his other dealings. Silently he turned over one after another of the paper designs skillfully sketched out by Katie. He studied them: the butterflies; the English birds; gay tendrils of vines twined about the borders.

"I will see to it that the silk merchants are informed of the lady's wishes," he said. "I do not know if they will want to take the time to command that the work should be done. However, if the lady wishes, and you wish," he said to Rupert, "it may be that a merchant will be agreeable. The contacts shall be arranged."

"It would be most gracious of your honorable self to do this," said Rupert. He dared not meet Selina's eye; she looked so scornful of all this talk directed to a man of the yellow race.

"The porcelain makers are accustomed to following the wishes of the foreign designers," said the mandarin very politely. "If you wish to suggest some designs for the porcelain you carry, that can be arranged."

"That also will be of great pleasure to us, as we have many commissions for coffee sets, tea sets, vases, and so on," said Rupert.

The mandarin now opened his "gifts" and permitted himself to admire the fine gold watches, a musical box of inlaid wood, a fine clock set in cedarwood, a clock of gold-tinted porcelain. This last he examined critically.

"Their work is poor," he said at last, disdainfully. "None of their porcelain is as fine as ours."

"We have not the many years of experience," said Rupert with a quelling look at Selina.

She blurted out, anyway, in her high voice, "But it is beautiful work, the best in England!"

The mandarin did not deign to give her a glance. "As you say, you have not the experience, nor do you have our good clay," he said decisively. He waited expectantly, and Rupert realized the gifts were not enough. Without the rude remarks made to the mandarin, the gifts might have proved sufficient. As it was, he must produce several other items, which the captain had advised him to have ready in the cupboard.

Rupert brought forth more gifts, more watches, two more musical boxes, and finally a box of gold coins fresh minted. The mandarin accepted them all graciously, then rose to signal his departure.

After the mandarin and his entourage had departed, Captain Potter asked the four of his employers to seat themselves again in the cabin which was their drawing room. His eyes sparkled with temper; his beard jutted out belligerently. However, he spoke quietly.

"There is something I must say to you all. I would have thought Mr. Douglas Llewellyn, smart as he is, would have explained all this to you. If you are polite to the Chinese and give them compliments on their excellent work, you'll do best. You won't have to pay so much cumshaw; the work they do for you will be accomplished more quickly.

"However, rudeness will meet with not more rudeness from them, but delays, hesitations, higher prices, more cumshaw requested. And much rudeness will result in all trade being shut off from you. You'll be closed out, definitely. No hong merchant will help you. The world will be out—no trade with Llewellyns. You'll go home empty-handed."

"Why should we bow down to those—those uncivilized creatures?" burst out Selina petulantly. "Why, their skins are yellow, they smell bad—"

"Because we are in their territory, Mrs. Selina," said Captain Potter. "To them, this is the center of the universe. Their emperor is not just their king; he's head of the world. Yes, this is the Middle Kingdom, between heaven and earth, and he dwells there. He's the greatest, the biggest, the tops of all. Bigger than our king, higher than everybody. That's what they believe. Trade is permitted only because they allow it. They say they don't need our goods; they have everything in the world they need and want. They trade with us graciously, they say, only because they pity us for not having the most beautiful silks and china and such only they can make." He paused for breath.

Terence said quickly, "Father did say something of this to me. I shall have to be more careful of my speech. It cost us more, didn't it, Rupert, because of what we said to him?"

Rupert answered him with care. He was angry with Terence and Selina, also, but he did not want it to show. It would be difficult enough to work with them in the months ahead. And if Terence chose to pull rank, Rupert would not be able to prevent trouble. "It cost about double, Terence. I had to take out some more watches and such from the cupboard. We won't have as much to trade in Canton now. With care, we may be able to get some good stuff and make a profit."

"I'll have to learn to keep my mouth shut or be as diplomatic as I am around the prince regent when he's in a temper," said Terence with a grimace. He turned to Selina. "And you, my dear, had best mind your manners! Pretend that they are the most snobbish of British lords and with power near the prince! Butter them up, that's what we have to do. You can do it well. I've seen you smooth the feathers of the most difficult and choleric of lords!"

Selina preened herself. "Of course I can. I know how to act in society! It is poor Katie who is ignorant of society ways. I must take her in hand!"

Rupert gave his wife an anxious look, fearful she would be offended. To his surprise and pleasure, she gave him a frank but merry look before turning to Selina. "It would be good of you to teach me society's ways, Selina. I would appreciate your training. As you say, I have been ignorant of their ways. I have no skills in this."

"We shall go out much in Macao while Terence and Rupert have to go to work in Canton," said Selina, looking more pleased than she had in a time. "We shall go out often and be merry! You must be guided by me, Katie. We shall have splendid times! And don't worry, Terence, I shall be very tactful and flattering."

"I knew I could depend on you, my dear," said Terence ironically. Rupert thought that Selina did not realize his irony and looked at the beauty more critically. Was she, then, not very intelligent?

The next day they went ashore. The mandarin showed them the house, and Rupert showed his gratitude plainly. The house had two floors of splendid size. On the first floor were rooms for receptions, a dining room larger than the one at the London town house, rooms for the servants at the back, and in the courtyard a fine large open kitchen.

On the second floor were six huge bedrooms. Rupert chose one for himself and Katie. Selina insisted on a huge bedroom for herself and her maid, Milbank, next to her husband's. They were across a wide hall from Rupert and Katie, but the younger brother could hear her lay down the law.

"No, Terence, you may not share my room! It is too

hot here in Macao! You must have a separate room, behind mine. I want the front one overlooking the harbor; at least I may have a view of this wretched place! Why your father insisted on my coming—it was only to punish me, I know! He hates me, and you will only make me miserable if you insist on sleeping with me in this horrible wet weather. Why, look how my clothes stick to me!"

Katie shut their door and sighed. Rupert sighed also. "I hope she will not complain constantly while we are gone, my dear Katie," he said gently.

Katie grimaced, then smoothed out her face. "I hope not, Rupert, but I shall have much work to do. I think it shall be all right between us," she said with determination.

"My good girl!" he said, and drew her into his arms and kissed her. In her ear he whispered, "I think if we had had this huge bed to lie in on shipboard, you would be with child already!" He smiled at her vivid blush and kissed her again.

After the turmoil of the day Katie was glad to go to bed that night. And not the least of her delights was that Rupert lay with her. In two more days he and the ship would proceed to Whampoa, the captain and he and Terence would go on by Chinese junks to Canton, and he might not be back for a month. He meant to return regularly, he had said, to make sure all went well with her.

Rupert came to her bed, and her mind was still going over all the details.

"How long will we be here, Rupert, do you know?" She was thinking of the supplies to be purchased, how much furnishing she should add for their comfort.

"I hope not longer than three months. The captain says it can take every bit of that. We are ordering special silks and porcelains, so that will take longer," he said, sighing. "However, Father will not be satisfied if we accept only what they will offer of their own choosing."

"No, that would defeat our purpose in coming," said Katie practically. "Well, we will have six servants, plus Milbank. The houseman in charge, Ho Chih, seems capable and understands my accent. And my maid, Lilac, will be a treasure, I feel sure. She is gentle of nature and willing to work."

"You must send a message to me by the mandarin if anything goes wrong," said Rupert. "I hate to leave you will all this arranging to do, and in a strange country. Dear Katie, you will take care, will you not?"

"Of course, Rupert. What could happen to me?" she asked in all innocence.

He stroked her back with teasing, intimate hand. "Oh, you are quite pretty, my Katie, and I won't have anybody running off with you." And he laughed.

"As though anybody would!" she scoffed. "Oh, that tickles, Rupert!"

He did it again and drew her closer. She cuddled to him and exchanged kisses with him. He had such a big, generous mouth, and she liked him to tease her with kisses, stroke her all over, caress her before taking her. In the big wide bed, with the windows wide open for the scented night air, the sound of the harbor below them down the hill, and a white mosquito netting seeming to shut them off from the world in a mist, she felt in a world of her own dreaming with the man she loved beside her, holding her tight.

He lay over her, kissing her, with more and deeper passion. Across the hall came the grumble of Terence's voice, his knock at Selina's door. "Let me in, Selina! It's only a couple of nights until I leave—" His pleading was in vain, the door was locked against him, and he finally padded away to "his" own room.

"If you shut me out," whispered Rupert, kissing her earlobe, "I would beat you!!"

"I would never shut you away from me," murmured Katie, and her hand curled around his neck, and her fingers played with the dark curls at its nape. In the dimness, with light from the sky coming in, she could see his intense blue Celtic eyes, like the lapis lazuli used in porcelains, she thought. And his lean, hard body was like that of a Greek god, broad shoulders, lean hips, a slim waist, long legs—

His legs curled around hers, then straightened again, as he brought them closer. His breathing was quickened, and she felt herself melting against him. There was a fire in her stomach, a need for him, so that she cried out softly.

"Oh, Rupert, darling—oh, please—"

"Do you want me?"

"Oh, love, do—oh, please—"

He smiled in pleasure and brushed his lips against her cheekbone as he came down to her. He held her tightly as he moved slowly inside. "Have you forgiven me for that first brutal night?" he whispered. "I have berated myself for that—your first time, to be so cruel—"

"Oh, don't think of it," she murmured against his bronzed throat. "It doesn't matter—oh, darling— darling—" Her voice stilled to nothing as he brought them to the height of passion with some thrust of his powerful thighs. She felt she was drowning in bliss.

He was so sweet to her those last couple of nights that she felt a terrible regret as she said good-bye to him. He had begun really to love her. He seemed to have a need for her. He did not hang about Selina anymore but kept busy during the day. If only he would stay with Katie for a time, he might forget Selina.

But the men had to go on, and they departed for Whampoa and then Canton, to live in the apartments over the British hong or warehouse and take care of the trading. They both seemed to be looking forward to a bachelor existence, especially as they had met men from the French, American, and other British ships already.

Selina began to whine before they were out of sight. "Oh, this dreadful Macao! I know I shall die of boredom! Why could I not have stayed in London or gone to Paris! Rupert can manage. Why did Terence have to come along?"

Katie knew better now than to blame Selina aloud for her part in the exile. Selina had much spite in her and found delight in petty little acts to take revenge. She was excellent in drawling disparaging comments about Katie before guests in a sweet, fretful tone that said how much she regretted Katie's gauche ways.

Selina presently left the room, still complaining. Katie went to consult with the dignified butler, Ho Chih. They decided on the menu for the next day. In the morning she and Ho Chih, with Lilac to chaperone Katie, went to the markets.

What a delight, and such strange sights! She found

it difficult to complete her purchases, to return before
the heat of the day, because it was so fascinating to
stroll from one shop to another, from fruit stand to
fish stand, from open-air market of flowers and vegetables down to the wharf, where the freshest fish could
be purchased off the boats.

Ho Chih thought it very strange that English missus
could speak his language. She spoke it well, not the
dialect of country peoples, but the pure Mandarin of
the scholars and upper classes. He dealt with the merchants who spoke only dialect; Katie insisted on
speaking to the others who could understand her.

They had to go to market every morning. The heat
and humidity of that tropical place was such that food
spoiled quickly. It was no hardship for Katie; she enjoyed the contacts with the smiling Chinese, the bold-
eyed Portuguese, the dark-eyed and beautiful Malays.
Roly-poly children spoke to her shyly and giggled
when she complimented them on their dress or their
toys. Their mothers gave her curious stares and some
shy smiles and occasionally spoke.

The mandarin was as good as his word and introduced Katie to several silk merchants. She examined
their goods with a critical eyes—amazing them—and
chose the types of silk she liked best.

"Not that kind," she said definitely, pointing to
some inferior silks. "Yes, I know that is popular. But I
wish to design for the thin silk of best quality. The
kind that can go through a wedding ring."

To emphasize this, she drew off her own engagement ring of sapphires which Rupert had given her
and placed it on her right hand. Then she drew off
her round slim gold wedding ring and took a piece of
silk in her hand. They watched, black eyes blank and

expressionless, as she took the glistening, excellent-quality silk and passed it through her wedding ring. The whole width went through it easily.

She replaced her rings carefully and smiled. "You see? Best-quality silk, only best."

With more respect then, they looked at her sketches. She was pleased when all were accepted with many nods. She had noted the colors on pieces of paper. A merchant took in what she said, as she pointed to the fabrics, and with a brush he sketched in Chinese characters the colors she indicated for each. Occasionally he would make a suggestion.

"This butterfly—more beautiful in deep blue, madame!" Or, "This flower, let us make yellow, in gold thread, madame."

She agreed with relief. They knew their business well and seemed interested in creating especially beautiful fabrics.

Rupert and Terence would be buying raw silks, bolts of it, in Canton for loading on the *China Princess* in Whampoa Harbor. Katie would turn in designs for silk-woven fabrics, and when the materials were completed, they would be sent to Canton for Rupert's approval, for purchase and loading on the ship. All had to go through Canton.

The merchants took her designs, went over them with her, made suggestions. All were amazed at her command of Chinese, and more respectful to her each time she returned. "Little English missus plenty smart," they said to each other, a couple of times in her hearing.

Selina's complaints died down. She was going out more, finding her own kind. She would invite guests to their home and weeded out those who bored her or whose language she could not speak. If they spoke English, they were invited back again. Her contempt for one woman who spoke only French died quickly when she discovered the woman was a princess of the old regime in France. For that, Selina would endure the boredom of the struggle to speak French to her.

Katie attended the teas, the dinners, suffered Selina's veiled insults, and watched alertly how Selina managed everything. Her sister-in-law might be unpleasant to her, but she did know how to curtsy in various depths for various ranks of person. She knew how to address correctly the wife of an earl, the wife of a baron, the daughter of a duke.

"Watching you and observing your good manners in society are an education in itself," said Katie to Selina on one of the other's better days.

Selina preened herself. "I was well educated," she said complacently. "Mother knew what was best always. If we are to advance in society, she told me constantly, we must be of the best manners, able to converse graciously or listen in silence to any conversation. Our attitude to our betters must be of the correct deference without being servile. To our equals we are familiar without being vulgar. We permit compliments; they are accepted with a smile if not too familiar, with a reproachful look if too vulgar."

Katie listened with interest and concealed amusement to these dictates. Milbank listened also, giving Katie a stern look if she thought Katie too amused. She was proud of her charge, she adored her, she was uncritical of her, thought Katie. Selina must be amused; she must be well-dressed; she must have her hot tea at any time of day she chose. She must not have work to do that would spoil her beautiful white hands. She must not go out in the heat of the day, when it would exhaust her.

So Katie did the marketing, planned the menus, except for the more elaborate dinners, when Selina told her what to have prepared. She sketched more designs for the silks. The mandarin introduced her to four porcelain merchants, and she went over designs with them, listened to their careful criticism. She learned much from them; they knew what could be done in china clay as well as the silk merchants knew the potentials of their product.

Katie rarely went out to teas with Selina; she had no time for many amusements. Milbank accompanied her mistress, to sit meekly in corners for hours at a time, drinking in the gossip, attending to Selina, obeying her in all things.

Several evenings a week Selina went to dinners or invited guests in. She was a beautiful hostess and became most popular in the closed little world of Macao. Some women remained for years with their husbands, while others were there as briefly as the Llewellyns.

The Chinese mandarins, however, kept to themselves. It was rare that the foreigners were invited to a mandarin home, or the mandarins to the foreign rented houses. Two closed little societies existed side by side in the beautiful city of Macao.

6

Katie was so busy that she was surprised to find three weeks had passed since they had arrived in Macao. It was now October, and Macao had turned slightly cooler. The winds blew gently across the harbor in the nighttime, and she had to wear a shawl or pelisse in the evenings. Selina often wore her best silk cloak with the border of swansdown. It was too hot to wear furs.

In her now-daily routine Katie went to the market in the early morning, with Lilac to accompany her. Ho Chih had taken over more and more of the routine of the household, and Katie was glad to leave to him such matters as the dusting, the supervision of the laundry in the back courtyard, the direction of the cooks and maids.

They had found a street, she and Lilac, which fascinated them both. It was narrow and dusty, as most were, but on it were the best shops, of finest porcelains, jade, jeweled objects, swords, herbs and spices. They turned in this direction that morning, after purchasing a day's supply of fish and fruits, vegetables, and a bit of meat. Selina disliked eating fish all the time, even though the meats were much more expensive.

Lilac carried the basket of groceries and deferentially followed her mistress the required three feet along the street. Katie had tried to get her to walk beside her, but the maid was horrified. She was an older woman, about thirty, with a patient, gentle air about her. She had become quite skillful in brushing and arranging Katie's hair in a loose chignon, with a soft arrangement of waves above her forehead.

They strolled along. Lilac was as eager to gaze in the shop windows as Katie. Katie had long been admiring the jade and thought of suggesting to Rupert, when he returned, that they buy some of it. It would cost some precious gold coins, but how beautiful it was. If his father was not pleased, they would sell it again at a good price for double the value. But Katie hoped he would allow them to keep it.

Her thoughts were absorbed in the jade when a small child dressed in skirts dashed in front of her on the walkway and out into the street. Katie's gaze went automatically to follow the little boy, with his mischievous dark eyes. She was all smiles until she suddenly heard the wail of the woman near her.

"Ay-eeee! Ay-eeee! My boy—my soul!"

Katie glanced where she looked and froze. A careening carriage was bolting along the narrow street, pulled by a frantic horse, white spume about its nose. Everyone scattered from its path—except the boy, who had halted to stare in frightened fascination.

That boy will be killed, Katie thought and immediately dashed into the narrow street to push him violently from the path of the horse and carriage. She felt the horse dash past her, the dangerous hooves just missing her feet. But the carriage did not miss her. It shaved past her, and a carriage wheel hit her, knocking her down.

Screams filled the air. Katie could not move; the

breath had been knocked from her. Then she felt herself lifted up, snatched literally out of the path of the next wheel. It all happened so fast she did not realize someone held her; it seemed a wind had come along and whirled her out of the path of the dangerous huge second wheel.

A curt voice said in pure Mandarin, "Bring a chair for the woman." She felt herself put down onto a chair; still, she could not get her breath. She raised her hand weakly and found blood on her palm.

Her leg stung now; she knew she had torn her gown and bruised and cut her leg. Lilac knelt beside her, wailing, the basket of groceries set down so the strong smell of fish came to them. Katie tried to get her breath. A man was above her. She wished she could lean on him because she felt dizzy.

A hand touched her shoulder and she bent her head back so she could see who it was. She gazed directly up into the handsomest face she had seen in Macao.

Her wide brown eyes gazed at him in amazement. He was so tall. And his face was not Chinese, she thought. In a glance she took him in, the broad, large face, the wide lips, the black eyes like jet under black eyebrows. And the hair was thick and dark, not pulled back so far, though he wore the usual pigtail, a big one hanging down his back. He wore the robes of a rich mandarin, but he did not look like a merchant.

His garb was rich and strange. Purple silk formed his coat, with embroidery of gold and silver threads in a dragon and wave pattern down the front. His pantaloons showed under the skirt of blue velvet and the embroidered hem of red. His shoes were thick and fine silk, with soles of leather. And on his dark head was an unusual round, peaked hat of leather and velvet. Rings were on his large brown hands; they glittered with gold and gems of rubies and emeralds and diamonds.

She looked back again at his face and by now had her breath back. She began to thank him in her best Mandarin.

"I must thank you, kind sir, for your generous quick help. But for you—I must—I must—" She faltered, and her face screwed up in an effort to hold back tears of shock.

He stared down at her. Amazement showed briefly in his formerly expressionless face. "You speak my tongue!" he said.

She nodded, weakly. "I have learned it. I hope my poor accent does not offend your august ears—" She had guessed he was a prince and would probably be offended that she spoke to him at all.

She brushed feebly at her face, which she guessed would be dust-covered. He ordered sharply, "Bring a glass of wine."

It was brought. She sipped at it, then submitted to Lilac's anxious attentions. Lilac had taken out a large silk scarf and tenderly wiped Katie's face.

A crowd had gathered, staring curiously at the sight. The man gave a few sharp orders. "Go on your way. Be off. Clear the street. Has no one gone to capture the horse? Where are your manners? Give air to the woman!"

They obeyed him at once, going off with looks over their shoulders. The shopkeepers retreated to their shops; the customers went inside or left the street at the other ends. Katie felt eyes still staring at her, but at least the people were not pressing around her.

She finally got her breath back completely and felt

better. "Thank you, sir, for your aid. I must return home now. My heart is most humbly grateful to you—"

"I will assist you in returning to your home," he said abruptly, arrogantly. "Where is your carriage?"

"I did not take the carriage today," said Katie. Selina always wanted it left for her, for her calls. "I walked."

The expression on his face was disdainful. He turned and spoke sharply to those who waited behind him. Katie now saw the sedan chair set down on the walkway, the four burly men, naked to the waist, who had carried him.

"Bring the chair to me."

They brought it quickly. He assisted Katie to her feet and was about to hand her into his elaborate gilt-covered silk-cushioned sedan chair.

"Oh, sir, I cannot take your chair, I can walk," she said, really horrified. She knew it simply was not done, for this grand gentleman to walk while she rode. And she a foreign woman, whom they despised.

"I insist," he said, and lifted her bodily into the chair. He motioned to the men, who started out at a trot. She rocked along the street, with the gentleman beside her and Lilac trotting along after them with the basket of groceries.

He must have obtained the directions from Lilac; she heard their voices briefly. Katie was leaning back in the immensely comfortable chair, her eyes closed. She felt dizzy again, and the pain in her hand and leg was immense.

She must have lost consciousness for a moment, for afterward she remembered little of the short journey. She came to as he was lifting her out of the chair, her weight seeming nothing in his strong, hard arms. He carried her up to the front of the house. Ho Chih hastened out, his face showing his shock.

"Missee! Missee! What happened to you?" he cried out.

The man carrying Katie brushed past him into the house. He glanced about, then took her into the parlor. Selina started up from the couch; she was beautifully gowned in blue silk, her curls brushed in long shining order.

"Katie!" Selina cried out, gazing at the man in surprise. "Katie! Whatever in the world—"

The man said to Ho Chih, "Bring water and bandage and salve. The mistress is injured. She saved a child from a maddened horse dragging a carriage. She is most brave." He sounded brusque, reluctantly admiring the foolish courage.

He set Katie down very gently in a straight chair. She tried to smile. "Thank you, again, sir, for bringing me home. How can you forgive me for causing you such trouble? May I know your honorable name so my husband can thank you when he returns from Canton?"

"I am the prince Chen Yee," he said flatly. "And your name?"

"I am—" She hesitated. She did not know her name in Chinese. "Katherine Adair, I mean, Llewellyn." She had been shaken so much she scarcely remembered her new name. "Mrs. Rupert Llewellyn."

He bowed his head briefly, with obvious arrogance. He had completely ignored Selina, though Katie introduced her briefly, in English, then in Mandarin. Selina curtsied deeply, but again he only bent his arrogant head.

Ho Chih returned with Lilac, a bowl of warm water, bandages, and so on. The prince murmured to Katie, "I wish you speedy recovery of your hurts. You are a brave, though foolish, woman."

Without waiting for her answer, he left the house.

Selina was wailing then. "Who was that man? What happened to you? Oh, you are covered with blood. I feel faint! And don't get it on the carpet; I have guests coming this afternoon! Whatever trouble did you get into?"

Katie told her briefly, wearily. She decided to go up to her bedroom and let Lilac tend to her. Milbank was in the upstairs hall. Without being asked, she accompanied Katie to her room, and with her usual dour expression she assisted in cleansing the wounds, then adding salve and bandaging the many little punctures and scrapes.

Katie lay down then, feeling a little tearful. The shock was beginning to be felt. She could have been killed! She wondered what had happened to the small boy and his mother.

She slept for a time, then got up rather stiffly and painfully. From the chatter of voices, clink of china, and laughter belowstairs, she knew Selina was having her guests.

Lilac brought her tea and dishes on a tray and showed her sympathy. The cook had prepared tempting delicacies for the injured "missus," whom they admired for her gentle voice, her fairness, her generosity.

Soup was in a dainty bowl of white porcelain with a red dragon pattern weaving about it. She sipped at it—it was hot and stimulating. With it were small rice crackers.

Then she ate the bowlful of rice, with a small side dish of shrimp and smoked oysters. For dessert, the cook had sent a caramel pudding that Katie had taught her to make.

She sat up for a time, then went to bed to sleep. In the morning she would feel better and up to her duties again.

The following day she felt much like herself and started about her tasks. When she returned home from the market with Lilac, she found Ho Chih in a state of suppressed excitement. With a ceremonious bow he handed her a long note on a silver platter.

She opened it and gazed with admiration at the beautiful calligraphy, that of a scholar, she felt. She read the note slowly.

> Dear foreign woman,
>   My wife and I request the honor of the presence of you and your sister at dinner in our humble home. My carriage will call for you at six o'clock. Come this evening, if you will.
>   Prince Chen Yee.

"Dinner!" gasped Katie. "at his house tonight!" She stared at Ho Chih, who beamed from ear to ear.

"Lady is much honored," he murmured. "Prince Chen Yee does not dine much with foreign people, not ladies."

"He says his wife and he—he is married?"

"Yes, Mrs. Katie." Ho Chih bowed.

"And has children?" asked Katie hopefully. Perhaps it had been his own small son she had rescued—that might explain his unusual gesture.

"Prince Chen Yee has no children; it is the grief of his honorable life," murmured Ho Chih. "He has wife, very high Manchu princess. He has brother, the prince Chen Lo, very young. He has many relatives, some cousins. No sons. No daughters to make him merry. He is much sober man."

'Oh, it must be a disappointment to him."

"Grief," said Ho Chih, using a term which meant a grief of deep intensity.

Katie nodded and went to find Selina. She had gone out for the afternoon and returned to change her dress before going out again to a friend's home. She met the news with a mixture of fury and curiosity.

"Well, if he doesn't have a nerve, asking us for tonight! He might have known I would be engaged! Demanding our presence and sending a carriage—I wonder if he is very rich. He doesn't seem so yellow as the other Chinese; I wonder if he is a foreigner himself."

"I am so sorry you have an engagement, Selina. I would love to see his house. I'll warrant it is as big as a palace! Could you not send your regrets to the place where you are going tonight?"

"It is Mrs. Shaw, our neighbor," admitted Selina grudgingly. She studied her reflection in the mirror. "I could put her off. I can go to the Shaws' anytime. But I must send her a note."

She did, to Katie's relief. An answering note came back at once.

What luck you have! Nobody has ever been invited to dine with Prince Chen Yee. Dear Selina, you must report all to us! What an honor! He is a very high Manchu, close to the emperor, and it is rumored his wife is very wealthy and haughty and gorgeously beautiful. Come to me tomorrow, for dinner, and tell me everything!

That note from Mrs. Shaw, the tactful woman, thought Katie, put Selina in a rare good humor for the evening. She dressed carefully in a fine gown of lilac silk, with her diamond earrings, rings, and bracelet. Over it she wore a white silk robe with ermine hem.

Katie worried over what to wear and finally asked Lilac, who took out a flatteringly simple dress of peach silk and a pelisse of deeper peach shading to rose. With it Katie put on her amethysts, a gift from her father: a pendant of a single large amethyst and a ring that matched and fitted well on her small slim hand. The earbobs were small but set off her small oval face and the peach and amethyst colors were well on her slim figure and set off her peach-bloom cheeks.

The carriage came five minutes early, and they set out in the late-afternoon sunshine for the winter home of the prince Chen Yee. The carriage was twice as large as carriages in London, with plump cushions and curtains of silk hangings to hide the occupants, yet give them air.

It was a long ride around the harbor, then up the steep hill behind the top fort of Macao. Breezes were blowing there, and it felt ten degrees cooler than down in the city. Katie was more and more excited the closer they came.

Why had the Chinese prince honored them so? Because Katie could speak Chinese? Or was there some other reason? She wished Rupert were here, to share this experience, to be with her and advise her. She was only nineteen, and Selina's advice could be questionable. The older girl was usually guided by her pride and vanity.

The carriage rode over cobblestones, then abruptly

on a smooth white surface. "Marble!" whispered Selina, who looked shocked and awed. "I do believe it is white marble!"

Milbank accompanied them. Her face had little expression, but her white hands kept twisting, her mouth moved in agitation. "I really don't think it's right, Mrs. Selina, to come to this foreign house without Mr. Terence," she finally said.

"Nonsense, Milbank!" Selina was impatient. "Why not? We go out many an evening with male escort. Someone always sees us home again."

"Not to foreign houses," said Milbank flatly, then was silent again.

A tall, imposing Chinese man met them at the pillared entrance to the huge house. His face was expressionless as he helped the ladies down to the marble pavement before an open entrance. They went up marble stairs lined with huge porcelain pots of flowers, crimson, rose, pale pink.

The man led them slowly along the way so they could admire the tiled walls, with glimpses of courtyards on each side—some planted with trees and flowers, some like rooms with basket weave chairs and tables inside. They walked through about five such courtyards, then turned to one side, and the man opened a twelve-foot-high latticed door of cedarwood, which still smelled faintly of the fragrant wood.

He bowed for them to enter. Selina led, followed by Katie, then Milbank. Inside, the prince stood at attention and bowed slightly to them as they curtsied to him. Katie followed Selina's example and curtsied as deeply as her sister-in-law. Then she moved a foot forward and introduced them again. The prince bowed his head slightly and turned to the tall, haughty, imposing woman at his side.

"Princess Chen Mei-ling," he said. The woman was garbed in exotic dress of black velvet embroidered in gold and silver. Her underdress was of thin, shimmering varicolored silks, simply and elegantly cut. On her long feet were silk shoes, softly padded. Her hands were covered with rings; she did not offer them in greeting but folded them together and bowed her head slightly. Her headdress was the Manchu one, wide strands of hair on each side over wire frames, giving an appearance of a black butterfly.

Her face was heavily made up, perhaps to conceal lines, thought Katie. The high cheekbones were covered with rouge, henna lined her eyes, and her eyebrows had been plucked to a thin black line. Her hairline had been shaved to make a high, broad-forehead appearance, with the hair beginning far back, giving her aristocratic features an even more forbidding look.

The prince then drew forward a boy almost as tall as himself and introduced him. "My brother, Prince Chen Lo."

The boy smiled broadly, the first smile Katie had seen from this family. He dipped his head in a brisk bow. "Welcome to Chen house," he said in a low shy voice in English.

"Thank goodness you speak English," said Selina to the younger man. The face of the older prince remained bland, but the black eyes studied Selina's face for a quick moment.

They all were led into another room, a large formal living room. The chairs were simple, of black wood, the tabletops lacquered in black or in red. On one table stood a precious porcelain bowl of a strange green-blue that shimmered in the light of the torches which lined the room. Thin cushions covered the chair seats of the straight chairs.

They sat down, the prince in the largest armchair. Katie took a seat at his right, and Selina sat across from them. Princess Chen Mei-ling sat next to the prince, her chair pushed back so she was almost out of the group. Milbank sat at the side behind her mistress.

Conversation was awkward at first. Only Katie and the prince Chen Yee seemed relaxed enough to speak, and Selina knew no Chinese. Servants brought in small trays with beautiful cups of fiery hot liquid. They drank, politely, and ate from other dishes of nuts, dried shrimp, and some food the English girls could not identify.

Prince Chen Yee, turning to Katie, asked her questions. His black eyes studied her face as she spoke, noting every expression. "Your husband is not with you in Macao?"

She had a definite feeling he knew all about it. But she spoke very politely. "My husband, Rupert Llewellyn, is with his brother, Terence, and Captain Abraham Potter at the port of Canton. The two brothers are carrying out the commissions of their honorable father, Douglas Llewellyn."

"And these commissions? What are they?"

She patiently answered about the silks, the porcelains, and the jade and ivory. He nodded, and Katie trranslated quickly for Selina.

"And your father and your family? They permitted you to make the journey so far without regret?" asked the prince.

Katie told him in her frank, open manner about her lack of family, the recent death of her father. At his questions she told him about her father, his work, his fascination with all the Oriental matters.

He listened thoughtfully, as did Prince Chen Lo. Another girl came in timidly as she spoke, and the prince turned to her when Katie paused.

He indicated to the girl she could come close and be seated near to him. His face had softened to gentler line.

"This is my dear cousin Moon Blossom, my third cousin on my mother's side," he said.

The girl bowed, giggled nervously behind her hand at Katie's greeting, straightened her face anxiously at a brusque low word of rebuke from Princess Chen Mei-ling. "I am happy to be introduced to you," said the girl. Her bright, inquisitive eyes moved from Katie to Selina, taking in every detail of their hairdresses and gowns and cloaks.

"Before the sun has set, I wish to show you a courtyard which may please you," said the prince, and rose, clapping his hands sharply. Servants appeared and opened doors. The prince led Katie, leaving Selina to follow with the others, displeasing her. The prince led Katie to the next courtyard, and she did gasp.

It was a smaller courtyard, with charming bays outlined with marble columns. In the center were three peach trees in full bloom, the pale pink blossoms just beginning to drop on the grass. The prince stood in silence as Katie gazed and gazed at the lovely peach trees, the roses in porcelain pots set about the four corners of the courtyard, the beautiful designs of tiles on the walls.

A rosy glow from the setting sun cast a pink light

over the trees, the blue-green tiles, the flowers, giving everything a gentle, happy appearance. The blossoms dropped as the breeze came up and flung some petals over them, some landing in Katie's hair. She had not worn a bonnet, only a thin scarf to protect her hair from the wind, and she had removed it when entering the house. The pink blossoms settled on her dark head, and one on her eyelashes. She removed it, blinked, and smiled radiantly up at the prince.

"How beautiful this place is. I shall remember it always. The blossoms, the setting sun."

"I shall write a poem about it for you," he said seriously, ceremoniously. Then he led them all into the next room, across another courtyard, under the trees, and to the far room.

The large lit room held a huge long table set for them. It could have easily sat twenty, but the chairs were all set closer to the head of the table. The prince took the head and again seated Katie to his right, Selina to his left. Milbank sat on a chair to the side, primly refusing both food and drink, her suspicious glance darting about to the silent servants as they brought in the platters of steaming hot food.

The courses were all very small, dainty dishes of elegant white china rimmed in gold, each dish holding some precious, exquisite bit of food. The servants came and went, quickly serving them. The prince explained each dish, and Katie again translated.

Selina later informed Katie there had been thirty courses. Katie tasted the foods, some hot and spicy, followed by a bland dish, followed by mild, scented dishes. Each was different, unusual, showing much thought and effort. They finished with fruit and nuts, pineapple, pine nuts, bits of coconut and nutmeg, pears so sweet and juicy Katie had never tasted the like.

They left the table, to go to still another formal room. This was furnished with blond wood chairs, against a background of soothing pale green tapestries.

Selina was completely out of the conversation and sulked. The prince had brought out thin tissue writing papers and ordered ink and brushes. He then proceeded to write a poem for Katie, in beautiful calligraphy, of the Court of the Flowering Peach, as he called it. She translated it for the indifferent Selina.

Guests come to the Court of the Flowering Peach.
The evening sun flashes in the west.
I wish the finest blossoms to honor my guests.
They respond by falling in homage at our feet.

Katie praised both the poem and the writing, and he seemed to respond with a more open manner. He even smiled once, when his younger brother made a nervous jest.

While Moon Blossom and Prince Chen Lo seemed shyly friendly, the princess Chen Mei-ling seemed to become more openly hostile and sneering as the evening proceeded. At last the prince's wife rose abruptly to her feet and spoke in harsh tones. "I am not well. I shall retire if you will it."

The prince stared at her for a moment, his black eyes direct. She stared back at him. He bent his head a moment. "You have my permission. My guests will excuse you."

Katie said quickly to Selina, "She is not well; she is retiring."

"She is probably as bored as I am," muttered Selina, smiling falsely as the woman bowed to her on leaving.

"Selina, please," said Katie desperately. She had a strong suspicion, reinforced by the look of the prince toward Selina, that their host knew English and could understand it well, if not speak it. Katie turned to him hastily, stammering a little, "You have been so kind to invite us to dinner and to show us your excellent writing. I do not wish to draw out your most hospitable feelings. Perhaps we should depart before long."

His eyelids flickered. "Before you depart, I would wish you to see one of my prized treasures. Permit me to leave for a few moments. This may intrigue you as you are interested in both silk and porcelain."

He left the room. Katie quickly told Selina what he had said. "Oh, jewelry?" asked Selina hopefully. "I do adore jewels, and his are simply splendid, and his wife's also."

Prince Chen Lo said, with his beaming, friendly smile, "Not jewels. I think my honored brother shows you his precious treasure which travels always with him. He never shows this to guests. However, I think—ah, yes," he ended as his brother reentered the room.

The prince carried with him a large round bowl with a half-inch stand. He carried it in both large brown hands, as though revering it and careful of its value and fragility. He set it down on the lacquer table before him. Katie leaned closer, catching her breath, holding it, as though a breath might damage it.

The bowl was of sheerest porcelain, so thin that when the prince Chen Yee set a candle inside it, they could see not only the light of the flame but the outline of the candle. The sides of the bowl shimmered like precious satin of rose color, yet showing other colors, like an opal, of palest blue, creamy white, yellow-green, depending on how it was turned and how the torchlights fell on it.

"You may touch the side," said the prince to Katie.

She looked at him for further permission; his black gaze met her wide brown look. He nodded. She reached out cautiously, afraid to tip over the bowl. The candle still stood inside where he had set it. She touched the bowl; it was warm, silky of feel, like sheer silk, intead of porcelain. Her finger rubbed slowly, cautiously over the surface, to the rim, where the edge had been carefully smoothed to roundness.

"I have never seen anything so beautiful," she said finally. "Never have I seen porcelain like this. It is indeed rare."

"It was created more than four hundred years ago," said the prince. "It has been in my family for that time."

She caught her breath again. He took the bowl away and returned again. Katie stood up, as did Selina, and they took their leave. The prince honored them by showing them to the door. Moon Blossom came after them shyly and spoke to Katie at the door.

"I am honored to meet you," she said to Katie, smiling. "I wish you good fortune and long life in our country."

Katie warmed to the young girl, who had tried to show more friendliness and politeness to make up for the princess Chen Mei-ling's rudeness. "You are most kind. I hope to see you again. If we do not meet, then my good wishes for your future life and happiness." She curtsied to the girl, who bowed low. Then Katie turned to Prince Chen Yee, who watched her curiously.

"Thank you again for your most gracious gesture of showing us your home. And you know you have my gratitude for saving me from the carriage wheel. My husband will wish to thank you also."

"He returns soon?" asked the prince abruptly.

"I do not know when he comes. He will come when he can," said Katie, feeling a little nervous; she did not know why, except the question had been asked with sudden intensity.

"I will escort you home," said the prince. While Moon Blossom gazed with wide eyes, he handed them himself into the carriage, all three of them, then sat with his back to the horses. Katie had a strong notion that he never did this! To take the inferior position!

But he did escort them home, talking politely to Katie in Chinese, drawing aside the rich silk curtains briefly to show to her the lights of the ships in port, the torchlights on the fort at the top of the hill, the glimpses of narrow streets and lighted houses and shops.

Then they were at their door, and he got down, handed them down, even Milbank, waiting until they were shown into the house by the attentive Ho Chih before driving away.

Selina burst out as soon as the door was closed, "Well, if that was not the dullest evening of my existence! Not a word of conversation to me, not even by his stupid young brother! And that one *could* speak English! You two monopolized the conversation, Katie! No wonder his wife left and was angry! You should know better!"

"But, Selina, she could have joined in the conversation," protested Katie uneasily.

"Well, don't ask me to go with you on another such evening! I had a feeling it would be dull and boring!" And Selina flounced up to her bedroom, grumbling to Milbank.

Nevertheless, at the dinner at the Shaws' the next evening, Selina boasted about being at the prince's home, his attentions to her, the many rooms of the house, the flowering courtyard, the jewels, and fine clothes. The others were most interested; as they said, none of them had ever been inside his home.

"He never invites us!" said Mrs. Shaw. And the rest of the guests said the same.

"He has had a winter home in Macao for many years; it was that of his family for generations. However, he has the reputation of staying aloof even from the other Chinese." One guest was very firm about this, having lived here for forty years. His elder-statesman views were yawned at by Selina, but he seemed to know what he was talking about in this case.

"He was probably charmed by Mrs. Selina," said one man, gazing yearningly at her blond beauty. "He must never have seen such a lovely blond woman. Their women are all so dark."

So Selina was restored to her pride and said no more of her boredom. Katie framed the prince's calligraphic poem and kept it in her bedroom. She would never forget that enchanted evening.

7

Two days later the memory of the evening was still vivid in Katie's mind. She sat in the large parlor as the rain poured down. How beautiful had been the prince's home. How gorgeous the roses, the peach trees. It puzzled her about the blooms of flowers and trees, for she had seen few such around Macao. And was it not the wrong season of the year for peach trees to be in bloom?

Selina was grumbling mightily. The thunderstorms were so heavy they dared not go out, for lightning flashed ominously over the land and waters, and Ho Chih said it could hit them should they venture forth.

"And I was to go to tea at the home of the French princess whose name I cannot pronounce," lamented Selina, striding up and down the large room. She glared at Katie, carefully drawing some calligraphy on a tissue-thin sheet of paper. "And what are you doing, pray tell? Those ridiculous letters—"

"It is calligraphy, a fine art here in China," said Katie absently. "I wish to draw it better."

"You would be better occupied drawing sketches for the silk or porcelain," said Selina tartly. "Or do you enjoy playing so much better, now that Rupert is not here to see how energetic and industrious his little wife can be?" She laughed disagreeably.

Katie flushed and bit back angry replies. They

made Selina all the more nasty. Without saying anything, she bent again to the drawing.

The sounds of a carriage drawing up took Selina to the window. "Can someone be calling? Yes, it is before our house! Ho Chih, go to the door!" she called out. The older man was already in the hallway, going to the door, to open it at the last minute so that little rain and wind would come in to wet and chill the hall.

"Who is it?" asked Katie, with regret for her work. She should not have spread it out in the front parlor, she thought, but today she had thought she would not be interrupted, and the light was better than in the smaller back parlor. She wiped her pen dry and closed the inkstand.

"Oh, damn!" gritted Selina. "It's that Chinese prince! All grand in yellow and black! Are we to have no peace?"

Katie's mouth twitched in humor. First Selina wanted company; then she wanted peace. But her own heart was beating with excitement as she went to the hall to greet the man. Her gown was too simple, she worried; she wore only a thin white chemise in the Empire fashion and over it a morning cloak of rose wool against the chill of the rainy day.

Ho Chih opened the door. In the doorway appeared the prince in a brilliant yellow coat over a black silk embroidered robe. He was protected from the rain by a yellow parasol of huge dimensions, carried by a servant. He was now taking from another servant a birdcage containing a small yellow bird.

Katie hastily greeted the prince. "How good you are to come in this weather, sir. I bid you welcome. Pray, allow your servants to take shelter in our courtyard in the back. It is covered, and they may warm themselves at the fire."

The prince gazed down into her wide brown eyes. Then he nodded and turned. He spoke brusquely to the servants. "You may take the carriage to the back courtyard and warm yourselves at the fire."

They nodded, soaking wet, and the servant with the parasol ran back to the carriage to help the coachman turn it and the horse around and into the carriage drive.

Ho Chih closed the door and bent his head anxiously, waiting to hear his orders.

"Pray, bring hot tea and cakes to the drawing room," said Katie. She smiled happily and unaffectedly at the prince. "I am so happy you could come on such a miserable day. We have been quite solitary."

She led him into the parlor and said brightly to Selina in English, "See who comes to us on this miserable day!"

Selina smiled charmingly and dipped into a beautiful curtsy, the discontented lines quite smoothed out. "Pray, ask him why he carries the birdcage," she said.

"Oh, I cannot do that!" asked Katie. "He will tell us when he is ready to do so." She shyly indicated a chair, a straight one with arms, of fine mahogany. The prince bowed and waited until the two ladies were seated before he sat down. He set the birdcage down beside him. The yellow bird gave a little *cheep-cheep!*

Was there a flicker of amusement in the black eyes? Katie could not tell. She thought there was a twitch at the corners of the large, firm mouth.

They talked politely for a few minutes, until Ho Chih and one of the maids carried in the silver tea service and the tray of porcelain bowls. Selina poured, as she did elegantly, and Ho Chih bowed before the prince when he offered the cup to him. The prince bent his head very slightly and accepted the cup politely. He sipped at it and ate a rice cake.

The prince then said to Katie, "I think I have interrupted your work. On what do you labor today?"

She flushed a little and said humbly, "I was trying to improve my handwriting in calligraphy, sir. I know I cannot attain the beauty of those who worked on it from childhood and are scholars. However, the loveliness intrigues me and causes me to try my best at the art form."

He set down the cup, rose, and went to the large table at the side of the room. He said to Katie, "Pray, come here. I will show you how to improve your lettering."

Katie quickly told Selina, who scowled, then gave a false smile. The other woman sipped her tea as Katie went over to the table. She seated herself, the prince leaned beside her, and when she took the brush in her hand, his hand folded over hers on the brush. She gave a little startled jump, but he ignored her nervousness.

"First, do not write at once when you seat yourself. Think, relax, compose your mind into beautiful thoughts. Move your hand in graceful motions in the air above the paper."

His strong hand moved hers and the brush with his. She obediently followed his slow, rounded gestures. It was more difficult to compose her mind as he stood so close beside her. He had a masculine scent, and it mingled with the scent of some jasmine perfume he wore. The silk and velvet of his robes brushed against her body.

"Now, think—think of some beautiful object."

"Yes, of the peach blossoms—" said Katie, rather breathlessly.

"Yes, good. What do you think?"

"I have wondered—how they could bloom—in this climate in Macao. I have seen no other."

He still continued to move her hand with his, in slow, graceful gestures over the paper. "You are observant. Yes, the peach trees would not grow of themselves. They are protected, under shelter, kept warm. My gardeners force the trees in warmth in Peking, and when we come south, they are wrapped in cotton wool and carried most carefully, as are the roses and .azaleas, the purple lilacs and the white. When we arrive in Macao for our winter here, the trees are placed in their large pots in the courtyard which can be covered against harsh winds and rain. I ordered the cover over the courtyard rolled back for your visit, that you might see the trees against the evening sky."

"Oh, all that trouble—I am most happy that you did this," gasped Katie. So it had been a special effect staged for them! She was overwhelmed at the thought.

"Now—try to write a letter; write the word for 'tree,'" he commanded, and as she moved her hand closer to the page, he still directed it. The result was a more rounded, graceful, beautiful line, the strokes curved slightly at the ends.

"Ah, yes," she said. "That is it! A more relaxed way," said Katie.

He released her hand and straightened to his usual height. "Try it again by yourself."

She moved her hand in an arc, striving for relaxation. She sketched the letter once more.

"That is good," he approved. He glanced over the other tissue pages on the table. "You permit? This is good, this is better—ah—I like this one—" He paused in studying the page, to gaze with approval on the sketch of a small child sitting on the ground playing with his puppy. His large mouth softened, gentled.

He then returned to his chair, Katie to hers. He lifted the birdcage. "I bring this gift to you from the woman whose child you saved," he said. "I went to see that the child was unharmed. She is a humble woman who runs a bird shop with her husband. She wished to give you a gift and hopes you will accept this with her great gratitude. The boy is her only child and the light of his parents' eyes."

Katie accepted the birdcage and listened to the singing of the canary. She gave him her formal acceptance and thanked him for his kindness in going to see the woman. He then stood, bowed, and indicated he was ready to leave.

Katie went to the door with him. He turned as Ho Chih opened the door, to indicate the carriage was being driven around to the front.

"The peach trees," he said abruptly, "have to be carefully sheltered, or they would not bloom in an alien climate."

He bowed his head to her, then went out under the yellow parasol. Katie watched him depart curiously. His words had been underlined, as though they were of significance to him and to her.

"Well, that broke the monotony of the day," said Selina, stretching like a cat. "I couldn't understand him, but I'll make a story for the Shaws. Imagine, coming to our house! Whatever did he say?"

Katie tried to tell her, but the woman soon lost in-

terest, went up to her room to take a nap. Katie asked
Ho Chih to purchase a stand for the birdcage and
meantime set the cage on her table. She studied the
bird carefully and began to sketch the little yellow
bundle of fuzz, as it stretched itself and fluffed up its
feathers and began to sing to her coaxing.

Three days later Selina was out for tea when the
prince called again. Katie went to the door with Ho
Chih and greeted him curiously. It was bright sunshine today, and the handsome tall Manchu prince
wore a stunning green embroidered coat and lighter
green gown with a wide band of embossed velvet
around the hem.

He was followed into the house by two servants,
who carried small boxes carefully in their hands. At
his nod they set the boxes down on the large table
where Katie worked and retreated, moving backward
to the door. Ho Chih let them out.

"Pray, ask Lilac to come to the room," said Katie in
a low tone. Ho Chih nodded; his mistress was aware
of the conventions.

The older woman entered the room, to sit in a corner, demurely, as chaperon.

The prince indicated he would take tea, and Ho
Chih hastened to have it prepared. Meantime, the
gentleman opened the boxes.

"I bring today several objects which will assist you
in your work; it is important," said the prince. "I think
you would like to understand our culture and inter-
pret it to your Western country, which does not understand us."

"You overwhelm me," gasped Katie. She swallowed.
"I do not think I should accept—" She was watching
him remove from a cotton-filled box a delicate porce-

lain bowl of an intense blue color. It was plain and simple, yet of such a color and sheen that it made the white porcelain and flower design seem blatant.

The prince frowned so heavily it was alarming on his dark face. "We do not speak of accepting or rejecting among friends," he said sternly. "Gifts are the symbol of our admiration and respect. No more and no less. I respect you and the work that you do in your female way. You try to do good work and to carry out your husband's wishes, though he remains away from you for many weeks."

Katie gulped at the tone of censure. "My husband has his father's work to carry out," she said finally. "We must all—make the sacrifice of being apart—and working hard—to fulfill his father's wishes and to aid the family business."

"I can understand this for a man," said the prince curtly. "However, a man does not leave his wife unprotected unless he has little regard for her." The shrewd black eyes studied Katie. She had flinched, and her face showed her hurt.

She lifted her chin bravely. "That is between my husband and myself," she said. "He—respects—me, and we work well together."

"And your sister? She works also?"

"She does not—know the work," said Katie uneasily, turning from his sharp gaze.

"Nor will she learn, as she flutters like a butterfly among the idle of Macao," said Prince Chen Yee, his voice condemning Selina. Then he shrugged and changed the subject. "Observe this bowl, Madame Llewellyn. You will note the deep blue color, which is unique to a province of China. The metals are added at the last moment, so they will not fade in the firing."

She listened to him as he briskly described the process of adding the metals. He indicated the sheen of the bowl and said that no Western nation had yet achieved this quality. She readily agreed, meekly.

He was dictatorial, and everything in China was far superior to that in the West. But he taught Katie well, explaining how the points of differences in the making and decoration of the porcelain made it superior.

He set the bowl aside on a table. He opened another box and took out several pieces of silk. Some were decorated in brilliant colors on pale peach or rose or blue background. They had been hand-painted in typical Oriental designs: the wave pattern, vines, stylized flowers—chrysanthemums and roses and lotus. He explained the various decorations. A strange design along the border was like, yet unlike, the Greek key design.

"This is the border that means everlasting joy," he said. "You will find it often in Chinese design."

She absorbed all this eagerly. He knew so much; he could tell her so much.

He opened another box, a very tall one, to reveal a carved ivory pagoda. He told her what it meant, how it was carved, how rare it was, how the Chinese revered their temples, pointing up to the heavens. Then he set it aside on another table, definitely, as though indicating that it was for her. She knew the object was priceless; it was far finer than any she had seen for which their owners had paid a small fortune.

"I hope you will use these designs in your sketches for silk and porcelain," he said seriously. "They will show to your people something of what we are and what we believe. This is important to their understanding of us. When we know what a man holds important, then we begin to know him."

"That is very true, sir," said Katie, nodding. "When I know what someone believes and clings to, then I begin to know that one." And she was thinking of Selina and her greed and her clinging to persons of high rank, no matter how stupid. And she thought of her father. "My father revered learning, wise books, Oriental teachings, and he admired beautiful objects, carved by the best hands, of jade and ivory. He taught me to enjoy beautiful porcelain and silks and the fine spices of the East. But most of all, he taught me to respect my own mind, to furnish it with beautiful memories and the best wisdom I could find. He said to me many times, 'A poor man with a good mind is to be more envied than a wealthy man with an empty mind.' For no matter the state of one's person, the mind is a continual blessing when it has these memories—" She stopped, blushing, recalling that she spoke to a very wealthy man indeed.

He gave her a genuine smile, the first she had seen from him, and amusement twinkled briefly in the sharp dark eyes. "I believe your father was most wise, Madame Llewellyn. He must have been part Oriental!"

She laughed slightly, pleased with his words, which were a compliment from him.

"How he would have enjoyed this journey," she said with a slight sigh. "How he would have reveled in meeting you, sir, and listening to your knowledge and wisdom. And to see these marvels! He enjoyed what we had so very much. We were permitted to keep in our rooms the jade pieces of lesser quality that belonged to Mr. Douglas Llewellyn. And our rooms were furnished with fine Persian rugs and one of Chinese make. How he enjoyed all these! And he would have loved to wander the streets of Macao, looking at all the shops."

"You speak of your father with affection and respect. That is good," said Prince Chen Yee. "I have thought you of the West do not respect your parents and your ancestors as you should. Yet you show due regard and reverence for your father."

"He was a good father to me, and I miss him very much," said Katie, and found she had to wipe her eyes with her linen handkerchief. He kept on staring at her; she found his close observance rather unnerving.

He turned then to a poem she had written and asked her to read it aloud. She did, and he gravely corrected her accent, gently nodding when she got it right. He would say a word over and over and insist on her saying it like that until she had the proper tone and pitch. It was like singing, for the meaning changed if the word was said at another level or tone.

Prince Chen Yee came again and again. The neighbors whispered when they saw the carriage coming each week and sometimes twice in one week. Katie told them he brought her objects to draw, and indeed, Mrs. Shaw insisted on seeing the designs.

"Excellent, Mrs. Rupert," she said gravely. "But does the prince come so often to bring you such? What does your husband say to this?"

"I have said to him in messages that the prince comes to visit and has been helpful. Rupert did not reply. I hope he received my notes," said Katie, her brow wrinkling. "We have had only two letters from him. He and Terence are very busy."

"*Hm.* I wish he would come soon," said Mrs. Shaw oddly. "I long to meet him, and Mr. Terence Llewellyn as well, of course." She was a sensible, practical woman, of middle age. Her husband had served as an agent of the British East India Company for some twenty years in Macao.

"I hope he will come. It has been so many weeks." Katie sighed. Her hand poised absently over the drawing she was sketching for Mrs. Shaw to see how to use a Chinese border of everlasting joy as a hem line.

Prince Chen Yee had shown her more attention than her own husband, thought Katie, feeling disloyal. But it was so good to be praised, listened to, approved of, instructed as her father had instructed her, sat with for hours while both in turn read poetry or spoke wisdom, or drew, or painted.

"It is very unusual for a Manchu prince such as Prince Chen Yee to pay so much attention to—foreigners," said Mrs. Shaw delicately. Selina was not present; she had gone out before Mrs. Shaw had come for tea.

"Yes, I am greatly honored," said Katie. Mrs. Shaw studied the serious downbent face and sighed again. Katie finished the sketch and held it out to her neighbor. "You see—this is how the border could be used, and it would give it an Oriental appearance, even though the flowers are English primroses."

"Yes, yes, very charming, I am sure."

Mrs. Shaw departed half an hour later, leaving Katie to her reflections. Were people gossiping about her? But she always had Selina or Lilac as chaperon when the prince came. And he had been so very helpful.

She glanced about her smaller parlor, where she now worked. Selina objected to having the larger front drawing room cluttered up with "Katie's work," as she said disparagingly. So the back table was filled with tissue sketches. Katie kept her folders there, and her ink and brushes, her watercolors and oil paints. It was there she had set the blue porcelain bowl, on a stand of its own, and the magnificent ivory pagoda. A box of finest red lacquerware, another gift from the prince, was filled with samples of the silks he had brought to her, painted lengths, thickly woven and embroidered velvets and brocades and the sheerest, shimmering varicolored silks.

The next time the prince came, Selina was preparing to go out for tea once more. Katie begged her in a whisper to remain. "For it is odd to some people that you go out when he comes, and I am alone with him except for Lilac," said Katie. "Do please remain, Selina. I will attempt to translate all the more for you."

"Oh—very well. I expect it is an honor," said Selina ungraciously. "Though he does not bring presents to me!" she added as she came down the steps to the hallway. "I don't know why I bother, except that Rupert will be terribly upset when he comes and finds you have a Chinese beau!"

"Oh, Selina, please!" whispered Katie, aghast. If Prince Chen Yee had heard her—! She entered the drawing room, where the prince stood waiting for them.

His expressionless face did not reveal whether he had heard and understood Selina or not. He bowed to them both. He sat down after them, in the Western fashion, and drank tea with them. Then he offered a fine black lacquer box to Selina.

"Madame Llewellyn, the elder," he said ceremoniously, as he always addressed her, "I wish to present to you some trifles which are expressive of the types of jewelry we have in our country. Pray, accept them, if your husband permits."

As Selina gasped and took the box with every evidence of pleasure, he turned and handed a red lacquer box to Katie, a box of such reddish rose that it was a wonder to see. She saw it was inlaid with ivory and precious stones. Her troubled brown eyes lifted to gaze at him. His black eyes were shadowed by his unusually long black lashes.

"Oh, how beautiful! How exquisite!" Selina was squealing. She had opened her box and drew out a long strand of gray-black pearls. After it came a long strand of oval ivory beads strung with round black jet beads between each ivory bead.

"You should not give us such expensive gifts," murmured Katie in a low tone to the prince. "It is too much—you have been too good—"

"I hope you do not mean to reject my humble gifts?" asked the prince. "I thought that between friends it was permitted? I am wrong about Western ways?"

He seemed angry and upset. Katie hurrriedly shook her head.

"Oh, no, it is correct—at least, I think so—only these gifts—you have brought so much—I mean—"

"Pray, open your box, and if the contents do not please you, I shall return them with anger to the merchant."

Oh, dear, thought Katie, and get that merchant into trouble! For the prince was very particular about any object that he bought and very critical about quality.

Slowly she opened her box. The first object was a strand of rosy white pearls wrapped in a shimmering square of pale rose silk. "How beautiful!" she said. "How—very lovely!"

"I am glad that you approve of that at least," said the prince sternly.

The next square of blue silk revealed an ivory necklace, simpler yet more beautiful than Selina's, of all carved ivory beads. And yet another silk lay there, and she opened that square to reveal a set of jade jewelry: a long deep green necklace of large oval pieces, a matching bracelet, another bracelet of pure green jade, and a golden ring with a large carved jade stone.

They thanked the prince, and he nodded, as though relieved. "You are welcome. Use the designs as you wish," he said to Katie.

Then he suggested that they should write another poem to increase her ability to speak and write. Selina became bored and wandered away, to show Milbank the jewelry he had brought to her. Katie sat at the large desk and drew carefully in the calligraphic way he had taught her.

He took her hand as she was about to sketch the next letter. "Move more freely, in a more relaxed manner," he said, and held her hand as he helped her sketch the letter. He was standing beside her, very closely; she could smell the jasmine perfume he wore and his own masculinity. And he was standing so very close that his garments touched her bare arm in the short-sleeved pale peach muslin gown.

She trembled a little and finally set down the pen. "I am a little nervous today," she said, excusing herself.

Still he held her hand. "Nervous? In my presence?" he asked in her ear.

She stood up quickly; he still held her. "I am sorry, it is all the excitement—the jewelry—you are too kind—I don't know what I should do—"

He gazed down into her pale face in such a manner that color came to her cheeks. Her free hand went to her face in embarrassment at his close scrutiny.

"But you are beautiful," he said in a choked voice. "But you are—exquisite—like the blossoms of the peach tree. Like a shy bird you speak, and the tone is music to me. Even your mistakes are charmingly spoken."

"Mistakes?" she quavered, trying to draw away.

Instead of letting her go, he drew her closer to him. Against her thin dress she felt the heat of him, even through his red silk embroidered gown. His arms went about her, he drew her to him. She knew she should push against him, speak her outrage— She gazed up at him, wide-eyed, startled.

Slowly his dark head was bent to hers; slowly he put his mouth on her opened mouth. She felt the heat and passion of his lips on hers, and she could not protest.

He held his mouth there, and the kiss deepened. She felt faint, dizzy, from the emotion she felt. She was trembling, shocked, yet unable to pull from him.

His arms tightened about her. They were alone in the room, and the sunlight blazed behind the drawn white curtains. They were alone in the world of passion he had built around them both, blazing with sudden desire. His mouth moved over hers, then to her blushing cheek of peach color, then to her dainty small ear, which he nipped in his teeth. It was the most erotic sensation Katie had ever felt, that little bite on her ear.

She shivered and said, "Please, you must not—" She spoke in English. He answered in Mandarin, savagely.

"Why not? Your husband neglects you; you welcome me. We meet as familiar friends; we laugh and talk together, knowing each other's minds. He is a fool!"

She swallowed and pushed him back from her. He slowly released her; his eyes blazed with emotion.

"You should not—have done that," she said with dignity, shy and troubled as she looked up at him. "I was wrong to—to permit this. I have no wish to—to betray my husband just because he is not here. Perhaps you should not come again. I do not wish you to think me a light woman—"

She was so dazed and upset she had not heard the loud voices at the door, the calling, the laughter and excitement. Then Ho Chih came to the door of the drawing room and opened it.

Prince Chen Yee had stiffened and moved away from Katie by three long strides by the time the door opened. Ho Chih glanced from one to the other. He spoke to Katie.

"Madame Llewellyn, your husband returns!"

Behind him Katie saw Rupert, and everything else flew out of her head. He was tired, dusty, but it was Rupert, it was Rupert, and with him Terence.

"Oh, Rupert, you have come home!" she cried, and hastened to greet him as he came into the room.

He had been smiling. Now he scowled and looked past her to the tall Manchu, in the impressive costume, his arms now folded across his chest.

"Who is that man? Why is he here?" demanded Rupert. "Why are you alone together?"

8

Rupert stared in dumbfounded wonder at the exotically garbed Manchu prince. Katie had written that a prince had rescued her from a carriage wheel, that she and Selina had gone to his home and received many courtesies. But in his rush of work, his absorption in the strangeness of Canton, worries over the dealings, he had not thought much about it.

In truth, he had almost forgotten he had a wife. He burned with jealousy when Terence spoke of Selina; he lay awake at times, too weary to sleep, his bones aching, and remembered the days when he was courting Selina and had such hopes that she would return his love. Then the bitterness when he realized she was accepting Terence's attentions and had become engaged to him would flood over him.

Now, here was this strange Chinese in his own drawing room! Rupert stared, frowned, turned to Katie. "Pray, introduce me," he said curtly. He vaguely noted that his wife seemed prettier than when he had left, pink-cheeked, sparkling of eye, in an attractive peach muslin gown.

Katie performed the introductions gravely. "Prince Chen Yee, may I introduce to you my husband, Rupert Llewellyn." She switched to English. "Rupert, this is the prince Chen Yee, who has been most kind in instructing me in Mandarin and in bringing objects for my drawings."

Terence and Selina had followed Rupert into the room. Terence had his arm about Selina, and she was cuddling to him in a way that made Rupert jealous all over again. Katie introduced Terence to the prince. The prince bowed his head slightly, his keen black eyes studying them intensely.

They talked for a few minutes. Then the prince said, "I regret I must leave now." He bowed to Katie, who curtsied deeply, then took his departure in the splendid carriage that awaited him at the door.

Rupert turned on Katie as soon as the door had closed after him. "Really, Katie, don't you have enough sense to have a chaperon with you? Where is your maid?"

"Selina was here when he came," said Katie gravely. "She remained for a time until—"

"Until he grew boring, holding Katie's hand while he showed her how to write!" Selina's laugh rippled maliciously. "Katie has a new beau! He brings her presents every time!"

"He brought jewelry to both of us," said Katie, and her wide brown eyes were troubled. "I wished to ask you, Rupert, if we should keep them since they seem so expensive. But he would be insulted if we tried to return them—"

"Speak for yourself!" Selina said with a gay shake of her beautiful blond curls and an alluring laugh to Rupert. How lovely she was, how he had missed her laughter and teasing, he thought. "I intend to keep my jewelry! Indeed, he has been our most faithful visitor. I count him a friend, and all society is jealous of me!"

"I don't like such a fellow hanging around you!" Terence was flushed and perturbed. "And a foreign chap! Is he rich? He must be—those clothes, jewels, the carriage— Selina, has he paid you particular attention?"

Rupert gazed worriedly at Selina also. She only laughed and sat down with a rustle of her silk skirts. "Oh, he stares at me with those black eyes, as though he would look right through me!" she proclaimed. "Of course, I cannot talk to him; he knows no English. But he shows me such attention—"

Rupert turned on Katie. "I wonder at you, Katie, allowing the man to come here! It is not as though he were English! These fellows that are Chinese have their own customs and beliefs. They have contempt for women and keep them in a low way. Some have concubines."

"We were introduced to his wife," said Katie slowly, sitting down on the sofa with a slow, weary movement. "She is a very high Manchu princess. And his home is of marble and very fine. He lives most of the year in Peking, he said. I believe he is only being kind to me—to us. He has sent some objects which demonstrate Chinese culture and the fine porcelain—"

"Don't change the subject," said Rupert sharply. He had a feeling Katie was hiding something, evading. Had the fellow been hanging around her, or Selina, or both of them? "I don't approve of this! I don't want you to have such a friend! Why can't you be satisfied to pay calls on the English and French crowd here? Selina is happy enough!"

"Oh, no, I am not!" snapped Selina. "I am quite bored! I long to return to England. Now that you are here, shall we sail in a few days? I can be packed in an instant. Milbank loathes this place also. She is sure we will all be dreadfully sick!!"

"My dear, we have scarcely begun the work," said Terence languidly, stretching out his long legs. "The orders are placed; we have bought some porcelain and some silks of the raw variety. However, the designs that Katie sent to the silk merchants have yet to be made up. They must set up the looms, weave the cloth, have samples approved—and the special design porcelain—"

"Oh, do not bore me with all those silly details!" cried Selina, pouting. "I am desperate to leave! Why can't we go on home and leave Katie to look after matters here? She knows the language, knows the work!"

Terence looked shocked. Rupert felt a little blaze of anger at Selina. Katie looked pale and thoughtful but said nothing, her hands folded.

Rupert said sternly, "We must all remain until the work is finished. It should be done within three months or so. However, good work takes time. We have a fine merchant, one Houqua, and he has been most helpful. Katie, we have purchased some jade—" He turned to her. Selina scowled at all this talk of trade and flounced up to her room. Terence went right after her eagerly.

Presently, as Rupert and Katie discussed the work, the sound of Terence's laughter and Selina's husky voice came to them. It was all too evident that they were in Selina's bedroom. Rupert lost track of what Katie was telling him; he stared unseeingly at the sketches she was eagerly showing him. The two of them, upstairs, making love—

He became aware that Katie had stopped talking and was silently turning over the sketches. He hurried to say, "These look splendid, Katie—"

She said in a low tone, "I was explaining, these are the sketches I have rejected as too ordinary. This pile here are the ones I thought much better."

"Oh—I see." He was embarrassed and turned hurriedly to the other folder. She waited in silence as he looked, but he could not concentrate. "These all look very nice, Katie. However, I am too weary to look straight at them. Let us wait until tomorrow, eh?"

"Very well, Rupert." She closed the folder. He noted the lovely yellow canary in the cage. He chirped at it, and it began to sing in clear, pure notes. "That is from the woman whose son I rescued," said Katie, noting his look. "The prince suggested that I use it in my drawings. He has also sent the blue bowl, there, and some lengths of painted silk."

"Tomorrow, Katie!" Rupert felt irritated at the repeated mention of the prince's name, and his gifts looked too elegant and expensive. "How well do you know this man?"

"He has been a kind friend," said Katie slowly. "He has explained much of Chinese culture, the patterns of designs—"

Another laugh from abovestairs; then no voices, but the sounds of the creaking bed. Rupert burned with jealousy and rage. He should have married Selina; she should have been his!

He realized Katie was speaking patiently, in a firm tone, as though she had said this before.

"If you will excuse me—"

"Yes, Katie?"

"I will go see to the evening meal." She left the

room, walking gracefully with her long skirts flowing about her slim legs. Katie was pretty; he had a fine wife, he reminded himself. But Selina was lost to him forever; she belonged to Terence—

Rupert went out to the carriage to see to the unpacking of the two trunks they had brought back. He had them carried to Katie's study, and then he began to unpack them. He was tired, but he could not go up to his bedroom to rest—not with Selina and Terence making love across the hall.

His own desires were raised, however, and when he went to bed that night and the house was still, he turned to Katie. She wore a light cotton nightdress, cool in the heat, and the windows were shuttered against a November storm. He could not see her; maybe he could pretend that she was Selina—

Then Rupert was ashamed of himself. Katie was a good girl; she deserved better than this. He forced his mind to her and began to kiss and caress her.

"Have you missed me?" he coaxed when she lay still and silent, flat on the bed.

She gave a deep sigh and put her arms about his body. "Oh, yes, Rupert. I have missed you—so much. As I wandered about Macao and did the morning shopping, I wanted to share with you the beautiful sights I saw—the shop windows with the beautiful green and white jade—and a small child dancing to the shrill of a pipe—"

He leaned his cheek against hers, holding her, forgetting to caress, his hand still on her waist. "I thought of you also, Katie. In Canton, such sights! Jugglers would come to the waterfront and perform for a coin. And stalls of fresh fruits would be set up each morning, and I would go with a servant to purchase some for our meals. And the narrow streets that lead into Canton where we are forbidden to go—how they drew me! We are confined to the waterfront and the hongs, you know. At evening, after the day's work was done, I paced the narrow gardens and longed to be with you."

"Oh, Rupert, really?" she whispered, and relaxed into his arms. He felt vaguely guilty because he had longed not so much for Katie as for Macao, where Selina was also, and for home, in London, with his family. "I have longed for you also. And when the sunset was especially rosy and beautiful on the hills, I have wished you to be there to share it with me."

He stroked her waist and down over her slim thighs, rounded and warm under the cotton nightdress. He drew up the hem and moved his hand over her slim leg and up her thigh and thrilled to the silky softness of her. He forgot everyone else; here was Katie, his wife, warm and yielding and sweet, her soft voice moaning in his ear as he caressed her.

They drew closer together, and the length of their absence made him all the more eager for her. His desire rose lustily, and he wanted her quickly.

"Oh, Katie, I want you now—I need you—oh, my darling—"

"I am—not ready, Rupert," she whispered huskily. "Oh, please—not yet—"

He drew back slightly, shaking his head at himself. He had promised her he would be careful, and she was small—

Carefully he caressed her, pressed his mouth to her lips, to her cheek, down to her throat. He held her breasts in his hand, teased the nipples, until they hardened in passion.

"You are adorable, my Katie, you are lovely in my arms," he praised her. If only he could truthfully say that he loved her. But for nights in Canton he had lain awake in the heat and thought bitterly of his lost love, Selina. One could not change one's heart so readily, he knew now. He should never have let his father persuade him to marry a woman he did not love. When one has loved so much, another woman could not completely fulfill a man's needs. Yet Selina was lost to him, Katie was his wife, he wanted a son one day—He turned again to Katie, and more feverishly he pressed his kisses on her.

At last she was ready, and he moved on top of her, holding himself off her by his elbows and knees. She was so small and slim she seemed even thinner than before. Had she lost weight here in this abominably hot climate?

He moved between her thighs, and her hands were flat on his back, as though she had forgotten how to caress him. He urged her, "Move your hands on me, Katie; show me how you care. Your little hands are so sweet; move them on me—"

She moved her hands slowly, then, on his back and thighs, and his passions built up. He felt the sweet moisture between her thighs and dared then to press gently.

She gave way before him, and he slid his big instrument carefully inside, into the softness of her, the sweetness of her, the tightness that excited him to passion. He surged back and forth on her, mindlessly, needing a woman, needing Katie, wanting a woman because he had not known one for weeks.

He came high in her, his seed surging into her, flooding her, as she moved under him. He enjoyed it so, the release of his need into his wife, the relief of the movements, the pleasure he had on her soft body. He rolled off, finally, and gasped with receding delight. She lay still, then pushed down the hem of her nightdress. He fell asleep as she got up to open one of the shutters slightly, to let in some of the cool night air. Dear Katie, she was so thoughtful—

The next days were busy ones. Rupert and Terence had meant to remain only a week, but Selina cried and pouted that she wanted to show off her "two beaux" to the society of Macao. She flirted with Rupert, and he was delighted with her attentions, though Terence was jealous even of his brother. Rupert could not help knowing that Selina still had much tender regard for himself.

Rupert did go shopping with Katie, however, and wandered the narrow strreets of Macao, while Lilac carried the increasingly heavy market basket. He helped purchase the fish, the shrimp, the jars of strange preserved fruits, coconut, pineapples, pears, greens for their salads. And then they would send Lilac home with one of the houseboys and proceed to shop among the more exotic stores. The jade shop, the ivory shop, the silks, and the porcelain houses—all drew them.

"Look," said Katie, pointing. "I always think the houses and shops are smiling at me. See how the roof points up at the ends, like a gay smile."

Rupert grinned indulgently at her fancies, but it was fun to go about with Katie. She did enjoy everything so much. Her cheeks flushed, her eyes sparkled as she pointed to the sampans in the harbor, flat-bottomed, carrying loads of cargo into Macao. Some were flower-decorated; some had elaborate cabins, hung with silk curtains, giving glimpses of brightly painted faces of women or merry ones of children.

"Which days does Selina go to market?" asked Rupert curiously after they had gone out together each morning.

Katie looked stunned. "Selina—to market? She never goes; she hates the smells and sounds. And besides, she goes out almost every night, then sleeps until noon the next day."

"Don't be ridiculous," said Rupert sharply, feeling angry with Katie, who sounded so disparaging of Selina, his beautiful ideal woman. "Tell me the truth—when does she go? She should take Terence with her; he would enjoy this."

"She never goes," repeated Katie, her mouth tight. She paused at a window full of jade. "Here is some beautiful jade, Rupert. Do you see the jade Buddha in the corner? That is especially good green quality."

He looked but scarcely saw it. His mind was in a turmoil, and he was furious with Katie, yet concerned. What if she told the truth? Was Katie doing all the work, while Selina gadded about Macao?

Something else had been disturbing him. He had persuaded Katie to go with them in the afternoons for tea, though she protested it cut into her working time. She seemed anxious to complete some drawings for him to take back to Canton with him. Some were for porcelain sets, and he admired the work intensely. Yet—yet when they went out to tea, fewer than half the persons there knew her. He was continually introducing his wife.

One man said, "Where have you been hiding this

little English rose?" and seemed to hang about her all the afternoon.

Mrs. Shaw, their neighbor, had remarked at the one dinner at her home, "My dear Katie, how splendid to see you again! It has been weeks. You must not work all the time, my dear young lady. The heat and climate will make you ill. We have you to thank, Mr. Rupert, for bringing Katie! She is so sweet and charming a lady."

Rupert went into the jade shop with Katie and admired the way she briskly questioned the shopkeeper. Pieces of jade were brought out for them; she examined them closely and chose eight pieces. Then she stood back.

"There, Rupert, do we have enough money to buy these?" she asked anxiously. "I have been looking at them, and I think they are the finest pieces in the whole of Macao."

The jade owner beamed and bobbed in curtsies. Rupert stared at the jade. "It is—much finer," he said slowly, "than what I bought in Canton. But I don't know if there is enough gold left to purchase it."

Katie's face fell. The shop owner glanced from one to the other and questioned her in a quick high voice. Katie must be explaining the situation. She turned to Rupert.

"He is bringing down the price," she said anxiously. "If it costs one hundred pounds for each piece, could we afford some?"

Rupert bit back his gasp of alarm. One hundred pounds for each piece? He picked up one Buddha carefully, examined it with his gaze and his hands. It was the smoothest, most beautiful piece of jade he had ever held. It put the ones now in the *China Princess* in Whampoa Harbor to shame.

He thought: If he purchased no more jade at Canton, if he cut back on the silks purchases—

"We could afford three of them, Katie," he said slowly.

Her face lit up. She studied them all, finally chose the jade Buddha, a figurine of a Chinese goddess, and a small temple with tip-tilted roofs. The owner said he would put them aside for the Llewellyns and save them for Rupert to pay for when he came again.

They left the shop, the owner beaming at them with gold-capped teeth showing and bowing them to the door.

Rupert's mind was the more confused. How did Katie know the quality of the jade? Why would the owner trust them for the price? Everyone in the market seemed to know Katie, all bowed to her, she talked to them with calm competency, and they replied with courtesy and interest.

Yet the society people, the British, the French, the Americans, the Germans, and Italians, did not seem to recognize Katie. Only a few British ladies knew her by name.

"Katie, do you not go out with Selina of evenings?" he asked abruptly when she paused to examine a window full of bright, shimmering silks.

"No, Rupert, rarely. It makes me too tired to stay out after midnight," she said absently.

"But surely you would enjoy the entertainment," he said helplessly. Could he believe her? Was she exaggerating? Did she want him to believe she was working all the time, while Selina was idle? He could not believe it. Selina was a fine lady with a good bringing-up, no matter what his father said. She would not run about all the time, leaving all the work to Katie.

"It makes me too weary. I cannot get up early to go to market the next day," she said patiently. "And I need the afternoons and some evenings to read and study and draw the designs, keep the books, and so on."

"But Selina could do some of that?"

Her slim shoulders stiffened. "What part?" she asked.

"Well, directing the servants. She can speak pidgin English, can't she?"

"I have never heard her."

Rupert never had either. "Well, Selina should not go out alone. It is dangerous for a woman of such beauty to be alone in her carriage at nights," he said. "I wish you to go with her, Katie."

Katie turned about and gazed up at him. He could not read the narrowed dark brown eyes. "She has Milbank," said Katie. "And I am not husky and big. I doubt if I could be of assistance should beautiful Selina be attacked." She turned abruptly and strode off down the street, her back expressive of outrage.

Rupert hastened after her and caught her up at another shop. He took her arm and forced her to a halt. "Now, Katie, I am concerned for your welfare naturally. But Selina is so beautiful she must be of great admiration to the foreigners. She is in danger, going out alone."

"Shall I learn to use a pistol?" asked Katie. He shook her impatiently and caused stares among the Chinese walking past them on the street. He saw several pairs of black eyes studying the pair curiously.

"Don't be ridiculous! It just looks better if two ladies go out together. Besides, you should have your amusements also; you work too hard."

"Thank you," said Katie. "But I am anxious to be done and return home. Did you not say we might return in January?"

"I hope so." He sighed. She sounded reasonable now and calm. They strolled on, the basket of small ivory pieces they had earlier chosen on her arm. He must return tomorrow with three hundred pounds for the jade. Three hundred pounds—for three jade pieces! Terence would think him mad. But need he tell his brother? Perhaps Terence need not know—he and Katie might keep the pieces for themselves. "Katie? Shall we keep the jade for ourselves? Surely we can afford them from our share in the supercargo? I hate to think of selling our best pieces."

Her face lit up in a blaze of delight. Her brown eyes sparkled with flecks of gold in them. "Oh, Rupert! Could we? I should like them so very much."

"Of course, I shall arrange it. It is merely a matter of bookkeeping entries. When I get them, we shall set them against our own accounts, Katie."

"Oh, I am so happy," she replied, and squeezed his arm with her gloved hand. "I can see our rooms now, with the pieces of our own jade, the porcelain vases, the ivory pagoda." And she sighed with pleasure.

He thought of the wing of the Llewellyn town house where he would live with Katie and later their children. And Terence and Selina in the grand rooms below theirs. Selina, the wife of Terence, the mother of his children—

He had thought that Selina would have started a child by this time. But Terence in a drunken furious mood had confessed to Rupert that Selina refused to have a child until they returned to England. It would be too uncomfortable and dangerous for traveling, she had said. "Sometimes I think she hates the thought of having my child," Terence had said.

Did Selina not love Terence then? Rupert's mind went around and around that point. If Selina did not love Terence, then perhaps—perhaps she still loved him, Rupert! What a tangle it was, all of them marrying the wrong person!

Rupert and Terence had to return to Canton after ten days. Selina wept to see them depart, but after they had left, she said to Katie, "At least when they come again, we can go home and leave this horrible uncivilized place!"

"Did Terence say that?" asked Katie in surprise. "Rupert hoped we could be ready, but there is much yet to do. None of the commissioned silk weaving is ready."

"We shall go!" asserted Selina firmly. "I mean to have lots of fun until we go, but I shall be glad to shake the dust of Macao off my shoes!"

And she went out that very night, to the home of the French princess, and did not return until dawn. There had been dancing, she said, yawning, the next afternoon, having arisen only in time for tea.

Katie had returned to work in the back parlor. She felt so far behind, having been gadding about with Rupert. And she felt sad, for she had felt, even as Rupert made love to her, that he thought of Selina. He still loved that blond woman who had made them all so miserable. She had wept silently over it, over the tangle of their lives, and wondered what would happen when they all returned to London.

She thanked God for work to do, to absorb her mind, make her forget for hours at a time the grief of being unloved. She had the errands to do, the marketing, the buying of a few more porcelain pieces. She was beginning to pack in trunks and packing cases the precious objects she had acquired. And then the second afternoon after Rupert's departure for Canton, several huge packages came for her.

Ho Chih and two husky men carried them into the back parlor, where Katie was drawing. Selina was entertaining guests in the front drawing room; she could hear the chatter of voices and the tinkle of silver spoons against thin porcelain cups.

Katie stood up, amazed, as the packages were brought in. The two strange men bowed; one handed her a large white envelope, then stood back, arms folded to wait.

"What is this?" she asked Ho Chih.

"The men come from the honorable prince Chen Yee," said Ho Chih, his broad face unprocessionless, his lashes lowered over dark eyes.

She opened the envelope, then sat down to read the long message. She translated it carefully, wonderingly. It read:

Dear foreign madame Katie,

I have pondered long how to cause you to forgive me for my reckless gesture when we met last. It was wrong, yet I felt your heart met mine in friendship.

I send to you some foolish gifts of little account, which I beg of you to accept in your forgiveness of my odd behavior. May they help you present to your foreign people in England over the waters the beauty of the best that China has made. You may say to them that here is the beautiful work our people can do. I wish you to do this, in remembrance of a hopeful friend.

                                        Prince Chen Yee.

Beside this letter was a long elaborate poem which took up many lines, and the scroll had to be unfolded wide to see it all. She saved it to read later.

She took up pen and paper to answer his note and send it back with the men who waited. She wrote hastily, yet was careful to use her best calligraphy, sketching the large clear letters.

Dear Prince Chen Yee,

You overwhelm me with your magnificent gestures of friendship. Yes, I forgive you for your gesture of familiarity. We must forget this. My husband has left for Canton, and when he returns, we shall depart from Macao. But always I shall remember your kindness, your goodness to me, your ways of showing to my people what magnificent work the Chinese people do.

Please accept my great gratitude for your gifts and for your most valued friendship.

                                Your friend, Katie Llewellyn.

She sanded the letter, then rolled it, and tied it with a small piece of silk ribbon. She handed it to Ho Chih, who handed it to one of the men. The two men bowed low and departed.

She asked Ho Chih to assist her in unwrapping the boxes. He did, his face inscrutable, yet she vaguely felt his disapproval. Whatever in the world was wrong now? she wondered, then forgot in the wonder of the magnificent gifts.

Two of the boxes contained the other five jade pieces she and Rupert had not felt able to purchase. She swallowed—five hundred English pounds! But she held the jade and stroked its silky, satiny surface affectionately. She would always think of Prince Chen Yee when she saw these beautiful pieces, she thought.

Another large box held long lengths of painted silk. On shimmering blues, or greens, or rose, Chinese artists had sketched and painted small figures or patterns, making the silk glisten with the gold or silver or red paint in the delicate little figures. A brief note in the prince's calligraphy indicated that these would make up dress lengths to be worn over a single white or black taffeta dress.

How intelligent he was, even about women's gowns, she decided. She held one up against her. The peach silk glowed, and she could picture it over black taffeta or dark ruby.

Other boxes held vases large enough to be set on the floor and hold huge sprays of flowers. A pair was in the exquisite famille rose design, with Chinese flowers on the rose background and white. She decided to set all these back in the fine packing cases of sandalwood and take them to England this way. They were repacked by Ho Chih, nailed shut, and set in the corner of the room, ready for sailing.

During the following weeks the prince did not appear. He did send with brief notes and poems, seasonal flowers—beautiful chrysanthemums, in yellow, orange, white, purple. He sent long sprays of lilacs in deep purple and white, for her to use in her sketches. After an interval would come more flowers, sometimes in an especially beautiful vase just suited for them.

Katie did not tell Selina about these gifts. She felt the woman would use them as an occasion for mockery. These were gifts to her, to Katie, the despised former clerk, who still worked as a clerk for the Llewellyns.

The presents and the words and letters and poems the prince sent to her were all balm for her sore heart. Rupert still adored Selina. But the great Manchu prince Chen Yee admired Katie so much he sent her very expensive presents.

In her innocence Katie saw no wrong in this. She knew that Selina accepted gifts, from her admiring beaux, of jewelry, plumes, fans of gold and ivory; she displayed them proudly to Katie when she saw her the next day after a late-night return from balls and dinners and parties.

Selina had her beaux and admirers. And she had Terence at her feet, and Rupert. Katie would revel in the admiration and friendship of a fine Manchu prince, a friend to her, a man who had great wealth, but also an appreciation of beauty and wisdom.

This man admired her, young Katie, plain and stupid in society's ways, the brunt of Selina's clever tongue, the one mocked by Terence and scolded by Rupert. It comforted Katie, at night in her lonely bed, to think there was one man in the world who admired her deeply.

Selina paid her calls, went out afternoons and nights, grumbled, and fretted. "I cannot wait to return to London. I am bored in Macao. I know everyone; I have heard all their jokes; their flattery is stupid," she said as she prepared to go out yet again, in a magnificent shimmering silk dress of purple that Terence had bought for her. "It is all right for you to like it here, Katie, but I am used to better, more comfortable existence!" And out she swept, with Milbank in her rusty black gown following her.

Katie grimaced behind her back. Milbank caught her at it and gave her an oddly compassionate look. Sometimes Katie thought Milbank did not think so highly of Selina any longer, but perhaps that was her imagination. Of course, Milbank adored Selina. Everyone adored Selina. Why not? She was so gorgeously lovely. And she could be sweet and charming when she chose.

Katie remained at home, weary, glad to relax in the plump sofa corner and sketch until she was tired enough to sleep. She should have been thinking of Rupert, alone and tired in Macao, but instead, she thought of the great prince Chen Yee and wondered if he would come to visit her again.

Rupert and Terence Llewellyn stared blankly at the interpreter and linguist, Wu Hsin, and then back at the hong merchant assigned to them, Houqua. The face of the elderly merchant was bland; they could not read it.

He was middle-aged, with a fine, long face of a scholar, dressed in a splendid crimson robe and a black cloak. Around his neck were long chains of gold and pearls; his embroidered silk slippers turned up at the toes. His hands were white, slim, flexible, expressive. Rupert had found him fair, even generous at times, having formed a respect for Rupert. Terence he greeted with stiff formality and rarely addressed any words to him.

Houqua now spoke to Rupert through the interpreter. "We regret the long delays, Mr. Rupert Llewellyn. However, the magnificent designs of your honored wife required much careful workmanship. Even now the looms have been set up, the threads chosen; many workmen are treading the looms day and night to complete your silk lengths. And the porcelain makers have expressed much delight in the unusual patterns sent to them from you. One such porcelain maker of many distinguished years sent word to me that the designer shows much sympathy for our culture, making use of our age-old symbols."

"But we want to get home!" cried Terence, interrupting the linguist rudely and turning to Rupert. His face was flushed. He had been drinking his breakfast when Rupert went to find him to set out that morning. Terence had become bloated with drink; his slim face was covered with a crude beard. What was the use of looking splendid when there were no ladies to see him? "I am sick of the Orient! And Selina will be furious at any more delays!"

"Hush, Terence, we will speak of this later." Rupert had noted the flicker of the hong merchant's eyelids. He had guessed the man understood English, as so many Chinese did, though they refused to speak the barbaric tongue of the foreigners. He was a brilliant man, the merchant, and it would be no wonder if he understood many languages.

Rupert turned to the hong merchant, one of the Cohong who managed the foreign trade at Canton and were solely responsible for the foreigners to the emperor himself.

"May I ask why there are such delays?" he asked with dignity. "We were assured a month ago that the work went well, that the goods would be ready in one month. We comprehend and respect the care of the silkmen and the porcelain men. We have received from your hands the most beautiful ivory and fine jade. Many of the ships will be ready to return home in January, but our hold is not one-tenth full."

Was Terence's rudeness causing delays, as the captain had warned it might, or was it the care given to Katie's designs—or some other, more sinister reason?

The linguist turned to Houqua and translated rapidly. Rupert wished, not for the first time, that Katie could have come along to do the talking. She was so good at it—if only they would permit women to come to Canton! He wondered again and again if they had in the past spoken of other matters before the hong merchant, secure in the fact that he did not understand a word they said. The faces of the two men were expressionless, but there was a strange tone—

The linguist turned again to Rupert and Terence. "Honorable Master Houqua regrets the delays so much, but it will be another two months before the exquisite goods will be ready. You see, Englishmen, the designs are of such complex nature, and unusual, they take longer to complete. However, we are sure you will be much satisfied when you see them finished." He bowed deeply.

Terence spoke in a dissatisfied way as they walked back to their own hong apartments along the waterfront. He had no eyes for the children playing in the narrow dirt streets, the men who set up the stalls of oranges and pears. Rupert paused to purchase a package of pears and take them back to the apartment. At this time of year they tasted especially delicious and juicy. He had learned that from Katie, in shopping with her. Dear Katie, he longed to see her and share with her what had happened. Maybe she would comprehend what was going on, why they were having these strange delays, when other ships were almost fully loaded and ready to depart.

"I'm sure they are going to cheat us," Terence was saying as they resumed their walk. His flushed face was turned to the mild winds. "Damn them all. Selina will have a fit and blame me if she has to remain another two months."

"Katie, now, won't mind," said Rupert rather proudly. "She has fitted in well—"

"Well—Katie!" said Terence. "She is just a clerk anyway; she isn't used to society. Old sobersides! Selina said she is a wet blanket at any party."

Rupert blazed suddenly. "Don't speak so of my wife! She works hard for all of us! I don't know what we would have done without her! She does all the housekeeping, the marketing, the designs—"

Terence looked his surprise. "Well, I didn't say she wasn't useful! But dashed if I know why you married her! It isn't as though she were pretty or wealthy after all."

Rupert could not answer because he was so swept with sudden rage against his brother. Terence had crowed enough about marrying Selina, he did not need to mock Rupert for marrying Katie. Of course, the girl was the daughter of a clerk, but Owen Adair had also been a teacher and scholar. And Katie had good manners—she was shy but polite. To treat her as a servant was wrong, and Rupert was beginning to realize that was what they all were doing. But Katie she was smarter than any of them, and she managed well in Macao. What would Selina have done if she had had to talk to the cook and vegetable sellers, direct the servants, rise early and go to bed late?

There was a long letter from Katie, enclosing more designs and speaking of everyday matters in Macao. Rupert lounged in his chair, reading it and laughing aloud at her vivid descriptions of a minor accident in a market street, with oranges and pears flying about, everyone screaming and blaming everyone else, children darting in and out to snatch the ripe fruit and make off with it, pigs let loose to run into shops.

"What is so funny?" growled Terence.

"Oh, this letter from Katie. She has a way of describing events!" Rupert continued to chuckle.

"Read it to me. Does she mention Selina? Does Selina go out with her beaux often?"

"Does Selina not write to you?" Rupert raised his head to gaze at his brother in surprise.

Terence flushed even deeper. "Never a letter," he finally confessed. "She hates to write. She says she will tell me when I come, but even then she says little. And that Frenchman hangs about her all the time and has given her an opal necklace. I am furious with her!"

Rupert did not comment on that but read portions of Katie's letter aloud to Terence. He was still thinking about her when they set sail on a swift small Chinese boat to return to Macao for Christmas and the New Year celebrations. He leaned on the railing to gaze at the gaily decorated sampans sailing along beside them and waved at small children with wooden buoys tied to their backs in case they fell into the water. How Katie would have enjoyed this sight! She enjoyed children so.

Patrolling the waterways was the official mandarin boat, with red sashes tied about the muzzles of the guns it carried and the gay flags of yellow and white floating above it. Rupert exchanged salutes with the man who stood in the center under a brilliant canopy. Another mandarin boat came alongside, surveyed them critically, then sheered off.

Rupert was still thinking. Would Katie want a child soon? She had never said so, yet he had observed her with little children in the market. And she had risked her life to save a child. Yes, he could be fairly sure that Katie would want his children when they came. And she would be a good mother, stern yet gentle, firm yet loving. He could see a serious little boy with Katie's dark eyes, a pretty little girl with her long, straight, silken hair and the golden flecks in the brown eyes. He half smiled, dreamily, at the boats racing past them.

It would be good to return to London, to settle down with Katie, to forget his hopeless love for Selina. To have children, to work hard for his father and help relieve him of many burdens, to love Katie and respect her for her intelligence and hard work—

Would that be satisfying? He wondered. It must be; that was his life to come, and he might as well resign himself to it. And it would not be so difficult. Katie was amenable, gentle, readily guided, and sweet and passionate in bed. He could wish that she loved him, but perhaps it was best to settle for respect and obedience. Selina loved Terence, but she led him a rare dance and enjoyed teasing him with her many beaux.

The two men arrived in Macao late in the same day and took a hired carriage to their home. They went inside eagerly, bowed to Ho Chih with teasing formality and received his low bow.

"Gentlemen Llewellyn," said Ho Chih formally. "Velly good see masters! Welcome, welcome."

"Where is my wife?" asked Terence eagerly. He went directly into the formal drawing room. It was empty.

"Katie!" called Rupert.

"Mistress Katie in back parlor, drawing much picture," offered Ho Chih. "Masters want dinner?"

Rupert went to the back parlor. Kate was seated at the desk, a single lamp lit beside her, sketching with such absorption she did not hear him come in. He came up behind her, put his hands over her eyes.

"Guess who?" He laughed.

She screamed with surprise and caught at his hands. "Rupert! You have come! Oh, Rupert!"

He let her get up from the chair, turned her into his arms, and kissed her. Her lips were fresh and sweet, unmarred by lip rouge. She was flushed deep pink with surprise, and her eyes were starry bright. "There, my little Katie, how is this for a surprise?"

"Oh, wonderful, wonderful!" she breathed. "We feared you would not come by Christmas!" Rupert hugged her tightly, deeply pleased with her welcome. She was so very sweet!

Terence came to the doorway. "And where is my beautiful wife?" he snarled with a scowl. "Off somewhere?"

"Yes, Terence," said Katie, turning in Rupert's arms.

"Where?" he snapped.

She frowned, thinking. "I believe—I believe it is to Lady Dawlish's tonight. Yes, it must be because the balls there last until dawn, and Selina said she would not be back until then. Why don't you go for her, Terence?"

The innocent remark set Terence in a rage. "Gone out all night, has she? My wife? Damn it all! Why can't she stay home to greet me?"

"She did not know you were coming tonight," said Katie, troubled. Rupert studied her face and thought what an open, honest face she had, showing all her thoughts.

"Why don't you go, Terence?" urged Rupert. "She will be glad to see you." It seemed easier to say it now that he was coming to terms with the fact he himself was married to Katie.

"Not when I tell her we are stuck here for another

two months!" And Terence slammed out the door, striking the doorframe an enraged blow which echoed through the hall.

"Another two months, Rupert?" asked Katie, raising her gaze to his face.

He sighed. "Yes, the materials are being made but will not be ready for one or two more months. We will be here for about two weeks, then must return to Canton. Selina will be disappointed."

Terence did not go after Selina but remained home and drank until he was insensible and had to be put to bed by Rupert and Ho Chih. At dawn Selina returned to go to bed. Rupert did not seek her out. Let Terence tell her the news and hear her scream and have her temper unleashed on his head.

The next morning Rupert was glad to go out with Katie to the market and miss the scene. They remained out, sending Lilac back with the market basket, for "Neither Terence nor Selina will be wishing luncheon," as Katie said.

They dined in an open-air restaurant near the wharf and were able to gaze through the radiant sunshine out to sea, where small sailboats flaunted their red and yellow sails and larger white sails stood to wind as they set out. Children flew kites on the wharf and ran about, laughing gaily.

Rupert put his hand on Katie's as she gazed out to sea. "Are you very disappointed, my dear?" he asked gently.

"Disappointed, yes, Rupert. Yet I had a feeling the goods would not be ready yet. It takes time to make the silks. And the porcelains. If we could be satisfied with lesser goods, we could return home the earlier, I suppose. However, I want to take the best back to Mr.

Douglas Llewellyn. He has been so very good to me and—to my father—" Her voice broke on the word "father." He squeezed her hand with sympathy.

"You still miss your father. He was a fine good man."

She managed a smile and withdrew her hand to wipe her eyes with a lawn handkerchief trimmed with lace. She whisked away the tears as the waiter brought their first course, a small white porcelain bowl with thin clear soup and a tiny cream-colored dumpling in it.

They ate and talked and caught up on the news. It was a comfortable two hours, and Rupert felt grand about it. They liked to talk together. Katie was an interesting conversationalist, and he enjoyed gazing into her pretty face. Had she become more beautiful as she matured, or was it his imagination? Had she always looked so lovely, with her clear pale skin, the pink of her cheeks, the sparkle of gold in the dark brown eyes, the dark brown swath of her hair against her cheeks? And in the rose gown she was lovely; the color set off her complexion, and the lines of the dress revealed her small, petite figure, the small, high breasts, the slim waist, the long, slim thighs. She was feminine, he thought, with surprise, not like Selina, with her larger breasts and wider thighs, her blond hair and vivid blue-violet eyes. People did not faint with admiration over Katie as they did with Selina. But Katie had her own looks, and she was like a shy bird with an unexpectedly beautiful song. He smiled at his own fancies and took her hand again as the soup dishes were removed.

"I have missed you, Katie," he said gently. "Thank

you for your many good letters. They helped make the days brighter."

She flushed brightly and lowered her eyelashes shyly. "You are welcome. I hope I told you what you wished to hear."

"Selina did not write to Terence at all," he added.

The smile faded. She withdrew her hand as the waiter set down the platters of fish and rice. She picked up her chopsticks and neatly opened the fish, to push away bones and skin, revealing the delectable white flesh. She squeezed some lemon on it and began to eat. She had not answered him, thought Rupert. Did she hate Selina? Was she very jealous of her because of her beauty?

They returned home to a torrent of abuse and weeping from Selina. She blamed them all hysterically for delaying the departure. Only the arrival of guests for afternoon tea stopped her, and the tirade continued the next day. Rupert withdrew to the quiet of Katie's study, and they discussed patterns with relief, leaving Selina for Terence to quiet. He had little success and calmed her only by purchasing more jewels for her, which made alarming inroads on their remaining funds.

Rupert was now comparing the two girls more seriously. How much more patient Katie was. How she took the delay calmly and only did more work, helping choose between patterns which Rupert had brought for the porcelain, discussing what they might sell in order to buy more silk. They finally decided to sell all the black pepper and the spices, and if necessary, they would cancel the orders for tea.

"For other ships will be carrying all the teas," said Katie. "We shall have unique goods, in the designed silks, the sheer silks of many colors, and the designed porcelains. Houqua assured you, did he not, that the porcelains for us would be of the best-quality porcelain, like the thin type I showed to you?"

"Yes, I took him the sample you gave to me from—from Prince Chen Yee—" And Rupert frowned unconsciously as he uttered the name. "He was surprised that I had such a piece and finally assured me a week later that the work could be done. He said not many foreigners wished such fine pieces."

"Good. That will be ten sets of dinner china and twenty-five of the tea sets, complete with coffee and tea pitchers, chocolate pitchers, and small cups, and the trays—oh, did they consent to making the trays of porcelain on silver, Rupert?"

He had to smile at the memory. "Yes, Houqua was so delighted by your design of the porcelain trays set in silver that he asked permission to have a set made for himself! I never heard him say that before, and Captain Potter said he never had either. Houqua has a magnificent palace of a house; he invited us once for dinner, quite an honor that. And I never saw such porcelain dinner service, lacquer-covered tables, and such."

Katie brightened; her eyes flashed with pleasure. "Oh, that is indeed a compliment of the highest order. I am beginning to realize, Rupert, that the usual China export porcelain is the poorer material, more gaudy colors that the Chinese would reject for themselves. I have seen such bowls, shimmering colors, purity of line, which the prince Chen Yee owns, that would make even your father's collection seem poor."

Rupert turned on her. "Have you gone to his home again?"

She jumped at his sharp tone. "No—no, only the time that I told you, Rupert."

"And has he come here to visit you?"

Her brown eyes were frank as her gaze met his. "No, Rupert, he has not come since you were here the last time. However, he has sent many things, many items for me to draw, some silks, and the parrot—" She broke into a merry smile, indicating the gaudy red and yellow and green parrot in its cage in the corner of her study. Its birdcage stood near that of the little yellow canary. "The canary is teaching the parrot to sing! It is too amusing—"

Rupert frowned again, though he felt better that the prince himself had not come. "I wish you would not see him, Katie; it is well that he has ceased to come."

"Why?" she asked simply. "Selina has many guests. May I have no one?"

He shook his head in exasperation. "It is not the same thing, Katie! Selina's guests are Europeans, like ourselves. Your guest is a Manchu prince, of great wealth, and he has given you enormous gifts."

"The French marquis has given Selina a diamond bracelet," said Katie in a low tone, gazing down at the watercolor sketch on her desk. "She is permitted to receive gifts, but I am not? Is that it?"

"No, no." He scowled deeply. "You say a diamond bracelet? Does Terence know?"

"I do not know," said Katie, and picked up a brush and dipped it into a dark blue color.

"The gall of the fellow! Taking advantage of our absence to court Selina! She must be protected from him!" He began to stride about the room, fretting over the fact that he could not offer his protection to Selina. He finally paused where Katie was working. "What is that design in the corner?"

"You have not noticed?" she asked, not looking up at him. "I always use it."

He bent closer, studied the little butterfly. "Yes, it is quite pretty, a butterfly, eh? And you always use it?"

"It is on every design that I make. Look." She pointed to a square of silk that Rupert had brought back with him, one of the best samples of materials from one of Katie's designs. The flowers and vines had several butterflies floating over them, and in each color block was a small butterfly in the corner.

"Ah, I see! The butterfly is your symbol," he said.

"And my initials in the body of the butterfly. See?" And she sketched quickly on a sheet of paper and showed it to him. "First I make my initials, a large *K* backward; then attached to the *K* is an *A* forward."

"*K* and *A*? But your name is Llewellyn," said Rupert, uneasily. "Do you always use that?"

"Have you never noticed?" she asked a little sadly.

"No, the butterfly was always there, but somehow, I never noticed; it is so small and fragile." He glanced at two other samples of silk; the butterfly was reproduced exactly as she had drawn it, sketched around her initials of *K* and *A*. "But you must begin to use the *L*, Katie!" he said. "Do you not realize you are a married woman?" He teased her a little.

Her head remained bent. She sketched carefully a *K* backward and then a larger *L* with curly tips and then a butterfly around it. "Like this?" she asked.

"Splendid!"

"Then I will do so," she said. The peace in the room was rent with a shrill scream from Selina. Both winced involuntarily.

"No, no, no, I will not remain at home tonight!" she cried. "I am so bored—bored—bored!" The sound of a crashing cup. "I am going to Lady Dawlish tonight. I don't care whether you go or not! I don't care whether you like her or not! I shall remain out until dawn! I shall remain until noon or night!" Another crash, heavier.

Terence's voice turned pleading. "But, Selina, you never stay home—I wish to love you—please, Selina, please, I want to be alone with you!"

A door slammed shut. Terence's voice continued to plead, muffled. Then heavy footsteps in the hallway upstairs, and another door slammed.

"Well, well," said Rupert unhappily. "Shall we go out for a time, Katie? We have not been out an evening alone for such a time." The quarreling made him feel very uneasy.

"I should like that. Give me half an hour to change my gown," she said eagerly, lighting up like a candle.

"I'll come up also and put on my fine blue silk suit," he said cheerfully.

As they went upstairs, they heard Selina ordering Milbank about. "No, not that dull blue, Milbank, you stupid fool! I want the bright purple one with the blue overdress! And my diamonds!"

Katie flinched and shut the door hastily. She unfastened her muslin gown, took it off, and put on a lovely rose dress with a gold overdress of painted silk.

"That is new, Katie?" Rupert asked pleasantly, as he noted the beautiful gown. "That will be a sensation in London!"

She smiled at him in the mirror as she began to smooth back her long brown hair and press combs into it. "Yes, new, thank you, Rupert. I am glad you like it."

"Did you have it made here?"

"I made it, of lengths of painted silks. You saw them when you were here last," she said with composure.

They went out and enjoyed an exquisite dinner at the restaurant they had lunched at before. The flaming torches at the railing that lined the room overlooking the waters made Katie look strange and mysterious, a dark-eyed beauty.

"I think you have bloomed since our marriage, Katie," said Rupert after a couple of cups of potent wines. His hand captured hers; he felt desire rising in him. "You are much more beautiful than when I married you."

"I have grown up perhaps," said Katie quietly.

"Perhaps that. Let me see—you are almost twenty."

She smiled and looked out across the waters. Some of the boats had torches hung from the tops of the masts, where they swayed and made flaming red patterns on the waves below. Someone was singing a Chinese song in a high falsetto voice. Another man took up the song, and his vibrant voice quavered in emotion as the restaurant guests paused to listen. The music, the flaming torches, the sound of the waves against the restaurant walls, the smell of the salt waters, and the scent of herbs and spices and perfumes made an exotic night sheltered by the black velvet of the sky.

Rupert and Katie went home to find the house still. Selina and Terence had gone out for the night to a dance, said Ho Chih. Selina had had her way, thought Rupert, sorry for Terence for once. He and his love would go to bed, to lie together, with the memories of the beautiful evening binding them.

He took Katie in his arms in their mosquito-net-hung bed and felt as though he lay in the mist with her, shut off from the world. He felt very close to his wife, glad to be with her. Canton had been lonely.

"I am so glad, Katie, that I married you," he whispered in her ear, and kissed the lobe. Selina was lovely, but oh, that temper! He could not have borne the humiliation if Katie had treated him so.

"Really?" she murmured, and she seemed stiff in his arms for a time. But he kissed her, coaxed her with honeyed words, and stroked her with his hand. His fingers searched her vulnerable places; he teased and kissed her mouth, the ripe nipples of her breasts, until she softened and lay curled up against him. Katie could be so sweet, her fingers stroking his hairy chest shyly, her kisses answering his, her little tongue flicking in and out of his mouth. They made love for a long time that night, and he finally slept, satisfied in his masculine desires.

He wakened in the night to find Katie lying awake, her hands behind her head, staring out the partly opened window at the night sky hung with huge white stars. They seemed so close one could reach out and touch them.

"Katie, awake?" He reached out and drew her to him possessively. "What are you thinking about?"

She did not answer. He put his hand to her face and found it wet with tears.

"Katie! What is wrong?" He was alarmed. "Are you ill?"

"No, Rupert. I—I just had a bad dream; that is all."

"Oh, my darling, come here," he said, and held her tightly to him. He kissed her mouth, her chin, her cheeks. "There, is that better, love? Are you wakened from the nightmare?"

"I am awake," she said. She sighed and rolled over, to lean against him and put her cheek on his bare chest. "Rupert, I hope you will not be gone long this time?"

"I hope not," he told her. "Maybe one month will do it. However, it may be two months. We shall need no more designs, I believe. What shall you do, go out with Selina? She needs companionship to make her less frantic."

Her slim body stiffened in his arms. She did not answer for so long he thought she slept.

She finally told him, "I think I shall paint in oils, Rupert. I have longed to have time to do this. And Prince Chen Yee has sent me an easel and many paints and brushes of the finest quality. Yes, I think I shall paint in oils. He thinks I have an unusual talent."

Rupert felt a strange stinging feeling in his chest. Could it be jealousy? "Why did he send you oil paints and easel?"

"He thinks I have talent. He—respects my creative abilities, he said in a note," said Katie with defiance. "He is the only person other than my father who praised me for my artistic ability."

Rupert was silent for a moment, in amazement. "But that is not true, Katie," he said gently, troubled.

"My father and I think highly of your talents. Why else would we have you design the silks and porcelains?"

"You never said you thought my talent was good," said Katie in a subdued tone. "You—just used the designs. It is flattering to be told I have genius."

"Genius!" Rupert gasped incredulously. "He said you had genius?"

"Yes. Prince Chen Yee said it."

"And your father?"

"Father used to encourage me; he thought I had much more talent than himself, dear Father." And she murmured a little longer, then fell silent. He thought she slept.

But this time Rupert lay awake uneasily. Why would a great Manchu prince, with all the world of the Orient open to him, encourage his little sparrow of a wife by telling her she had genius? Genius. That was a strong word for Katie! Could it be true and he had not fully appreciated her? Or—or did the prince have other motives?

Uneasy thoughts lay in the back of his mind as he and Terence once more departed after the New Year and its wildly gay celebrations, to return to the dullness of work in Canton.

10

Katie wondered what she would do to fill her days after Rupert and Terence had returned to Canton. The marketing occupied her mornings, and she consulted with the cook and planned the meals.

However, Selina often went to luncheon with one friend, then went to tea with another, and returned only to change her gown and go out for the evening and night. She treated Katie as a housekeeper, never asking her to accompany her, and ordered her about when she did see her. Katie was glad to see little of her petulant sister-in-law.

She shuddered to think what it would be like on the ship, unless Selina calmed down on the voyage home. Selina's temper was often on the edge of hysteria. She hated Macao, for all her running around. She hated everyone there; they bored her to death, and she could not wait to return to London. She would never again permit herself to be pushed around as her father-in-law had done.

Katie went out mornings for the shopping, ate a solitary lunch in the massive dining room, then retired to her study to paint. She had both oils and watercolors, and she enjoyed using the colors to draw pictures. In these she did not have to confine herself to patterns which could be reproduced by a silk loom or a porcelain bowl or cup. She could use her imagination and draw and paint what she chose. It was a wonderful creative experience.

On one day she had just finished luncheon by herself when Ho Chih knocked politely at the open door.

"Yes, Ho Chih? There is a problem?" She laid down her brush and turned around.

"You have a visitor, Madame Rupert," he said solemnly. She caught a flicker of expression on his bland face. "The honorable prince Chen Yee is here."

He had not come for more than a month; she had not seen him, had received only notes and messages from him. She jumped up, her face lightening in a blaze of delight. "He is here? Oh, I will come—" She glanced down at her gown, was pleased that her maid had put on her today the peach dress with the high Empire waist and deeper rose ribbon at her throat.

She went out to the hallway, where she found the prince, gowned in a black embroidered coat and lighter azure blue undercoat, with tilt-toed black slippers embroidered in gold.

They bowed to each other solemnly, but she could not refrain from smiling brilliantly with delight. She had not seen him for so long! He also began to smile his rare smile that lit up his somber face.

"Madame Katie," he said softly. "It is good to see you. You are well?"

"Quite well, thank you, sir. And—and you?" she ventured.

He bent his head. "Well, I thank you. I hope you will consent to coming to my home this afternoon. I have a surprise which I wish you to see."

"A surprise?" She clapped her hands together like a child. "Oh, what is it?"

"Come and you will see."

Ho Chih listened to this exchange with quiet disapproval, which showed on his usually bland face. Katie turned to him.

"Request Lilac to come with me. And bring my rose pelisse and bonnet," she said.

"Yes, madame."

He went off to fetch Lilac, who soon came down the stairs hurriedly, garbed in her usual black gown and black cloak. She carried the rose pelisse and bonnet, which she proceeded to assist Katie in donning.

"Your maid will not be required today," said the prince, with his usual calm authority. "Moon Blossom will welcome you and chaperon you. She waits in the carriage." He indicated the huge closed carriage waiting at the steps.

Katie hesitated, noting the brief disapproval which crossed Ho Chih's face at these words.

"If you do not object strongly, I wish Lilac to accompany me. She is my maid after all," said Katie.

Prince Chen Yee nodded and then escorted the two women out to the carriage. He handed her inside. Moon Blossom sat on the seat with her back to the horses. She beamed happily and bowed her head again and again, her bright young face pink with emotion and the wind.

Prince Chen Yee sat with Katie on the backseat, and Lilac sat beside Moon Blossom. The prince proceeded to show Katie, as before, the many sights of Macao, pointing out houses of wealthy foreigners, of many Chinese, the harbor where one of his ships rested. It was a large one, with huge white sails and a flag at the front of it on the high platform.

"That is the banner of my house," he said.

The carriage wound uphill, and around and around, with more views of the harbor and city. Katie practically hung out the window—she was so entranced—and the curtains were kept aside for her to look. Many people glanced at her, at the bright face of the white woman, the dark form of the Manchu beyond her.

Just before they drew up to the house of the prince, he turned to Katie. "I hope you will not mind if the princess Chen Mei-ling does not appear to greet you today. Her health is uncertain," he said gravely.

"Oh, I am so sorry. Pray convey my regrets to her and my wishes for her recovery."

He bowed his head. "My brother, the prince Chen Lo, studies hard for his examinations. However, he will join us for tea. My cousin Moon Blossom is our hostess today." And he smiled kindly at the girl.

She blushed under golden skin and giggled behind her hand. She was becomingly dressed today in a silvery dress with rose embroidery and a fine wrap of deep rose over it.

"It is my great pleasure and honor to welcome you," she said shyly as they were helped down from the carriage by the prince and two men servants.

"Thank you, Moon Blossom," said Katie. "You are most kind."

Indeed, she was relieved that the princess would not appear. Katie had the strong conviction that the woman despised her! She probably hated more strongly than she loved, if she loved at all. Katie wondered if it had something to do with the fact that the prince had no children. It would be a great humiliation to his proud wife not to provide him with heirs.

The prince led his small party through several rooms and courts until they arrived at the Court of the

Flowering Peach.-Small tables and comfortable chairs were set out, and in the center—

Katie clapped her hands in wonder and delight. "The peaches are ripe!" she exclaimed.

The prince smiled and nodded to her as she drew closer and gazed up at the beautiful small balls of pink and cream fluff of the perfect little peaches.

"We shall have them with our tea," he said. "But first—pray be seated here."

He indicated a chair, set before a slanting table that contained sketching paper, colored chalk and colors, brushes, pens in a bewildering array.

Katie sat down, confused. Had he brought her here to work? He was watching her face, smiling slightly, his eyes bright. Lilac had seated herself demurely in the background, in a corner of the court where Katie could see her beyond the peach trees.

And around the peach trees, in their large red pottery jars, were more blooms. She saw now the long sprays of purple and white lilacs, the pots of roses in bloom, of rose and white and red.

"How beautiful," she breathed. "I shall enjoy drawing these beautiful blooms."

"I hope that you will," said the prince, still standing near to her. "However, that is not the surprise I have for you."

He nodded to Moon Blossom and clapped his hands sharply. As the sounds reechoed around the court, she went to the doorway into the huge house and reached out her hand. Out came a small child, a little girl, with solemn eyes and black bangs and a most beautiful gown of almond embroidered in blue. Behind her came a little boy in a deep blue dress with a ball. And behind him another boy and another girl, until about a dozen children were parading about the court, around the peach tree, pausing to bob curtsies and bows to Katie and the prince.

Katie clasped her hands in delight. No more beautiful children could be imagined! What laughing eyes, what pretty little faces, what graceful limbs as they began to play, throwing the ball to each other, two girls dancing together to the soft sound of an invisible flute.

The prince did not watch them as much as he did Katie's face. She was obviously delighted with the adorable children, the roof rolled back from the court, the sunlight playing on them as they danced and on the brilliant blooms, the peaches, the green tiles of the roof, the blue tiles of the court floor.

"Oh, oh, how delightful!" cried Katie in English, then in Chinese, turning to the prince. "What a wonderful surprise! These are the prettiest children I have ever seen!"

"They are the children of some neighbors of mine. I have invited them here for a party. You may draw them if you like."

He then showed her a beautiful porcelain bowl, which he put into her hands. It was a crimson color and around it the figures of small children were painted in quaint green colors. The children played with balls, kites, little toys she did not recognize.

"You see how such designs can be utilized," he explained, pointing to various figures. "However, I hope you will also wish to make oil paintings. You are working with oils, I believe?"

"Yes, sir, with the most beautiful equipment you sent to me, in your kindness," she said. "I have completed the designs for the silks and the porcelains.

They need no more." And her face shadowed. "The work is taking so long we will be about two more months in Macao while my husband waits in Canton and loads the ships."

"You are sorry for the delay?" he asked sharply.

"In a way I long to return home to England," she said with her usual honesty. "Yes, I long to return home. However, Macao is so beautiful I shall be sorry to leave it."

"Ah—quite so." Then he fell silent. Inspired by the delightful scene and the laughing children, she began to sketch on the fine white paper he had provided.

What a beautiful day it was! The sun shone brightly, yet a cool breeze swept through the court to cool them. The children played happily together. When they tired of the balls and the dancing, servants brought out small kites, which they attempted to fly in the little breeze.

The prince sat in a large armchair near Katie, where she could see his face as he watched the children. A small girl, temporarily weary of play, came to him and leaned on his knee, sighing with weariness. He leaned down to her and tenderly picked her up and set her on his knees. She leaned against him naturally and began to whisper to him, cuddling against him.

Katie began to sketch them quickly, the prince's bent head, the tender look, the little girl in her deep blue dress against his black robe. The small hand lay confidingly in his big one, with the long, scholarly, sensitive fingers, the well-manicured nails, the large rings of diamonds and rubies and sapphires.

She sketched again, another drawing of two girls dancing together. Then another sketch, quickly executed for further development in the quiet of her study, of several small boys in their absorbed study of some toy ships and boats. Another boy played with a top, sent it spinning, and she sketched that.

The hours sped past. She had about half a dozen sketches completed and several others outlined in colored chalks when a tea tray was brought out into the courtyard. With it came Prince Chen Lo, his shy face beaming with pleasure as he bowed to Katie and greeted her.

"How go your studies, sir?" she asked him.

He grimaced. "Poorly, I fear," he said.

His elder brother shook his head. "He is too modest. He studies well; his tutors are most pleased with his intelligence. He will be much smarter than his elder brother."

Why, he was even teasing his brother! Katie was delighted to see this side of him. All of them seemed much more at ease than in the presence of the haughty Manchu princess Mei-ling.

Servants brought out a number of small tables and chairs, and the children were seated. Tired with play, hungry, delighted with the food offered, they fell to eating, very politely, though, with good manners, as young as they were.

They ate rice cakes, puddings of cinnamon and vanilla and drank weak tea of a light straw color. Their elders hungrily ate more rice cakes, richer cakes of chocolate and coconut, and stronger tea. It was very refreshing to drink the hot tea in the cool breeze of the shadowy courtyard as the afternoon sun moved farther to the western sky. Bowls of water were brought, peaches picked before them, reverently by the servants, and the peaches washed and offered to them. Katie bit into hers, and juice ran down her chin!

She was embarrassed and wiped it off quickly. The prince smiled at her.

"That is a part of the pleasure of eating the peaches," he said with unusual kindness. "The juice drips from the ripe peach and is of such profuse variety that one is covered with the sweet, sticky fluid. I can remember as a child one of the delights of this time of year in Macao was when our peaches were ripe and my brother and I were allowed to eat them. You remember our honored father, Chen Lo? You were so young when he went to the heavenly place set for him—"

Katie was suprised at the intimacy of the conversation today. It was as though the children had softened him so much he could speak so.

Prince Chen Lo answered, "Yes, my brother. Our honorable father would take me on his knee, as you now take the small boy. He would hold a napkin beneath my chin and tease me as I ate. How I respected and revered my kindly father. I can see him yet, his scholar's face with the narrow white beard, his fine eyes—" He sighed.

Moon Blossom had scarcely said a word. Now she spoke shyly. "How kind he was to take me into his home when I was but a baby. The death of my parents caused him to come to me, in our poor home, and bring me and my brother to live with him. And now the honorable prince Chen Yee continues in the tradition of his honored father, caring for all his relations in the best ways that Confucius commended."

"You cause me to feel warm with embarrassment," said Prince Chen Yee with a smile at her, and with a wave of his long hand he cut off the conversation.

The children finished their cakes, played a little

more, then grew sleepy and fussy. Moon Blossom had them all bow to Katie and the two princes, then led them away. The courtyard seemed suddenly strangely quiet.

Katie had returned to her sketching. She noted that the prince had sent for a writing table and was now absorbed in composing something, with a fine brush, black ink, and elegant writing paper. She continued her work, thinking she would like to make an oil painting of one of the scenes today.

Presently the prince had finished two pages and lifted his head. When she also paused in her sketching and laid down the chalk and stretched her fingers, he said, "May I read to you two of my compositions today?" His mouth curved whimsically. "There is poetry in the very air!"

She smiled. "I would be most pleased to hear, sir."

He picked up the first page of a shorter poem and read.

The peach branches have blossomed, and the
　　rain has washed them away.
Now peaches hang heavy on the bough, to be
　　eaten by children, laughing, the juice on their chins.
Soon the winds will blow white sails north to
　　Peking and I with them.
Will anyone see our shadows on the wall and
　　remember the sound of our footsteps?

He looked at her for her comment. She said, "That is very beautiful, very touching. Does—does it mean that you—you leave Macao soon?"

"Presently," he said. "And you also?"

"When my husband returns, with the ship laden," she said. "Perhaps in six weeks to two months. It will be late, but the orders are being done painstakingly and slow."

He looked satisfied, for some reason. "Now, the other poem," he said, and lifted a page of longer lines of characters.

> The merry children circle 'round the courtyard.
> How the ball bounces, how the kite streams in
>   the air!
> Laughter comes as readily as juices from a peach.
> How my heart delights in young pleasure.
>
> Evening comes with its lengthened shadows.
> Torches flare where the little ones ran.
> I think I see a small one in the corner, hiding,
>   teasing—
> No, it is but a lilac branch stirred by the
>   night wind.
>
> The day seemed full of never-ending joy.
> Forever the children laughed and ran.
> How quickly came the end of singing voices.
> How empty is the courtyard and my heart.

She complimented him correctly on the poem. Then she added shyly, "I think the poems both show much sadness, sir. I believe you enjoy the children so much and regret not having any of your own—as I do."

He looked stern and thoughtful, as though unwilling to express in ordinary conversation what the poems had said. Then he nodded slowly, and only Lilac in the corner could hear what he said. Moon Blossom had not yet returned; Prince Chen Lo had returned reluctantly to his studies.

"Yes, regret. A man who has no sons to follow in his footsteps is empty. It is as the saying goes, 'I had no sons, none to mourn me during the feasts of the ancestors. The gods will not remember me either.'"

"Oh, that is so sad, sir. I wish—I hope that one day your wishes will be fulfilled, that you will have a son," she said impulsively. "Surely you will—" She blushed at her own thoughts that he was so masculine, so virile he must have a child. Why had he not? Was there some strange medical ailment that prevented him?

"You are most generous in your thoughts. I wish for you also a long life and many sons and daughters." He bowed. Then he stood. The courtyard was almost dark. "I regretfully return you to your home, before your people worry about a precious woman out after the darkness falls."

During the next days Katie thought constantly of that joyful afternoon, the courtesy of the prince, the lovely scenes of the children. She began to work on an oil painting of the courtyard and the children.

In the foreground was seated the prince, turned sideways from the viewer. The small girl in his arms was fully visible, the weary yet happy droop of her head against his black embroidered coat, glimpses of other children playing in the background, at one side the heavy peaches hanging from the boughs. She painted the little girl with her deep blue dress and the other children in their reds and rose and greens. It was a pretty scene, and the tenderness of the prince's arm about the child was sketched carefully. She did not show his full face, only the proud profile, the bent dark head, the fine hand.

She was not surprised when the prince came within a week. Somehow she had thought he would come again. Ho Chih showed him into her parlor and sent for Lilac to sit, unregarded, in the corner. Katie had sprung up when he entered and went to him, holding out her hand. She knew that one did not touch hands with an Oriental, yet he was so close to her thoughts she had forgotten and wished to greet a friend. The big, strong hand closed about her slim hand and held it tightly for a long moment.

"I am so happy to see you!" she said in English, then in Chinese. Again she thought he did understand her English.

He smiled his rare smile, which lit his deep black eyes. "And I to see you. Today you look like a small songbird. I think to hear you break into music!"

He gazed at her in the yellow muslin gown, with her ribbons of golden brown at waist and throat, looked her up and down as though he could not gaze enough. She blushed deeply and drew away her hand.

She gestured to him to take the armchair, but instead, he went, as though pulled, toward the easel. "The painting!" he exclaimed. "What have you done?"

She wondered if he was displeased. But by the look on his face he was not—he was happy. He gazed and gazed at it.

"It is yours," she said impulsively. "The oil is not yet dry, but I will send it to you—does it please you, sir?"

"Please me! Please me! So this is how I seem to you? The tender expression, the child in my arms—" He paused. She could not see his face as he turned it fully to the painting. In a low tone he added, "I cannot express to you my keenest pleasure. All is understood; all is known. One reads the other's heart; we are friends, I think."

"I hope we are friends," said Katie simply and honestly. "You have done so much for me, aided me here in this land new to me, helped me in my work. You have enriched my mind and my heart. Yes, I hope I may be permitted to call you friend."

He turned around slowly from his gazing at the painting to look fully into her face, upturned to his. He seemed to drink in the sight of her lovely face, her bright brown eyes, the dark curve of her hair against the porcelain white and peach of her cheek. He nodded slowly.

"I have never had a friend before who was a female," he said. "I have never spoken of thoughts to a woman before. You are different. You have a mind to comprehend, a heart to understand, an artistic hand to paint eloquently—yes, a genius, that is what you are. What a wonder is this!"

She laughed a little, embarrassed yet so pleased. She begged him to sit down. He did, but first he handed her a parcel wrapped in silk.

She unfastened it, cheeks growing more pink. "You bring me too many gifts," she dared scold him.

"It is only my hope that the poor thing will please you," he said, watching her curiosity and her eager fingers.

She opened the silk square and gasped at the contents. She held up an elaborate blue silk overdress of thick velvet, embroidered in colored silk threads, a Manchu gown like his and Moon Blossom's, with a border of deep rose embroidered in gold. "It is too beautiful!" she cried in rapture, holding it to herself. "It is too lovely! How can it be for me?"

To please him and herself, she had Lilac assist her in putting on the overdress on top of her yellow muslin gown. She left the robe open so that the yellow might set off the deep blue. He was very pleased; she knew by his smile.

Then they sat down and talked; Ho Chih brought tea for them; they talked and discussed and talked some more. The hours flew.

They talked of Oriental wisdom, the sayings of the wise Confucius, or Master K'ung fu-tze, as Prince Chen Yee called him. The prince expounded on the sayings, which Katie had been reading slowly in Chinese.

" 'To live in the presence of a man who is at his best is the most excellent possible manner of living. When a man has the choice, how can he be considered as possessing wisdom if he does not choose to live in such a presence?' " the prince quoted, and began to explain what it means.

And again, puzzling, he said, " 'A man who is a man living at his best will always know which men to love and hold to and which men to hate.' "

"I do not understand that, 'which men to hate,'" said Katie thoughtfully. "In our Christian religion we are taught it is wrong to hate. We should love all men, no matter what evil they do. For it is the evil thing which is wrong, not the man."

"How can you separate what a man is from what a man does?" asked the prince, leaning forward with interest. "Do you separate this? How?"

She frowned, in puzzlement. "I do not know," she said frankly.

"Let us take an example. A man injures a person you love. What of this man who does such a vile deed? You take him by the hand, you say words of love to him? If he has wronged the person you love, say, he murders him with a sword, what would you say to this man?"

"He would be put into prison."

"Why? He has done you, not the state, harm."

"What would you do to him?" asked Katie.

"Kill him," said the prince.

"Yourself? Kill him yourself?" she cried, eyes wide.

"I would kill him myself or order my servants to do so, yes. For a man who kills once, for spite or greed or malice, will kill again if he has the opportunity. There is evil in this world; there are evil men—and women, Mistress Katie," he said, and his voice was a caress as he spoke her name. "You are young and too innocent for this world; you have been sheltered by a scholar-father from the madness which infects some. Know this, there is evil about you which would do you harm. I would have you guard yourself since your husband does not remain to do so."

She blushed. It was not the first time that he had criticized Rupert. She changed the subject, feeling guilty enough that she had received this man in the absence of her husband. She could not listen also to criticism.

They spoke for a long time over tea. She could have gone on forever, she thought later. But as dusk came, he rose, bowed, and asked to take the painting with him. She granted it, delighted that he was pleased with her work.

She worked on other paintings in the following weeks, more paintings in oil, more watercolors. She enlarged her sketches, no longer bound by the restrictions of working for silk weaving and porcelain designing. No more could be done for that this winter. And soon Rupert would return, the ship laden, and they would go home.

She would miss the prince. He came again and again those weeks, bringing her gifts, accepting her gifts in return. She gave him a watercolor of lilac blossoms which pleased him, the painting of a still life of a precious bit of porcelain on a lacquer table, and a painting of the canary in its cage, singing in the sunlight with a vase of roses nearby. He praised her glowing colors, the purity of her line, her subject matters, so simple yet with such warmth of emotion.

And she bloomed in his praise. She enjoyed their talks, especially since Selina was never home to disturb them or mock her. She loved to match her speech against his, to improve her Mandarin, to know more of Oriental wisdom, to argue gently with Chinese ideas versus European. Surely there could be nothing wrong about this conversation, these few visits. After all, Selina ran about Macao with other men! It did not mean Katie was disloyal to her husband, any more than Selina was. Selina knew correct behavior, and she did it.

Sometimes Katie thought of Rupert with wistful longing. He was her first love, her only love, her husband now. Yet he had never praised her, never appreciated her mind, never seemed to long to be in her company as the Manchu prince did. He did not hang on her words; he did not speak with her for hours on end; he did not watch her paint with such intensity; he did not write poems to her!

She flushed at herself, shook her head, reproved herself, vowed not to show so plainly her pleasure in the prince's company. Yet when he would come unexpectedly to her door and smile and enter, her heart bounded with pleasure. After he had left, she would count over like jewels the precious words of admiration he had voiced, the way he had gazed at her as though he liked what he saw. She would savor his criticism, try to improve her drawing so it was even more simple, letting every line count, as the Oriental artists did. She valued his critiques, for he praised even as he criticized, and he was never destructive. He made her feel more confident.

She longed to return home to England—yet she wanted to remain here, near to him, this strange exotic friend who had made in her loneliness. She would miss him sorely; she hardly dared look ahead to the days of Rupert's return and their departure. Her heart would be wrung at leaving. Yet it must be.

11

As February drew to a close, Selina ordered Milbank to begin to pack her clothing and household articles. "Surely Terence will return soon, and we can leave this dreadful place!" she said.

"They have not written for two weeks," Katie said worriedly. "I hope nothing has gone wrong. We must leave by the end of March, earlier if possible."

"I am anxious to leave, but why do you say we must go by the end of March?" Selina paused in adjusting the bow of her attractive blue silk and lace bonnet.

"Because the monsoon winds change, and begin to blow toward Macao and to the east, instead of toward Africa," Katie explained. When she saw Selina's puzzled frown, she added, "The winds change twice a year. When they blow toward Macao from Africa, the sailing ships can come here. That is April or May to about December. Then, in January, the winds begin to change and blow the other direction. Then we must depart. Many of the ships have left already."

"I cannot wait to go! And we must not be left behind! If Terence does not come soon, I will leave without him!" cried Selina anxiously. She flounced out of the house with Milbank in faithful attendance.

On the second day of March Katie was working in the back when she heard a carriage drive up. She thought it might be the prince, and she hastened to the hallway.

The door was open. She saw a strange carriage, and in came Rupert, helping carry a limp form. Two Chinese sailors assisted him.

Katie put her hand to her mouth, staring. Rupert saw her. "Katie, have his bed made up at once. Terence is terribly ill!"

They all flew about. Ho Chih was sent for an English doctor. Lilac came with medicines and poultices and cool water and cloths to place on Terence's forehead. The man was out of his mind, raving in delirium.

"How long has he been like this?" The doctor's ruddy face was grave and anxious. He had lived in Macao only two years and was not familiar with all the possible fevers yet.

"Three days. He came down with it, I thought he would recover and stayed up with him, but he began to go out of his head. I looked for injuries, I thought it might be from an infected scratch. But no, no injuries. He kept vomiting also." Rupert was pale and anxious—so tired that Katie's heart ached for him.

The doctor shook his head slowly. "I don't know what is wrong. I will consult with other doctors who have been here longer."

But none knew what it was. Some strange fever, a tropical disease, said one doctor. All they could do was keep him covered, cool his head with cold-water packs, feed him broth that would strengthen him, and wait out the fever.

Selina refused to go near him. Wild with fear, she had hysterics and wept whenever Katie begged her to come. Terence was asking for her in his delirium.

"No, no, I will catch it and die! Yes, I will die!" cried Selina, weeping. "I'll never get back home. Don't ask me to come! I cannot!"

"Poor child," said Rupert to her. "Of course, you will not have to go near him. We can nurse him."

He and Katie took turns nursing Terence that night and the next day. Lilac and Ho Chih helped with medicines, cold packs, hot tea, hot broths. The house settled into an anxious silence, punctuated by Selina's weeping and Terence's moans and his cries. "Selina! Where are you? Selina, I want you! Oh, God, I cannot see, it is so dark—am I blind? Mother, Mother, Mother—"

"I wish I could get him on the ship and take him home," Rupert said worriedly to Katie as she prepared to sit with Terence that night. "The winds will soon change; we must go—"

"But a six months' journey—and no doctor aboard—dare we risk it, Rupert?" asked Katie.

Selina hovered in the hallway, listening. "Why can't we take him?" she asked sharply. "We cannot remain here another year! My God, I would run mad!"

Terence heard her voice and opened his eyes. "Selina? Are you there? Selina?"

She backed away, fear in her blue eyes. "No, no, I cannot come—I won't get that fever! I'll go stay with Mrs. Shaw—"

But before she could carry out her threat, Terence died. Katie was with him early in the morning, about three o'clock, when the spirits sink lowest and the worst seems to happen. She had been half-asleep in the large armchair Rupert had brought up to the room, rising at times to bathe his forehead. She had drooped against the arm of the chair, her head down, when she heard Terence speak.

"Mother—Mother—" he said. She jerked awake and got up to go to the bed. His sunken eyes had opened; his thin yellowed face turned up appealingly. Sweat beaded his forehead and he pushed at the covers with one thin hand. In a few days the fat from his heavy drinking had seemed to fall from him; his bones showed on his face, his arms, his legs.

"Mother?" he questioned as Katie placed a cool pad on his burning hot forehead. He gazed up at her, half smiled. "Mother," he whispered, and closed his eyes.

"Yes, Terence," she whispered, thinking it might comfort him.

"I was wrong—wrong. You were right—about Selina," he whispered. "Wrong—wrong, sorrry. But I—loved what I thought she was. Sorrrry. Sorrrry. Selina, oh, Selina. If only I had not loved her—"

He fell silent. Katie bathed his forehead again; again he seemed to cool. Then he was quiet, lying so silent; his heavy breathing, so harsh, had seemed to turn quiet.

And she remembered her father. She went quickly to the door and called softly, "Rupert! Rupert! Come—"

He was so sound asleep that he did not hear her. Lilac came, and saw, and shook her head. Ho Chih, half-asleep in the hall outside, came in also and said, "He is dead, madame."

Lilac went to call Rupert. He stumbled in, said, "Oh, my God, it cannot be—when did he go?"

"Just now—so quickly—"

"Poor fellow." Rupert gazed down tenderly at the peaceful face of his brother. "He never wanted to come here. At the last he said we would never leave, he would never get home again. And now he must go home"—he choked—"in a casket—"

Katie did not answer. She was remembering what the doctor had said quietly to her, "Bodies decay rapidly in the tropics. If he dies, he will have to be buried at once, here. The authorities in Macao will insist on it."

"What did he say at the last?" Rupert was asking. "He must have said Selina's name—"

"Yes, he did," said Katie ironically.

Rupert's face lit. "I will go and awaken her and tell her. She will be comforted that he spoke of her at the last."

And Rupert left the room and went to waken Selina. Katie could hear her weeping and Rupert comforting her. When she went to ask him if they should call the authorities, he was sitting on her wide mosquito-net-hung bed, holding her in his arms. She wore a pale blue low-cut nightdress, and he was holding her close to him—

Katie went out again without disturbing them. Her heart raged with futile anger. She thought bitterly: If Rupert had not married me, he would now be free to marry Selina, his first and only love!

She consulted with Ho Chih, who said he would go to the doctor as soon as dawn came. Katie left the tending of the body to him and to Lilac and retired to her room. Rupert did not come; she could hear his soothing voice speaking to Selina, her bitter weeping, as she fell asleep. She was so exhausted she could not even care, not just then.

The house was filled the next morning with the doctor, the men from the health department of the

Macao government, men from the funeral house. They took the body of Terence away, burned it, and a brief service was held as they buried his ashes in the cemetery.

Selina could not go, she said. She was exhausted from weeping, and besides, she had not a suitable black dress. Rupert and Katie went, and Ho Chih and Lilac, and Mrs. Shaw came and expressed her sorrow.

The other friends of Selina did not bother to come; they did not care for funerals, and the disease might be contagious. The whispers had swept around that Terence had been ill of a strange malady that had taken him very quickly.

The doctor told Katie and Rupert, "He was in poor condition. He must have been drinking heavily, a fault of some men in the tropics. When his condition was poor and when he got this fever, whatever it was, he did not have the strength to throw it off. A man cannot be too careful in the tropics—we are not accustomed to their fevers and must remain in a very healthy condition to resist them." He himself recommended cold baths each morning, and lifting exercises, and some running about his patio, which he did faithfully.

They returned from the funeral to find Selina hysterical, ordering Milbank to pack everything so they could go at once. Rupert went to talk to her. Katie sank into a chair, unable to move further for a time. She closed her eyes to try to shut out unpleasant thoughts, but it did not work.

Selina—and Rupert. Rupert—tied to Katie. Selina—free. Selina would find some way to win Rupert. Katie could not think how, but she knew Selina.

Her tired brain went around and around. Rupert

still adored Selina. He did not love Katie. How he must regret having married Katie in such haste. If only he had waited, if only he had waited—

Poor, poor Terence. Dying here in a land he hated. Coming to realize what a poor bargain he had in a wife, but too late. Dying for it. Dying—a fate too heavy for his foolishness.

What would his parents say? His poor mother, who doted on him. His father, with such hopes for his elder son.

She opened her eyes and stared blankly at the window. Rupert was now the only heir! Rupert—heir to the Llewellyn estates, fortunes, ships, all the wealth. Oh, Selina would want him now!

Rupert's heavy steps were heard on the stairway. Ho Chih stood respectfully waiting. "Does the master want tea?" he asked.

"Yes, hot tea, Ho Chih, thank you. In the drawing room."

Rupert came in. Katie had not even removed her dark blue bonnet, the closest she had to black.

"Poor darling, you look so tired," said Rupert, and came over and gently removed her bonnet for her and cast it aside. "Have I thanked you for your faithful care of my brother? You were so good to him—"

At the unexpected words Katie's eyes filled with tears. She was so tired, and her bones seemed to ache as though with the rheumatics. She was too young for this, she thought, and managed to sit up straight. She was just tired; a night's sleep would put her right.

"I have been thinking, Rupert. About your parents. Is there any way to send word?"

He nodded. "Two English ships are leaving tomorrow. I have scribbled letters to be sent by each Captain. Father will hear a couple of weeks before we arrive home." He sat down, sighed, put his head on his hands. "Poor Father, how unhappy he will be. He will blame himself for sending Terence on this journey."

Katie opened her mouth to speak hotly in defense of Mr. Douglas Llewellyn, then closed it again. Had Rupert forgotten so soon that Terence had brought this on himself by marrying Selina, by dueling for her? No, it would do no good to rake up old coals.

Ho Chih and Lilac brought in tea. Their faces were grave and weary. They too had been up for long hours, helping.

Katie thanked them. "You have been most kind, both of you," she said formally. "I cannot thank you enough for your goodness."

Selina came in, her face swollen with tears, and sank down. Rupert jumped up to pour some hot tea for her, to urge her tenderly to drink it.

"How soon can we leave, Rupert?" she asked wanly.

"Well, I must go back at once to Canton and finish loading the ship. Then—"

"Finish! Finish! Isn't that wretched ship finished yet?" she cried out. "Let us leave at once! You said other ships were going—"

"We must take the *China Princess* back, Selina," he said firmly. "It is almost full; the last silks and porcelains should be ready when I return. Then, in a week, we shall go. You can wait another two weeks, can you not? A week to finish loading, a week to finish and be ready to depart from Macao!" He smiled at her, coaxing her. "Come, bear up, you have been brave so far!"

She pouted. Katie braced for a tantrum. But instead, Selina smiled at Rupert, took his hands in hers, and said, "Dearest Rupert, I do not know what I would have done without your strength to support me! Poor Terence, poor, dear Terence, he had not your courage, your fortitude." Her long lashes slowly lowered over her blue-violet eyes; she was the picture of demure grief, of wistful longing.

Katie longed to throw the teapot at the blond head. If only Rupert would see through her! But no, men doted on flattery; they fall before it as though before a bullet. She watched, with new cynicism, as Rupert squeezed the small hands and comforted her yet again.

Rupert decided to leave two days later. He asked Katie to supervise the packing, "for we must leave as soon as I return. Selina cannot endure much more."

"Of course, Rupert," said Katie wearily. She herself was so weary, so exhausted she felt listless. She felt warm, and her bones ached. She hoped she was not catching a cold or, worse yet, the fever that Terence had had. Still, she was a healthy person and was careful of the food she ate.

Katie kissed Rupert good-bye at the door, but Selina ran out after him, flung herself into his arms, and cried, "Do be sure to come back at once, at once, dearest Rupert! I cannot abide the waiting!"

Rupert kissed her cheek and said, "I shall come as soon as I can, dear Selina. Do not fret, we shall take you home soon, and London shall be merry for you. You are young yet—do not despair and mourn for what is past."

Katie leaned against the door as they went through this prolonged leave-taking. Rupert glanced back at her, and she saw his eyelids flicker as she watched them both gravely. He let Selina go, then waved to

Katie. She lifted her hand and saw him enter the carriage to go down to the port.

He was out of sight now. Selina returned slowly to the house and went upstairs.

Katie turned to Ho Chih, who had stood silently surveying the odd sight of one wife seeing off the husband of another. Strange foreigners, he thought.

"Well, Ho Chih, we must do much more packing. I think the good china today; we shall not need it much longer."

"Yes, Miss Katie. You return soon to your own country?"

"Yes, in about two weeks, Ho Chih. Thank you for your good work. I shall give you good references when I leave."

He bowed low and thanked her humbly, as did Lilac, standing nearby. Katie went wearily up the stairs to survey her bedroom. She would first pack most of Rupert's belongings, then her own.

Milbank in her usual dark dress was in the upper hall. She paused as Katie came toward the front. "Mistress Katie," she said in a low tone, "I wish to apologize for not helping to nurse Master Terence. Indeed, I would have, but—but Miss Selina refused to let me. She was afraid of catching the fever—" She hesitated, head turned alertly to the front bedroom where Selina was.

"I understand. Thank you anyway," said Katie, her tones tired.

"You best lie down while you can," whispered Milbank. "You look weary to death."

"Yes, I would like to rest. But there is so much to do—"

Selina came from her room. "What are you whispering about?" she asked sharply. "I asked for my dark blue dress, Milbank! And the flowered navy hat with the cunning white rim."

"Yes, Miss Selina," said Milbank, and scurried toward her.

"What were you saying?" Selina asked Katie.

"I am rather weary," said Katie.

Selina looked at her crossly. "Well, I'm going out for luncheon at Mrs. Shaw's. *She* understands my grief!"

"You are going out so soon?" asked Katie involuntarily.

"Yes, I am!" And Selina went into her room and slammed the door shut.

Katie shook her head and went to her own room. She opened Rupert's trunks and began to fold garments into rice cloth and silks to ready them for the journey. She laid aside the garments to be washed or cleaned and packed others, slowly.

Her head ached so. She felt so queer, as though she might fall down.

Selina went out, followed by the faithful Milbank.

12

Katie felt odd all afternoon. She finally went down to the front drawing room and had some tea. She was probably very tired; she would have an early night.

She could not eat anything, but the hot tea tasted good and revived her somewhat. She was sitting with her head back on the cushioned seat, resting, when Selina returned with Milbank.

Selina came into the room, looking attractive in her smart blue.

Katie opened her eyes with an effort. Her head was pounding. "Selina—I think I am—ill," she said slowly. "Will you please, send Ho Chih for the—doctor—"

Milbank exclaimed and came in also. Selina stood gazing at Katie, with a look of fear in her blue-violet eyes.

"Ill? You cannot be ill," she cried out. Then she hesitated, her face strange, her mouth twisted. "Milbank, get the carriage. We will take her to the doctor!"

"Oh, Miss Selina, she should be put to bed and the doctor called!" protested Milbank. The voices seemed to waver in Katie's ears, coming and going like the waves of the sea.

"Do as I say! Bring the carriage around!"

Selina and Milbank left the room. Katie tried to get up to protest she did not want to leave the house. She would just go to bed and rest.

Lilac came in with Katie's cloak. Her face looked startled when she saw Katie's condition. "Missee sick!" she exclaimed as she saw her mistress.

Selina, who followed her, said sharply, "No, she is going out with me! Help her into her cloak!"

Ho Chih hovered in the hallway, looking very puzzled. His face also wavered before Katie. Lilac was assisting her to the outer door. Katie tried to say, "No, no, I do not want to go out—" but heard herself mumbling.

She was put into the carriage. Milbank was saying, "I could nurse her, Miss Selina!"

"Be quiet, Milbank!"

The jolting of the carriage, on and on. No one spoke. Katie wanted to beg to return home, to beg to be put to bed; she wanted the comfort of a warm bed; she felt chilled. Then she felt hot, and everything was swimming before her eyes.

Then came Selina's sharp voice to the coachman. "Up that hill there. To the house of the prince Chen Yee!"

The carriage turned, jolted on the cobblestones, then onto a dirt road. Milbank was protesting. Katie nodded against the corner of the carriage. Her head hurt; she could not see or think clearly.

"Miss Selina, this is wicked!" said Milbank in a low tone. "You cannot take Mrs. Rupert to that man's house!"

"He can nurse her!" said Selina shrilly. "He is her friend, her lover! Let him take care of her. She shall not prevent us from sailing! I will not catch that fever and die in this horrible country!"

"Oh, Miss Selina, God forgive you! You must not do this! I have ever obeyed you—"

"Then keep on obeying me, Milbank!"

Katie felt as if she were in a nightmare; this was not happening. She was dreaming, tossing in her bed, alone, without Rupert, missing him. What a dreadful dream, and she was so hot; she must get up and open the window—

The carriage rattled on. Why was she in a carriage? She had thought she was in bed. She wanted her soft pillow; she wanted cool sheets about her—no, she was cold, a warm blanket—and hot tea—she was cold.

Voices came faintly. Milbank was arguing with Selina. Strange, they never argued. Milbank always said, "Yes, Miss Selina," and adored her mistress, and praised her beauty—

"This is terrible wicked, Miss Selina, you will never forgive yourself—"

"Milbank, one more word, and I will dump you here in Macao! You can stay here and nurse Katie, and catch the fever, and die! Yes, I shall leave you here, and you shall never see home again!"

"Oh, no, no, Miss Selina! I have ever served you faithfully. No, Miss Selina, do not leave me here in this heathen place!" There was cringing fear in the low voice.

"I will if you say one more word!"

There was silence then, quiet, and Katie seemed to sleep. She wanted her bed; she wanted to rest—

The carriage jolted her so. And she was raging hot; her body seemed to burn in the thin dress and dark cloak.

They jolted to a stop. Katie vaguely heard voices; they spoke in Chinese. She forced her eyes open. She had been lifted, turned, carried. Now she stood on the steps of the prince's home. How odd—had he sent for her? Had it been his carriage?

She saw the wide eyes of Moon Blossom in a creamy face, her startled staring, the blank expressions of the burly servants in dark blue, then the prince himself, face impassive, as Selina spoke to him.

"I brought her here—you can nurse her—I will not have that horrible fever—this horrible country—" Selina was weeping, screaming at him. "Horrible, sickening people—"

Then Katie felt herself lifted and carried, and her mind was blank. She could not see or think, she could only feel, and presently she was in a cool bed, and there were cool compresses on her forehead. Good, they had taken her home; finally she could rest. She remembered no more for a long time.

Rupert worked long hours in Canton, rising early, retiring late. The silk goods had finally arrived, and the porcelains as well. The porcelains in huge wooden crates were loaded in the lower part of the ship for ballast. The precious fragile silks were loaded in the upper parts, out of danger of water spoilage. The jade and jewels, the ivory, the few remaining kegs of spices were kept in his own cabin.

Captain Potter was equally relieved when they cleared customs, paid the hoppo in charge of customs a large number of gifts for his clearance of them, and set sail from the harbor at Whampoa and down to Canton. It was a long day's journey, and they arrived at night.

Captain Potter stayed aboard. They would begin loading the personal effects of the Llewellyns tomorrow and with luck could sail in three or four more days. He kept a watchful eye on the winds; they must be off before the monsoon winds changed, and it could happen any day now.

Rupert hastened by carriage to his home. He was anxious to see Katie, have her report on the progress of the packing. And poor, dear Selina, he was anxious about her too. He hoped she would begin to recover from her grief on the journey home. They must be careful and tender of her.

The carriage pulled up at the silent house. No one came to the door; he had to knock. A strange man opened to him; a bland Chinese face stared into his.

"Where is Ho Chih?" asked Rupert blankly.

The man bowed low. "Ho Chih gone. What can poor Lang do?"

"I am Rupert Llewellyn; this is my home. Where is my wife?" He was angry and anxious as well. Katie was always here to welcome him.

"Mrs. Llewellyn go out."

"Where?"

"Lang not know."

Rupert searched about. It was strange. Katie was not there, nor Selina nor Milbank. Ho Chih was gone, and so was Katie's maid, Lilac. How odd, had they all gone to a party? Or had something dreadful happened to them all? He thought of the fever and went cold with dread.

He went to the kitchen; it was empty, but the cook was in the back patio. He spoke to her haltingly in pidgin English, but though she beamed in friendly manner, she only shook her head at his questions. "Missus go out, missus very busy."

He returned, went up to his bedroom. It seemed empty. His trunks stood open—Katie had begun to pack his clothes. Yet there was a slight layer of dust over the trunks. How strange. Had she stopped packing? He fingered the dresser, another layer of dust, over the furniture, over her brushes and combs and mirror, her small jewel box

Rupert sat up in the drawing room, waiting. He had never felt so helpless except when Terence had been taken ill. Katie had helped then, dear little Katie, so faithful, so strong for all her slightness. He longed to see her again, to see her smile and have her welcome him. On the journey home he would make up to her for the long absences, for her heavy work. She had done marvelously, handling a strange home in the tropics, handling the servants, doing such great work in the designs.

He thought briefly of Selina and tried to thrust her from his mind. She was free. He felt ashamed that he still desired her, his brother's widow!

If he had not married so hastily, if he had waited, Selina could have been his bride one day. If only he did not have such a strong sense of duty—

His mouth compressed; he passed a weary hand over his face. He must not think along these lines. Beautiful Selina, free, but still not for him. He was tied in bonds of marriage and duty to Katie. Lovely Selina had been freed by death to marry again, but he could not marry her—

He muttered, "Forget her, forget! You must treat her tenderly as your sister—but that is all!"

And he was very fond of Katie now. She was his wife, and he rejoiced as he thought of her. She could be so sweet and generous in her loving. Yes, he must desire only his Katie. She alone was due his love and his loyalty.

Determinedly, he turned his thoughts to the work, the voyage before them. They could set out within a few days, they must, before the winds changed.

His father would be very pleased with the marvelous goods they brought back. Rupert stretched out his long legs in contentment. He was very tired, but it would be good to get on the ship and have a restful journey home with Katie. She was such a dear. They would get off at various ports, and he would take her about and show her the marvels of the various places. Dear Katie, she loved such things.

He had fallen asleep when the sound of a carriage awakened him. Lang was opening the door; he heard voices, subdued laughter, a French accent of a man's voice. When Rupert reached the door, he saw Selina waving good-bye and laughing as the Frenchman retreated. She wore pale blue; her face sparkled with laughter and was flushed with wine.

"Selina!" Milbank turned about at his voice and went pale. Had he startled them so? "Selina, how good to see you! Who was that man? Where is Katie?"

"Good heavens—Rupert!" Selina gasped, then recovered. "Oh, dearest Rupert, thank God! We can leave this dreadful place!"

Selina came toward him impulsively and tried to fling herself into his arms. He caught at her arms and held her off. He was a married man, he had reminded himself again and again in Canton. He was married to Katie and would remain loyal to her. She was a gentle girl.

Though Selina was excitingly beautiful, adorable—

"Where is Katie?" he asked gently, looking past Selina.

Selina drew back, lowered her lashes. "Rupert, I

hate to tell you like this. Let us go into the drawing room—"

Milbank took her cloak and went upstairs. Selina took Rupert's arm and urged him to the room. Her arm trembled with nervousness.

Rupert tried to hang back. "No, where is Katie? Was she not out with you?"

"Rupert, I have something dreadful—to tell you. I must find the courage—to support you—but you must understand."

"What is it? What happened?" he asked sharply. "Did Katie get the fever?"

He felt her hand quiver. "No, of course not, darling. She—she left you."

"*What? What?*"

"She left you. She went to her lover—the prince Chen Yee."

Rupert put his hand to his forhead. "What? I cannot believe it. Katie?"

Milbank had returned and stood in the doorway. Selina turned on her. "That is all, Milbank!" she said sharply. "Leave us! You may wait upstairs for me!"

"Yes, Miss Selina," said Milbank in a subdued tone.

Selina waited until she was gone. "There. That woman is becoming insolent!"

Rupert stared at her blankly. What did it matter about Milbank? Katie had left him! To go to the handsome tall Manchu prince! "What happened? Why did she go?"

"Rupert, darling, I hate to be the one to tell you. However, Katie has been acting so odd for months. She kept going to his home, accepting extravagant presents from him. And he would come here and spend hours alone with her in the study. They would talk and laugh—everyone was whispering about them! Ask Mrs. Shaw, she spoke to me about it. Everyone thought it odd, her, an Englishwoman and married, and him, Chinese!"

"What—happened?" He had to force the words. He had suspected something was going on. But Katie had looked at him with her honest face and wide brown eyes and had denied that anything wrong was happening. And yet she had fallen in love with that—that Chinese! And run off to him!

"She could not bear the thought of leaving him. Right after you left, she took a carriage and went to him—and never came back! She had dismissed her maid, Lilac, and the butler, Ho Chih; she said it was for insolence. I heard them arguing with her in Chinese. I did not know what they said, but I soon suspected that they tried to persuade her not to leave you, not to go to that Chinese person."

He rubbed his forehead; he felt as if he were in a terrible nightmare. It could not be, his faithful, good Katie. His fine, responsible, dependable Katie! Selina had turned away, her hands over her face.

"If you doubt me," said Selina with a sigh, "just go into her study. You will see poems he wrote to her, in those odd letters they use. You will see drawings she made of him. Many drawings! And pictures she drew which could only have been in his house! She went to him again and again!"

"Why would Katie—do this?"

"She loved him, Rupert," said Selina, turning back to him, her head lowered, fingers fluttering. "I could at least understand that. When one has married the wrong man and finds oneself still in love with the right man, what a dreadful position to be in! I have wept at nights, you must believe me." And her beautiful eyes filled with tears, and she pressed her handkerchief to her lips.

Rupert felt flattered yet uncomfortable. Did she mean only Katie? Or did Selina mean herself? From the way she gazed at him wistfully, he wondered. Yet he must think of Katie.

"I must go to her, persuade her to return," said Rupert abruptly. He started for the door. Selina clung to him.

"Not tonight, Rupert, you are so weary! And—and I had heard a rumor that the prince has left Macao." Her head was bent against his chest.

"I could not sleep while she is away," Rupert told her sternly, and put her away from him. He went out to the carriage, found the horses just being unhitched. He had them put to again, and in spite of the fact that it was two in the morning, he went to the home of the prince.

He saw no lights as they approached. When he arrived, no man came to the closed and barred gates. He peered beyond them. It all looked so empty, the courtyard with leaves blowing in the wind, no servants at the entrance, no torches flaring in the courtyards. No lights in the windows, no signs of life— could that rumor be true?

He had to return home without seeing anyone. He scarcely slept. The next day he rose early and went to the ship. He told Captain Abraham Potter the story bluntly. He must enlist his aid, and he could be sure of the man's discretion.

The red-haired captain scratched his chin. "It surely does seem strange, Mr. Rupert," he said. "Doesn't sound like Mrs. Katie; she seemed such a sensible lot. Was she sick?"

Rupert shook his head. "Selina said no. She said she went in her carriage willingly to the Manchu prince because she loved him and could not bear to leave him." He felt bitter and incredulous. The captain frowned and shook his head.

They finally decided to go with the Chinese linguist to the home of the prince Chen Yee and discover where they were and where Katie was. The carriage took them up the winding hills, with the splendid view of Macao. Rupert thought of Katie traveling about Macao in the carriage, of her bright, eager face and sparkling eyes.

Katie had loved the Orient and all its culture and art, the people, just as her father had done. Was that it? Had she fallen under the spell of the Orient? But why had she departed in such a manner? Why not have remained and told Rupert in her frank, honest manner that she wished to leave him? Had she been afraid to face him? That was not like Katie.

They found the house of the Manchu prince empty. An elderly gardener was finally discovered working at scraping up dried leaves and hailed to come to the bolted and barred gate. He shuffled over to them. The Chinese linguist questioned him, then turned to Rupert.

"He say—Prince Chen Yee leave one week ago. He point to harbor, like this." The linguist raised his long hand and pointed down to the harbor. "He say prince's ship raise white sails, sail north to Peking. Go home for rest of year."

"Ask him what happened to the white woman,"

urged Rupert. He felt sick with fear. Surely the prince would not have dared take Katie with him way up to Peking!

The linguist questioned; the old man stared up curiously at the other two men and shook his head.

The Chinese linguist interpreted as the old man answered questions. "He say he saw no white woman. He did not see the persons departing. He is only an old gardener, employed to keep the place clean until the prince returns."

"When does he return?"

"Sometime in the autumn if he comes. Other times he does not come."

Rupert returned home very depressed. The captain accompanied him, puzzled, yet worried about the voyage. "We must go soon, sir, or not go at all. The winds will change any moment—"

When Selina heard the argument, she turned white with fear.

"We cannot remain here! Don't be foolish, Rupert! The silly chit has gone of her own will; there is nothing you can do!"

"I will follow her to Peking," said Rupert stubbornly. "She is an Englishwoman. They will treat her badly. I must go after her. They may harm her!"

Captain Potter shook his head gravely. "You cannot follow her, sir. It is impossible. No European can enter China without permits, which can take years to obtain. And you cannot go to Peking, and the Imperial City, without permit from the emperor himself!"

"Then I will begin to apply for permission!"

Selina began to weep. Milbank stood watching them, worry on her lean face.

"I will not remain another week, much less another

year!" cried Selina hysterically. "I will die, I know it! This is a horrible, terrible place! I will get that dreadful fever and die! I long for home. I long for clean, civilized England. Will you deny me, Rupert?"

He rubbed his hands over his tired face, trying to think. "I will send Selina home with you, Captain. That is it. I will remain and go in search of Katie. She is my wife, I must do this—"

"But she left you!" cried Selina. "I tried to persuade her to remain, but she would not! She loves that terrible Chinese man! They were always together! And she loves the Orient. I could not persuade her to remain!"

Milbank spoke up suddenly. "But, Miss Selina, it is only right if we remain to search. Perhaps she will wish to return after a short time—"

Selina whirled on her, her tone sharp. "I did not tell you, Rupert, Milbank is also enamored of the Orient. She said she would like to remain—did you not, Milbank? *Did you not?*"

Milbank clutched her thin hands until the knuckles showed white. "Oh, no, sir, no, sir! I don't wish to remain. Miss Selina—she jests, oh, sir, she jests," she said in agony. She looked green in the face to Rupert. "I want to go home, sir, oh, home to beautiful England, please, sir!"

"You shall go home, Milbank, do not worry," said Rupert. "And Selina will go in the company of the good captain. But I must remain and search for Katie."

"It will do no good, Rupert," said Selina. "Come, Milbank, let us go and finish packing! Captain, I shall go to the ship tomorrow morning. I cannot wait to leave!" And she marched up the stairs, Milbank following her meekly.

Rupert consulted with the captain and finally went around to see Mrs. Shaw. The Englishwoman was a sensible creature and might be able to explain what had happened.

He found her surprised at Katie's disappearance. "Well, Mr. Llewellyn, I did not know her that well, but it does seem unlike the girl, such a young, shy girl, not used to company. The little I saw of her, she seemed so young to run such a household, but since she spoke Chinese, she did well."

"Did you know—guess—of her interest in the prince Chen Yee?" Rupert forced himself to ask.

Mrs. Shaw answered reluctantly but honestly. "Well, sir, she did come and go with him in his carriage. And Selina did speak of his many presents to her. Many a day I would pass by in late afternoon in my carriage and see his grand barouche parked at the door and Selina not there. There was much gossip about them in Macao. I thought to speak to her; she is so young, you see, but—well, I did not know her well."

"I could wish you had spoken to her," said Rupert. "She is much more immature than I had thought. She is but nineteen, and had little experience in society. I thought Selina would aid her in that."

"I don't think they were much together," said Mrs. Shaw slowly. "Indeed, Mrs. Selina—forgive me, sir— seems a frivolous piece and not fit to instruct any young girl in society. I have wondered at her at times, encouraging the young dangerous French marquis, accepting his lavish gifts, out to all hours of the night, even till dawn, especially so soon after her poor husband's death! But there, I'll say no more. I dislike gossip."

"I should not have left them alone in Macao," Rupert reproached himself tautly. "It was my fault—yet I felt I should be in Canton; I had to be there to bid for the goods. I feel torn in two, Mrs. Shaw. What can I do to rescue Katie from her impetuousness? For once in my life, I do not know where my duty lies."

He talked with Mr. Shaw, a ruddy, hearty type who had been long in the Orient. "You'll get nowhere chasing the prince north," he advised bluntly. "They'll never let you get near. You cannot even go into Canton. And if you sail up the coast after her, they'll stop you the moment you try to go inland. Very conscious of their privacy, they are."

Mr. Shaw advised him to go home and return another year.

"She may be tired of the life by that time," said Rupert. "Enamored as she is of the Orient, surely she will miss England and our life there."

Rupert finally decided to accept their advice and aid. They offered to keep Katie's clothes for her, and her personal possessions. And they would write to Rupert should the prince return and they were able to send word to Katie.

Until then all he could do was to write to Prince Chen Yee, beg him to return Katie, and then go home to England. It might be a year before he would hear.

With a heavy heart he returned to the house to find Selina had already removed to the ship with all her luggage. The maids assisted him in finishing the packing. In the study downstairs he found crates nailed shut, piles of them, and he sent them also to the ship, not knowing what they were, but guessing they were the jade and other objects Katie had planned to take home.

Near the end of March the *China Princess* slipped

out of Macao Harbor and headed south and east toward the coast of Africa through the Indian Ocean. Rupert leaned on the deck railing, staring blankly back at Macao, his heart heavy and anxious.

Rupert wondered if he had done right to leave Katie, but he was also angry with her. She had encouraged the attentions of a Manchu prince, accepted his gifts, drawn his image—Rupert had found a half a dozen sketches of him—and finally gone to the man Selina called her lover.

"Katie, you foolish, foolish girl!" he muttered, and banged his fist on the railing. "How could you have done this!"

Then he blamed himself. He had left her too much alone, and she was very young. But what else could he have done? He had always done his duty, and his duty had lain in Canton, bargaining with the merchants, purchasing the porcelains and silks for his father's business, supervising all that work. Terence had been the main supercargo, but he had known little of business and had finally began to drink heavily through boredom. Rupert had had to take over.

"I could do no else," he muttered.

He wondered if his father would see it that way. What a deal he had to tell his father: Terence's death; Katie's defection.

Well, he had six months to think about what to say and what to do next.

Selina came up on deck presently, attired becomingly in her dark blue dress and blue bonnet edged with white. She slipped her hand in his arm, with silent sympathy, and together they watched the harbor slide away from them, and the large white-sailed ship moved out into the sea.

13

When Katie wakened from time to time, she felt the swaying of a cradle. Sometimes the cradle rocked violently; sometimes it was just a gentle movement. But she was so hot. She pushed aside the heavy quilts and gazed up in bewilderment at the thick blue silk curtains around the ornate red laoquor bed.

Then a hand would come and soothe her, and cold compresses would be placed on her head. She scarely understood what was said, but it was comforting, and she would fall into that heavy blank condition again, not sleep, but like falling into a dark well.

She could hear voices dimly; they made no sense. Someone would lift her up, hold her, and put a cup to her lips. Her cracked lips, so painful. She moaned, but they insisted. She drank a warm broth, and it tasted good to her parched mouth.

Sleep, rocking, heat, and cold, pain in her mouth, and then soothing drinks. She saw light and darkness; they seemed to come and go.

One night, she thought it was night because it was so dark, her spirits had fallen so low. She dreamed that her father was there, holding her hand comfortingly.

"Oh, Father," she murmured. "Oh, Father, I thought you were dead."

A large hand pressed hers.

"Oh, Father, I am so glad you came to me. I thought you were dead. I am—so alone. No one understands—no one—I can talk freely—to no one. I have missed you so much—"

She thought she saw her father's face smiling at her, in his understanding way. And her mother was there, her gentle, sweet mother with her soft brown eyes and her sweet singing voice.

"Mother? How wonderful, you have come! Oh, they told me you were dead, but you are here—"

Murmur of voices from behind the thick draperies. Strange voices, but Katie brushed them from her. She was gazing at her parents, holding hands, standing beside her. How young they looked, as they had many years ago. She reached out longingly to them; they held out their hands to her.

"Mother, Father, you have come for me! Come closer—lift me—I long to go where you are—where are you? Where are you?" They seemed to be in a hazy cloud, like puffs of cotton around their feet, swimming toward her, walking as though on air.

A deep voice spoke in a strange tongue, but she seemed by some miracle to understand what he said. "She is very low. She dreams as those who are near to death. Bring herbs and burn incense! Pray to the gods. And bowls of water, cloths; we must bathe the fever from her—she burns to the touch—"

None of that made sense to Katie. She was seeing her parents; they looked tenderly at her. And she seemed to see pearly gates behind them and such a beautiful green view! Oh, look at the flowers, and the little burn rippling beside them. It must be Cornwall. Yes, it must be, for there was the blue and silken sea on a calm day. They were walking together on a beach, with the hot sun burning down. And all around them were glorious flowers, crimson ones, and rose, and white, that smelled of strong incense—

Her parents were fading, drifting away, walking away from her. Katie cried out yearningly and held out her arms once more to them. "Do not leave me—I cannot bear it! You are the only ones who love me—don't leave me—"

But they drifted away, and she began to weep, heartbroken. Someone lifted her; she heard voices; she heard a strong beating under her cheek and ear. Someone comforted her, soothed her. And she rested against him, thinking it was her father.

"Father, do not leave me," she muttered.

"No, I will not leave you," said the deep voice.

She rested for a long time, so long that her bones ached and she could not move them in the bed. She ached from her head to her toes. How odd that even her toes ached. Someone rubbed her briskly from head to foot and put cold cloths on her. She shivered, the cloths were removed, and a blanket was put on her. Then she was hot again, but soothed, and she slept.

She wakened, drank hot broth, slept again. The bed rocked violently; she thought she would fall from it. But someone came and held her in strong arms, and she smelled a perfume that she knew. Why did she know this? She puzzled about it, but it was too much of an effort to think, and she desisted.

Then came a time when she lay between wakening and going to sleep again. She was cooler, yet she could not sleep. She heard voices, the deep one that comforted her at times and a lighter, higher voice.

"She is better, my prince."

"Yes, better, my cousin, but still she does not waken. If only she slept more calmly."

"Perhaps if I sang to her, as to a baby—"

"Do you know such songs? You are not much over a baby yourself, little Moon Blossom!"

"You choose to tease me." And there was a little faint giggle.

Katie smiled and tried to open her eyes. The eyelids were too heavy, but she could hear, and she listened with pleasure to the soft voices above her.

"Perhaps I could sing a lullaby, my prince—"

"Sing then."

And a pretty voice sang to Katie. She listened to it, comforted, rocked in the cradle; she was a child again, and her mother was singing.

Hush now, my child, the moon is new.
Good fortune attend my lovely one.
Cease your soft wailing; none shall cause harm.
    Close your eyes and sleep.

Hush now, my child, the stars will attend
And swing in the heavens to amuse my babe.
Look how the clouds form patterns for you,
    A dragon with long curling tail.

Hush now, my child, the sun will rise soon.
The earth will show glories to amuse my babe.
You shall walk in meadows of flowers.
    Now close your eyes and sleep.

Someone said, "That is a lovely song, and you sing it well."

"Thank you, my prince." And the song came again, soft and pretty, over and over, and Katie slept.

When Katie opened her eyes next, she was confused. She had been with her father and her mother; her mother had sung a song to her. Now she lay within a cocoon of heavy quilts, tucked snugly about her, and gazed at tall red lacquer posts.

She turned over slowly, painfully. And she found she was facing a latticework of beautiful red lacquer which formed the side of the bed. Above her was a blue canopy. Silk curtains of the same deep blue were drawn back and fastened to the posts, so the sun from the windows could shine in.

The sun felt good on her face and her hands. She held up her hand to feel the sun. How odd, her hand was so thin and white and frail, and it shook. Her fingers trembled.

Someone came; a darkly yellow face bent over her, a round good-natured face, a servant, she thought. Oh, yes, she was in Macao. But this was not her usual bed.

"Where—am I?" she asked faintly in English.

The smile broadened; the woman stroked her head and nodded, satisfied. She went away, returned with a cup of hot broth. Katie drank it, tried to think how to ask in Chinese, but all her linguistic knowledge seemed to have faded for now. She smiled faintly and closed her eyes to savor the sunlight and warmth.

She knew then when Prince Chen came in and when Moon Blossom came in and smiled at her. She smiled faintly back at them. How good of them to come and visit her. She must have been ill.

Was it time for Rupert to return? She remembered the ship was being loaded in Canton. Then they would return home, she and Rupert, Selina and Terence. Or—had something terrible happened? She crinkled her forehead, trying to remember.

The days slid past; nothing seemed to matter, but eating, sleeping, smiling faintly at the faces above her.

"It will be slow," said the deep voice. "She was very ill."

Who had been ill? Oh, yes, Terence had been ill. Something dreadful had happened to him. What was it?

She dreamed of her father, but it was of his dying, and she wakened in terror and cried out. A man came and held her, his voice quieted her, and she slept against his chest. Her father—no, it was not her father, for her father was dead, and she wept for it.

Someone soothed her. "Gently, now, my dove, my pigeon, my little songbird. Gently, now, no more tears. All is well; you are safe."

"Safe?" she murmured. "Safe? No harm—"

"You are safe from all harm," the voice reassured her.

The dream went away, and blankness came again, a nice blackness where she could rest.

There came a day when Katie wakened and her mind was calm. She lifted her shaking hand and saw the thin fingers, how thin—she could almost see through her hand.

Moon Blossom came in, gazed at her, smiled questioningly.

"How good—you are—to visit—so often," murmured Katie in slow Mandarin speech.

Moon Blossom beamed broadly. Her round kind face shone; her dark eyes sparkled with pleasure. "You are yourself once more, Mistress Katie!" she said softly.

"Yes, yes, of course. I think—I think—I should get up—have I been ill?"

"Yes, very ill, but you are better. No, you cannot arise yet!" added Moon Blossom in alarm as Katie tried to sit up.

"Oh, I cannot—get up—" It was scary not to be able to sit up in bed.

A servant came, a plump woman Katie seemed to remember. She lifted Katie gently, and Moon Blossom stuffed two pillows behind her. Katie lay against them limply and stared at the bed, frowning.

"Have I—a new bed? I don't—remember—"

"No, very old bed, very venerable," assured Moon Blossom. "Best bed on this ship. Very fine bed. Comfortable, yes?"

Katie had caught at one word. "Ship?" she asked. "Ship? The *China Princess*?"

"No, this ship is the *Red Dragon of the North*," assured Moon Blossom, beaming happily. "Fine ship, very large ship, belonging to the honorable prince Chen Yee."

Katie puzzled over that. Moon Blossom went away, returned with a cup of hot broth and some chunks of soft bread, which she dipped into the broth and fed to Katie. It tasted wonderful.

"Soon you will eat egg and then chicken and meat," said Moon Blossom.

"I do not understand—why this ship?" mused Katie. She was comfortable, they were kind, yet it puzzled her. Why was she on the ship belonging to the prince Chen Yee?

She fretted a little, but she was very weak yet. They took away the cushions, and she slept in the sunlight.

When she wakened, Moon Blossom came again, smiling with pleasure that Katie was alert and in her right senses.

"How long was I sick, Moon Blossom?"

"Many days and many nights," said the girl.

Katie realized the girl did not know how to count or was indifferent to the passing of days.

She struggled to make her comprehend. "I must return to my house in Macao. My husband comes soon. We must leave Macao."

"We have left Macao," said Moon Blossom simply.

"Left—Macao? We are not—in the harbor?"

"No, no, at sea! Regard how beautiful is the sea!" Moon Blossom went to the paper-thin silk curtains at the windows of the cabin, drew them back, and gestured with her graceful hand.

Katie gazed in horror. All she could see was the open sea, no land in sight! No other ships near—nothing! Only the vivid blue sea and the waves that rolled away from the ship as it plowed its way through the azure blue.

Then she saw another ship, nosing up closer, then dropping back. "Another ship? A harbor?" she asked eagerly.

"No, madame. That ship is one of the three of the honorable prince Chen Yee. Three ships. This one the greatest of them all. Three ships, in case of pirates, also to have much room for all the honorable prince's household. The princess Chen resides on other boat." And she pointed to the one close by.

Three ships. Where were they going? Why was she on the ship? Katie forced her weakened mind to consider it.

"Why am I on this ship? Where do we go?"

"Where go?" Moon Blossom seized on this question as one she could answer. "We go to the huge beautiful house of the honorable prince Chen Yee in Peking!"

"Peking!" Katie lay back, staring wide-eyed at the other young girl. "It cannot—be true. It cannot—be true!"

Katie began to weep because she could not make the girl understand that this could not be true. Moon Blossom tried gently to soothe her, the tears still fell, and Katie wept bitterly. She wanted to go home; she wanted Rupert; she wanted England, dear green and lovely England!

"I want to go home," she said, sobbing. Moon Blossom went away and finally returned with the prince.

Prince Chen Yee entered into the bedroom and made it seem smaller with his height. He came to the bed, drew up an armchair of polished redwood, and seated himself. He gazed down at Katie; his dark eyes softened.

"What is it, Katie, little songbird? What goes wrong? You are sick again?"

She shook her head fretfully. "No, I cannot make Moon Blossom understand—I want to go home!"

"But you go home with us," he assured her complacently.

"To Peking?" She gazed up at him and stretched out her hand pleadingly. He took it and held it carefully in his large, strong hand. She felt the warmth of it; it felt vaguely familiar, as though such a strong hand had held her many times and had given her strength and courage to come back from a long distance.

"Yes, Katie, to Peking. You shall live with us and be happy. We shall care for you and make you laugh again."

"I do not comprehend what has happened to me. Why am I not in Macao?"

"You came to us in a carriage."

"I do not remember." She frowned, trying to grope in the mist of her faulty mind.

"It does not matter now. Just rest and become well again. Soon I shall take you up on the deck, and you shall lie with the gentle winds in your face and regain your lovely color. Your cheeks shall turn to peach blossom once more; your lips shall put the rose to shame."

She flushed a little, and he smiled, his black eyes sparkling. Moon Blossom stood nearby, with head bowed, not gazing at them.

"You said—in a carriage. When was this?"

He hesitated. "Many days ago. You were ill of a fever then, and we put you on this ship to take care of you."

"But—but where is my husband? Where is Rupert?" Her voice rose in her dismay.

"He has taken the foreign woman with the hair of ashes back to their home in England. The *China Princess* sailed a week ago. I have had word from my men in Macao, by the means of swift horses galloping to the ports where we paused to take on water."

She rubbed her forehead. "It cannot be! Rupert would not leave without me!"

The prince did not reply, but he was no longer smiling at her. He seemed to have withdrawn the warmth of his approval from her, yet his hand still held hers.

"Rupert would not leave me," she muttered. "Rupert—where is he?"

"On the way home to England, where he belongs!"

"But I belong—in England also."

"No. You love our way of life," he said firmly.

"Of course—yes—the Orient is very—beautiful," she said weakly, tiring quickly after the long conversation. "But England—is home!"

"Peking will be your new home." He rose, detached his hand from hers, bowed slightly, and left her.

She turned in bewilderment to Moon Blossom and questioned the patient girl. "I do not comprehend," she said very slowly, so the girl would understand her speech. "How did I come to—this ship?"

"By carriage, in the arms of the honorable prince himself. He would allow no other one to carry you." Moon Blossom smiled. "What a fortunate woman you are! He cares for you; he will take excellent care of you!"

"But how—did I come—to his home?" Katie tried that angle in worn voice.

Moon Blossom timidly sat on the edge of the arm-chair where the prince had sat. "It is a dark night," she began dramatically. "The sun has set. There is the sound of a carriage. Who can it be? The household of the prince Chen Yee is preparing for sleep. We have been packing; soon shall we leave for our home in Peking. The men run out. I follow, in curiosity, for some-one calls it is the foreign women!"

"The—foreign—women? Who?"

"Why, it is you!" she said. "And the woman with the hair so pale, like the ashes after the fire has died. And the dark woman who is her maid. She pushes you into the arms of the man who opens the door. She says, 'Here is the woman,' so said our prince when he comes. She closes the door; she drives away; she leaves you to us. You are pale, sick with fever."

Katie leaned back on the pillows, her mind whirling. It could not be true! Selina hated her, but mostly she treated her with cold indifference. And no one would play her such a trick—no one.

A voice echoed in her mind, the distressed voice of Milbank. "But this is wicked—wicked—wicked—" The voice faded; she shook her head; she must be hearing strange voices, as a dream.

Moon Blossom tiptoed softly away as Katie lay with closed eyes. Katie was not asleep this time; she was going over and over the terrible cruel thing that Selina must have done.

But why?

Selina must have realized Katie had a fever. She did not want to remain in Macao. She hated Katie. And Terence was dead; Selina now a widow. It was all returning to Katie,—those dreadful days. Selina had been terrified of catching the fever from Terence. She would have been very upset when Katie became ill. They had delayed their departure because of Terence's illness and death. Then Rupert had returned to Canton to finish loading the ship. Selina had begun packing. So had Katie—

"Oh," she said aloud. "I did not finish packing for Rupert. I was packing for him—"

But Selina must have realized that now Rupert was the sole heir of his father, heir to his estates, heir to his fortune, heir to his business, which continued to return vast sums to them all. Rupert, the only son—and married to Katie, who had caught the dread fever—

"That would be wicked!" said Katie again aloud. "Wicked! Nobody could do such a thing—" To take her from the house, deposit her like an unwanted sack at the doorstep of the prince—

Fretfully she regarded the open window. She saw the other ship nose up briefly; she thought she glimpsed a proud Manchu face and a slim form in beautiful red robes on the deck of the other ship, gazing toward them. Then the ship fell back once more behind them.

The next day Katie felt stronger. A servant washed her under the supervision of Moon Blossom and put fresh clothes on her—new clothes.

"Where did these come from?" asked Katie. "My clothes, my dresses—"

"You had only the dress you wore to us, and the cloak," said Moon Blossom, and opened a red lacquer wardrobe on the side of the cabin. It revealed one European dress and one cloak and a multitude of other gowns, in the Chinese style, beautiful silken garments, velvet embroidered robes. "The prince, your protector, brought many garments with us and ordered more to be made. You will be garbed like a princess!"

She was dressed in a pale rose silk gown, with an overgown of deeper rose velvet, to protect her against a draft. Presently the prince entered, eyeing her with approval. Her hair had been brushed briskly and was regaining its luster after the drabness caused by her illness. Her cheeks had some color, added by the skillful fingers of the maid.

"You look like yourself once more. That is good. Congratulations on the improvement of your health," he said formally, bowing slightly before seating himself by her chair.

She looked at him in a troubled fashion. She braced herself to argue with him. He must turn back.

At his gesture Moon Blossom bowed and left the room. The two of them were alone.

"Your kindness to me and that of the people of your household is of such great generosity," began Katie, as formally.

"I will not hear praise. It is what would happen between—friends," he said.

"Beyond friendship," she said. She glanced uneasily away from the steady regard of his black eyes. "You have—kept me from death, I think."

"You were near to the brink, I believe. Fortunately we knew this illness and were able to bring herbs and give you strengthening medicines."

"I am—more grateful—than I can say."

There was a slight pause; she braced herself then.

"Your Highness," she said, very formally, "I beg you now to return me to Macao. My husband—will wish to see me—to take care of me."

"He has departed from Macao. He goes home with the foreign woman of no dignity," he said.

"No matter," said Katie. "I—I will await his return. I will stay in the house where we lived, and he will return for me."

"He will not come back. He is bewitched by the foreign woman."

"Yet we are married to each other." Katie forced herself to continue. "It is his duty—to take care of me. He always—does his duty. My husband—was an officer—of the king. He always—does his duty."

"More than one man has been enticed from his duty by the wiles of an evil woman."

She put her face in her hands and gulped back tears. The words spoken so calmly in a foreign language drove the truth home to her. Rupert did love Selina. He adored her, even though he was married to Katie.

"I have to go back!" she cried. "No matter where he is, no matter whether he ever returns for me, I must return to England! It is my duty—and I love him!"

"How can you love a man who deserts you? You will recover from this feeling, just as you will recover from the fever," pronounced the prince firmly.

She began to weep, the tears dripping down her fingers as she pressed them against her wet cheeks. He said nothing, only sat beside her, not touching her. She wiped her face with her handkerchief and tried to compose herself.

"I am grateful to you—oh, Prince—but please, please—you must take me back! I cannot go to Peking—"

"We are going. Presently we shall go inland and take the dragon boats along the canal, for many beautiful miles. You shall see and learn to love my beautiful land, as you loved Macao."

"I shall be a foreign woman in a land strange to me. I shall weep for my own country, my green and beautiful land! Let me go home, Prince Chen Yee! Please let me go home!"

"No," he said.

She turned to face him fully; he met her gaze unflinchingly.

"Why?" she whispered.

"Because I want you."

She shook her head violently. "No, I am a friend, no more! I am a foreign woman, you feel contempt for me—for us all—and you cannot take me to Peking, it is forbidden!"

"Nothing is forbidden to me. I am a prince of the House of Chen," he said sternly. "The emperor himself will not forbid me to do as I wish, so long as I do not any harm to our gracious kingdom, which is the center of the world."

She forced herself to try to think of more arguments. He did not respond to her weeping, to her pleadings. "But why? Why? Your—your wife will hate me; she will not endure me in the house!"

"My wife will do as I tell her. My eunuchs will protect you from her wrath," he said calmly.

"Wrath! Yes, she will be furious with you! Do you wish dissent in your peaceful household? Take me back to Macao, or send me with your men—any way at all!"

"There will be peace in my household because I command it," he said quietly. "No harm will come to you because I will prevent it. I am the prince of the House of Chen, powerful among my peers, commander over my many peoples. You shall be gowned in precious silks and jewels. You shall have servants at your command. You shall live in a precious courtyard with any toy at your will. You shall draw, paint, or idle your days as you will."

She was shaking her head, so the fine, dark, straight hair spun about her shoulders. "No, no, no, that is not my life! I am a worker, the wife of an Englishman. I shall always be a stranger; you will come to despise me; I am not Chinese—"

He drew a deep breath as though to command patience. "You came often to me; you permitted me to come to you. We spoke much of ancient wisdom; you admired ours. I wrote verse to you; you did not reject it. I gave you gifts; not one did you return to me. You accepted my attentions, my gifts, my verse, my presence, often with no chaperon. You even gave gifts to me, and I honored you by accepting them, though you were foreign. I knew you had come to love me, as I had reluctantly come to love you."

Katie cried out, horrified yet thrilled somehow—trying to deny him yet unable to. She did love him—yet she loved Rupert. She could not love this Manchu prince—yet his touch affected her, his attentions; no, she had not been able to refuse his attentions. Her pride—yes, her vanity had been pleased. But more, she had hungered for his visits, she had longed for them—

"I cannot love you, I cannot be—with you!" she cried out. "I belong to Rupert. I am married to him; he is my husband!"

"He neglected you. He left you for long weeks without his protection. The merciful gods brought you to me. Fate has willed it. You will live with me. I shall honor you, give you presents, command all to give you the honors due to a woman of your position in my household—"

"My position," she gasped hysterically. "You are married to the princess Chen Mei-ling. I am married to Rupert Llewellyn. What position will I have? It is impossible!"

"Not at all," he said soothingly. He stood, clasped her hands for a moment in his, then laid them gently in her lap. "I will leave you now to consider your future. Rest. Be calm. Know I will take care of all your needs. You shall never want for anything. One who is loved by the prince Chen Yee shall be indeed precious to him—you shall see how precious."

"But what position?" she cried again. "It is impossible; I am nobody; I am not anything in your house—"

"Yes, yes," he told her quickly, at the door turning and smiling his rare smile. "I cannot marry you for my second wife because you are a foreign woman of Europe. But you shall be my first concubine and of much value to me!" And with that he left, gently closing the door behind him.

14

The prince did not come to see her again that day. Katie had long hours to think over what he had said. It could not be true! She, an Englishwoman, married, had been taken away from her own people by a Manchu prince to become his concubine!

She shook her head, dazed. Could she still be feverish, dreaming this? She pinched her hand; it hurt. No, she was awake, her forehead cool, eyes seeing the blue of the ocean outside the wide windows.

Evening came; Moon Blossom came to her, with her tray of food. She carefully fed Katie a bowlful of soup, soft bread, a sweet pudding. Everything tasted good.

The next day she was dressed in a silk gown of jade green, and a robe put about her. When she was ready, her hair wound up in a chignon, her feet in tilt-toed slippers, the prince came in.

"Ah, you look much better! The color returns; your eyes sparkle!" he said. Then he bent down, and as Moon Blossom gasped, he lifted Katie right into his arms.

Her eyes widened; she stared up into his deep dark eyes. "Where—are we—going?" she asked faintly.

As he carried her, he gave crisp orders. "We go on deck. Air the bed; shake out the mattresses; open the

windows to the sea air. Let all be cool and composed
in this room."

He smiled slightly at Katie's surprise. He carried
her up some stairs, out onto the deck, and set her
down carefully on a long lounge chair, covered with a
thick mattress of rose silk and surrounded by cushions. The sun was warm; a canopy had been erected
over the couch, and a table and a chair placed beside
it.

She drew a deep breath. "Oh, how good it smells!"

The sea air had the cool fragrance of salt and wind,
the sun shone golden, and the two ships sailing beside
them looked like paintings, so perfectly set with large
white sails. On their fronts were dragon head carvings, so they seemed like immense red dragons plow-
ing through the azure sea.

"It pleases you?" said the prince, seating himself
beside her.

"Oh, yes, it is beautiful." She could not be angry
with him; she could not quarrel this morning. It was
good to be alive, to be lying in luxury, to feel her
strength returning, to gaze at beautiful scenes. She
smiled and held out her hand to the breeze. "It is like
wine to the senses, this air."

"Yes, like golden wine," he said. He reached into
the deep pocket in his sleeve, of blue velvet today,
embroidered with golden butterflies. He drew out a
long jade necklace with a pendant on the end and
slipped it over her head. "Look, the pendant is a songbird, like you."

She examined the pendant, holding it in her hand
awkwardly. Another present! Should she refuse it? His
smile would depart; he would frown and be cold. She
sighed a little. "How lovely," she said hastily. "This—is

the songbird—design?" She fingered the cold jade, and it turned warm in her hand.

"Yes. Jade is a lucky stone for us; we use it for our most precious Buddhas, our goddesses, to decorate our homes, to wear. For us, it has for centuries been more valued than gold or silver. I have some pieces handed down by my family that have been with us more than five hundred years. You shall see them in the palace in Peking."

He talked to her charmingly that day, idle speech, telling her of the beauties of Peking, of how she would enjoy the journey north, how the spring would be there when they arrived, with many flowering trees. The gardens she would visit would all be radiant with spring flowers; there were pools with great golden carp in them.

Katie wanted to argue with him again, to beg him to take her back home again. But her strength was still frail. And somehow she knew that no argument would prevail over him. Prince Chen Yee was accustomed to doing as he chose, and nobody stopped him. He would have been faintly, politely amazed if anybody had tried.

His voice faded; she closed her eyes against the bright sunlight and slept again. When she wakened, he was gone, but Moon Blossom sat beside her, carefully embroidering a piece of canvas, about a foot square.

She laid it aside, smiled brightly, and signaled a servant, who brought a cool fruit drink. Katie drank it slowly, watching a bird wheeling and dipping near the side of the ship, hoping for scraps. It was a glorious white sea gull with wide wings, a large bird.

"A sea gull," said Moon Blossom.

Katie nodded. She longed for strength to draw it. Presently the prince returned. "You are weary?" he asked, studying her face. "I think it is time to return to your cabin."

Again he lifted her in his strong, muscular arms and held her against his velvet-clad body as he carried her down the steps and into the hallway, then to her room. Moon Blossom padded after them to take care of Katie, along with the plump servant.

The evening came, and the prince visited Katie after her light supper. She had finished everything on her tray, and he was pleased. "Your strength will begin to return now," he said firmly, and she thought: I cannot refuse him! She wondered if the wind would cease at his command!

She eyed him shyly after he had set her down to lie against the cushions on the red lacquer square bed with the red lacquer side. One side was open for her to slip in and out; the ends and the other side were of exquisite red-lacquer-covered sandalwood—she could smell its faint fragrance.

The prince wore his favorite perfume of jasmine and its odor was strong on her from contact with his robes. His handsome, brooding face was more open this evening; his carved mouth wore a faint, enigmatic smile as he studied her.

Moon Blossom saw her comfortable, then slipped away with the servant. Katie felt vaguely uneasy.

The prince took her hand and smoothed her fingers gently. "So thin, so tired, this little hand which is so skillful," he murmured. "I hope for the day when it is strong again and able to draw and paint as before. Do you also, little songbird?"

She nodded. "I feel—so useless," she said. "I am accustomed to working hard and doing my duty."

He listened soberly. "You will never have to work again," he said positively. "You shall always do just as you choose. Your duty will be to please yourself, to be happy, to laugh and sing, to smile when you see your master come."

She gulped. Her future was a dangerous subject, so she sought to change the conversation. Yet it made her tingle with embarrassment to feel his gaze on her, to think of what might lay ahead. Nothing must happen! She must persuade him somehow that an Englishwoman did not become the concubine of a Manchu prince!

"What colors please you best?" he asked.

She sought frantically for an answer. "Why, rose color, and peach, and almond," she finally answered. "I like the cream colors and some blues, the deep blue of the sea, the soft blue of a summer day."

"Our summer days the sky is a hot, intense blue," he told her. "In Peking in the summertime we seek the shade, for the hot winds blow and the sky burns with fire. The spring and the autumn are pleasant—you shall enjoy them and our flower gardens. In the summer we seek coolness. You will see how it is."

Her eyes began to sparkle. This was an adventure! If only her father could share it, if only it could be an innocent travel adventure! Even so, despite the circumstances, Katie began to look forward to seeing this strange country.

"Is the land green?" she asked.

"In places the land is green where the Yellow River and other great rivers flood the lands and make the grains grow. Other places you will look up and see great mountains towering over you, as our boats go through gorges carved by the rivers over thousands of years. The gaunt cliffs are crimson in the sunset, painted so by our artists of many years. They show how small are man and his boats, how great is the mountain, as the gods are great over small men."

Presently, as he talked, her eyelids drooped. He rose and bent over her. "You will be undressed by the maid and go to sleep," he said softly. "Tomorrow we will talk again."

And he touched her lips firmly with his, his hard mouth softening against her pale mouth. He lingered over her, kissed her again, her round chin in his palm. He smiled down at her, amused at her shyness, the way she tried to turn her head. His large hand reached to stroke the thick, soft, loose hair. His fingers ran through the hair lovingly.

"You will sleep well," he said.

"Thank you," she murmured. "You are most kind. However, Your Highness—I must say to you—"

"Not tonight. And you will call me Elder Brother when we are alone together, as now. It is what my household calls me, and it will please me to hear this name from your lips."

That seemed safe enough. She smiled and nodded. "Thank you—Elder Brother."

He touched her lips with his again, and his mouth pressed more firmly. A tingle went down her spine. It had been so long since Rupert had made love to her, and she was a woman—not a young girl, but a woman. She fought to keep from answering his lips. He held his hand to the back of her head and pressed her closer.

"You will kiss me," he commanded in a low tone.

She could not disobey him. Something made her move her lips, and shyly she answered his kiss. Her mouth seemed to melt against his hard mouth. His hand stroked down her hair once more; then he raised himself. He was smiling, his eyes shining.

"Good night, my songbird."

"Good night—Elder Brother."

He went away. Moon Blossom and the maid came to undress her and put on her a pale peach nightdress and slip her back into bed. She slept, dreamlessly, for a long time and wakened only a couple of times in the night. The maid was always there, to give her a sip of wine and water and to cool her forehead if she wished.

The next day she felt much better. She was dressed in an almond gown with a pale rose pelisse over it, with fur-trimmed sleeves, and was ready to go up on deck. The prince came and carried her up as before. The sun was bright again today, but clouds hovered in the west.

"There will be a storm tonight," said the prince. "In a few more days we will arrive at the great port of Shanghai. There we will leave our great sailing ships and take the smaller dragon boats along the Grand Canal. You will see how beautiful is the land."

As he spoke, he reached into his pocket sleeve and drew out a long strand of perfect matched pearls with a faint glow. The white looked as though it had been slightly washed in peach bloom, so the pearls glowed pale pink.

"Pearls are made to be worn by a beautiful woman," he said, and slipped the strand about her neck. The pearls hung down to her waist. She gasped and lifted the strand in her fingers. "Does it please you? They rival your cheeks at the moment, though they cannot match the perfection of your face."

"You are most kind. But I cannot accept any more—please, Your Highness—"

The smile disappeared; a frown came, a frown of deep displeasure. "You forget my name so soon?"

"Elder Brother," she said faintly. "But please—" She tried to remove the necklace.

"If it does not please you, I shall return it to the sea!"

"Oh, no, you would not do that!" But he would; she saw it in his face. "Please, do not. I—I think it is very lovely. And you are most kind—"

"So—you will keep it." And he leaned back, satisfied. The subject was closed. "I do not usually go the route of the Grand Canal, for it is longer. We could take our sailing ships up to Tientsin and go inland by carriage. However, I wish you to observe much of my country, and so we go this way. The Grand Canal leads overland past the Yellow River and so up to Tientsin. From there carriages will convey us home to Peking."

He talked in a quiet manner, telling her much of the countryside she would see. When she wearied, he left her alone to sleep in the fresh air. She wakened to a darkening sky—the storm had approached sooner than expected—and the prince carried her down the stairs to her cabin. He ordered the windows shut and locked and the curtains and draperies drawn, so she would not see the violence of the storm.

The ship rocked, but it went slowly and took the waves well. Katie did not get sick. The three ships turned inland, Moon Blossom informed her, and into the shelter of the land.

Each day the prince came to her on deck and brought her gifts: a silk-lined lacquer box which played a tune to hold her pearls and jade necklace, the finest linen for her garments, more silk dresses and robes to match them, of velvet embroidered with silk thread, and hairpins of jade with tips of pearls and diamonds, which would be thrust to hold her chignon in place.

They arrived in Shanghai. Prince Chen Yee and Moon Blossom went with Katie for a little tour of the city in a carriage with curtains hanging about. They could peer out at the wonders of the huge city, its shop-lined streets, the trees now in bloom, the crowds, without being seen. Merchants ran up to the carriage when they paused, and the prince would buy from them and lay gifts in the laps of the two girls. Katie wondered what the princess Chen Mei-ling would have said if she had known what gifts they received!

The prince put a couple of bright yellow oranges in her lap. She smiled "That pleases me," she said. She liked oranges.

As casually, he piled in her lap a necklace of ivory, a little jewel box of sandalwood inlaid with other woods, beautiful earrings of long strands of gold and pearls, a bracelet of opals set in gold, a pair of Persian slippers of gaudy embroidered silks and with long curled-up toes.

She giggled at this and held up one slipper. "It is so cunning! Like that of a child!"

"For your petite feet," he said, embarrassing her. She had realized, but pushed to the back of her head, the knowledge that he had helped bathe her naked body when she was deathly hot of the fever.

The end of the carriage ride was beside the harbor

of the Grand Canal. There half a dozen huge dragon boats awaited them. In one of them sat the Manchu princess Chen Mei-ling, her haughty head covered with a high headdress half-concealing the butterfly wings of stiffened black hair. She glared at them as they left the carriage and did not lift her hand in welcome.

Prince Chen Lo came up to them, bowed to his elder brother, and smiled at Katie. "I was on another ship; I have not seen you. How my heart rejoices that you are well again!"

She thanked him; the prince watched them indulgently, then escorted Katie to one of the dragon boats. He left her in her cabin.

"He goes to the princess Mei-ling," whispered Moon Blossom, glancing furtively at the maid. "She is very cold, very angry with him, because he neglects her for you. All whisper about it. How he loves you! He will be very good to you!"

"Oh, but I do not want his wife to be angry with him!" Katie exclaimed in distress.

Moon Blossom looked her approval. "You have a good heart. You do not wish dissension in the household. Mei-ling will adjust to this; she must know that he would take a concubine since he does not have children of her body. A prince must have an heir." And she nodded wisely.

Katie went cold. Everyone took it for granted that the prince was her lover! The relationship would be dreadful—she could not be the concubine of anyone! It was against her principles; it was against her moral upbringing, her very nature. She sat silently in the chair as her hair was brushed and restored to order. She was dressed in a fine red silk dress, with a coat of silky soft fur against the chill of the early-spring evening.

Prince Chen Yee returned within an hour, his voice cold as he snapped the orders which caused the dragon boats to begin their journey along the canal. When Katie went to have dinner in the small salon, where Moon Blossom led her, she found him expressionless; only his black eyes blazed.

His wife must have insulted him, berated him, thought Katie. Nervously she spoke of Shanghai.

"What a great city it is! It must be larger than London. And such shops, such a wealth of goods. Much trade must pass through its harbor."

He relaxed a little, lifted the wineglass, and toasted her. "To your most pleasant journey in our land, to our home," he said.

She raised her glass to him. "And my gratitude for your great care of me, sir. May your household be blessed and peaceful under your wise leadership."

This pleased him. He nodded and drank, and so did the others. There was Moon Blossom, an elderly man, who nodded over his dinner, and another woman, of uncertain age, perhaps a cousin or aunt.

The conversation turned to the journey. They told her what she would be seeing, and presently they all went up on deck to watch the land sliding past them. It was much more intimate an experience to be on a canalboat and see the fields of wheat and barley, the forests, the figures of people finishing their day's work and returning to their lighted houses in the distance. Some paused to watch the dragon boats glide past and bow their heads to the ground.

The following days were even more interesting. Katie sat on deck most of the day, sketching, fascinated by the sights. The prince had ordered a small sketching box with a slanted lid brought up for her. Inside were crayons, brushes, pots for ink, fine white paper. She could sketch all the day if she had the energy, for one interesting sight followed another.

She drew the small figures of people working in the fields, one man carrying two buckets of water at either end of the long pole over his shoulders. Children worked and played, industriously digging in the fields and planting rice, as the prince had told her. The fields shone with water, the rice planted in the mud beneath it.

She sketched again the dragon boat ahead of them, tiny against the mountains in the distance. She drew with colored chalks the little houses with tip-tilted roofs of tile, the women who came from the houses with wet cloths and hung them on low bushes to dry. She sketched a scholar in his garden, glimpsed from the boat, his head white and his beard pointed, as he drew, not even looking up as the boats passed.

They came to the deep canyons of the Yellow River, and she was amazed at how high and dangerous they were, those cliffs above them. How small men did seem against them, and she drew in the Chinese manner a small man in a small dragon boat and above him the writhing cliffs and the trees that seemed to tip over the edge.

The prince was with her almost constantly, watching her work or taking a desk and paper himself to draw and sketch. She was surprised to find he had a fine artistic ability, which he had not shown her before. He smiled at her amazement.

"We all are taught to draw as children," he said. "It is part of our education to appreciate nature in her awesome majesty, to show how small is man against the gods. The finest of painting is calligraphy, but the pictorial arts are not despised."

The trip drew to a close, and reluctantly Katie left the dragon boat. It had been a lovely experience. The prince was attentive, but without bothering her with his caresses. Perhaps the smallness of the boats prevented him, for they were constantly in the view of others.

Carriages were drawn up at the dockside as they left the boats. Katie sat in a rest house, eating lunch, while the carriages were loaded. She enjoyed her food now, her illness quite gone, and the egg dishes, the broth, the delicate fish—all were pleasing to her palate. The meal ended with pudding and hot fresh green tea with a mint flavor.

Then she went to her carriage, a barouche, with Moon Blossom attentively beside her. The prince did not ride with them today. He rode in the first carriage, and it was a fine procession of more than twenty-five carriages as they drove along the road to Peking.

The journey was carefully planned so that each night the carriages halted at a rest stop. The rooms had to be shared, but the beds were comfortable, and Moon Blossom was always paired with Katie and another elderly aunt.

And finally they came to Peking and entered the elaborate gates of the city. An official came out to welcome them formally, the carriages and barouches and carts of luggage all halted for two hours while the greetings were expressed. Then they went on, up a winding dusty trail, to the country palace of the prince, just on the outskirts of Peking.

It was dusk as they entered. Great torches were lit in the main courtyards as they entered the grounds. Katie leaned from the carriage, breathlessly wondering at the size of the place. She had thought the house in Macao was large; this was ten times as large! The grounds she could just make out seemed to go on endlessly.

The prince came to her and escorted her and Moon Blossom to a courtyard through a narrow gap in several buildings. "This is the Court of the Flowering Peach in my Peking home," he said. "I have ordered it made ready for you. You shall have this courtyard, for its flowers and trees are the right colors for you. Eunuchs shall guard the four entrances, and no one shall come to you without your permission. You may feel quite safe and sheltered here."

Katie felt instantly chilled. Why did he speak of being safe here? Why did eunuchs guard the entrances to her courtyard and rooms? Was there danger? She thought abruptly of Chen Mei-ling, the proud Manchu princess who hated Katie. Her hatred could be deadly, thought Katie.

She slept uneasily that night, alone in the great bed, with a maid sleeping on a couch in the corner of the room. The air was cool, the bed did not sway as on the ship, yet she could not sleep peacefully.

Danger was around, and the prince knew it. Oh, why, why had he brought her here? She would not be welcome.

15

Peking was glorious with spring colors. In the Courtyard of the Flowering Peach were several flowering peach trees, the blossoms pale pink, the scents a faint, beautiful, lingering fragrance like perfume.

In the corners of the courtyard were sprays of lilac bushes: two corners purple, the other two corners white lilacs. Around their roots had been set tulips, of purple, gold, red, yellow. The rest of the courtyard was tiled in peach and almond colors, of precious small tiles, each one individually fired, as the prince explained to her, then colored and fired again.

She had four rooms to herself, all set about the court. One room was a huge bedroom, with an immense bed of unpolished sandalwood, emitting a faint odor, set in the center. The large wardrobe matched it and was now filled with dresses and robes for her. There was a low dresser to match, with a large mirror surrounded by gilt figures. The low dresser seat was padded with rose silk. On the floor of sandalwood were spread priceless carpets of traditional Chinese designs—cloud designs in dreamy pale rose, blue, and yellow; pearl border designs exquisitely woven; and sea waves with gay little sea horses dancing over the waves.

The bed canopy and curtains were of almond silk,

embroidered with rose silk thread, in more cloud patterns, soothing to the eye. At the end of the bed was a large chest of sandalwood, which held thick quilts and blankets for the bed, along with silk sheets of pale almond and rose.

Another room was Katie's sitting room, with the simple furniture favored by the Chinese: a sofa of open latticework and cane seating, with cushions to make it more comfortable; chairs to match, in the same scented woods; small tables for tea and to hold images of the Buddha and of goddesses, in ivory, porcelain, jade. Along one wall were hung paintings which she thought were quite old and valuable. They were scenes of mountains, lakes, and tiny figures of people, all in almond, gold, and cream—gentle shades that attracted one's eye again and again for the intricacy of the patterns which gradually revealed themselves to the observer.

Another small room at one side of the court was a kitchen, in which the cook prepared dishes for Katie and her staff. It was a little world of its own, this court, and no one could enter it but the prince and Moon Blossom, unless Katie chose.

The fourth room had been empty when she arrived, but it was soon furnished as the prince commanded, with desks for her work, easels of varying sizes, a chest of white papers, inks, brushes, oils in jars, palettes. Anything she wished for she had only to request, and it promptly appeared.

Except her freedom to leave the court. Katie was not allowed out of the area unless the prince was beside her or he had given specific orders. She was amazed, shocked, protesting. But he was inflexible.

"It can be dangerous for you. You shall not go out without my permission," he said firmly. "I will take you out in a carriage to see Peking, and the gardens, and many fine buildings, temples, and so on. But you never leave this court without me."

To Katie, accustomed to running out on the street in London, to greet the bread man, the country farmers, the crier of oranges and to go out in the carriage to the warehouses, down on the docks, to go anywhere she liked—this was a terrible condition. In London she had gone with a maid to the shops, bought her own bonnets and dresses, ordered cloaks made up, had shoes fitted, talked freely to tradesmen, shopkeepers, street people, friends over tea, warehousemen; it was dreadful that she could not even speak to an aunt of the prince without issuing a formal invitation for the lady to come, getting permission from the prince to have a guest, and going through such channels that it made her weary to think of it.

She protested in vain. She moaned about it to Moon Blossom. The girl said, shaking her head, "But it is a scandal to the Chinese in Macao that foreign women are permitted so much license! That is why they have bad reputations. They go out even with a man!" She looked very shocked and added, "This is why your sister with the hair of ashes was much despised by the Chinese. It was generally known she permitted the attentions of many men and went out day and night with them!"

Moon Blossom had come with an invitation to a dinner. It was a very special occasion and would take place in midafternoon in the court of the dowager princess, the mother of the prince.

Moon Blossom went over the dresses of Katie very critically. She finally chose a fine silk gown of almond and a thick rose brocade overdress. The slippers had to match exactly.

Katie was bathed by her maid, a broad-faced, beaming middle-aged woman who was named, she said, Third-Born. It meant that she was the third daughter of her family, she explained, and she had no other name. Because the woman beamed constantly and seemed so happy to have a kind mistress who was the object of the curiosity of the entire family, she was laughing and happy all the day.

"I will call you Joy," said Katie, resigned to the attentions of the woman.

Jasmine perfume was added to the water. Then she was liberally anointed with more jasmine oil after she had been dried and powdered like a baby, she thought. The prince had sent a large porcelain jar of the oil for her express use. It was his favorite perfume.

Then the underclothes were put on: the pantaloons; the long linen garments; the thick stockings of silk. Over it went the almond dress, covering her from throat to toe. Then the headdress was conceived. About her head was set wire mesh, and over it her thick, brown, long hair was wound and coiled, until she had a simplified Manchu headdress, about half the size of that of the princess Chen Mei-ling.

It would not do, of course, for a mere foreign woman to have a headdress of the size of that of the wife of the household! Katie was glad she did not have to have one so large; even this one made her head ache.

For over the hair was added a headdress of stiffened gold wire, hanging with butterflies, flowers, pearls, jade stickpins, until her slim throat drooped from the weight of it all. Then she was carefully fastened into a rose brocade robe of stiffened gold embroidery in patterns of the prince's household, designs of clouds, waves, sea horses. Evidently they all were typical symbols of his household.

Finally she put her feet into tilt-toed slippers of rose brocade. Moon Blossom set an ivory fan into her hand, a handkerchief into her sleeve, and she was ready.

Moon Blossom, already attired in very formal robes, led the way, and two of the eunuchs who guarded Katie followed her. They went all the way around winding lanes, through and past wide courtyards where elderly ladies sat in the sunlight, and as Katie passed by, they got up and followed her. They were rather incredible old ladies, painted and powdered, garbed in gaudy colors, gray hair wound up in hairdressing like hers, stumbling along in tiny slippers. Some had had their feet bound as children, though the Manchu despised that habit as a decadent habit of the Chinese. All were distant relations of the prince or his wife and as such had lifelong posts in the household.

The prince, his wife, and an elderly woman sat in thronelike chairs at the end of the huge room into which Katie was conducted. Several men were ahead of them. The men went up to the three and bowed until their heads touched the floor. Moon Blossom waited, then conducted Katie up to the three as well. She also bowed low. Katie dipped into a deep curtsy in the English fashion but did not put her head to the floor.

The elderly woman muttered, "Is this the foreign one? She has no courtesy!"

The prince said, "She bows according to the customs of her country." His voice was deep and smooth, expressionless.

Princess Chen Mei-ling ignored Katie; her gaze went over Katie's head out to the courtyard as though she were indifferent. However, her long, slim hands were clenched tightly on her fan, so her knuckles showed white.

Katie was then shown to a place at the very long table which went around the room, three sides of a square. She was seated at the side where the elderly ladies were seated, with Moon Blossom beside her. After everyone had been greeted and had expressed more or less elaborate greetings on the return of the prince and his family from Macao to Peking, the three main figures were seated in the center of the central table.

The dinner went on for three hours. There were many toasts in golden and white wines. The courses were comprised of so many small dishes that Katie lost count. It began with clear broth, proceeded to fish dishes, bits of delicious snails and shrimp and oysters. Then there was a larger fish course, of a delectable fish like trout. The meat courses followed, one dish after another, accompanied by tiny fragments of greens, bowls of rice in exquisite porcelain, tiny cups of green tea, then orange-spice tea, then mint.

Everyone ate and drank with much enjoyment. After the first formal remarks and toasts, everyone seemed to relax and talk to everyone else. The chatter went on in low voices, then in higher-pitched voices as the wines took effect.

Katie glanced shyly toward the head table from

time to time. The prince was courteous, smiling at his
elderly relatives, kindly toward his smaller young
ones. There were even some children there, round
Chinese faces with big black eyes. Katie thought more
than one hundred people were present, plus servants
padding about, seeing that everyone had the right
food and wine at the right time. Trails of servants
came and went from the kitchens, bearing trays and
trays of food and drink.

She caught the look of the dowager princess. The
elderly woman was tiny but spry. She looked frail, her
cheekbones showing in a yellowed face, her gray hair
thin over the wire frames. But she sat erect, her shoulders back, carrying the heavy brocades sturdily. Her
throat was yellowed and wrinkled but covered with
long strands of pearl and jade.

The look of the dowager princess, Princess Chen
Hsiao-yin, was cold on Katie. She did not approve of
the foreign woman in her household, it was evident.
Yet she was as frosty to her daughter-in-law; they exchanged few remarks, and Katie thought the smiles
were more like grimaces.

When the dowager did smile on a relative who
toasted her, it softened her harsh face, and her black
eyes took on a gentle look. She could be kind, like the
prince, thought Katie.

Toasts to the princess Chen Mei-ling were much
more formal, speeches carefully framed, nothing spon-
taneous, as though all feared her. She accepted their
flatteries with a cool nod of her heavy Manchu gold
headdress, the butterfly wings of her black hair shining with lacquer, sparkling with gold and diamond
headpins.

Toward the prince there was much more enthusiasm. They spoke, stammered, smiled, nudged each other at his answers, delighted when he tossed a jest in their direction.

A servant came and whispered to Moon Blossom. She leaned toward Katie. "After the dinner is over, the dowager princess wishes you to come to her court for speech."

"Oh! Goodness," said Katie faintly in English. Then she said, "Is it permitted?"

She hoped it was not. Moon Blossom nodded. "She has asked special permission of the prince Chen Yee. He wishes you to become acquainted."

"You will come with me?"

"I will take you there. She may permit me to remain. I never dare speak even a little lie to her," said Moon Blossom naïvely. "She sees through the head down to the heart and the stomach! She knows what is in the head and whether one tells the truth."

A formidable woman, evidently, for all her tiny build. Katie suppressed a sigh. The long dinner had wearied her, and she dreaded the ordeal to come.

The dinner having been concluded, the most elderly of the household offered a final toast in a fragile voice, and all drank. Then the prince left, followed by his mother and his wife.

Moon Blossom led Katie through a maze of corridors into the main section of the huge palace. All the surrounding courts were in the gardens; the prince and his wife and mother lived in the main palace. She was conducted past armed guards, along shining polished floors, past corridors of marble leading in all directions, past tables of precious objects of gold, silver, porcelain, jade, ivory. Faded carpets of ancient weaving covered some of the marble floors; others were allowed to remain uncovered so the beauty of the wooden floors would show.

Into a huge, thronelike room Katie stepped, as in an Arabian nights' tale. The dowager princess sat in a golden chair on a dais. She beckoned Katie to approach with an inperious finger.

Katie was not invited to take a seat. She curtsied, and Moon Blossom bowed to the ground until her head knocked on the carpet. Katie stared back steadily at the dowager.

"Why did you come to our country?" came the sharp question in a high, shrill voice.

"I came with my husband on a mission of his father, who is a trader of much distinction in England."

"A trader, a merchant! *Paugh!*" The nose wrinkled in disgust. "What do you not return home with your husband? Are you an unfaithful wife?"

"I was ill of a fever. The prince brought me on his ship."

"Why did you come? Why do you not go home?"

"I wish to go; the prince will not permit it." Katie kept on answering honestly, remembering the words of Moon Blossom, who had slid quietly to the back of the room, waiting.

"*Hm.*" The thin brows frowned over sharp black eyes. She tapped the arm of the chair with long, sharp fingernails. "What is your impression of China?"

"It is a very beautiful land, and the people value beauty and have much good taste," said Katie carefully.

The face did not soften; the frown remained. "China is the center of the world," she said. "All countries wish to come and bring tribute to us and to our honorable son of Heaven. Is that why you come?"

Katie studied the question. Finally she answered, "No, Your Highness. I came to purchase many precious objects of porcelain, silk, jade, and ivory to carry back to my country, England. Many persons there will pay a high price to obtain such objects and value them very much. It is of a profit for my father-in-law."

"You design on paper for these," shot out the dowager.

"Yes, Your Highness. It gives me much pleasure to draw and design."

"You may go." The dowager nodded abruptly, and Moon Blossom came forward to escort Katie to her room. More bows and withdrawing backward from the room—

The two eunuchs were there at the entrance to escort Katie and Moon Blossom the long way back to the court where Katie stayed. She arrived with relief and at once took off the heavy robes, the thick headdress. The maid Joy helped her, soothing her, rubbing her neck, as though she knew without being told how uncomfortable it was.

Moon Blossom departed, leaving Katie to her somber thoughts. She was not wanted here, except by the prince. If only he could be persuaded to let her go! The palace was stifling in its formality. She felt hated by some of them, especially the princess, and the dowager disapproved of her and her presence here. Why did he not let her go?

She was alone for two days, long enough to think and worry and figure out how to plead for her freedom. She worked on some sketches, but in an absent-minded way. It was not so important to work as to plan how to win her freedom and persuade the prince to send her south to Macao. There she could stay with Mrs. Shaw until someone came from England. She could beg her way home; surely some Englishman would be gallant and take her.

Prince Chen Yee came the following day. She began to frame the way she would ask for her freedom. He was smiling as he sat down beside her under the flowering peach tree. The petals blew in the breeze; some had fallen on her loose dark hair.

"You are very beautiful today, my songbird."

"Thank you. There is something I wish to discuss with you."

"Anything. Except for me to let you go."

Did he also read minds? She looked at him wretchedly. "Your mother will hate me as well as your wife. The dowager princess strongly disapproves of me."

"No, she approves of you. At first, before she met you, she disliked the idea that I had brought a foreign woman here. Then she saw you at the dinner, as I had planned, looking beautiful, almost Chinese, in our robes, our headdress. And she said to me that the songbird from England has a delicate figure, with beautifully fine hands, a soft voice that can scarce be heard (like a court lady, she said), and honest eyes."

Katie was silent, dazed. Had the dowager thought this of her? Or did the prince read more into her polite speech than was warranted?

The prince picked up the page on which she had sketched the lilacs. "Your mind wanders," he said gently. "This work is vague of line, not crisp."

"I have been worried," she told him. "I think I should depart before I cause—dissension in your household."

"Your thoughts do you honor. But this shall not happen. You shall be welcome." He took her hand in his and looked at it. "Such a lovely small hand." He raised it to his lips and kissed the fingers, each one from tip to palm, fhen the next. Her hand burned with his touch. She tried to draw it from him; his hold tightened.

"Today," he said, "I shall take you in a carriage to visit one of the beautiful gardens of Peking. There you will see ponds in which swim golden carp."

Each day thereafter he took her out driving in the city or in the countryside, showed her the beautiful palaces of Peking, from the outside, not the interiors. They did not visit anyone. She gazed from behind curtains at the shops; he snapped his fingers to have merchants run to him with some special gift. And on the way home he would hold her hand, kiss her lips lightly, brush his mouth against her cheek, praise her beauty, tease her from her anxiety, talk to her of Chinese wisdom, quote poetry, or make up poems about her.

His attentions increased daily. Nervously she held him off, permitting him no liberties with her person, though his large, strong hand would stray to her waist, once to a soft, small breast. She pushed him away, her eyes wide and alarmed.

In early May she found the weather growing warm. The peach blossoms were gone; the peaches were forming on the tree. The lilacs had disappeared, abruptly replaced by summer flowers of gaudier colors, gladiola in tall spikes, larkspur in vivid blue, brilliant red roses.

And one evening after dressing Katie in her night-dress of almond, Joy left her at her dressing table in the midst of brushing her hair. She must have heard some sound, for abruptly she had slipped out of the room. Katie was puzzled but went on brushing her long dark brown hair, lustrous and glossy again after her illness.

Prince Chen Yee stepped in the room. She started, seeing him in the mirror behind her. He wore a crimson velvet robe over his dark blue silk gown and dark blue slippers. He seemed pale, determined, coming to her at the dressing table. He put his hands on her shoulders. The brush fell to the tabletop. She nervously clasped her fingers together.

He bent and put his lips to her throat, and his mouth seemed to burn against her flesh. He said nothing, only lifted her in his arms and carried her to the bed. The maid had left only one oil lamp burning, and it cast a soft glow on the rose draperies of the bed.

Katie found her voice as he placed her on the sheets. "No," she said hoarsely. "No—you must not—no—"

He said nothing, merely discarding his robe, removing the underdress, his slippers. He lay down beside her and drew her into his arms. She tried to back from him, only to find the side of the red lacquer bed against her back. He smiled faintly and bent over her, and his lips went to her cheek, her earlobe, her throat.

"I have longed for you," he whispered in her ear. "I have longed for such time that now I burn intensely. Do not deny me, my songbird. Sing for me, in your throat, as I take the delight that is waiting for me."

"No, no, no," said Katie, trying to push him away. "I cannot do this—I must not—it is not right—"

"You are my woman; we both know it. Ah, how sweet are your small, delicate breasts—" He had uncovered them, drawing back the low-cut nightdress, and now lips large and firm touched them, touched the small pink nipples.

She felt the nipples rising to his touch. She moaned a little, pushing at his strong shoulders. She might as well have tried to move a large boulder as he bent over her. His shoulders were wide as a mountain above her; she was a small person at the foot of the mountain. Her mind was dazed, confused, as he went on caressing her. Something was burning inside her, a softening heat, a tremulous longing—

She thought his eagerness would make him plunge right into her. He was large, larger than Rupert; he would hurt her—

But he did not. Again and again his hands moved over her small body. He removed the nightdress; he removed all his own garments, so that his hard, lithe body moved on her small naked form, languidly moving so that every bit of her flesh was touched by his, caressed by his body, by his hands, his lips.

All desire to repulse him had gone from her. She lay in his arms, liquid to his fire, her hands on his head, his throat, his smooth, hard chest. Her fingers delicately touched his body, and he encouraged her with soft words.

"Touch me, my songbird, my little pigeon, my dove. Touch your lover and learn him. Do you feel my flesh burning for you? Do you feel the heart that throbs for you? Yes, touch me there, move your hand—ah, my dove—" Her hand had moved lower, by some drive beyond her conscious will, and had touched his thighs.

Still he did not take her. He went on caressing her, from her head to her feet and up again. He moved over her, his lips touching, caressing, praising her with words and touch.

"Softness, sweetness, fragrance, gentleness," he murmured against her breasts. "The body of a girl, the heart of a lioness, the spirit of a winged bird, the fragrance of a flower." He caught her lips delicately in his, savored them, sucked at them, until her mouth answered his lips, and her tongue timidly touched his large tongue.

He lay on his side, her body against his, chest to her breasts, his legs holding hers between his thighs. His one arm was about her; his other hand moved up and down her side, then held a breast in careful fingers, teasing the nipple with his thumb, moving it, brushing against it with a soft touch. She shivered and drew closer to him, her arms about him, her breath catching.

He thrust his tongue into her mouth and moved it around to learn the feel of her tongue, her teeth, her lips. The way he touched her was like a thrust into her body. Still he lingered over her, though she would feel from time to time the brush of his thighs against her and knew he wanted her. His body was hard, large, and suddenly she wanted him. She had melted; her thighs burned at his touch. His hand went to her thighs, and his large fingers moved on her, again, again, his one large finger thrust gently into her.

"You are dripping with the soft oils of love, my pigeon," he murmured. She flushed with deep embarrassment at his intimate words. He kept on whispering to her. "How I enjoy your lovely soft limbs. How silky you are, how scented. I feel your heat rising; you have a fever of love in you. Do you not? Tell me, my dove, do you burn with the love fever?"

"Yes," she muttered. Her head tossed back and forth; her dark hair whipped at his shoulders and hers. "Yes, yes, I am—burning now—oh—oh—please—"

"For what do you plead, my lovely one?" He whispered it in her ear and thrust his tongue gently inside, an erotic touch that made her shiver with delight. "Tell me, for what do you plead?"

"You—you—" she murmured. "Oh, please—"

"Call me love—"

"Love—love—"

"And I am love—my love—I am your lover—"

"Yes—yes—"

His finger was thrusting again and again inside her. She convulsed, and against his hand she came, again, again. He uttered some words of pleasure. "You are an angel of delight; you are a goddess of joy—"

Then he moved above her, and into her still-quivering body he gently pushed his own instrument. She moaned with the strong, heady delight of it; she came again in ecstasy at the power of his body pushing against hers. In and out, slowly, so slowly, in and out again, again— She came again and cried out.

He let her rest against him, still holding strongly inside her; then when her breath was even once more, he began to thrust again. She had never dreamed of such power in a man, not even in Rupert's arms. Rupert had made love to her, let her go, and slept. This man could not sleep; he desired more and more.

Then his body began to quiver and grow tense. She lay limply under him, but as he thrust more hotly into her, she began to tense. Her fingers dug into his hard back; her moans were against his hard mouth; she could not get enough of him. Her body thrust up against his; her softness demanded more from him.

He seemed to be singing something. Poetry? His voice went higher, stopped abruptly; he held her in his hands under him and thrust once more, deeply. Then he came, a gushing torrent of seed inside her quivering depths.

In the erotic feel of it she came once again. She seemed to open her whole self to his entry; she was wide and receiving and desiring and wanting him. Her thighs were shaking; her whole body shook but not with a chill. She was so hot, so full of needs—

She fell asleep in his arms, completely worn out with the wild embrace. Sometime in the night she wakened, thinking she dreamed. He was kissing her delicately all over her naked body under the silk sheet. She felt him under the covers, his mouth brushing against her waist, his hand on her thigh.

"Lover," she whispered. He went tense and still, then came up to gaze into her face in the dimming light of the oil lamp. She smiled up at him, and tenderly he brushed back the long, thick hair from her forehead, from her cheeks. "Lover—" she said.

"Again—oh, my love—I must have you again—" he said in a choked and broken husky voice.

"*Ummm,*" she agreed, still half-asleep. He came over her, but he was not rough and quick.

His lips parted hers; he thrust his tongue into her mouth. His body slid slowly over her wet body; he seemed to wind himself about her—like a dragon about his pearl, he whispered.

"I am the dragon, breathing fire into you. You are my pearl, my pink pearl with the silky lining. I must have you—I must absorb you into my very being—I am aching with desire for you, I burn—I feel my hand, my heart—"

Her hand curled about his strong virile throat, moved down his hard arm to his hand. He caught her fingers in his, moved them to his lips, kissed every finger with passion. He rubbed his body sensuously against hers, wakening her erotic emotions once more. He nibbled at her underlip; she had never felt such a sensuous kiss.

He moved her hand to his thigh, made her hold his large instrument in her fingers. She slid her fingers over it shyly, wonderingly, all reserve gone. It was so big, so hard.

"When you wish it, take it to yourself," he whispered, and kissed her earlobe, nipping it between his teeth. She felt such a hunger, and she turned and drew the instrument to her body and pressed it inside, wanting him with a direct simple primitive hunger.

He lay, half over her, letting her make the advances, and their bodies came together again. She pushed her hips against his, needing him, wanting him. She felt him swell even larger; could she take him?

She lay back gasping, a little afraid; he was so big. He came over her then and came into her slowly, slowly, pushing farther and farther—until she felt the tip of him deep inside her. Not crushing, but so full, so good—so good—

Out and in again, out and in again, moving so deliberately, so erotically, that she caught at his shoulder over her. Her fingernails dug into his flesh. "Lover—oh, lover—I wish it now—oh, please—"

"Tell me in words what you wish," he teased. He pushed in, then drew out slowly.

"Oh, yourself—please—come—come—"

"Tell me more—"

He gently made her say more words to him until they both were so roused that he could not wait any longer. He moved more rapidly, then swiftly, and she felt the spasms beginning in her. Still he held his response back until she was beating at him with small fists, pushing at him with all her strength.

Then he came powerfully, as though it were the first time in long days and nights of wanting. As though he had not touched her before, he kissed her wildly. And his strong seed spurted in her, sending more ripples of response through her, causing deeper and deeper answers in her body to the push of his. She seemed flooded with the waters of love, burning hot with the sun of desire, naked to his every caress, spinning higher and higher—

She spun up to the heavens, and he was with her, holding her, bodies welded together by the wet heat of the storm. She did not want to come back from the heavens; it was so marvelous up there in the clouds, in the hot sun, in the intense climax that shook them both.

Finally it was over, and they spun slowly, lazily down to earth once more, lying tangled in the bed-clothes, limbs wound together, bodies wet and limp.

He laughed a little when he had recovered and had drawn her to him and straightened out the sheets to cover them both.

"Ah, my love, it was worth the waiting for you!" he whispered against her hot cheek. "You made me long for you until I would have burned to death, but it was worth the long nights alone—to have you now!"

16

Prince Chen Yee came to Katie's bed almost every night. When he did not come, she missed him. Rupert had never been so ardent, so demanding, yet so gentle and considerate.

She was shocked at her own responses; they left her shaken and limp. He drew wild responses from her, not with cruelty, for he was never cruel or rough. He would woo her through the afternoon, with his close presence, his speech, poems, attentions. When he came at night, he lay long with her, caressing her with his clever hands, whispering to her in words that increased desire in both of them until they could not endure waiting any longer. Then they would come together in a wild rush or in a slow erotic mating that went on for hours.

He wooed her continually, by his voice, his look of approval on her slim rounded body, by his thoughts for her pleasure. He did not need to touch her, only to look at her, and she would flush hotly and avoid his glance, thinking of the night to come. He would touch her knee, and she felt a flood of response from deep inside her. He would sit and say nothing, sketching beside her as she sketched, and she felt his presence so keenly that her hand would shake.

He smiled more now. His face was more gentle and relaxed. He rarely frowned, and never at her. He lavished gifts on her; her wardrobe was overflowing; another wardrobe was brought for the many gowns and robes of finest hues, almond, peach, rose, azure blue, crimson, golden yellow. All the flower colors, he said.

They were talking one rainy day in her beautiful drawing room. The winds lashed the petals of the flowers, but the room was peaceful, the curtains drawn against the rain and dark sky. She scarcely heard the punishing beat of the wind and rain, the growling of the thunder, the crack of lightning.

They talked of literature, of the wisdom of the Chinese sages. Prrince Chen Yee was speaking of fate. "How can we rail against fate? What will be will be. We can only be the best person that one can become and let the fates do what they will."

She considered that, lying back in the rose cushions. He sat in a large armchair facing her, his long legs stretched out idly before him. He was more relaxed in her presence now, his mouth amused from his hard strength, his black eyes waiting eagerly for what she would say.

"Do you think then that fate plans our lives?"

"Yes, fate plans our lives," he said. "We fight against it, but it comes around and strikes from behind. A strong man can force his own destiny, but others must accept meekly whatever happens. And all of us are swept by the winds of fate."

"What if a strong man has had poor advice all his life? He is strong, but he is not wise. Not because of any fault of his, but because his advisers are lacking in wisdom?"

"Then he is not a strong man," said the prince positively. "He is crippled by lack of wisdom."

"Then it is not fate, but his upbringing, that hampers him. His counselors, not fate, are at fault."

He began to laugh, softly at first, then more loudly, and she laughed with him. "Oh, you have caught me a bit, I think, my songbird! But what is fate? Perhaps it is a combination of our birth, our parents, our counselors, our learning, and our own efforts."

"Where does fate come in? You have not mentioned it this time."

He thought, then answered, "It is the circumstances that whirl us around. We do not live alone, but with others. Forces from them and forces from nature, such as storms at sea, cliffs which break off and fall, raging rivers, and floods—all can change our lives."

"Again it is not fate!" she said quickly, laughing again and brushing back her long dark hair. "All you have said are natural things. People and nature."

"Ah—but there are gods," he said, smiling with pleasure at her quickness. "If the gods choose, we are struck down. Or if they find favor with us, they lift us up."

"You are a strong man," she said thoughtfully, musing, her finger at her rosy lips. "What has happened to you that you can blame the gods for?"

"That they brought you to me, and for that I am grateful!"

She shook her head. "I have told you the circumstances that caused my marriage, the fact that I knew Mandarin languages, that my father trained me in Oriental ways and customs, that I can draw. All this brought me to Macao."

"Fate threw a small child in the passageway before a maddened horse and caused you to rescue him and me to notice you."

She reflected. "The horse was maddened for some reason we do not know, probably ill-treated by a person. The curiosity of the small boy led him into the street. My nature made me wish to rescue him."

"Ah—but why was I on the street at that moment?" he asked triumphantly.

"*Umm.* Maybe we would never have met. You did not go to the homes of the foreigners."

"Nor did I invite foreigners to my home," he said quietly. "And certainly the reputation of your sister would have prevented me had I not been so desirous of seeing you again."

"Even then?" she asked, gazing at him tenderly. He was so good to her it was only in small moments of time that she wished she had never come.

"From the moment I saw you and heard you speak."

He came over to sit beside her and draw her into his arms. His strong hand came to her small breast and cupped it through her dress under the robe. He bent and brushed his lips against her cheek.

"From that moment I was lost," he breathed against her ear. "From seeing you, observing your loveliness, hearing the soft coo of your voice, small as a bird, strong and willful as a spring breeze, graceful as a willow, fragrant as blossoms. I was lost, lost, and gloried in it. Never had I believed the poets who sang of love. I had never known it—"

"But you are married—" she dared say.

His strong face shadowed; the dark brows met over the black eyes. "It was arranged for me," was all he said. "My grandmother arranged it; the girl was Manchu and of good family . . . My dove, do you wish to sketch today, or is it too dark?"

She accepted the change of topic. She had dared

more than she should have done. "It is too dark," she said. "Shall we have tea, or would you read to me of poetry and tell me what its layers of meaning are?"

They decided on both. Joy padded in with the trays of tea; the prince read to her in his beautiful musical voice; they discussed the poems at length.

Another day he came while she was sketching in her court. He looked critically over the small sketches and turned over the pages in her drawing book.

"It seems to me that these are English drawings," he said finally. "What is this strange lovely flower?"

"That is an English primrose, Elder Brother. It is yellow of color and grows in the English countryside, over hedges, over fences, making the fields glow."

"Ah, so simple, yet so lovely," he said. "Katie, would you like to make more designs for the English market?" he asked so suddenly that she caught her breath.

"How can I?"

She had no contact with merchants now, no contact with anyone outside his palace, and not much outside her court. He and Moon Blossom were her only links to the outside world. She had wondered if Rupert would try to write to her and, if he did, if she would ever receive the letters.

"I have no interest in trade," he said. "However, I admire your work. And I think you like to work for a purpose. Shall I contact silk merchants for you and let them use your drawings for the English trade in Canton?"

It was much more than she had dared hope. It would give her something definite to do, and it would be a link with Canton. She stared at him eagerly, her brown eyes glowing. "Oh, will you do that for me?" she breathed.

"More than that. You are my life," he said simply. "I will do whatever is best for you always; that is my vow. Now, would you like to choose sketches to send?"

"These are only rough drawings," she said. "I—I would like to do something finer and then send them. I am most grateful to you for your offer." Formality had come into her voice. He eyed her gravely, then set down the sketches.

"It shall be done. Give me the sketches when you have prepared them," he said as formally. Abruptly he changed the subject and took her with him in a carriage for a ride in the countryside.

But the conversation had given her hope. It was her wish and her duty to return to Rupert, to explain to him what had happened, to beg him to take her back. She was an Englishwoman; she missed her country, her relative freedom, her life there. She must try to return however she could and must plan for that. A strong woman, she thought wryly, would work firmly to do as she must do.

However, she was wrestling with herself. Did she want to leave the prince and his household? She felt so safe here, so secure, so loved and protected. And no one could ask for a more considerate and ardent lover. The nights in his arms were like paradise for the girl who had lived such a quiet, friendless life. It was like one who had lived on bread and water suddenly given a veritable feast that was overwhelming and told to live on this now. But was it right? That was what bothered her. Her upbringing told her that this was wrong, that she was immoral to live with a man without marriage, and she was married to another man and owed him her loyalty.

Katie thought over the matter the next morning. She was dazed by the night before, when the prince had come and made love to her the entire night, not sleeping until dawn. They had not risen until the sun was quite far up in the sky; he had had breakfast with her; his laughter had rung out in the courtyard; he had teased her by feeding her with bites of sweet rolls, bits of egg, putting the morsels into her mouth with his own fingers.

Now he had left. He had to do some work, he said ruefully. She sat back in her chair in the sunlight, her pencils idle on the desk, the white paper unmarred by any line or sketch.

What should she do? It was her duty to try to escape, but how? She could never find her way south to Canton; she would be murdered for her money; she had heard enough stories to know that bandits abounded in the countryside. The prince would follow her, be angry with her; he might even kill her himself.

Moon Blossom had told her what the princess Meiling had once done. A maid had displeased her soon after her marriage by pulling her hair as she brushed it. She had had the girl's head cut off by a guard right before her. The prince had been coldly angry with her and had not gone to his wife for a year. But such things did happen, even in so kindly a household as that of the prince.

Katie was beginning to understand the coldness between the prince and his haughty wife. The woman was cruel and feared. She beat her maids, unless the prince found out and prevented it, and that he could not always do. She seemed to find pleasure in hurting persons under her, and most of the palace was inferior to her station.

Katie shuddered when she thought of the brief stories Moon Blossom had reluctantly told her when Katie insisted: tales of torture by pincers when a guard closed his eyes at her door, an elderly woman struck when she stumbled into Mei-ling's path, cats and dogs tortured for her laughter. Only the prince and his mother were immune to her; she dared not touch them.

The prince despised his wife, thought Katie. He was good and honorable, fair to and thoughtful of the people he ruled. He considered all his extended family. He went often to the palace of the emperor, who was his friend and valued the fair judgment and thoughtful wisdom of Prince Chen Yee, comparatively young though he was. All honored the prince for his balanced mind and his caring heart, as Moon Blossom put it. No wonder he could not live with Mei-ling or make love with her and create a child. This explained much to Katie, that a man of such passion had never had a child. He was too fastidious to take any woman, and his own wife had his deep contempt.

Yet he had shown such wild masculine need to Katie . . . and she had responded so. . . .

Then Katie remembered. And picked up her pencil to draw. A flush came into her cheeks. She must at least get a message to Rupert, try to tell him she was alive and wished to convey words to him.

Into the sketch she added the initials *K* and *L*

in the device they had discussed, with the butterfly wound around the initials until they were almost invisible. But they were there for anyone who might be looking for them.

She drew all the day, steadily, sometimes biting her lip. She felt as though she were betraying the prince, his love for her, and her love for him. Yet she belonged to Rupert, by English law, by her own long love for her boyhood friend, her devotion to his family. And she was English, an Englishwoman. She must make the effort to get a message to Rupert. Perhaps a Llewellyn ship was even now on its way to Canton. Mr. Llewellyn sent one every year. Rupert would be on his way home, perhaps passing that ship on the way, perhaps sending a message to her. She must do her best to reach him in a subtle way.

And so she sketched out several designs and in the corner went the initials *K* and *L* for Katie Llewellyn, with the butterfly about it.

Prince Chen Yee praised her sketches and had his secretary, Wu Hsun, wrap them and send them off to the silk merchants. Katie felt very guilty. The prince was so warm in his praise, so eager to please her. . . .

Yet she was married to Rupert. No matter how much desire Prince Chen roused in her, her first love was Rupert, and her first duty was to her husband. She must find some way to return to him. . . .

She was surprised one day as she sat sketching in the afternoon to have a visitor—the dowager princess Chen Hsiao-yin. The woman walked in sturdy strides with an elderly lady behind her. She went past the guards with a contemptuous wave of both hands, as though shooing off flies.

Katie rose hastily and went to greet her. She curtsied low and was amazed to find the woman bowing slightly in return. The woman behind her bowed low and gave her a wide-toothed grin.

"I have come to visit you," announced the mother of Prince Chen. She sat down in the large armchair he usually used, and though her feet dangled from the ground, she managed to look like an autocrat. Joy hastened to set a footstool at her feet. The older woman, clad in dark flowered blue, sat down behind her.

"You are most gracious." Katie hesitated; an imperious hand waved her back to her seat.

"You may offer me tea."

"Thank you." Katie turned to Joy, and the plump woman was already scurrying to the kitchen to prepare it.

"I came yesterday; the guards turned me away!" Outrage filled her frail voice. "I had to get permission in formal way from my own son!"

Katie suppressed a smile. "It was good of you to persist," she managed to say. "You are most kind."

"It is a sad thing when a mother cannot visit the concubine of her own son without his express permission!"

Katie winced at the term, and her smile faded. The woman watched her sharply and said more gently, "He is careful of your safety. He is a wise man."

"Yes, he is most—protective—and wise."

"I have heard that laughter comes often from this court when the prince visits you. Elderly ones living nearby tell me this, and we are all happy that you make him laugh. He has not laughed much in recent years."

"I thank you, Your Highness. It is a pleasure to—to make him laugh."

"And to bring pleasure to him." The woman nodded complacently. "A wise woman makes the man of her life happy and laughing, giving him joy and pleasure of her."

Tea was then brought.

"When is the date of your birth?" asked the dowager abruptly, dusting cake crumbs carefully from her yellow silk skirt. She was elegantly gowned in golden colors today, her coat a deep gold brocade with the skirts a lighter saffron, all embroidered in clouds, waves, and sea horses. Her hair was pulled back in a simple gray chignon, clasped with jade pins. It made her look gentler, more vulnerable, as though she were an ordinary woman anxious for her son.

"My birthday is April third."

"And the year?"

"I do not know the Chinese year. It was in England 1797."

The woman frowned. "I will ask Wu Hsun to compute it for me. Then I will give the information to the makers of horoscopes and see what your future is."

Katie started. "Oh, I do not believe in that," she said without thinking. "I am sorry, I do not believe—"

The dowager glared. "It is well known that people of the outer world are stupid and ignorant of many well-known truths," she snapped. "At what hour were you born?"

Katie tried to think, knowing she had blundered. "I believe it was about dawn, perhaps five or six in the morning. My mother spoke of the rising sun after my birth."

"*Hm.* I will note that. We shall see if there are any auspicious signals and signs about you. Perhaps there will be as you make my son happy."

"You are most kind to trouble yourself."

"It is my duty. I always try to do my duty as well as I am able. Is that your way also? Or are the outer world people so different from us?"

The piercing black eyes seemed to want an answer.

"I try always to do my duty," said Katie gravely. "So do—other persons of honor in England." She thought of Rupert, trying so hard against difficulties, against Terence's drinking, Terence's idle nature. Her face softened. "My father tried always; he worked very hard and with much intelligence."

"Tell me of him."

Katie thought later how oddly natural it had been to sit in this foreign courtyard, surrounded by eunuch guards, telling this little yellow-faced woman with sharp black eyes the background of her life. As they drank tea and ate rice cakes and honey cakes, she spoke of her father and mother, of her life in Cornwall, and of her brief education, how her father had schooled her in sketching, in Oriental matters. Her talking went on naturally to the story of Terence and his marriage, of Rupert and how unhappy he had been.

"But his elder brother spoke for her!" snapped the dowager, breaking her silence after listening long.

"Yes, but Rupert saw her first and loved her. It was he who introduced her to Terence."

"Did not go-betweens arrange the marriage?"

"No. In fact"—Katie hesitated—"his father and mother were—wary—of the marriage. It was well known that—that Selina was frivolous of nature—"

"They should have stopped the marriage!"

Katie sighed. "Terence would have run off with her."

"So then what happened?" The dowager seemed as fascinated in her well-bred way as any woman or girl interested in the stories of others' lives.

Katie told her, and the two women and Joy listened with great interest. Her own marriage, the duel—at which they gasped in amazement—all the events that had happened. She stopped short when she came to the arrival in Macao. "So that is how I came to China," she concluded.

"An amazing story," mused the dowager. "You had no guidance as a child. You are but twenty years of age, a little over a child with no mother or aunt to guide you. Why did not the mother of your husband assist you in your problems?"

Katie hesitated, thinking of Mrs. Mathilda Llewellyn. "She had much grief over the duel of her son and his being sent away," she said finally. "I think that was why I did not burden her with my troubles. Also, I was not accustomed to confiding in her. And she did not ask. My father-in-law was anxious for me to marry Rupert; I did not ask him for aid. And my grief over my father—it all seemed unreal and strange, as though things were happening to someone other than myself."

She had not thought the dowager would understand. But the older woman nodded her head; her hand went to Katie's, and she patted it for a moment. Then, as though regretting her action, she frowned and drew herself up.

"All very regrettable and unfortunate," she rapped out. "Those in the outer world do not order themselves well. You should have had more guidance and protection in your youth and a woman of the family to instruct you and educate you in the ways of taking care of a household. I understand you work in trade and go out among men in that land of England?"

"Yes, madame. That is true."

"Disgraceful! No wonder they are decadent!!"

Katie's mouth twitched; her sense of humor was affected by the snort of anger and contempt. Her brown eyes danced with laughter, and the dowager looked at her a long moment. Then unexpectedly she, too, gave a cackle of laughter.

"Soooool I will tell you of another world, how another culture should live? Well, well, it is ever so. Old women like to give advice; young people like to resist it! That is true everywhere!"

"It is very true, madame!"

"Soooo, we are agreed!"

She got up to leave as abruptly as she had come. But though her manner was cool, they had shared a moment of laughter and understanding. Katie thanked her for coming.

Katie bowed low in the Chinese manner, and a flash of pleasure lit the little face. Then she departed, leaving a waft of lilac behind her.

Prince Chen Yee came to her that evening for dinner in a very good mood. "Mother enjoyed her visit with you. She said you have intelligence beyond your years, though your education is sadly neglected."

Katie grimaced. "I was educated, but not in the matters she considers important. And perhaps she is right. If I had known more of the world and its ways—" She might not have married Rupert, hoping to win his love, she added mentally.

"You please me very much as you are." And his arm drew her close to him. He gazed down into her face, and as they were alone just then, he kissed her forehead where the hair lay on her brow. His big hand stroked the long swath of hair down her back, then continued down over her rounded hips. A shiver of delight went through her, and he smiled.

They sat in the courtyard long that evening. The late June evening was warm, and summer would be hot, he had warned her. If it grew unbearable, they would retire to his summer home in the hills. However, he would rather remain in Peking because he had some family affairs to attend to.

She understood that his interests were wide. As head of the House of Chen he was responsible for all his relatives, no matter how distant, who chose to throw themselves on his mercy and pity. He also owned lands for some distance and was accountable for their good working. He felt responsible also for the workers on his lands, even though they were not relatives, and visited them at times to see how matters went. Evidently he was both judge and jury, dispensing justice when needed.

He was young to have taken on so much. However, she realized he had been strictly trained in such matters by tutors and his father. His tutor, Wu Lung, brother of his secretary, Wu Hsun, had trained his father and then himself and was now training his younger brother, Prince Chen Lo.

The prince had found time that day to compose another poem to Katie, and he recited it as the moon came up, murmuring the words in her pinkened ear. It was very erotic, very intimate, and she thought he would not dare print it! Yet their ways were different from English ways; perhaps he would!

The shadows fell in the courtyard, moved as the

moon moved, and still they lingered. The guards stood with their backs to the court, leaning against the wall or lying in the tiled narrow streets, composing themselves for rest. They would lie where no one could enter without disturbing them.

Joy had departed also, along with the cooks and the other maids. They were alone in the fragrant court, with only the flowers, the shadows, and the moon. Now a few stars came out, pricking their way through the purple velvet sky.

Prince Chen Yee rubbed his cheek against Katie's hair. He was talking in a murmur, as though thinking aloud. "I must go away in a few days to a small village where there is quarreling. You will miss me, yes?"

"Yes. How long will you be gone?"

She did miss him whenever he did not come. The days were long and lonely, even with Moon Blossom's cheerful visits.

"Not long, perhaps four days. Will it seem long to you?"

"Yes." She sighed and turned around in his arms. Their lips met and lingered. Presently he picked her up and carried her to the bedroom. His hands caressed her as he undressed her, removed the light dress, the undergarments of linen, the small slippers. He laid her in the silk sheets of almond.

He removed his own garments quickly, impatiently, as though eager to be done with them. She lay on her back, watching him in the dimness—he had not lit a lamp. She saw the strong, muscular body in outline as he turned, his arms over his head as he pulled off an undershirt.

How strong he was, how virile, how very masculine.

Yet so understanding of her needs, so gentle with her small narrow-hipped body—

He lay down with her, his arms going about her hungrily. She put her hands on his shoulders and ran them down his arms. Hands moved over her, learning her all over again. "You are beautiful, oh, my beloved, you are the silk of my sword, you are the vessel of my passion. How I think of you during the days when I am away from you! I feel you in the back of my head, in the body of my loins, even when I am away from you. And by the time I come to you my need is very hot."

She blushed even in the darkness at his whisper. How very frank he could be!

"Tell me words," he coaxed, stroking her with his clever long fingers. His long fingernails scratched lightly over her nipples and made her shiver. "Tell me how you feel, how you miss me when I am not here!"

"I—think of you—" she whispered shyly at his urging. "I think of how we lie together—and you are so gentle to me—so good—so careful of me—and how we come together—like the earth receiving the rain, like the clouds unleashing rain on the parched ground that hungers for it—and a storm rises in my heart, lashing me, until you come."

"*Ahhhh*," he murmured against her ear, and thrust his tongue inside her delicate ear. She shivered with pleasure and desire and squirmed closer to his warm hard body. "Tell me more—"

When she could not, for shyness, he laughed softly. In the darkness he caressed her with his hands; his lips spoke words that were like poetry. "You are so lovely, my love. My beloved, you are rounded like an orange that I would bite into you and find the juices of you—" And his lips gently bit at her nipples. "Your arms are like alabaster, your lips like petals of the rose, your waist like the trunk of a slim tree. And your thighs are enticing to me—I long to lose myself in the treasure box of you. Your slim legs are like the limbs of the pine tree, swaying in the wind. Your toes are as small snails, so sweet to eat—" And he nibbled at them, going up and down her body like a gourmet contemplating a meal!

He came back to her lips. "Your mouth is like wine, and I would drink of it—

"And your tongue is sweet as an apple—crisp and good.

"And your throat is soft as white jade. . . .

He was kissing her all over, praising her as he went. She nestled into his arms, and her hands went slowly over his smooth chest, caressing him with her fingers, down to his waist, down to his thighs. . . .

He caught his breath, lay still as she held him. The rod rose in her hands, growing, swelling.

A groan of eagerness came from his throat, a soft cry like a song, and he moved to lie over her, but not wanting to disturb her fingers. "Put me inside you when you wish, my beloved," he commanded softly.

She played a little longer, delighting in her ability to make him react. She had forgotten the world—it meant nothing; it was all beyond her. This was the center of the earth, here in this bed, with him. And the bed was swaying with their passion, creaking with their faster movements.

She cried out, and quivers of ecstasy rocked her, and she said words that pleased him in the violence of her passion. All modesty was forgotten, all reticence, all shyness. He made her forget all else.

He held back while she came and he made love to her again and again, in the wildest passion. She felt no pain; he caused her no hurt; she received his thrusts with pleasure and happiness and felt again the pure ecstasy of rising with him to heaven, up to the very clouds.

Then they rested, wound tightly in each other's arms, limbs entwined. And he sang softly to her of his delight in her.

17

June turned to July, and the days grew hot. Prince Chen arranged to do his work early in the day or later in the evening, for the hot, dry wind blew constantly in Peking during midday, and all wanted to rest then.

Katie lay in her wide bed, waiting for the prince to waken. She contemplated his strong face seriously, as she lay turned to him, held in the loose clasp of his arm. She studied the broad forehead, the dark eyebrows, the thick lashes, the strong, firm mouth so carved and large, like a jade Buddha. And his hard throat, his wide chest hairless and smooth, narrowing to his slim waist.

She had reason to stare, she thought wistfully. Her child would probably look like him! She must tell him soon, for even now her maid would be preparing hot tea and a biscuit for her to eat before rising. Joy had guessed, though she said not a word to her mistress. Her black eyes sparkled, her beam was broader than ever, and she took great care in bathing Katie.

If only she had been with Rupert, if only the child would be his! It might have happened on the *China Princess*, coming to Macao, and then—all events might have been quite different. Surely Rupert would have been delighted and more devoted to Katie, even have forgotten his love for Selina.

If only the child were Rupert's, if only all this had not happened—

But *if* was a fine thing, thought Katie wryly, remembering sayings of her childhood in Cornwall. *If* was the wind blowing where it would. *If* was the wishes of the fairies. *If* was the elf of mischief, leading one's thoughts astray for what would never be.

Prince Chen opened his dark eyes, smiling to see Katie's small, serious face beside him. He touched her cheek gently with his long finger.

"You waken early, my little songbird."

"Early. Good morning, Elder Brother."

He leaned closer, his hard mouth closed on hers expertly, and they were silent for a time, kissing, pressing close. Gently he drew her to him, his lean hand on her hips, and they came together slowly, playing.

Presently he drew back. "Your mind is occupied with another matter, I believe," he said.

Could he really read her mind? She thought he could. She smiled a little, brushed back her mussed dark hair, and nodded.

"There is something I would tell you, Elder Brother."

His dark eyes studied her thoughtfully, his face closed so he seemed enigmatic. "What is it? You are troubled?"

"No—or yes," she said, confusingly.

"Tell me, you can speak of anything to me," he said.

She thought: No, I cannot. But of this matter she had to; there would soon be no hiding it.

She took a deep breath. "I must speak of the matter to you—I—I wish to tell you—"

"You have trouble finding words, my dove," he said gently. "Tell me what is in your heart."

His gaze grew troubled as she bit her lips. He caressed her cheek with his fingers. She finally blurted it out.

"Elder Brother, I am—I am pregnant—"

He stared. "What do you say?" he asked in a low tone.

"I am—pregnant—with your child. I— am not sure if you will be pleased—or not."

"Pregnant—with my child?" He seemed strangely stupid. He stared at her as though unbelieving. "You are sure?"

She began to worry. Was he not pleased? "Yes, I have been sick some mornings and have—have not bled, you know. It must have happened soon after you—you first took me—" She began to blush furiously, remembering the first nights. How deeply he had made love to her, keeping her awake all the night.

"You are—to have my child?" His hand went to her waist, felt the faint swelling there. His face began to light; his dark eyes glowed. "You are—to have my child?"

"Yes." She put her hand shyly on his broad shoulder; her eyes gazed directly into his. "You are—not pleased?"

He shook his head, leaning up and over her. "Pleased? I am dazed. I cannot believe—I am incredulous with joy! How can this be? I have had no child—I thought, feared—" He broke off abruptly. "When is the wonderful event to happen?"

"I think in the middle of February by the English calendar."

He thought about that, gazing down at her, his dark eyes glowing more brightly until his whole face blazed. "In the middle of February—my adored—I can scarcely believe it! A child—to the House of Chen—"

"By a foreign woman," Katie dared remind him soberly. "What will your mother say? And others?"

He shook his dark head impatiently. "They will rejoice with us! You are happy, my songbird?"

He asked her anxiously, his hand caressing her throat.

She considered it, then nodded; it would make him happy, and she—somehow—wanted to give him this joy. "I am very happy, Elder Brother, if this is what you wish. I am both happy and worried, anxious—"

"Anxious? Worried? Nothing will happen to you but good," he assured her gently. "We shall have utmost care of you, the best women to care for you."

She met his gaze again bravely. "I think—your wife—will hate me the more."

He nodded but said quietly, "I shall increase your guards. And only I and Moon Blossom shall come to you."

She compressed her lips, then burst out, unable to contain the words. "Oh, I am so lonely and afraid! I am sorry—I should be braver. But I worry—and when I am alone, the worry returns and plagues me. I wish I were braver—"

"My bird, my bird," he said tenderly, and put his cheek against hers for a long moment. "Nothing will happen to you. And I shall think of ways that you will not be lonely. Give me your trust and confidence; none will harm you, my dove."

He kissed her, murmured to her, and left her reluctantly. There was a court in session this early morning, in the cool of the day, and he had to preside. But he left with a light step, joy on his face.

The word swept around the courts, and Katie could hear the chatter and laughter and high-pitched voices from where she sat in the early afternoon. Joy was beaming, pattering about with tea, preparing her lunch tray carefully, bubbling over that her mistress was to give the prince Chen pleasure, great joy, and honor by having his child. What an honor for herself, what a great delight, to take care of his mistress!

Moon Blossom came to her, to share her lunch, on the prince's orders. She was smiling, and happy, her black eyes shining.

"All of us have heard, by the prince's command. He sent word to every court. There is to be a feast planned in a week. His mother asked me to speak to you, to ask if there is aught she can do for you."

"Is she angry with me?" asked Katie bluntly.

"Angry?" Moon Blossom stared, sinking down into the chair beside Katie's under the awning which protected them from the hot sun. "Angry? His honorable mother? No, she rejoices that His Excellency is to have a child. She prays already that it will be a son!"

Another worry. Katie grimaced. "What if I give him a daughter?"

Moon Blossom dared press her slim hand with her own plump fingers; her face was kindly and encouraging. "My dear cousin-by-marriage, permit me to say that any child of the prince will be joyously welcomed. He has been married these many years; he has been unhappy in his barren state. His own mother urged him to take a second wife, but the princess Mei-ling—" She stopped abruptly.

"Go on, Moon Blossom. I would know your wise words—"

Moon Blossom nodded reluctantly. "It is best that

you know. Princess Mei-ling is very angry. She says rash words. Whenever his dowager mother suggested a second wife, Mei-ling went into a torrent of rage, breaking mirrors, making threats. The prince turned from her in cold anger, and yet he liked no woman enough to make her his wife. When you came, so foreign and different, we all wondered, for never had we seen him act so with any woman. He loves you as a miser loves gold, as a shepherd loves his sheep, as a farmer loves his trees and land. You have the core of him."

Moon Blossom had never spoken so eloquently and passionately. Katie gazed at her in wonder, saw the deep blush on her cheeks, the flash of her usually quiet eyes. She guessed the girl's secret: She loved and adored her third cousin, the handsome great prince. But it was a quiet, selfless love, wanting only his good and his happiness.

Katie put her hand on the girl's arm. "Thank you for telling me, Moon Blossom. No one but the prince has been as good to me as you are. I hope we will always be friends and be able to speak honestly with each other."

"You do me too much honor," said Moon Blossom, blushing even more deeply with pleasure. "It is my joy to wait on you."

"No, no, you are my friend, not my maid! Oh, I would like to see you more often, Moon Blossom. Could you not come daily when the prince does not come? Perhaps we could talk to each other; I have been lonely— And as the child makes me heavy, it will be—more difficult—for me—"

"I will ask permission from the prince if it is your will."

"Thank you. Perhaps you have other duties—"

"My aunt, the dowager, will release me from all other duties. And she wished me to say to you, again, if anything can be done for you, you have only to ask."

"Yes. I have thought," said Katie slowly, "I know nothing of having a child and caring for it. Perhaps if she would be so gracious, she would ask one or two of her women to advise me."

The guards were doubled at every entrance to the courts. Katie heard from Joy that Princess Mei-ling was furious. Her maids had fled from her in terror in the first moments of her outraged cries. She lay in her room, refusing to eat or talk now.

Katie was sorry for her; she knew how she felt, the jealous anguish that another woman, and a foreigner, was to give birth to the child that should have been hers. But remembering the spite of the woman, her arrogance and cruelty, she shuddered. She just hoped that Mei-ling would stay away from her!

"You must have a care," Moon Blossom warned Katie. "Do not attempt to go anywhere without guards. For the woman can be dangerous. I dare speak to you because you are my friend and I love you."

"You are good and kind to me, and I am very grateful."

"Your food will be carefully guarded," said Moon Blossom, in a matter-of-fact tone. "Your cook is loyal to the prince; she rejoices that you are to have his child. She herself will taste every portion before you are given food or drink. And Joy will also do the same. Dogs will be kept nearby to taste any other questionable foods or candies. They react swiftly to poison."

"Poison!" said Katie faintly, her hand to her mouth.

"Yes, that is the path of the jealous woman, and Mei-ling knows of such poisons. Her own mother was poisoned by the jealous concubine of her father."

"Good—heavens!" said Katie, her hand to her head. It was all another strange weird world, this one in the Orient.

Music came faintly to them; it had an Oriental twang of strange instruments. Even the air was strange, with hot, sultry scents day and night. And she felt stifled sometimes, practically a prisoner in the Court of the Flowering Peach.

A beautiful prison, but a prison still. For a moment she felt wildly rebellious and longed to run away, no matter what happened to her. She had never felt so penned in, so trapped. Even in London, working in the quiet apartments with her father, rarely going out, seeing few people but those of the household, she had not felt so trapped. She had been so unimportant that nobody noticed her; she had felt safe. She could go out if she really wanted to; Mrs. Llewellyn would take her shopping with her and on a rare visit with friends. Or her father would take her to the warehouses and docks to see the ship coming in from the Orient, their own ship, the *China Princess*.

She felt a wild longing to see that ship again, to be sailing back to England. But it could not be. She was here, pregnant with the child of the prince of the House of Chen, and she must stay and have the child. No escape now for a long time, many months, even if Rupert should contact her.

And Rupert might never contact her; she might never hear from him again, not in this life. A pang went through her, a terrible homesickness, a longing to see England and its green fields, the white cliffs of

Dover as the ship came home. London streets, dirty, smelly, but lively and bustling. Women strolling in their full skirts and bonnets, maids at their heels, peering into shopwindows. Men striding about, peering into shop windows. Men striding about, late or coffee in the coffee shops, their pipes being puffed vigorously. All the street scenes of London, the orange barrows, the sellers of lavender, the old clothes peddlers, the newsboys, the carriages trotting through the streets with fine horses prancing and tossing their manes.

"The dowager princess asks when she may come to see you," said Moon Blossom, and Katie came abruptly back to the present.

"When she will," she said listlessly.

"Will tomorrow be all right, for luncheon? The dowager does you honor by asking," warned the girl.

Katie nodded. "I am honored. She may come and have luncheon with me. I will inform Joy."

Moon Blossom studied the downcast face, nodded, and presently she left Katie to her thoughts.

Prince Chen came in the cool of the evening. His face blazed with joy as he questioned her again. "It is certain you are to have a child by me?"

She nodded, smiling; he was almost like a young boy in his eagerness. "I think you are very much pleased." She dared tease him. "I have not seen such a smile in a long time!"

He did smile down at her again, his arm curved possessively about her still-slim waist. "You have made me so happy; I cannot tell you how happy. I had quietly despaired of having a child," he confessed. "My honorable mother advised me to take a second wife or a concubine. However, I had little interest in this. One wife was quite enough, I told her."

Katie concealed her revulsion of such talk. It was their custom, and she had to accustom herself to such.

"I thought all the day during my meetings of the joy to come," he told her. "I hastened back to you to have you assure me I had not dreamed what you said."

"It is true, Elder Brother." She leaned against him, pleased that in spite of all her troubles, she had brought pleasure and happiness to him. He was a good man, with many responsibilities. He had done much good for others; he deserved to be happy. She could look ahead and figure out what would happen. Perhaps she would remain here all her life, bearing his children, helping raise them, learning to reconcile herself to the loneliness of being an Englishwoman among Chinese.

"I have spoken to my former tutor, who now studies with my younger brother, Prince Chen Lo," he said presently. "We have consulted together and also with my mother. It is not good for one with your lively mind to be much alone. And I must be away sometimes this summer and autumn. So I have thought of a plan, and they have approved it."

"What is that?" she asked cautiously.

"Moon Blossom wishes to learn from you; she admires your learning, your ability to write our language, to add, and to compose poetry. Would you be willing to teach her?"

"I should like that very much!" said Katie eagerly. "Oh, she could come every day and be with me—if you approve!"

"Yes, each day for a couple of hours when I cannot be with you. Also—" He hesitated, then continued. "It is not usual, for men to be with women in this way. However, I have asked my distinguished tutor to come for two hours each afternoon, with my young brother, to learn English from you and what history you wish to tell them. My tutor, Wu Lung, is a good and gentle man, with a scholarly reputation, and he would like very much to widen his knowledge. It is most unusual to have a woman teach a man, yet he realizes, as I do, that you have much to teach. You would do this?"

Katie's brown eyes widened. This was indeed a concession, she realized, knowing how the Chinese and Manchu felt about women and learning. The Manchu had much more respect for women than the Chinese had, and many Manchu women directed their households for long years while their husbands were away at battle. They were clever women, autocratic, like the mother of the prince, with imperious manners. But for one to teach!

"It would be a great pleasure for me if they will learn from me," she said slowly. "Perhaps it could be a combined teaching. I will teach them English, and the history of England, and our customs. And Wu Lung would teach me more of the Mandarin language, Chinese customs and ways and correct my writing."

"That will be good. I do not wish you to tire; you must stop at once when you are weary and protect your health. However, I believe you are happiest when your quick mind is busy and your hands are sketching and writing." He smiled down at her with such understanding that impulsively she hugged him, throwing her arms about him. He was not shocked at her action, but rather pleased, and hugged her carefully and put his cheek against hers.

"Oh, thank you! It is so wonderful to be understood!" she cried, tears starting in her eyes. "It feels so—so lovely that you comprehend how I feel!" She wiped her eyes quickly as he looked his distress. She managed a smile. "Only my father knew my feelings and cared about them."

"But of course I do," he said quietly, and sat with her on his lap in the big armchair inside her drawing room. "I think that is an important part of loving, to understand the important things of the beloved, what means most to her. One cherishes as one's understanding grows. The more of you that I learned, the more I loved."

She pressed her cheek against his broad chest. "That is very wise," she said, her voice muffled. If only Rupert had known and understood that, how different their lives would have been! They had been married such a short time, though, and Rupert had lived much with men at war. Even so, Terence had shown no such understanding; so perhaps this was rare in men. The prince was a rare man, she thought, and she said so. "I believe you are different from most men—above them, for your understanding of people is profound."

That pleased him. He disliked empty compliments, disdaining flattery. But Katie had learned that honest words frankly spoken did please him. She was revising her opinion that all men must have flattery to please their egos. The prince had no such need to build his ego; he was head of the House of Chen and owed obedience only to the emperor himself. It was like the English royal family, thought Katie. None of them needed flattery, for their worth was obvious, yet their courtiers set themselves to flatter, not knowing how many could see through them.

The prince stayed with Katie all that night and many other nights. He did not attempt to make wild love to her; he had told her bluntly that he might damage the child. Instead, he caressed her, spoke poetic words to her, talked tenderly of the coming child. She had never felt so loved, so protected, so cared for. Nothing was too good for her.

He showered gifts on her, such as gowns with fuller waistbands, and fans huge and impressive which her maid would set to work by a tapping of her foot, so both were cooled in the heat of the day. He gave her long chains of gold with sparkling gems on them of rubies, diamonds, emeralds, jade of all sorts and varieties, in jewelry and in statuettes of goddesses and Buddhas, little houses of jade, intricately carved objects, and little ivory pagodas and large carved ivory balls.

Every day he came with gifts, and when he could not come, he sent them in silk cloths by way of Moon Blossom. He kept her supplied with oil paints, fine writing paper, brushes of excellent camel hair. Beautiful tapestries would appear on the walls of her room. A gorgeous parrot in red, yellow, and green was brought, reminding her of the other one he had given her which had remained in Macao. A huge cage of several canaries arrived and brightened her day with song.

The dowager princess had come to luncheon. She had been so kind and warm that Katie had confided in her.

"I am afraid because I do not know much about giving birth," she said. "I have never been around when a birth—happened. I know nothing of it, having been raised by my father."

"But of course. I will help you," she said. "I will tell
you anything you wish to know," the dowager said
pleasantly, and like a mother, she informed Katie of
the processes. She talked about care of herself during
pregnancy, abstaining from sex during the first
months until it was certain the baby was well set in
his little womb.

The dowager also spoke of the women who would
attend Katie. Two had been present at the births of
her own sons, and other younger women would come
to assure all went well. They were skilled in mid-
wifery and had brought many many children into the
world.

The dowager seemed pleased to have her advice requested. She set women to working on small clothes,
and weekly the little garments were brought to Katie
for the fragrant cedar chest in which they were kept.
Other women knitted blankets, and the dowager consulted Katie earnestly over the patterns, what colors
would please her, which designs were good omens for
her. When Katie requested colors of both rose and
blue, these were made. When she asked for flower
patterns, these were promptly carried out by her designs. Garments of all sizes were created, for a child
from one to three years.

Her afternoons were happier also; she was rarely
alone except when she wished to be. Moon Blossom,
Prince Chen Lo, and his tutor, Wu Lung, came daily.
They sat in the shade under awnings and worked or in
the lovely airy drawing room during the hot days of
July and August and September.

Katie taught them English slowly, first words, then
phrases and sentences. She corrected their speech,
going over and over the first few words until they

were right. Then she would go on to more difficult words and longer expressions. They progressed rapidly, all three of them, including Moon Blossom. She was so eager to learn her face glowed, and she practiced every morning and night as she sewed, she confided.

Katie found that Moon Blossom could not read or write in Chinese. So she began to instruct her in that also, and Wu Lung indulgently helped them both. She taught them all about arithmetic and writing in Arabic numerals and how the English added, subtracted, and so on. She would talk to them for an hour or so every other day on the subject of England, and they listened with fascinated wonder at the marvels. She told them stories, finding that was the best way of all to teach, stories of going out to shop on a London street and what they would see. Stories of Cornwall, and walking along the cliffs, and seeing the fishermen returning from a night of fishing.

She would stumble sometimes, searching for the right words in Mandarin to describe such sights. Her own vocabulary was of trade words, polite speech, words about art and painting, jade and porcelain. She searched for words to say "fisherman" and "bonnet-maker" and dancing a waltz or forming a set in a cotillion. But Wu Lung was quick to help, and he had a scroll on which were printed many English words. He would unroll it rapidly, pursing his lips over it, and come up triumphantly with the right word and phrase, his graying hair standing up on end as his fingers had run through it. Often their sessions were punctuated with laughter as they vied with each other to find the right words and laughed at their mistakes.

Moon Blossom had been a third cousin, lowly in the

household. Now she glowed with the attentions given to her. She was devoted to Katie because her gentle nature had drawn her first to the girl, and now she wanted only to help her through this difficult time. And she was learning! Her mind craved learning. She worked day and night to do her sums correctly, to write with fingers curved about the brush in the correct manner, and to read.

Prince Chen Lo was a serious young man, yet with a keen sense of humor. He had an engaging, shy young personality, and he added much to their sessions. The tutor, Wu Lung, was about fifty years of age, and his scholarly face had heavy lines; his chin was covered with a long gray beard. But he was kindly, understanding of their mistakes, and patient in correcting over and over.

As the heat of the afternoon faded and lessons were coming to an end for the day, Prince Chen Yee frequently would arrive and listen. He would watch and observe thoughtfully, and they all tried hard to please him and show him what progress they had made. He listened to Katie's recitation of a poem in difficult Mandarin, showing how her accent had approved. He listened to his brother recite a résumé of English history about the times of Henry VIII. Or Moon Blossom would shyly read aloud a little essay she had written about what she understood of English ways.

He gazed at her in surprise sometimes, his little third cousin, with glowing face and sparkling eyes reciting. She had a good mind, in addition to her gentle heart, he said to Katie, and Katie agreed. "Yes, a quick mind, she is learning very rapidly!"

"She is young and female, yet she seems to absorb knowledge as a sponge absorbs water. I did not know

Chinese women of her class would wish to study such matters. In fact, I know of no women who do but you."

"Perhaps others would wish to learn if they had the opportunity."

He shook his head dubiously. "It is not the custom to teach women anything but household matters. Yet it does make a female more interesting to a man, I believe, if she can read and write and speak of important matters to him. *Hmmm*, I wonder if girls should be taught in academies, as you said. My mother is very wise, but she cannot read and write and says she has no wish to learn."

"There are many kinds of wisdom, and your mother is both wise and virtuous," said Katie tactfully. "Her good heart causes her to be loved as well by all in your household."

She had soon learned that because of the way other women acted toward her when they came with the dowager to luncheon with her and Katie. Only one person was feared here, and that was the haughty and cruel princess Chen Mei-ling. It was too bad that marriage had ever been arranged, was Katie's opinion.

18

It was early September. Heat lay heavy on the courts, and people stretched out to sleep where they lay. Katie smiled to see her cook and maid, Joy, stretched out, both snoring, on the cool tiles under an awning.

She had been so hot and uncomfortable that night she had slept little. She was still sick in the mornings, and after eating a biscuit and drinking some tea, she had refused breakfast. She had strolled around and around the court and finally settled to draw the parrot in his cage.

He squawked, and she glanced up absently, feeling heavy in her cool cotton dress. It was a simple gown; one of the elderly ladies in the next court had made it for her of the peasant blue and white embroideries. Katie had been delighted with it, for the heavier warm silks and brocades were almost unbearable in this blistering heat. Her praise had pleased the lady so much she promptly set to making another gown, and other ladies did also, of the quaint peasant embroideries on cotton: designs in butterflies, little houses with children playing in them, a fisherman in his boat, all decorated in blue and white cotton.

Katie had been so pleased that she had asked if the ladies might make some little gowns in this material for her child-to-come. She thought they would be much more comfortable for a child than the elaborate gowns and robes coming in a steady stream from their clever fingers.

She had explained what she wanted to the dowager princess, and the orders had been promptly made. The little ladies were giggling with pleasure that the mother of the prince's child-to-come wished the work of their hands, and practically a small factory was set up in the next courts. Some cut, some stitched, some embroidered, and over their chatter and cups of tea they worked eagerly, glad to have a little part in the excitement over the coming child.

Katie yawned. It was such a hot morning. She had not slept well; the prince had not come. He was planning a journey of some days beginning this morning. He had said farewell the evening before, holding her tenderly for a long time.

She would miss him; he was so kind and understanding, anticipating her wishes, doing all he could to make life sweet for her. She was sinking into a state natural for women in her condition, so the dowager assured her, of resting much, walking some, her mind turned to the child, nothing else much of any matter.

Even the guards lay in the shade, snoring, all of them. That was unusual. Usually some of them stood erect, on guard, their long poles lightly laid across the passageways, in symbol that none might enter without permission.

Katie sketched again, gazed at the pattern. Perhaps an unusual color combination might be of interest. She was drawing some peasant scenes, like those of the women, remembering the trip by canalboat from Shanghai to Tientsin. She drew the rest of the scene, a small figure of a scholar seated at his table, drawing, absorbed, as the dragon boats slowly passed near him on the narrow canal.

Then she picked up her box of oil paints to choose the first colors. Beginning to become very absorbed, she paid no attention to sounds. The squawking of the parrot roused her from her work.

She glanced around, the smile of welcome freezing on her lips. For it was not Moon Blossom coming, or a small party of the dowager and her ladies.

Several men in dark blue garments, big men, tough-looking, were coming toward her past the sleeping guards! They crept on stealthy bare feet, massive, intimidating! They saw her staring at them, and with a bound one reached her and grabbed at her.

Katie found her voice and began to scream. Her easel fell over; the box of paints fell with a clatter on the tiles. Joy and the cook did not stir, snoring on the tiles. The guards did not move. What was wrong?

The man who reached her first slapped her face with such a shocking force that she could not scream again. He clapped his dirty hand over her mouth then, cruelly holding her jaw tightly. Another man came, close, staring at her with curiosity.

He said, "This is the foreign woman. Look at her white skin, and she paints with brushes."

"But why does she not sleep? Enough was put in the food—"

Five men crowded around, muttering. Katie was in a daze of fright, her hands still clutching her brushes.

"Quickly, let us go, this way—to the carriage—"

One man picked her up. The first man still held her head in his hard hands, so she could not speak or scream. They carried her quickly from the court in a direction she had not gone before, through empty courts, over grassy parkland, toward the dirt road where a carriage sat. On the tiles she had dropped one brush.

One muttered, "I do not like this. The prince of Chen is all-powerful." Katie dropped another brush on the parkland.

"She assured us he would not interfere. He goes on a journey." Katie flung down another brush as they reached the road.

"But to rape and kill this one—"

Katie went cold with shock. To rape and kill—She—who was she? Mei-ling, of course—she had finally struck!

One man glanced nervously over his shoulder as they pushed Katie into the crude dusty carriage. She landed on the floor with a thump. Oh, my baby, she thought, and began to scream. She yelled with all her might, and she called for the prince.

"Prince Chen—help—help—helllppp!" she cried in English, then in Chinese.

One man landed on the seat above her, grabbed for her. While he groped in haste, she continued to scream, striking out savagely, clawing with her fingernails.

"This is a little beast!" said the man angrily, and he slapped her deliberately hard with his big hand. She slumped and lay half-conscious on the floor of the carriage.

"By the gods, some come—" cried a man, and all piled into the carriage. One caught up the reins, clucked at the horse, and drove off wildly down the rut-filled dusty road. Katie lay bumping in the darkness, huddled to protect the child, curling up in a defensive gesture to protect her stomach and thighs. Her arms were wrapped about herself. Her shoulders and hips ached where she had fallen after being flung into the carriage. If only she had the strength to throw herself out, but in her dazed state she could not move. She moaned on the floor, moaned again. "Oh, Elder Brother," she moaned. "Ohhhhh, Elder Brother—"

"What does she say?" muttered one man worriedly.

"Elder Brother."

"Is it the prince of Chen? Is she so close to him? Oh, we are in much trouble—"

"*She* said it was a filthy foreign woman of no account," said another man furiously.

"*She* gave too much money. We should have suspected—"

"Some come following us!" cried another, and the horse was whipped up. Katie lay very still, listening.

She heard cries of "Stop—thieves—stop!" as they rode along. But the carriage went rapidly, bumping on the roads, and the cries were left behind.

It was no use; if anyone had followed her, he would soon be left behind on foot. She prayed then, desperately. "Oh, God, help me, help me. I am so lost—so alone—in this strange country—no one cares. Oh, God, please—help me—help me—help me—"

She was murmuring in English; they paid no attention. The men were preoccupied with their worries, muttering to each other. They must have entered the main city and had turned into a narrow alleyway. She saw gray walls about them. She knew then they were in one of the many hutungs of old Peking, where gray tiled alleys with blossoming plants in pots were lined with houses. Only doorways faced the alleys, and one entered to find a bright house built around an inner courtyard. One after another in a maze; no one could find her—

They would take her into one of those places, rape her as ordered, for they were blindly obedient to orders. After hours of agony she would be killed.

It was her last chance. They were dragging her from the carriage; she clung to the carriage door, to the step, forcing them to use violence to hold and drag her. And all the time she was crying out.

"I am of the House of Chen—help me—help me. I am of the House of Chen—House of Chen—help me!"

She saw people in the distance, men, women, children, an old gray-haired woman staring, coming closer, in spite of the cursing of the men.

"She is my woman, a disobedient, dishonest female!" cried one of the men in fear. "She has wandered away from her duties!" And they tried to drag her into the doorway of one gray house.

Katie clung to and clawed at—by nails, by fingers that were raw—the doorsill, a plant in a huge pot. She kept crying out, bit a hand that tried to silence her, cried again.

And into the narrow hutungs, in the lanes, came a grand sedan chair carried by four enormous men naked to the waist. The curtains were flung back, and the prince himself was inside. He ordered the chair down, and he stepped outside with a terrible look on his face.

The half-naked men had been running; their bronzed chests and backs dripped with runnels of sweat. But they scarcely breathed hard as they let the chair go and went after the men in dark blue. The men let Katie go and scattered, screaming with fear.

The prince stood over Katie, directing his men in a

firm, loud voice. "Get that one—there—he tries to escape—"

A sword cut down the man, and he screamed once, and then his head rolled from his body and landed in a gutter. The people gasped, backing away, too fascinated to leave the scene, too caught in the drama to think of escaping.

A carriage rolled up near the sedan chair, and more men poured from it.

The men in dark blue gathered their courage and turned knives on the coming men. Maybe they knew their hours were numbered, even their minutes, and they fought with desperation, knife against knife, clashing, so the narrow alleys were filled with the cries of fighting, the clink of metal, the groan of an injured man. Katie lay against the gray wall, exhausted, watching with incredulous eyes as the men fought just beyond her, kept from her only by the prince with his drawn knife. He stood above her, only glancing quickly at her from time to time to make sure she was all right. She lay pressed against the wall, and his legs stood sturdily above her prone body as though he dared anyone to take her from him.

One man clashed with two burly men and lost, one sticking him in the chest with a knife that went through to his backbone and came out the other side. He fell with a cry, still alive. Another's chest was covered with bleeding cuts; still he fought on, his eyes wild with terror.

The prince watched all impassively. His arms were now folded over his chest.

It seemed to go on and on, but finally it was over as abruptly as it had begun. One man lay moaning, two guards with knives and swords over his body. Another lay still and silent. The other two gave up, arms about their bodies, cringing.

The prince motioned. The men were caught by the arms and dragged before him. "Who has ordered this?" he asked harshly, his voice guttural.

The men stared proudly, for all their wounds. He stared back at them.

"One more opportunity to speak before going down to the dog of hell! Who ordered this?"

They did not speak. "Kill them; cut off their heads," said the prince.

Katie could not believe this was happening. He stood over her as the men were made to kneel, heads back, and one man held one by a pigtail. Another man slashed; the head was severed from his body. The other one was grabbed, his head held by the hair, his head slashed off. The other two were lifted up, and likewise, their heads knocked off.

The prince watched in somber silence. When it was over, he beckoned to an elderly man who shuffled up and bowed down to the bloody alley floor.

"I am the prince of the House of Chen. You will have these men shoved into some hole in the earth and dirt flung over them. All shall know them for the dogs they were."

The man kowtowed to the ground. "It shall be done, Honorable Prince."

The guards were wiping their swords and knives, faces inscrutable. Any cloth would do; they wiped the blood on their loincloths or the garment offered by an old woman from her clothesline. The little crowd was silent, eyes wide, watching and listening.

Prince Chen stooped then and gathered Katie up into his arms. "It is over, my beloved," he said, and carried her to the carriage near the end of the hu-tungs' entrance. She saw dimly curious faces watch-ing, the gray walls, a small pot of a bright red gera-nium, like blood against the gray wall. Then she was being lifted into the carriage, carefully, and the prince held her in his arms. The curtains were lowered, the guards sprang up to the seat, and the horse was turned about in the narrow space. Other guards fol-lowed. They picked up the sedan chair with its trim of gold and velvet and carried it to follow the carriage.

Katie felt faint and sick, half-numb, half-cold with fear that remained. She thought of the thick gouts of red blood and wanted to vomit. But the prince held her closely and wrapped his own robe about her to warm her and stop her shocked shivering.

"It is all over, my beloved," he kept crooning to her as he rocked her slowly back and forth in his arms, like a child. "All over, you are safe."

They drove slowly, carefully back over the dirt road to the walled home of the prince. The carriage drove right inside to the prince's court, before the massive columns.

"Not there," Katie managed to whisper as he would have carried her inside. All she could think of was that Princess Chen Mei-ling would be there, malevo-lently, like a snake ready to strike again. "Home—to my own—court—please—"

The prince nodded, face inscrutable. He carried her in his own arms down the long passageways through other courts, past small courts of the elderly people. She saw there was a great commotion among the courts. Younger women bent over the elderly ones. Other strong men were raising guards, holding them up, arms about them, carrying them away.

"What happened—to them all?" Katie asked.

"They were drugged, all of them, with some strong sleeping potion," said the prince shortly. "Do not talk now; do not trouble yourself over others."

In her own court Joy was being raised by two burly servant women, but the maid hung limply between them, her head hanging, her eyes shut, snoring. The cook was in as bad a way.

The prince carried Katie to her room, laid her down gently on the bed, and began to examine her injuries. Her hands were bleeding, scraped by her efforts; several fingernails had been torn. Her head bled at the forehead, and her clothes were dusty and ripped. She felt bruised from head to foot.

The dowager princess rustled in with several of her women, her face disturbed, her gray head with a formidable headdress on it, her gowns elaborate. Evidently she had been disturbed in some formal ceremony. Then Katie remembered: The prince was going away today, and there was always a great ceremony on his departure.

"Have the women bring hot water," said the prince curtly. "Bandages, herbs, salves. She has been hurt."

"The child?" breathed the dowager, hands at her breast.

Katie managed to speak. "I protected him—as much as I—could. I think—it will be—all right—"

"Hush, do not speak, rest," urged the prince, bending over her. His black eyes burned like coals, but his voice to her was gentle and soothing. "You will be bathed; you will rest and be very calm. Was a drug administered to you? Do you feel very sleepy?"

Katie shook her head. "I did not eat breakfast this morning," she recalled. "My stomach was still upset."

She closed her eyes and rested, trying to calm herself, as they moved about her and murmured to each other. She must be controlled, she must relax, or the child could yet be damaged. The shock had been terrible.

She heard the prince say, "It must have been in the breakfast food of them all. The guards—more than twenty of them? Yes, the older women also? All the ones around here, more than forty-five persons! Also her cook and personal maid. How could this be? Who dared to administer all the drugs to them?"

"I will investigate," said the dowager in a low tone. "Forgive me, my son. I was in charge of their food; it must be some neglect of mine. If this is so, I shall accept my punishment," she added humbly.

Katie opened her eyes. "No, it was not your fault," she managed to say.

The prince asked sternly. "What do you know of this?"

And she remembered. When he had caught the men, he had ordered their heads cut off! If she pointed a finger at Mei-ling, the woman would be beheaded as well! Much as she feared the woman, she could not condemn her to death.

"I would trust—your mother—with my life," she said quietly. "It was not she." And she shut her eyes again, but not before she saw the gratified look on the older woman's face.

The prince went away to discover what he could and gave orders for the care of all those who had been drugged. The dowager assisted generously in the care of Katie, ordering her bath water to have healing herbs in it and personally supervising the salving of her hands and the bandaging of them.

She crooned over them. "Poor, dear hands. Poor, dear hands. How dreadful this is. My poor daughter-in-law. How dreadful." She had never called Katie this before.

Katie was just settling down to rest in the silken sheets once more when Moon Blossom came. The girl had torn her hair; it lay about her shoulders in a dark, misty cloud. Her face was pallid, shocked. She flung herself at the foot of Katie's bed.

"You are saved, saved," she whispered. "Oh, thank the gods of heaven!"

Katie was puzzled at the look of the girl. Surely she did not blame herself! She felt too weary to question the girl, though. Her body wanted only to sink into the mattress and to sleep.

The prince returned, however, and Katie was amazed to see Moon Blosom prostrate herself at his feet, her head on the dusty tiles. The maids were just clearing up the bath water which had splashed from the tub, and two were carrying out the heavy copper tub of warm water. They bowed to the ground and managed to carry out the tub at the same time—no small feat.

The prince tried to raise Moon Blossom. "What troubles you?" he asked kindly. "I owe you a debt of immense gratitude—"

"But my rudeness was so dreadful!" she whispered. She would not rise from where she groveled on the floor. "How my heart is full of gladness that Mistress Katie is saved. But my mind is shamed, I am shamed, that I was so rude to you. I screamed in my lord's presence. I flung myself at his feet, preventing him from moving. I prevented his departure with my miserable body. I interfered with his plans."

"And you caught my legs in your very hands to prevent me from moving," said the prince with a twitch of his fine large mouth. He looked at Katie, his dark eyes reflecting both the humor and the agony of the moment. "Imagine, if you will, my beloved. The formal gravity of a departure, the sedan ready, all giving me their good wishes for a safe journey. The priests scattering incense, all in auspicious embroidery robes. And in hurls this small one and flings herself at my legs and clasps them in her hands and screams at me."

"Oh, miserable me!" moaned Moon Blossom. "What rudeness, what peasant manners, I do not deserve to remain here. Fling me into the countryside whence I came; crush me down. To touch your honorable person so impolitely. I am a miserable poor wretch!"

Even the dowager smiled gently at her bowed head. The prince bent and lifted her up firmly and held her by the shoulders. Still her head hung down, the hair hiding her pallid face.

"I have not heard yet how you came to know what was going on," he said more seriously. "What warned you? How did you know Katie was being carried away?"

"I was going to take luncheon with her, having heard she had no appetite for breakfast. I saw her tray returned to the main hall. I wondered at it, for usually her cook prepares all. As I walked along, I saw the courts of the elderly ladies, your esteemed cousins and aunts, and all lay asleep, most unusually. One lay snoring on her back in a most undignified position, her embroidery still in her hands. And then I saw the guards, all—all lying asleep, their poles disturbed. I stared, I wondered—I feared— I heard Katie scream; I

knew it was she. I glanced down the long path; I saw
the dark blue clothes of peasants. It was then I ran to
you, oh, Honorable Prince."

He nodded. "And your warning came to me in time.
I took the sedan chair and followed the paths. I came
to the outer courts and saw one of the paint-brushes
on the ground. We saw the men in blue clothes as she
told me," he said to Katie. "We saw the carriage drawn
up, waiting, saw you being dragged along. I urged my
men faster, but the carriage went off. I was in an agony. My men ran as never before; I must reward them
all."

He put his arm about the shivering child beside
him; the girl looked up at him adoringly.

"Forgive my miserable self for my impertinence,"
she whispered.

He smiled down at her. "Forgive you? There is
nothing to forgive. I owe you the life of my beloved
and that of my unborn child. You shall ask of me what
you will; nothing is too much to give you for what you
have accomplished today: the foiling of the kidnap
and murder of my love."

Moon Blossom blushed and hung her head. Her
voice was muffled. "I ask only to serve your beloved,
Master. And to serve the House of Chen, which has
sheltered and cherished me all my days."

"Your sentiments do you honor," he said quietly.
"But we shall see you have more rewards. Your courts
shall be better; you shall have maids of your own; you
shall be honored for protecting the House of Chen.
Ask what jewels you wish, they shall be given, gowns
of more formal attire, a finer place at my table. And
you shall be called by me Little Sister."

She tried to bend to the ground to kowtow before

him, but he refused to permit it, holding her before him. He pressed a formal kiss on her forehead. Then he said, "Withdraw now, and rest, and make yourself clean without ashes on your forehead and hair. There is no shame and no need for forgiveness. You have done well."

"May I speak something to Katie first, Elder Brother?" she whispered. He nodded. She came over to Katie, bent over her, kissed a bandaged hand. "How thankful I am," she said. "How thankful I am—" Her voice broke.

Katie smiled up at her drowsily. "You have been such a friend to me, Moon Blossom. How can I thank you also?"

The girl shook her head, tears in her eyes, and went out, bowing, moving backward to the entrance of the room.

"If she had not come, if she had not insisted on interrupting the ceremonies," murmured the prince. He shook his dark head. "She had the courage of our family; she has a bright mind and good appearance as she grows to maturity."

The dowager nodded her huge headdress. "She shall have a good husband; we shall arrange a fine marriage for her," she said. "She now deserves it. I am surprised that I did not recognize her good qualities. She seemed always humble and shy."

The prince frowned slightly. "Do not arrange anything yet. I may have some plans for her."

"Yes, my son," said the dowager, and bowed her heavy head. "Only permit me to assist as I may."

"You are very good to your devoted son," he said politely. He glanced at her; she bowed and withdrew from the room, leaving him alone with Katie.

He sat down beside her on the bed, smoothing back her loose hair. "Does my songbird feel a little better?" he asked gently.

She nodded. "I will sleep. Do you—go on your journey now?"

He shook his head. "No. I shall not leave you. I shall plan otherwise."

And he did not leave, to her great relief. Instead, he ordered his younger brother, Prince Chen Lo, to take his place. The younger lad was flattered at the great honor and went out with his tutor on many journeys, learning how to deal justly and fairly with their people and many problems.

Prince Chen Yee did not openly accuse his wife of having arrange the mass drugging of his people or the carrying off of Katie. However, the princess was sent to her family for a journey of six months. She was to remain until after the birth of the child. People whispered behind their hands and nodded wisely. There was much talk, but no answer to their questions. No one said for sure. But one had heard screaming from the princess's quarters; she had torn her hair, someone said. The prince had been cold and judicious. She had not confessed to anything, she had denied all, the whisper went around.

Katie had nightmares about the beheadings of the men. Prince Chen Yee soothed her. He said that dispensing of quick justice was the only way to handle such criminal acts.

"It is the best way to deter crime so that people will see it does not pay to do evil. They will be deterred, if not by the good in their own natures, then by the swift punishment that will come from criminal acts. What man would think to accept a bribe to carry off a good woman, knowing that he will be caught soon and his head cut off? No, it is best to do what must be done, swiftly and before an audience, so that word may be carried to all."

She was badly shaken by it all, but knowing it could only hurt her child if she brooded about it, she tried to put it from her mind. She filled her days with work. Moon Blossom came each afternoon. The prince came more often. The dowager came with her ladies, with good advice, with embroidered objects for the child.

Katie took pleasure in handling the little clothes. She invited the little elderly relatives of the prince to come for tea, a few each week. She gave them rice cakes and honey cakes and coconut cakes, which they ate greedily. The elderly ones craved sweets and crunched away on them with their few remaining teeth, sucking up the sweet hot tea with loud appreciation.

On these occasions they would bring their gifts wrapped in rice paper. When the tea drinking was over, they would hand the gifts to Katie and watch with bright, wise eyes as she opened the papers and exclaimed over their embroidery.

What loving care went into the fine little stitches! Each little blue and white peasant cotton cloth was finely made. She admired the little dresses, the vests, the tiny pantaloons, the small slippers with curled-up toes. And some ladies of the dowager's court brought fine velvets embroidered in the symbols auspicious to their house, the sea horses especially. And there were the symbols of ever-lingering joy, lasting good fortune, honorable estate, conquering over all evil, and so on.

She filled her days with receiving guests, meeting the dowager and hearing advice, getting acquainted with the many relatives of the prince. And best of all was the frequent visiting of Moon Blossom. She was such a comfort, devoted to Katie's well-being, beaming at being a special member of the prince's family.

The prince visited her morning and night. He rarely slept with her now, anxious about her body as she grew heavier. The nights grew colder; he would sometimes come in the middle of the night to make sure enough blankets were over her and furs tucked about her.

It was a relief and kept her from feeling more stress to know that the princess Chen Mei-ling and her servants were far away, more than a thousand miles, said Moon Blossom. That malevolent presence close to her would have been distressing and a constant reminder of what the woman had tried to do.

At least for these months she would be safe, and she settled into a routine which would be best for her and for the child to come. She worked some at painting and designing. She walked about the court, slept well, ate the foods planned for her as best for an expectant mother. And she occupied her mind much of the time with reading and listening to books being read by the tutor, Wu Lung, when he and Prince Chen Lo returned from their journeys.

All seemed in a pleasant conspiracy to make her feel comfortable, wanted, cared for, amused, and entertained. It was a good life for those months, and Katie settled into enjoying it. If she was not under stress, it would be all the better for the child.

19

Prince Chen Yee had decided not to go to Macao for the winter. Katie had thought he would not go because he was worried over her condition. Yet it was in a way a bitter disappointment. The traveling might be dangerous, but in Macao she would have been close to other English people; she might have got word to a ship of her father-in-law that she was alive and well.

Still, he might not have welcomed such word, knowing at the same time that she was with child by a Manchu prince! Katie could not plan anything; her life was bound up in the coming child, and all must wait until the birth was accomplished.

As the cold winds of autumn gave way to the bitter winds of winter, Prince Chen Yee insisted that Katie should leave her own court and move into the warmer palace. The elderly ladies and gentlemen were already moved in, and the palace rang with their chatter and laughter and the patter of their feet. It was crowded but comfortable; everyone ate together in the great hall and exchanged gossip over tea.

Katie agreed reluctantly to move. She liked her own court and felt more at ease there. She knew Princess Chen Mei-ling had left and would not be there for months, but still, that evil presence seemed to linger in the great palace.

Katie had feared she would not have any more privacy. But the prince had arranged for her to live in a small suite of rooms on the sunny side of the palace, near his own suite. Her maids came with her, and Moon Blossom attended her daily.

Her rooms were large and airy. The bedroom was huge, with a formidable but comfortable four-poster hung with thick crimson silk draperies which were pulled at night to keep out the unhealthy night air— and also any cold drafts that might creep in around the windows and doors. The prince had ordered her bed furnished with silken sheets, quilts, and furs, so she curled into them at night with a feeling of utter luxury and warmth.

Her drawing room was also large, with tables, chairs, and sofas in the Chinese manner, of beautiful red cedarwood and lacquer. Sofas were covered with thick velvet cushions. She could sit up straight on a cane seat in one of the wide armchairs or curl into a sofa with cushions, according to her mood. Her painting easel was brought and set in an alcove with bright sunshine or at least some light even when the skies were gray and stormy.

She had her own bathroom, and hot tubs of water were brought when she wished. The rooms were warmed with charcoal heaters, and if she did not wish to travel the long halls to the great dining room, she could have trays in her rooms.

Prince Chen Yee came daily to see how she did. He would linger whenever he was not holding court or being requested to attend the emperor, also in residence in the Imperial City. They would talk, and sometimes he read to her of history or poetry, literature or travels.

The lessons were continued whenever she felt well

enough, and that was most of the time. Moon Blossom came for instruction, seeming to soak up learning with the eagerness of a child. Her mind was bright; her willingness, endless. The prince nodded in approval. She had her own rooms now and her own maids and sat closer to the head of the table in the dining room, near Katie. Her modesty kept her from gloating over it; her face showed that she had the approval of the man she adored, her cousin the prince.

Occasionally the prince took Katie out when the sun shone and the winds were not keen. Wrapped in a thick fur coat of white ermine or of lustrous sable, she would walk with the prince along the long paths through the now-deserted courtyards, gazing at the brilliant blue sky, the distant snowy mountains, the city of Peking, or the Imperial City with its red lacquer gates and high walls.

They would walk slowly, sometimes talking, sometimes content to be silent, his arm about her, helping her so she did not stumble with the weight of the child.

"The women say you will have a large son," he said one day in late December, helping her carefully over the tiled walk where some fallen leaves made the path slippery. "You carry the child in such a manner, and your belly is very large."

"Either a large child or twins," she said ruefully. "I had not dreamed I would become so big. I hope they are right. You wish a son, of course?"

What would happen if she had a large and ugly daughter? Would she be discarded in disgrace? Perhaps then he might allow her to leave!

He did not smile. "I have not dreamed ahead of what will happen," he said seriously. "I am holding my breath that I am to have a child—can it be true? Such joy, I had thought, would not be for me. I was planning a good marriage for my younger brother, to follow me with his children. I had thought I might never have a child."

She squeezed his arm impulsively. "I could not believe that. You are so virile, so masculine." She blushed at his look. "The very first night," she said shyly. "I could not believe how you—were with me. It must have happened very soon that I became pregnant."

"I had so longed for you, so hungered, so desired—I could not hold back," he said quietly. His arm held her close to him. "I had never felt so with any woman. I had been—fastidious in my youth, much occupied with learning, with my duties. I had little time to play and no wish to idle my precious time with loose women, as many men of my wealth could do. It was distaste that kept me from doing so. I did not wish to think I had a woman many men had had. And I hated disease," he said frankly.

She nodded. What she had not known about men she had been learning from the women whom the dowager sent to her. Along with teaching her about pregnancy, childbirth, and caring for a child, they would gossip and giggle about the prostitutes, the court ladies, frivolous and idle women whom men had in Peking.

She was beginning to realize how sheltered she had been in London. Selina's coquettish behavior was beginning to make sense. Terence and Rupert probably had had their doxies, as they called them, though Rupert had been gone so long at the wars she had heard nothing of them. Katie had known that Mrs. Llewellyn, in spite of disapproving of Selina, had accepted her with resignation—she was not so bad as some of the London "ladies." And of course, Selina was young and beautiful and did not have the reputation yet of a loose woman, however popular she was with the rakes and Corinthians.

Remembering Terence's last words, Katie realized he had become disillusioned at the last with his wife's frivolous behavior and her longing for the company of other men. How was Selina behaving in London now? Katie wondered. Was she—perhaps—still chasing Rupert? Or had she found other, wealthier men who would be attracted to a rather well-off widow?

"Of what do you think and sigh?" asked the prince as she was silent for a time.

Katie glanced up at him. His eyes were keen, and she must be honest, she decided. "I was thinking of Rupert, and Terence, my brother-in-law, and Selina, now his widow. I wondered what my husband was doing in London."

The prince frowned heavily, something he had not done in her presence for a time. "I thought you had forgotten him," he said curtly.

Katie shook her head in the white ermine bonnet. "No, I cannot. He is still my husband." She held her breath, waiting for his response to that.

"He neglected his wife; he did not deserve her." And he deftly turned the subject. "Look at the evergreens, how beautiful they are in their winter green coverings. We do not notice them so much in the spring and summer and autumn. Then the peach attracts us, and the plum in its delicate bloom, like ghosts in the moonlight. We admire the crimson maple and the shivering willow. Now, in the winter, we can admire the green trees that bravely keep their trim when all else has blown from the other trees."

He spoke so poetically to her and so gently she accepted the change. She did not want to make him angry. Yet it was true, she was still legally married to Rupert.

"Tomorrow I will go into the hills to see how the woodcutting progresses," he said. "I could send someone, but I prefer to go myself and show the men that I am interested in their good work. Would you like to go with me if you feel well?"

"Oh, I would like that!" she said eagerly. "Any chance to ride in the carriage and to see something more of China is most welcome! Shall we truly go into the hills and mountains and perhaps see the snow?"

"Yes." He smiled indulgently at her. "You shall see the snow, and the white rabbits which run about, and the few birds that remain to sing to us in the winter. And perhaps we shall sight the deer that live there."

And he did take her the next day, with a sizable retinue of his men. The men rode in splendid procession on their magnificent sturdy and beautiful horses, showing off for their prince, veering away from the carriage and back again.

The carriage drove steadily up into the hills, so high up in the mountains that the snow was there, white and pure in the sunlight and blue in the shadows under the thick evergreens.

There was a patch of trees lacking their leaves in a clearing where smoke came from a hut. The men were gathered about the hut, some drinking tea, some stacking the wood they had cut. Others were among the trees, steadily sawing wood.

The prince left four men to guard Katie in the carriage, where she sat wearing her sable coat and wrapped in other furs so only her small face peeked out. She watched with keen interest as the prince walked among the men. He shook his head when they made to kowtow and laughed with them at shy jokes. She could hear the ringing of their voices.

Two men had a contest to see who could chop down the tree the fastest, and it ended in a tie. The prince shook their hands gravely and gave them presents.

He observed the cutting, walked around the thick, high cords of wood, and nodded approval. He drank tea with them and finally brought Katie a beautiful porcelain cup filled with hot smoky tea. "They ask you to drink with them to the honest work of wood-cutting," he said.

She smiled and drank eagerly. "The tea is excellent, strong as the men and with the odor of the woods," she said.

"Thank you. I will tell them your words," he said, and took the cup and went back to them.

They left about noon as the men were ready to eat their midday meal of bread and thick cheese and drink more tea. They gathered around the carriage to see the prince and his woman drive off. The broad peasant faces beamed at them.

The prince said after they had left the clearing, "These men are the fortunate ones. They are healthy; they work hard and earn money for their families. I am worried about other men—those who are sickly and unable to work and die young. Their families are distressed; even the smallest children must work if any work is found, or they starve to death. Some

princes are cruel to their people, demanding more and
more in taxes and work. I cannot endure the injustice
of it, but what can be done? China has millions of
people; bandits roam the countryside ready to make
the people rise up against their masters. Guards must
put them down—"

He seemed to be talking to himself, frowning, gazing out at the snowy landscape. Katie was quiet, letting him talk, yet wondering about him. She had seen
poverty in a couple of their carriage journeys, especially in Peking, where children played in gutters and
small boys carried heavy loads. The women seemed
gray and old, but they had small children with them,
which meant that they themselves were not old, but
worn with the burdens of poverty. The prince was a fair
and compassionate ruler. His responsibility was not to
be envied.

January came and went. Katie stayed more and
more in her rooms or only walked in the long hall-
ways, with a maid on each side of her. The prince was
worried about her, though he tried to conceal it. She
was so heavy with the child, and she felt slow and
awkward.

The women murmured. "Narrow hips," they said
again and again, glancing furtively at her. The dowager hushed them sternly, but Katie knew they were
upset, fearing she would lose the child on whom their
hopes for the prince's heir were set.

Moon Blossom stayed with her much of the day.
Now they did not study, but the girl played her lute
softly and sang many songs, soothing songs.

Early in February Katie wakened in the night with

pains. Her moaning roused her maid, who came to her sleepily, anxiously. The maid put her hand on Katie's stomach and nodded. "I must get aid," she said, and ran out.

She returned quickly with several women who were midwives. The dowager came soon after them, her hair in a hasty bun, her nightgown showing under her elaborate robe of deep blue. Their faces were anxious. "Too early," they said. "Two weeks early; the child is anxious to be born—"

The prince came, but he was shooed away for all his importance. He said as he left, "You must send me news regularly," and his anxious face was all Katie had to comfort her.

Moon Blossom was not allowed in Katie's room through the hours and days that followed. The birth took long.

The waters had broken, and Katie moaned with pain as the midwives tried to bring the child. They gave her pain-killing drugs, then stopped when the birth pains ceased. They feared the drugs would kill the child.

She heard voices about her as in a daze. The pain hazed her mind; she did not want to move in the warm bed, for movement brought on more pain.

"She has narrow hips," said one.

"I think the baby is turned wrong," said another.

"She is too small—"

The pain went on and on. Day turned into night, and back into day; all was gray to Katie. A lamp burned continuously in the room, and the charcoal heater was sometimes too hot and sometimes too chilly. Drafts curled around the bed as the women worked over her.

The pains came and went. Finally they came often, again and again. The dowager remained nearby, her mouth set, her eyes anxious. She consulted in low tones with the midwives.

"It is the third day," Katie heard dimly. The pain was wrenching her insides out. She thought her hips were broken, they hurt so much. "Something must be done, or the child will be born dead."

"No, no," moaned Katie. Not the child—not after all this time, this pain—

The women conferred, and two tried to bring the child. Katie screamed with the pain, and the baby started to come.

"Shall we give her more drugs?" asked one woman. "Opium will ease her—"

"No," said the dowager sharply. "It might relax her so much she cannot bring the child."

"But the pain is killing her; she bleeds very much. Shall we send for the prince?"

"No, no," said the dowager again. "The child is all important. Bring the child. The foreign woman does not matter as much."

The words rang through Katie's mind as the pain wrenched through her. She lay mostly unconscious, but something penetrated from time to time. The words had reached through the gray fog surrounding her mind. She heard their echo again and again.

Her own screams roused her. The child was being taken from her body. Oh, how it hurt—it hurt—her hips were broken—her body was broken—she felt weak, so weak, struggling against those firm, cruel hands—

"The foreign woman does not matter—bring the

child—bring the child—the foreign woman does not matter—"

She moaned feebly. She no longer had the power to scream, to beg them to leave her broken body alone. Oh, the pain, the pain, the burning, crushing pain—

Was this what it was to die? This pain, was it dying?

She had not felt so with the fever. The fever had burned her, but it had been clean and pure and calming. She had drifted away gently on a stream of smoke—

"*Ahhhh*, the child—it is a boy! The prince has a son!"

Katie heard the women laughing and crying. The voice of the dowager, her commands—

But then she fainted and knew no more.

When Katie came to, the night was gray, the curtains drawn around her. Only a faint cold draft crept around them and had wakened her with its chill on her face. She was numb except for the pain in her hips. She heard the crack, crack of rifles. . . . What was that?

She stirred; the maid, Joy, crept to the bed, peered around the curtains with concern. Her beam shone broadly as she saw Katie's eyes were opened.

"*Ah*, you are awake!" Her piercing whisper penetrated. Katie tried to lift her hand; she was so tired, so very tired—

"I will bring hot tea, some hot broth," whispered Joy, as though she might wake someone. She went away to return presently with the hot broth and the dowager.

The woman bent over Katie. "How do you feel; is the pain less?" she asked kindly.

All Katie was able to think of was how the woman had directed, "Bring the child. The foreign woman does not matter as much." Her eyes filled with tears.

"You will eat, then rest," commanded the dowager.

"How is—the baby?"

The woman's face crinkled into a broad smile, as wide as that of Joy. "You have brought forth a son! My son has given me a grandson! What a big strong boy he is! Did you hear the fireworks?"

"They still continue," said Joy as Katie sipped at the broth. "May I have permission to open the curtains?"

Katie nodded weakly. Joy turned and spoke to someone, and a woman opened one side of the bed draperies, then the thick window draperies. Katie's eyes widened when she saw the great colorful rockets of light as fireworks burst over the palace grounds. Great massive white light became red, then blue. And then huge lanterns burst forth, from which came smaller and smaller ones, all blazing colors of light.

Katie watched in wonder as the fireworks went on and on. She heard cheering faintly in the distance. "For—my—son?" she whispered.

"For the son of the House of Chen," said the dowager proudly. She patted Katie's shoulder kindly. "You will rest now. You have done well. We are pleased with you!"

But they would not have minded if she had died so long as the son lived, she thought, and weak tears rolled down her cheeks. She felt so alone and afraid. Nobody cared if she lived or died. In her weakness she felt frightened that no one loved her. No one cared about her. She was important to no one in the world.

Only the child was important. She was not important. If she lived or died, it was of no matter. No one cared—

The maids closed the curtains softly, and she composed herself for sleep. It was the next morning when she wakened. She could see the daylight creeping through the line of the draperies at the windows.

She lay gathering her strength. If she could only leave—

But it was impossible. She could never get away—

She felt so helpless, so weak and tired. Her body felt wrenched to pieces; her hips ached; her breasts hurt.

And the child—where was the child? When Joy opened the bed-curtains and smiled at her, she croaked, "Where is—my son?"

"He is safely in the rooms of the dowager princess," said Joy. "He is in the hands of the wet nurses most carefully chosen."

"Wet—nurses?"

"Those who will feed him milk from their breasts," said Joy. "Only clean ones were chosen; you may be certain of that! The dowager herself questioned the women."

"I want—my son—here."

Joy was puzzled and afraid. She went away, returned with the dowager.

"What is this?" asked the princess calmly. "Why are you upsetting yourself?"

"I want—my son," said Katie obstinately. "Bring—my son—here!"

The dowager frowned. She was elaborately dressed

today, and the Manchu headdress in great wings over false black hair made her appear strange and formidable. "That is impossible. You are not well enough to care for your child. You must first recover your strength. Do not worry, I shall take great care of my grandson!"

"But I have not even seen him!" Katie said angrily, and began to weep. The dowager muttered to one of her women and went away. Presently she returned with the boy wrapped in a thick white blanket.

The child was set gently beside Katie. She turned herself painfully in the thick bedclothes and peered at his face. It was a small miniature of that of the prince!

The small face was an imitation of his father's, dark brows, a firm chin small as it was, a fuzz of black hair, a strong nose. She gently opened the blanket, and the dowager smiled indulgently.

"The boy is perfect," she assured Katie. But Katie had to see for herself.

She examined the little hands, counted the fingers. They were long and slim, like those of the prince. His feet were large for his legs, firm and well turned. He would be a big boy; he was large already. The eyes opened; the vague eyes looked up toward her. And her heart turned over.

He was exactly like his father. And yet so small, so helpless, the small fists waving as he wakened. His small pink mouth opened; even the lips were the same shape as those of the prince, large and molded firmly. Katie touched his pale pink cheeks; he gurgled and a bubble came from his lips. She crooned to him, "Oh, how pretty you are, my son! How handsome you are— oh, my son—"

"What do you say?" asked the dowager, and Katie realized she had spoken in English to the baby.

"I said—he is perfect, he is so handsome, just like his father." Katie sighed.

It was an effort to speak Mandarin; she was so tired. She lay back, folding the blanket over the baby's legs. They moved to take the child; she protested.

"No, no—I will keep him! Bring his crib here!"

"You are not well enough to care for him," said the dowager firmly.

Katie protested again, but they took the baby away. She lay weeping softly, tears of sheer weakness. Presently the prince came in, and smiling broadly, he approached her bedside.

"What is this? Tears? Are you not happy, my beloved, the mother of my son?" He sat down on the bed beside her and bent to kiss her lips.

"They—they took—the baby away," she murmured. "I want him here! He is my son! I mean to care for him!"

"But you are so tired from the birth, my adored," he said gently. "I will not have you disturbed. My mother and the wet nurses are caring for him, and two midwives assigned to him. They will have every care for him. I see him morning and evening and sometimes in the afternoon also." He smiled, his black eyes shining. "What a handsome child you gave to me!"

She relaxed a little and managed to smile. Gently he wiped the tears from her cheeks. "I am weak, yes," she admitted. "But when I am recovered, I want the child here in my rooms. I want to feed him and care for him. It is the English way, and I will not be parted from my son!"

"Of course not," he said to soothe her. "You shall have him in your care."

"You promise this?" she asked sharply. She had the strong feeling that the dowager would be reluctant to give him up.

"I promise it," he said. "The child belongs to you as well as to the House of Chen."

She thought of Princess Mei-ling returning. She wanted the child out of the palace before the woman returned. But she did not have the strength to worry about that now.

She lay back in the pillows, feeling the hurt in her body. The prince was stroking her thin hands. "You are much better now, my adored?" he whispered. "I came to see you several times, but you were unconscious at first, then sleeping. I was worried about my beloved."

His concern was soothing. "I feel—better. The birth—was difficult, was it not?"

He nodded. "Yes, I feared—that is, I prayed to the gods for your safe delivery and the birth of the child. Many of us prayed and sent up much incense."

She had been close to death then. She brushed aside the thought, but it lingered beneath the surface.

"How do you like your son?" he murmured, brushing his lips against her cheek.

"He is very handsome."

"I think so also. Very big and strong and handsome."

She smiled, managing to tease him feebly. "He is the image of his father!"

The prince grinned widely. "I know! My delight is beyond bounds! You heard the fireworks? I ordered many pounds of them and feasts for all the people in my palace. When you are better, you shall have another feast, and all shall bow down to you and my son." He sighed. "I never thought to be so happy. A son, and in my image! A strong boy, who already knows his father's voice and opens his eyes!"

He stroked her hands as she began to drowse, unable to remain awake for long. "You will sleep now, my beloved," he whispered. "When you waken again, I shall show you the gifts from our gracious and much-honored emperor, the son of heaven. He sends many gifts to my son and wrote a poem for him."

"I shall be—most pleased—to read—the poem—" But sleep was overcoming Katie. She felt comforted, soothed as the prince's large hand was smoothing back her thick, loose hair about her forehead and cheeks. He was close; no harm would come to her—no harm—now—

20

Katie was slow in recovering. Her torn body rebelled at movement. She had to force herself to get up out of bed, to hobble about the room. However, she was determined to recover soon, to take over the care of her child, and to leave the palace. She wanted herself and her son out of there and back in the Court of the Flowering Peach before the princess Mei-ling returned.

Unfortunately she did not achieve her goal. The princess had returned with great fanfare in less than two weeks, Moon Blossom informed Katie.

"Oh—she is back?" Katie could feel the chill of the news, as though a great deadly snake hovered over her, hooded, malignant.

She must have gone pale. Moon Blossom patted her arm, soothed her, spoke honestly. "Your guards have been increased, and none may enter without the permission of the prince. Only the dowager princess and I may enter without this. You need not fear her, though she is very jealous of you and the child."

"The child," whispered Katie. "I must have him with me—"

Moon Blossom nodded, understanding, but she dared not say much. Katie saw that in her worried face.

When the dowager came in next, as she did every afternoon on informal visits, Katie spoke to her at once.

"I am now recovered, madame, and wish to have my child with me."

"But the wet nurses attend him regularly. You must not be disturbed," said the princess complacently. "He is quite content in my quarters."

"Prince Chen Yee promised me that the boy would be with me as soon as I was able to have him. Now I am able, and I will nurse him myself!"

The dowager raised her hands gracefully in horror. "No, no! No woman of the House of Chen nurses her own child! No, you will have the best wet nurses!"

"I wish to nurse the child myself!" Katie realized she was going to have a battle on her hands and steeled herself for it. If she lost this battle, she and the child might die.

"Only peasants nurse their children," scoffed the dowager.

Katie studied her and thought quickly. "Peasant children are very strong," she finally said.

"Strong?" The dowager frowned, looked amazingly like her iron-willed son, with black brows drawn together.

"Strong," said Katie. "Their mothers nurse them. They receive strength from their mothers' breasts. It is true, I have observed it in my country," she said very firmly, not at all knowing if it was true.

All she knew was that she had to have her child. For him she would lie, she would cheat, she would do anything. For the first time she understood how a person could kill. To protect the child, she would do whatever she had to do.

The dowager hesitated. "I will consult with my son," she finally promised.

And Prince Chen told her to take the baby back to Katie. It was borne back by the dowager herself and regretfully laid in the crib prepared by Katie, a wicker basket on legs, with downy mattress and pillows and cotton sheets.

"I put him in silk; he is a prince," said the dowager.

"Cotton is more comfortable for his little body," said Katie firmly, holding the baby securely in her arms. She managed to smile at the older woman, whose hungry look told of her love for the child. "You must come often to visit him so he will know his grandmother well."

The dowager relaxed and smiled, pleased. "Already he opens his eyes more often and looks about him," she said fondly.

When she had departed, Katie tried to nurse the child. Her breasts ached with milk, but she feared she had not enough for the large child. How relieved she was when after the first day or so the milk came freely for him.

Prince Chen Yee came in the morning to see the child. He watched as Katie fed him, his look causing her to blush. "I must write a poem on seeing my woman feeding our child," he said softly. "It is a beautiful sight."

"How large and strong he is, see his little feet," she said, caressing one of the feet in her hand, as the baby fed at her breast. "He will be a tall man, I think, with such feet."

The prince leaned to look at the foot, caressed it and the small arm. A hand groped for his, and fingers gripped his thumb firmly. The prince gasped; his black eyes glistened.

"Why, he is strong already!" he exclaimed.

"Yes, is he not wonderful?" The grip held; the prince sat quietly while his son held the thumb in his small fist. There was such pride and joy in his face, such wonder, as he looked down at his son.

When the feeding was over, Katie reluctantly put the boy down in his crib. He needed the sleep, much as she loved holding him. He lay quietly, his body relaxed, his wee face calm. He had such serenity, she thought. He was not red-faced and fussy, as she had seen other babies be. He was a much loved and much wanted child, and he seemed to sense it!

The prince had brought with him some gifts today. Now that the feeding was finished, he set them about Katie and watched her open them. They all were silk-wrapped, and several were bound in golden yellow ribbons.

"These are from the emperor, the son of heaven," said the prince, indicating those. Opened, they revealed many honorable and costly presents: a jade rattle, tiny enough for the baby's hand; dresses of crimson brocade of several sizes; robes of costly embroidery in gold and silver. And a ball that bounced! Katie held it curiously, wondering at it. She had never seen such a ball. "It is from some southern country, brought in tribute," said the prince.

There was a beautiful musical box also—lacquer-inlaid decorated with gold scenes of children playing. When opened, the box played a little tinkling tune, very soothing and amusing. And there was a fine gold watch made in England. She touched it and thought:

The young prince will not be ready for this for many years!

"As soon as you are well enough, there shall be a great formal reception in the grand hall of the palace," said Prince Chen Yee. "The baby shall be named at that time, and all shall kowtow to him. I wish to ask you about his name."

He spoke kindly, but Katie thought he had probably already chosen the name. "What names are—auspicious—for the House of Chen?" she asked cautiously.

By his smile and look of approval she knew she had asked the right question.

He told her the names, and between them they chose several for the child. The name Chi-chi was one of them, and she decided to call the child by that one because it sounded small and adorable. Then she added, "Would it be appropriate to add the name of your tutor, Wu Lung? He has been most kind and is a man of much wisdom."

"That is a magnificent thought and would honor and thank him for his dedication to our family." The prince was very pleased. "I shall make him the other father of the child, as some of you say, the godfather."

The prince surprised her at times with his knowledge of England and its ways.

So in a couple of days the great hall was prepared. The dowager chose the clothes for Katie and for the baby and accompanied them down to the hall with her women in a great procession. Joy carried the baby carefully in her arms, not on the pillow, for Katie had protested against his being carried on a slippery pillow. The child was garbed in a soft white cotton cloth dress, embroidered in blue peasant embroidery. It was more comfortable for his small silky body, Katie had insisted. Over this and concealing the peasant dress was an elaborate robe made from a gown given by the emperor, which hung two feet below the baby's legs. The robe was of crimson silk velvet, embroidered in gold, with signs of sea horses on waves, a wave border, and an auspicious continuous-happiness hem. The same decoration covered the wide long sleeves. The baby had been fed, and he had slept before the event. As Katie sat down in her chair in the great hall, he was set on her lap, and she held him so he could look out over the hall and also be seen.

She wore the gown the dowager had chosen for her. It was more formal than any of her others. The undergown was an elaborate silk robe of royal blue embroidered in silver. Over it was another deeper blue robe, also in silver, with a wave pattern on the hem of the gown and sleeves. It was embroidered all over with auspicious symbols of the House of Chen, sea horses, peach blossoms, pearls, a fan, a sword, and an elaborate phoenix matching the one on the baby's robe.

The prince took his place on the top level of the chairs, his chair of gold and his robe of gold and crimson. On the next level on each side sat the dowager in crimson and his wife, the princess Chen Mei-ling, in black and silver. On the third level was Katie's chair, directly below that of the prince, and the baby was in her arms.

First, the prince came to kowtow to the child, and he then bent and kissed the small fist of the baby and then his forehead. His dowager mother came next and bowed deeply, her face serious.

Next came the princess Mei-ling. She bowed low,

gracefully, but as she rose, her black, malevolent gaze was fixed first on Katie, then on the child. Katie shivered as the gaze swept over them. It was like a promise of evil. She held the child closer to her.

Next came the prince Chen Lo, then Moon Blossom, and then the tutors of the court, including Wu Lung and his brother, Wu Hsun. Wu Lung, as the godfather, then took his place standing beside Katie's chair, a staff of wisdom in his hand. His face was dignified and proud; his beam flashed out uncontrollably from time to time as people congratulated him on his honor at giving his name to the child.

All during the ceremony, as one after another the people of the court came up to kowtow and promise loyalty to the small prince, Katie kept thinking of the evil in the look of the princess Mei-ling. She meant them harm, Katie knew. And she was powerful, and cunning, and wealthy, able to bribe whom she wished.

The ceremony took long, for all the people had to come up and peer at the baby's face. The baby finally yawned widely several times and fell asleep. That did not stop the ceremony; it flowed on around him as he slept, quite unconcerned by the babble of voices, the laughter, the comments about him.

"What a beautiful child. Very auspicious birth!"

"What a handsome baby. Just like his father!"

"He is strong, brave, good. Just like his father!"

The polite comments were always just loud enough for the prince, his father, to hear them and be pleased.

Gifts were piled on the next step: large and small gifts, all wrapped in silk cloth and tied with bright ribbons. Katie's arms ached with the child after a while, but she would not stop the ceremony; all wanted to see the child. She smiled at the little elderly ladies and gentlemen, who had been so kind and interested and had done so much beautiful embroidery and sewing for the baby. She recognized many of them and was able to call them by name and thank them.

And last came the guards, marching past, with staffs erect and backs stiff, coming to pledge their fealty to the baby. He was sound asleep by this time, or he might have been frightened as the guards saluted him with staffs slapping smartly on the polished wooden floors.

Always, in spite of her smiles and gracious words to the guests, Katie was aware of the princess Mei-ling just above her and to the side on the next step. The princess sat very quietly, as one accustomed to such ceremonies. However, from time to time the slippered foot near Katie would begin to tap-tap-tap, impatiently, as though fury were bursting in her and must show in some way in her stifled body.

It was a relief to have the ceremony over. Everyone remained for the long dinner that followed. Katie was excused, though, and allowed to return to her own rooms with the baby. It was time to set him down to sleep peacefully until his next feeding. She rested, then ate a more simple meal from trays brought to her.

The next day she began to think how soon she might return to the Court of the Flowering Peach. She felt restless in the palace, and very uneasy, for all the guards. Mei-ling had managed to reach her before; she could again. But a snowstorm had come, and bitter winds raged through the empty courts, knocking down trees, blowing off tiles from the tiny gay roofs with their upturned corners like little smiles. She could not return until the winter ended and spring came.

The prince came in the morning to assist in the opening of the many gifts. Moon Blossom helped also and then carried away the gifts to be kept in fragrant cedarwood chests against the time the prince would need them. Some of the garments were big enough to fit him when he was eight or ten years of age. All would be kept forever, into his old age, and handed down to his children.

At noon the prince said he would share in Katie's luncheon. He had something else for her, he said.

"More gifts?" she protested, waving her hands. "I am overwhelmed with gifts! You are much too generous!"

He smiled at her, his face open and pleased with her; his gaze lingered on her body. She was the mother of his child, and his look approved the fuller breasts, the wider hips, the languid air of her recovering limbs. She wore today a loose cotton robe of blue and white and over it a warm robe of blue silk with fur hem and cuffs of mink. Her hair lay loose on her shoulders, thick and glossy brown.

"This gift is your own making," he said to her surprise, and his smile broadened. He went over to the table and took some lengths of silk which she had thought contained more presents. He brought them back to her and laid them on the table in front of her. He sat down beside her on the sofa and lifted the first length. "Do you recognize this, my adored?"

Katie stared, lifted the end doubtfully—then saw the sprays of peach blossom and the little butterfly in the corner. The designers of silk had copied her design exactly, even to the little betraying mark in the corner of her initials circled by the butterfly. She gasped.

"Oh, my pattern!" she said. "For the silk merchants!"

"Yes. They have sent to you samples of all the designs they made up of your patterns. With your approval now they will send these off to Canton to be sold in the English market. You will look them over, and I will send your approval to them if you will. These lengths are long enough to make fine gowns for you should you choose."

He opened another length, flung it across the table. The English primrose looked a little stiff, but it glowed in pale yellow on the almond background, surrounded by lengths of ivy vines. And in the corner a butterfly hovered over a single rose.

He opened another length, and lotus blossoms of rose and unusual azure blue floated on pools of pale blue brocade. The lengths were heavy and luxurious silk. He then opened other lengths of lighter fabrics, some so thin and fragile they could slip through a wedding ring. The colors were marvelous: shimmering white, cream, pale rose, smoke blue, celadon green, blue-green of the sea, violet, silver, gold.

Katie slid her hand under one length of almond cream, and through it her hand could be seen clearly. Even so, it had been done in a pattern of spider-web delicacy, with wide-winged butterflies hovering over a field of daisy-shaped flowers.

"I have never seen such delicate fabrics in my life," she exclaimed in awe. "The workmanship is beyond compare! The English will be wild with delight—and my father-in-law will make much money in selling them," she added absently.

"That pleases you?" the prince asked gently, studying her face.

She nodded. She glanced up at him, her gaze shadowed. "I cannot help—thinking of them," she said awkwardly. "I am sick for home at times. Forgive me," she added in a low tone as a shadow came over his face.

"The year just past has been the happiest of my life," he said deliberately, holding her hand carefully in his. "I had hoped that it was somewhat happy for you also. I have never known such joy, such happiness in a woman, such pleasure and delight in knowing that my child was coming. I was distressed at your pain on the birth, yet this is natural, I am told. I had hoped—the birth of the boy was a delight for you also."

She was silent but clung to his hand. She searched for words.

She did not want to hurt him. Yet she had to be honest, for it seemed he could see right through her and know the truth, whatever her words. She lifted her gaze to his and met his look.

"I will tell you how I feel," she said delicately. "First, I owe you much joy and happiness. Never in my life have I felt such—" She began to blush, then went on bravely. "I have never felt such pleasure in my body and mind. You are an exquisite lover. You have given me so much joy—I cannot with any modesty tell you—" She was blushing wildly now; she felt hot from head to foot.

He pressed her hand. "That is how I feel," he murmured, his eyes glowing. "I cannot say in words, though I have tried, how much delight I had in our nights together. Such joy, such ecstasy."

She nodded, and her head bowed. "And your gifts, your kindness, your thoughts for my comfort. All that— it was so strange to me to be cherished." She struggled to put her feelings into words and groped for them as he watched her gravely. "Never in my life, except a few times with my father, have I felt cherished, for I was—of little account, I thought. You made me feel— important, wanted—the object of much care and attention."

"I wished you to feel that way," he told her. "And what is wrong, my songbird? You are troubled in your mind, for all my concern for you. Does the incident of last autumn still haunt your dreams?"

She nodded, gaze averted. "I am haunted by that, yes. And your wife—hates me. I fear for my son!" she blurted out. "I cannot tell you—how I felt in the great hall. All the kind people, but her—her malevolence—"

He lifted a hand, halting her impetuous speech. "You speak of my wife so. I cannot allow it. Yet I comprehend. All is done to protect you. And I have warned Mei-ling she is to honor my son on pain of her death!"

"You have—warned her?" Katie wondered how much good it would do to warn the woman. She was so clever—

"Yes, so you need have no fear of her. What else then?"

Katie thought of the dowager's words: "Bring the child. The foreign woman does not matter as much." She knew the woman would have great care of her grandson, but what if Katie had another child, what if she remained and insisted on her own way of raising the boy?

Yet she could not speak all these vague complaints to the prince. She drew back from him, her face troubled. He studied her keenly. "Anything else?"

She finally shook her head. "Only," she said in a low tone, "that I am homesick for my country. I long for the green fields, for speech with my countrymen and women. I feel like a stranger here, a foreign woman. I fear I always will feel like a stranger. How can I remain, and my son?"

He was silent for a time, then finally rose. "You will be more comfortable," he said firmly. "I shall see to this. Now I will leave you to rest. In the next few days look over the lengths of silk carefully. If you disapprove of them, so mark them. If you approve, I will send a letter to the silk merchants to allow them to send the lengths on to Canton. You will let me know soon? It is almost the end of February; the English ships will have all left soon."

"Yes, I will let you know." She felt a little chilled at his formal departure. He was disappointed that she was not completely happy for all his care and presents. But it was not presents she craved; it was security besides love.

She feared for her life and that of her son.

She rested for a time, then got up and went over the lengths. She was pleased to find that each block of design had the butterfly around her initials, so delicately made that it was not noticeable. But Rupert would know. If he saw these silks, he must notice her initials, the *K* and the *L* that he had wanted her to use. If he ever saw them—

Perhaps one of the English ships in harbor now at

Whampoa would carry these lengths to England. Rupert must be watching for a message from her if he cared at all. He was a man of duty and obligation. He would make it his duty, she thought with longing, to make sure he did all possible to find Katie and know what happened. Perhaps he would return to Canton, to Macao.

Finally she decided. It would take courage, and skill, to write the correct letters. And it would take much luck—or fate, as the prince would say—to send a message to Rupert. However, she must try in desperation. She longed for the familiar look and smile of Rupert, his brisk English manner, his hard work, his dependability. He had loved—probably still loved—Selina. But he had cared for Katie, and she was his wife.

She wrote first a message formally to the merchants.

> I, Katie Llewellyn, now of the House of Chen, commend you for your most excellent work on the silk lengths. These from my patterns have been accomplished with much skill and dedication and artistic ability. Please send them to Canton consigned to English merchants, for they are patterns much appreciated in the English market. I wish them sold only to Englishmen.

She signed her name in the characters and then turned to another page.

> A message to Rupert Llewellyn in care of the merchant Houqua. Dearest Rupert, I am in the House of Chen in Peking. I miss you and wish to

return home to England. Pray try through our embassy to contact me, and do not give up trying to reach me. I wish to return home to England.

Signed, Katie Llewellyn.

She sealed this message, wrote Houqua's name in Chinese characters on the front, and put it inside the message to the silk merchants. She did not have great hope it would reach them, but miracles could happen, and she would pray daily that the message would reach Houqua and, someday, Rupert.

She could scarcely sleep that night. She was awake with her worrying when the baby wakened and began to cry. She got up before Joy and, taking the baby, slipped back into bed and began to nurse him. She whispered in English to him, "Oh, little Chi-chi, we may go home one day. I will show you England, and you will forget this land of your birth. You and I are not safe here!"

She brushed her lips on the baby's soft, silky head with the fuzz of black hair. She wondered if he would look Chinese or Manchu so much that people would point at him and stare and whisper. But he was her son! She must keep him close to her and protect him.

The next day the prince came to see her. After the usual greetings he sat down.

"I have looked over the silk lengths and approved them all," Katie told him nervously. Was he looking at her curiously today? Could he see through her? "I wish to send a message to the merchants, thanking them for their good work."

"Where is the message?" he asked.

She had been afraid of that. "It is in a silk cloth envelope, all sealed," she said bravely. She pointed to the table, where the silk envelope lay beside the scattered lengths of silk.

She had fastened the envelope neatly and brushed the name of the merchant firm on the front of it, so that any opening would disturb the address. She had hoped the prince would not wish to read it.

He got up in a leisurely way and went over to the table. He fingered the silk lengths, scattered there, and she realized she should have folded them neatly. Their disorder spoke of her own state of mind, worried and disorganized.

Then he took the silk envelope and deliberately ripped it open. She could not keep from gasping. His face was enigmatic, grave. He opened it fully and read the message to the merchants.

Then he turned to the other envelope of white paper, folded neatly, with the name of Houqua on it. And again it was opened. But he could not read English, she thought wildly, her hand to her breast.

He lifted the page and began to read silently. She knew by the way his eyes moved that he was reading! He could read English! She had thought he understood it when one spoke, but to read it—and he had never told her.

Aghast, horrified, she watched as he read it deliberately, once, twice. Then he stood up, and went over to the charcoal stove. He had the two letters in his hand. She cried out, "No, do not destroy it, do not destroy it—"

She cried out in English, then in Mandarin, and she knew he understood. But he deliberately opened the iron door of the charcoal stove and pushed the two letters inside. He watched them burn, his back to her, and she began to weep.

Her hands went to her face; the tears were running down her cheeks. She fumbled for a handkerchief and pressed it to her eyes. She sobbed aloud.

"Oh, you should not. I must get a message to Rupert—oh, how could you? I must leave here—I am not safe—I must leave—I have to go home!" She wept like a child.

He came and stood before her. Through her lowered eyelids and the tears, she could see his strong legs planted before her. He was furious; she felt it emanating from him. She gathered the courage to look up at him, to gaze into the burning black of his eyes. He was very angry. Would he kill her? In her desolation she thought it did not matter; her agony would be over.

Her heart was full of grief. He gazed down into her face dispassionately, yet the black eyes burned still. He watched her gravely, as she wiped the tears from her face. Then abruptly he turned and left the room without speaking a word to her. He had never done this before in all their days and nights together.

21

Little Prince Chi-chi grew daily, or so it seemed to his fond mother. She held him as he fed at her breast, and she gazed into the calm face as he pulled vigorously for his milk. At two months he was well formed, growing nicely, his face round and handsome.

Katie was much happier. Just this week, the first week of April 1818, she had been moved back to the Court of the Flowering Peach. It was her birthday, April 3, and she was twenty-one. How happy she was to be there! She had never felt at ease in the massive palace, and had confined herself to her rooms, fearful of encountering the princess Mei-ling in a corridor or on the great stairs.

Now she was in the open air. The spring winds were kind today. The peach trees were in blossom, and the beautiful petals of creamy rose drifted at each passing wind. They scattered over the almond and blue tiles of the court and cast their fragrance also. She gazed up at the trees, remembering that first sight of such trees in the prince's palace in Macao. How much had happened since then!

She was more homesick than ever. Not a word, not a letter, not a message had come from the silk merchants and from Canton. No word from Macao. None, of course, from England. She wondered if anyone had tried to write and the prince had intercepted the messages. Or had Rupert and his family forgotten her, written her off as worse than dead?

She sighed as she gazed down at her child. Was there any hope of taking him to England? She began to sing to him as he finished feeding, and the dark eyes slowly closed. What long lashes he had on the pearly cream cheeks. How his firm large mouth reminded her of the prince. She brushed her lips against his forehead and sang.

She sang a folk song in English and talked softly to him. "Oh, my little treasure, what am I to do? How can I get home again? The days and nights are so long. I dream of England. Oh, if only my father were alive, he would try to get me home! He would not forget me!"

She sang again, but tears overcame her. To Joy's distress tears rolled down Katie's cheeks.

Neither noticed the dark shadow in the corner near the entrance to the little court. "Mistress, why do you weep? The child is well!" exclaimed Joy anxiously, coming up with a large white handkerchief.

Katie accepted it and tried to smile. "Spring has come, Joy, and I think of—home—far away."

"This is your home. Your man is here; your child is here," Joy dared to say, standing with feet planted far apart, hands on hips, gazing down at the Englishwoman and the child.

"Yes, yes, I know," said Katie forlornly. She dried her face, stood with the child. "I will lay him down to sleep for a time," she said.

The shadow moved; Katie turned sharply, her eyes wide with automatic fear. Ever since the attack she had been jumpy. Eyes startled, she saw the prince approach.

"Forgive me, I did not mean to startle you," he said easily, but his face was grave. He came to her and looked down at the child. "Let me take him," he said, and held out his arms for the baby.

She put the baby in his arms and wrapped a blanket about the little one because the wind was a little cool today. The prince sat down in the armchair and looked, absorbed, at the tiny face.

"How he sleeps," he said. "He does all with such single-minded attention! He eats; he sleeps; he laughs; he sobs."

"That is a baby," said Katie, smiling a little. She sat down opposite him and watched them both. His long arms curled about the child carefully, and he seemed as assured as ever.

"He does look like me, I can see it," he said thoughtfully.

Katie laughed, a little tinkle of pleasure. "Of course he does! He has your features exactly. Look at his eyebrows, they are yours, and the chin, even the ears. And his hands, just like yours."

After he had held the baby for a time, he allowed Joy to take him and put him into his crib in the bedroom. Then he sat gazing at the peach trees and their blossoms. He seemed grave today, not smiling much.

"You are happy and comfortable in your court?" he asked presently.

"Yes, Elder Brother. Thank you for allowing me to return early."

His eyes sparkled a little. "You have started an exodus from the palace. All the little elderly honored relatives have asked to return to their courts, eager for the fresh spring air. Moon Blossom has returned to her court."

"Oh? I have not seen her for two days," said Katie. It was odd, now she thought of it. "I suppose she was moving."

"Yes," said the prince. "I had thought perhaps you might wish to continue the lessons now that you are well. Is it your pleasure? My younger brother has asked if I will request it."

It would fill the days for her, and Katie nodded. "Oh, yes, it would be good. Does he not go on journeys now?"

"He will be home for a month. I will inform him that you wish to continue the lessons. Moon Blossom is to be instructed further in writing and reading in Chinese. She has a good mind. Wu Lung tells me she has an eager willingness to learn and much quickness in absorbing information."

"She is very intelligent," said Katie. "She is quick and eager to learn; one need only tell her once, and she remembers."

"Good, good," he said absently, slightly frowning, still gazing at the peach blossoms. "She has an honorable position now and must take up some duties in the palace with my dowager mother, learning the formal etiquette. It is my wish."

Katie wondered if he planned a marrage for her. Suddenly it occurred to her that maybe the prince was planning for her to marry young Prince Chen Lo! That might be as he was anxious to plan a good marriage for his young brother—one that would be happier than his own had been.

"Well, it is arranged then," said the prince. He arose and asked, as an afterthought, "You wish anything, my love? Shall I send anything to you?"

She shook her head. "I have paints, paper, all I wish. Thank you for your kind thoughts."

He bowed and departed. She wondered again. He had not come to her bed since months before the birth of the baby. She had been relieved, for her body had taken long to heal after the birth, and only now could she walk without stiffness. Yet he rarely touched her now, rarely kissed her, even on the forehead. She missed his attentions, missed his kisses. Had he tired of her?

She felt torn in two with indecision. Her own emotions were confusing to her. She wanted his love and caresses; she missed his expert and gentle lovemaking. Yet she had conceived so quickly with him—If she was going to leave him one day soon, if he permitted her to leave, then she had best not be with him. She could not travel if she were with child. He had not allowed it last year.

She bit her finger, nibbling at it anxiously. He had said no more about the two letters he had burned, yet she had felt a coolness between them. He was gentle, kind, thoughtful of her comfort. But there were no more caresses, no attempts to make love.

What did he plan? She felt sure he had something on his mind, he was so grave and somewhat absent of manner. Yet it could be only some problem of his little empire, some trouble among his people, some problem to be solved. Sometimes he was called to the Imperial City to give advice, and he would work for weeks on his report anxiously.

Well, they would not be visiting Macao until autumn, and that was five months away! Determinedly she turned to her painting and making of designs. She would not whine and mope about; that was not her way. She would keep busy, and that would make her more content and cause the days to go more rapidly.

The following afternoon the tutor, Wu Lung, Prince Chen Lo, and Moon Blossom appeared at the usual time for lessons. They gathered about the small cedarwood tables eagerly, scrolls and writing paper spread about, and began to work. Wu Lung began with reading a long essay on the history of the Chinese people.

Moon Blossom listened intently. There was something different about her today, thought Katie, her thoughts straying from the long recitation of dates and events. Moon Blossom looked radiant. Her cheeks were pink; she wore a rose gown covered with a deeper rose robe lined with silk. The hem and cuffs were of mink. Her hair was dressed high, with more dignity, in the wide butterfly pattern of the Manchu ladies. It shone glossily in the sunlight, and peach blossoms fell on the folds of smooth brown hair like jewels.

She was older; perhaps that was it, thought Katie. The girl was now about seventeen, and the dowager was grooming her for future plans. What were they? Katie was curious but knew she would have to wait to find out.

The lessons went well. About five the prince and his tutor bowed to Katie, thanked her for her hospitality and tea, and departed. Moon Blossom lingered, her eyes revealing a certain dreamy, quality that seemed to surround her.

"I am admiring your beautiful dress and gown," said Katie presently.

A very deep blush, the girl's face was rosy. "Prince Chen Yee honors me with his gifts," she said formally.

"And your hairdress, it is different and most beauti-

ful. Of course, your hair has always been lovely, but
now it is more—grown-up," Katie dared say.

"Yes, I am a woman now," said Moon Blossom, the
blush dying. Her head was up with dignity. "I am seventeen and must learn many lessons from my dowager
aunt. I must not run about and giggle aloud in company," she recited, touching her fingers as though she
were counting. "I must listen demurely and not inter-
rupt my elders."

Katie concealed a smile. "She has been teaching
you."

"I go each morning at ten to her," said Moon Blossom.

Katie then had to hide her surprise. Each morning!
That was why Moon Blossom had not come; she was
being strictly and rapidly groomed. For what purpose?

Moon Blossom excused herself presently. "I will return again tomorrow for history and writing lessons,"
she said. She peeped at the baby, then departed, moving gracefully along the narrow lanes until she was
lost from sight. The guards had lifted their lances respectfully to her as she moved among them.

Katie ate her supper alone; the prince did not come.
In fact, he had not shared her meals with her since the
baby had come. Was he still furious with her over the
incident of the envelopes?

But she did not allow herself to worry. She took
care of the baby with Joy's eager assistance. She
worked on silk designs as carefully as though they
would be made up, even though she was not sure that
would happen. She painted a picture of the baby
asleep in his crib, another of him lying gurglingly
awake on a blanket placed on the tiles in the sunshine.

She showed him in the latter picture with one foot kicking up, his arms flung out, blinking at a butterfly that hovered above him and peach blossoms that fell on him.

The prince came to see them in the mornings, about ten each day. He would linger for an hour, perhaps two, watching the baby play or sleep, talking idly to Katie. He was delighted with her paintings and asked permission to keep them. She gave them gladly, happy to please him.

There were no more poems written to her; his face did not glow at sight of her; he did not attempt to kiss her or suggest he would come at nights. Did he now despise or hate her? But there was no real sign of that. He was as considerate as ever, although more impersonal. She sensed it was as though he were waiting for something.

One afternoon in May their session of learning was unusually long. Wu Lung had been discussing the ancient wisdom, and they had gotten into a long talk about that. Moon Blossom had contributed her thoughts in a spirited, eager manner, and Wu Lung had listened respectfully, his long white hand stroking his gray goatee thoughtfully.

"Yes, Moon Blossom," he said finally. "I think you have comprehended the matter correctly. I am most pleased with your progress."

Her face glowed; she smiled and thanked him. Just then Katie noticed that Prince Chen Yee had entered the courtyard and stood motionless in the shadows, listening. She did not indicate his presence by a movement; she was curious.

He stood listening as Moon Blossom continued eagerly, speaking of the joy of doing one's duty. "There is a satisfaction that fills one's self with pleasure in the right accomplishment of the work," she said. "It is also good to have the approval of those one respects. The approval of others is pleasant but may be idle flattery. However, the approval of one who is high in wisdom and goodness himself is a sign that one is fulfilling her life."

Wu Lung caught sight then of the prince and rose to bow. The others became aware of his presence; he came forward in a leisurely way. "Pray continue your speech," he said.

He gestured that the others should remain seated and sat down in an armchair which Joy hastily brought for him. He listened in silence as they spoke, his gaze going from one to the other. Conscious of his close attention, the others became self-conscious, and the session was gracefully concluded by Wu Lung.

Wu Lung departed; so did his pupil, Prince Chen Lo. Joy brought out little Prince Chi-chi, and the prince took charge of him, holding him for a short time in his arms. The baby looked up sleepily at his father; Moon Blossom watched them both with a tender expression on her face. The baby kicked out and laughed as his father patted his stomach.

"You have brought your lute?" he said to Moon Blossom. "Pray, will you play for us? I think the child will enjoy the music and your gentle singing."

She flushed and bent over the lute. She sang in the Chinese manner, in a soft high voice, over the sounds of the plaintive lute. It was lovely; they congratulated her. She sang another song on the urging of the prince.

"You sing and play very well. Have you ever played the ch'in?" he asked.

"No, Elder Brother, I have never had that opportunity," she said. She turned to Katie, who looked her question. "The ch'in is a musical instrument of seven strings," she said.

"In the West it is called a zither," added Prince Chen Yee, further confirming to Katie that he could speak and understand English. "It is very lovely. I must obtain one for Moon Blossom and an instructor for her."

"It would be a great pleasure for me," she whispered, blushing.

"It is our pleasure that you play and sing for us. I am happy that you are so willing to take instruction in the feminine arts of music and song."

Katie was half listening, wondering if she should invite the prince, and perhaps Moon Blossom, to remain for dinner with her. She had been lonely lately—

However, the prince rose in a few moments and handed the baby boy back to Joy. "I must leave now. Moon Blossom, I will escort you back to your court and carry the lute for you," he said graciously.

She handed the lute to him in silence and gathered up her scrolls and writing paper and brushes. She bowed to Katie formally, a little question in her face. Katie bowed back, smiled, said, "Come soon again, Moon Blossom. I will see you tomorrow?"

"Yes, I come tomorrow afternoon at the usual time. Thank you for your hospitality." And she bowed deeply and gracefully.

Moon Blossom turned to leave, and her foot slipped on the blossoms in the tiled court. Before she could go down, the prince's hand had shot out, caught her firmly by the arm, and held her upright.

"Oh, I am so clumsy!" she gasped.

"Are you all right? Your foot did not turn?" asked Prince Chen Yee in concern.

"Yes, yes, I am fine. Thank you—"

They moved away together, the tall prince and the short pretty girl with dark hair. She wore pale blue today, and her long hair streamed down her back, caught in a blue bow, making her look quite young and lovely. Her small blue slippers with turned-up toes pattered along beside his feet.

Katie was gazing after them in amazement, the facts coming all together. The prince—and Moon Blossom! He touched her, spoke to her with a special timbre in his voice. She was maturing, glowing, a new confidence in her manner. And when she glanced up at him shyly, the turn of her head and the appealing look caught at Katie's heart. She knew the girl had long loved the prince—

But that he had taken her for his concubine!

Turning from the sight of them walking slowly down the path between the courts, the prince's hand still holding Moon Blossom's arm firmly, Katie caught the sideways anxious look of her maid, Joy.

Joy knew. All the courts must know, all the maids, the guards, the little elderly relatives. Only Katie had been blind. When had it started? Perhaps in the palace, as Moon Blossom had begun to glow with happiness and the prince had not come nights to Katie.

She sat thoughtfully as the dusk came. Her meal was brought to her; she ate alone as the petals of the peach blossoms drifted slowly to the tiles. Darkness came, and Joy lighted a torch to gild the courtyard; still Katie sat, thinking.

She was jealous! She missed him, longed for his arms, hungered for his expert caresses. She missed his close attentions, the way his eyes had lit up for her. They no longer did; his looks were for Moon Blossom. Katie put her hand to her face; it burned. How dreadful she was; she had hurt him by her frank speech of homesickness, by the note to Rupert. Yet she still longed for him, though she had in effect pushed Prince Chen Yee from her.

Joy's voice roused her. "You come in now, missee? The wind grows cold for you." And she put a soft cashmere shawl about Katie's shoulders.

Katie nodded and went inside to the bedroom. The baby slept soundly in his wicker basket, and she touched his cheek lightly with her finger

It was early, but she did not feel like drawing or studying a scroll of history or art. She undressed and went to bed. The prince would not come to her; he had a new mistress. . . .

Lovely Moon Blossom. An intelligent girl, bright girl, gentle girl, who would be safe in her soft hands, thought Katie. She would not hurt him by her coldness or cruelty; there was none in her. He might make her his second wife or chief concubine.

If only Princess Mei-ling let her alone!

The prince would guard his own. And if she gave him a child, then Katie would be free!

She lay thinking about that, torn between jealousy and relief. If Moon Blossom conceived and gave birth, as she very well could, then Katie would be released. The prince had already grown weary of her. He still adored his son, though, and would until he had another son, an all-Chinese, all-Manchu son!

Katie could not sleep. She lay awake in the darkness, alone in the wide bed where she had lain with the Manchu prince and known the ecstasy of his caresses. She remembered how he had whispered poetic words to her, how his hands and lips had roamed over her. How he had thrilled her, how they had lain awake the whole night, lying in each other's arms, unable to sleep for sheer delight.

The nights had been short then.

Now they were dark and long.

She remembered how he had spoken of "the one year of happiness." Yes, she also had had one year of great happiness, along with worry and terror when she had been captured and thought to be killed. She still had nightmares about that.

But the joy in his arms, the great pleasure, which even Rupert had never given to her—

To be so adored, so loved—for one year. Was it enough to last a lifetime?

But perhaps she was being too extreme, she thought. Perhaps the prince liked to roam, as she had learned many men did. He might yet come to her, alternately with Moon Blossom! She writhed in the bed, knowing now she was madly jealous. She loved Moon Blossom, admired her, was glad for her—yet!

In the days and weeks and months that followed, Katie was to know jealousy very often. The prince did not come to her, but he did to Moon Blossom. All the inhabitants of all the courts knew; they whispered and nodded wisely and followed the progress of the romance with satisfied looks. Moon Blossom was one of their own, not a foreign woman. Now that the prince had had one son, it was sure he could have another!

A daughter, a whole family! He could conceive; he could have many concubines. He could be like many emperors; he could have dozens of children! He was all-powerful, all-kind, all-generous to his people, all-wise in ruling. Yes, it would be good if Prince Chen Yee conceived many children with his women!

Prince Chen Lo was being groomed for marriage, and the whispered rumors were that he would be married to a fine Manchu princess of a good family, not related to Mei-ling.

The princess Chen Mei-ling went about in black and silver and gold, trying to attract the attention of the prince. Now she also longed for a child. But he did not go to her bed; her maids whispered that she screamed in fury nights when her perfumed letters to her husband went unanswered. She tried to get the dowager mother to plead for her, but the prince did not listen to his mother's pleas for him to go nights to his own wife.

Katie wondered if she would strike again, this time at Moon Blossom, and dread filled her for the girl.

The guards had been doubled in the courts, especially around the Court of the Flowering Peach and the Court of the Moon, where Moon Blossom lived in luxury in rooms of moon white, blue, and crimson. She had new gowns of those colors, and the prince showered her with favors. She wore long chains of jade in intricate carvings; her small ears had many changes of earrings of gold and silver, ivory and jade. When Katie took the baby on a little walk to visit her, she shyly showed Katie the boxes of black lacquer and gold filled with jewelry and perfumes.

"He is very kind to me," she said, her eyes glowing.

"You are favored," said Katie, trying to stifle her jealousy. "You are a fortunate and wise girl. Be good to him always; know he is a busy man who longs to relax with you. I see him laugh with you; that is good."

Moon Blossom bent her head. "I am more fortunate than I have ever dreamed," she whispered.

"You have loved him always," said Katie slowly, playing absently with the baby's small fingers.

"Always," murmured Moon Blossom. "From the time I was a small child, brought here by his own carriage, away from poverty and disease and starvation. My own parents had died; he rescued me from a cruel woman, and from then on I was cherished."

"He will always protect his own," said Katie, wondering how to say what she wished and finally finding the words. "He will protect you as he can. But you also must be very wary and alert, Moon Blossom. Keep your maids alert about you, and do not listen to false messages. Remain within the court as much as you can, or in mine."

Their looks met. Moon Blossom nodded, her face a little apprehensive. "I will take care, my sister," she said shyly.

Katie bent and kissed her cheek. "May good fortune attend you always, my sister."

Then she laughed. "Look how Chi-chi tries to talk!"

He was sitting up in her arms, his mouth bubbling with milky air, and saying, *"Ummm—ummmm—ummmmm!"* very emphatically.

"He will talk early," said Moon Blossom admiringly. "May I hold him for a little time?"

Katie gave him into the girl's eager arms, and together they played with the child and laughed softly at his cunning ways and bright laugh. A shadow lay over the Court of the Moon, but they bravely ignored it.

22

As September approached, Katie and others wondered anxiously if they would remove to Macao for the winter. Moon Blossom was not pregnant, to her quiet sorrow; she had hoped to conceive for her prince. But he continued to come to her.

Katie was painting idly one day when he came about ten o'clock in the morning. He absently gazed at her painting, at the scene of an English countryside in Cornwall, the steep cliffs, the dashing water of the sea, and the foamy waves. A tiny figure of a fisherman in a boat was the only sign of human life.

He did not speak of the painting. Instead, he said, "I have decided that we shall go to Macao for the winter as usual. I have business there, and we shall all be happier for the easier weather. Does this please you!"

Her face had become radiant; she could not hide her joy and expectation. "Oh, yes, yes!" she cried. "Oh, I long to see—Macao—again." And she hoped desperately to see Rupert, or someone from the Llewellyn company, and get word to them that she was alive. She scarcely dared hope for her freedom, but it would be the first step toward it.

He nodded briefly and sat down. "My honorable mother and her women will not go with us; the journey is too difficult for them. My brother, Prince Chen Lo, remains with her this time, as does his tutor. He has much work to do for the examinations in the spring. The emperor is pleased with his maturity and has arranged work for him to do in my absence."

"But that is splendid," gasped Katie. "And the prince is so young! It is indeed an honor for him." Her eyes shone; she liked the young happy prince so much. He was gentle, tactful, and gaining in maturity and wisdom under the guidance of Wu Lung. "You must be very proud of him."

Prince Chen Yee nodded. "I am proud, yes. He is an honor to the family. Moon Blossom accompanies us. My wife, the princess Mei-ling, also goes; she has expressed an urgent wish to see friends in Macao." He said this rather dryly, with a quirk of his mouth.

Katie bit her lips anxiously. Did the woman mean mischief? She could not help thinking so. Prince Chen Yee put his hand briefly on her hand. "Do not worry," he said. "I protect my own."

"I worry now for Moon Blossom," said Katie bravely.

He looked faintly surprised. "You do? But she will be guarded, and besides—"

"She is not a foreign woman," said Katie bluntly. "But I fear the jealousy of your wife—for any woman on whom your attention falls."

He was frowning heavily, eyebrows drawn together blackly. "You must not speak so of my wife," he said automatically, adding, "Why do you fear for Moon Blossom as she is Manchu?"

"I have seen the eyes of your wife in her presence at dinner," said Katie gently. "Forgive my rash words and my impertinence. However, I love Moon Blossom. She is my sister, and I wish you—I wish you much happiness with her. She is gentle, good, and becoming wise. There are some who are envious of the happiness of others. Unable to give of themselves, they are jealous of those who can give with open, generous hands."

He sat silently, thinking, his frown set. She was silent also, wondering at her daring. There were things one could say to the prince and other things one should not. But he had never directly punished her for her honesty. Only by depriving her of his attentions had he shown his disapproval and hurt at her impulsive wish to return to England. He was an honest and honorable man, for all his subtly impassive manner.

"Well—" He roused himself from his musing. "I came also to inform you and your maids"—he glanced where Joy sat silently listening, respectfully—"that we shall sail in a week. Trunks will be brought for you in which you will pack all your garments, jewels, paintings, and so on. The baby's clothes shall also be packed, for ready use on the ship. We shall sail from Tientsin, after carriage rides to the three ships. From there we sail south along the coast, past the port of Shanghai and Hangchow, around the coast to the south and east, to Macao. There we shall remain for the winter. This pleases you?" he asked gently.

"Oh, yes, thank you!" She looked at him frankly. She meant to be very honest. "You know—I long to see if I may make contact with my people again."

"Your husband deserted you."

Her face showed her pain; his narrowed eyes watched her keenly. "I know," she whispered. "But I have my duty to him. And I am homesick for England. Will you—permit me to leave you?"

"That is in the future, in the lap of the gods," he said gravely. "Now is not the time to speak of this. You are not happy with us?"

She bent her head. "I have been more happy and more afraid and more ecstatic and felt more pain than in all my other days on earth," she admitted. "My mind is confused. I cannot think what is right to do. How I wish I could go to some wise person and ask, 'What is right and correct?' For I have my duty to the man I married and to his family who raised me. I have my memories of my good father, and yet I do not know how he would counsel me. And to you I owe a debt of gratitude for saving my life of the fever—"

"I do not wish gratitude!" he said abruptly, briefly showing anger and hurt. "A man must aid one who is ill, one who has needs and no one to help. I did what I had to do. And I wished to help you, for I admired your courage and spirit. I felt no one appreciated you; all worked you hard but did not love you. Your own husband deserted you for weeks and months, and when he came home, his admiring eyes turned to his forbidden sister-in-law! No, you were a little songbird with no one to listen to your plaintive song."

"Except you." Impulsively she put her hand on his large hand resting on his embroidered knee. "You listened to my song and gave me confidence in myself and my own worth. I am now a woman, where I was a lost child. And for your attentions, your love—" she added softly. "How can I thank you for that? I have never known such love, and it wakened in me—" She began to flush under his grave look. "I felt such emotions, I learned how to give and receive love—"

"The year was all happiness for me," he said quietly. "One is fortunate who knows even one year of joy and love. I loved completely, and my joy was complete when you gave me a son, for which I had longed in vain. Could we not have such joy again?" He was looking directly at her.

She gasped, hesitated. "I do—not know," she said, thinking of Moon Blossom, thinking of Rupert. Yet— yet she longed to lie in the man's arms, the man who had given her wild feelings of ecstasy and rapture. She glanced at him timidly; his head was bent.

"Soooo," he said with a shrug of his broad shoulders. "We shall begin in a week a journey of many miles and some discovery. Perhaps we shall learn more of ourselves and our souls on this journey." He stood up slowly, gracefully, and bowed to her as he left.

She remained with her thoughts, her brush idle. Then presently two men began bringing to her court three immense trunks. It took both of them to lift the trunks when empty.

The massive trunks were about five feet long and almost three feet deep and wide. They were of thick fragrant sandalwood, reinforced by black iron corners carved in the dragon pattern with heavy feet and massive rails around the bottom. Two long handles were on the end sides. The wood was lightly embossed with patterns of the sun rays and sea horses, with a stamp of the House of Chen.

Joy bustled around those days, filling the trunks. One trunk held the winter garments they would use on the ship, for it would be chilly in the winds. Another trunk held the summer garments for use as they sailed into southern waters and lived in Macao. A third trunk was of household goods for Katie's rooms: silk sheets; woolen blankets; thick quilts.

Katie wondered as she directed the packing of her jewelry in lacquer boxes, some of three drawers, some of five. Was he having her take all her clothes and jewels, and the baby's possessions, because he was going to let her go to Rupert?

However, when she briefly visited Moon Blossom during the hectic days of packing, she found the girl also packing all her garments in massive trunks like Katie's and all the jewelry. "There will be many parties," said the girl in excitement. "Prince Chen Yee plans to introduce me to some of his relatives who will be in Macao for the winter. There will be much entertaining! He says I shall be his hostess on some occasions when Princess Mei-ling is out visiting!"

She was bubbling with excitement. Katie felt jealous pangs again, but after all, she herself could not be hostess for the prince, not in Macao and probably not in Peking. Always she was "that foreign woman," even though she had given the prince a son.

And the dowager was not grooming Katie for anything!

The carriages conveying the trunks set out first, to have all ready on the ships. Then one grand day the formal procession of the barouches of the prince's household prepared to depart. There was a ceremony on the marble steps before the palace, as the dowager stood with her ladies, making formal farewells to her son. Prince Chen Lo, looking manly and fine in scarlet, stood beside her, his tutor behind him, gray hair blowing in the slight wind.

The tenderest farewells were for the baby, Prince Chi-chi.

"When you return, you shall be more than a year old." The dowager sighed, kissing his forehead. "Bless you, may the gods be kind to you." He gurgled up at her and waved his arms, pleasing her immensely.

Katie wondered. "When you return," the woman had said confidently. Did she not guess the prince might let her go? This might be the last the dowager would see of her grandson. Perhaps she hoped that by that time Moon Blossom might be pregnant and would give the prince another son, who would be more acceptable to them.

The farewells were over. The dowager even kissed Katie on the brow and wished her well. Then finally they were all in the barouches and waving from the windows as the procession got under way. The prince led the way, Moon Blossom with him in the barouche. Princess Mei-ling and her women were next.

Katie, Joy, and Prince Chi-chi had the third barouche, which gave her some concern. Was he now demoted to third place? Yes, that was the case. She worried a little about the ships, hoping fervently she would not be alone on a ship with the venomous princess Mei-ling.

She was relieved when the carriage journey was over and they arrived at the port of Tientsin. The prince made short work of their loading, and soon the great beautiful ships set out. Katie was on the same lead ship as the prince, Prince Chi-chi and Joy with her in their rooms. Moon Blossom had her own rooms on the same ship, next to the prince's rooms.

Princess Mei-ling was on another ship, sailing to the side and behind theirs. Sometimes Katie, on deck under an awning, could see the haughty Manchu princess under a crimson or yellow awning, gazing across the waters toward them.

How humiliated the princess must be as the prince

gave her only courteous and formal attentions! Everyone knew he never slept with her; she had little hope now of producing his heir. Unless—unless she managed to eliminate her rivals. However, the prince detested her for her cruelty. If she did manage to kill her rivals, he might even set her apart and dismiss her to her relatives. Or kill her! Katie remembered the men who had kidnapped her.

The journey of several weeks was pleasant, except for one storm which plagued them for three days. The rest of the time they were able to spend days on deck, painting, talking, reading aloud. Moon Blossom was practicing her calligraphy much of the time under the prince's direction, as well as her reading and playing the lute and beautiful zither, or ch'in, as they called it. She had worked very hard on the ch'in and was already accomplished, and the evenings were usually filled with the plaintive, beautiful sounds of music. She taught Katie several of the songs, and Katie would sing along with her, to the quiet smile of the prince as he lay back in his chair.

As the ships drew into the harbor of Macao, Katie leaned on the rail eagerly, scanning the harbor for signs of the *China Princess*. However, her unaccustomed gaze could not recognize any ships. Besides, the Llewellyn vessel might have gone on to Canton, or perhaps it might not have yet arrived.

Her heart pounded as they went ashore. It was not a long process, but she was impatient to be settled and able to go about Macao by herself, searching for some word of Rupert. She would try the Shaws, for surely they would know—they knew all the gossip.

As Joy unpacked some of the trunks and hung up the garments in the huge cedarwood wardrobes in Katie's rooms, Katie went out into the hallway. Prince Chen Yee met her there and smiled at her.

"Where do you rush to, Katie?" he asked softly, and she thought his eyes glittered.

"I wish to go out in the carriage, Elder Brother," she said eagerly. "I will call upon the Shaws; surely they know of the Llewellyn ship and perhaps Rupert—" She halted as he slowly shook his head, his face turning impassive.

"I cannot permit you to go out alone," he said.

She stared at him, her hand on her heart. It was beating rapidly. "But why?" she burst out. "I must find out about Rupert—if he is here—it he will come and talk to me—if—"

"I will have inquiries made for you," he said curtly. "It is not permitted for you to leave the palace." And with a slight bow, he turned away.

"But, Elder Brother!" She ran after him, touched his arm.

He turned; his black gaze burned at her. He was furious; she knew by his rigidity.

"You will obey me, Katie!" He turned her shoulders and pushed her gently back to her room. When she was inside, he closed the door on her and walked away. She could hear his footsteps, louder than usual, as though he were stamping.

Joy was staring at her. Katie managed to shake her head. "I will help unpack," she said nervously, and went to set out the lacquer boxes of jewelry mechanically. What would Prince Chen Yee do? Why did he deny her wish to go out in the carriage? She had had to be protected in Peking; she was a foreign woman and a stranger, every feature of her hands and face making it evident to the Chinese that she was foreign.

But here in Macao, where so many English, Spanish, Portuguese, Dutch, even Americans were, why could she not go out?

He was keeping her a prisoner inside, she finally realized. He did not permit her to go out beyond the gardens, and even there her maid shadowed her and guards stood politely against the gates, their poles crossed.

Katie began to feel frantic. What if Rupert were in Macao and could not come to her? The palace gates would be closed to him if that were the wish of the prince. How could he reach her? How could he contact her if his letters were stopped and he were prevented from coming to her?

In the hallway one morning she was strolling with the baby just outside her own rooms. She could go out into the courts, but today rain swept across the tiled roofs and poured in a steady stream down the gutters. She felt dreary, desperate, as gray in mood as the gray sky.

Toward her came Princess Mei-ling, stately in her black and silver robes, walking alone for once. Katie turned to go nervously back into her own rooms.

"Wait!" said the princess imperiously. When she came closer to Katie in one of the wider areas of the hallway where chairs and tables were set, she stood and beckoned with her long finger. The long fingernail at the end of it glittered with gold dust. "I would speak with you!"

Katie feared her, and she had the baby with her. Yet Princess Mei-ling rarely bothered to speak to her, and she was curious. She moved a little closer. "What do you wish, Your Highness?" she asked formally.

"Your husband is in Macao. Why do you not go to him?" Princess Mei-ling flung the words at her contemptuously, her black eyes snapping.

Katie gasped, her eyes wide. She clutched the baby closer to her. "How do you know of this?" she asked after a pause.

"I saw him while I was out in the carriage. All the long noses look alike, yet I remembered him. Rupert Llewellyn is his name, is it not? And he lives in a house of the foreigners in that section of Macao."

Katie wet her lips and searched the princess's face. "Why do you tell me?"

A vast shrug, veiled eyes. The woman wanted to be rid of her, thought Katie.

"Why do you not go to him?" asked the princess. "You do not belong with us."

"I wish to see him, but the prince Chen Yee has forbidden me to leave the palace."

The black eyes glittered. She hesitated. Then she said, flinging the words away as of no account, "I will take a message to him. Write it."

Katie stared. "Why?"

"If you do not wish to meet him, then do not write." The woman moved to turn away in disdain.

"Wait!" Katie cried. "I will write—I will—"

"Hurry then. I am going out in my carriage."

Katie ran back to her rooms and dumped Chi-chi in Joy's arms. She sat down at her desk, took up pen, and began to scrawl.

Rupert, I have just learned you are in Macao. I long to see you, but I am forbidden to leave the palace. I am in the House of Chen, under the protection of the prince Chen Yee. Princess Mei-ling offers to take this message to you. I beg you to try to see me. What has happened to you? Please, please come.

Katie

She longed to say more but dared not keep the princess waiting. She rolled the page into a small scroll, fastened it with a ribbon, and ran out again. The princess was seated in a chair in the hallway, gazing indifferently into space. When Katie went to put the scroll into her hand, she pointed to a small table near her. "Put it there," she said.

Katie set it down nervously. The woman rose quite indifferently, as if she had all the time in the world, picked up the scroll with two long fingernails, as though not wishing it to touch her skin. She strolled away.

Katie gazed after her, biting her lips. The woman was impossible! She doubted if the princess would even bother to deliver the message, much as she wanted to get rid of Katie. Perhaps she was tormenting Katie with hope, only to dash her down. The Chinese and the Manchu could be subtle in their cruelty.

She returned to the drawing room of her suite and sank down into a chair. Joy was tucking the baby into bed in the other room. Katie put her hands to her head. Would the message be delivered? What would Prince Chen Yee say if he discovered it? What would Rupert do? Was he here in Macao to find her or only to carry out Llewellyn business?

That last thought did plague her. What if Rupert had come only to do the trading and did not care about her at all? What if he would be surprised to find her about and be displeased that he must concern himself with her?

And worst thought of all—what if he had thought her dead or lost forever to him, had obtained a legal divorce and married Selina? Katie got up and paced the room in deep agitation. All her previous feelings for Rupert returned in a rush. At one time she had adored him, thought him the finest and most honorable man in the world. No matter what else, he was her husband, and she thought of their good times together. How protective he had been on the ship, how they had laughed and talked together, in spite of Selina.

She could scarcely eat when her lunch trays were brought. She drank cup after cup of hot tea, then got up again to pace the room. How soon could she expect an answer? Tomorrow, a week, a month? How long would it take for Rupert to come, to get past the barriers of the guards? Or would he not want to come? She half expected a stiff note of refusal.

About three o'clock she fed Chi-chi, then closed up her gown again. The rain made her nervous, pounding on the tiled roof, thundering down the gutters to the ground. The trees looked drenched; the flowers trembled and hung their heads. She held the baby close and paced to the windows and back again, whispering to him.

"Oh, my darling Chi-chi, what will happen to us?" She wondered if the prince would come today and inform her that she might go out and see Rupert. Or was he angry with her? She had scarcely seen him since they had arrived in Macao.

The door opened abruptly. The princess Mei-ling

stood there, splendid in her brilliant gown. Joy started up from her corner and went to stand in front of Katie defensively, startled.

The gaze of the princess flicked them all with contempt. "Your husband is here," she said abruptly, and left the room.

Rupert came in.

"Oh, my God in heaven!" cried Katie, and started for him. She burst into tears, still hugging the baby. Rupert started toward her, then saw the child. His face changed from eager anticipation to wonder, to shock.

"A baby?" he gasped. She never forgot that his first words were about the child. "Why—how—oh, Katie!"

He came closer and put his hands on her arms. He gazed into her face as though seeing her almost for the first time. Then he looked down at the baby dubiously.

"It is my child?" he said with doubt. He could not tell how old the baby was, she realized.

She shook her head. "It is my child by Prince Chen Yee," she told him bluntly. He flinched. "Oh, Rupert, I longed to see you! What has happened? Is Selina—"

"In London," he said. "Of course, she did not come. I had to try to locate you; Captain Potter is making inquiries in Canton as he trades. I said I would search in Macao first. Oh, Katie, how could you have run off as you did?"

"Run off!" she gasped. "I did not! I was delirious with the fever—Selina took me in a carriage to the prince and left me here! Didn't she tell you?"

"No!" he said blankly. "She told me you dismissed Lilac and Ho Chih and was angry with her because she scolded you for seeing too much of the Manchu prince. She said she tried to persuade you not to go—"

Katie gazed at him blankly in shock. Had she been so sick she didn't know she had gone of her own will to Prince Chen Yee? No! She did not believe it. Selina had lied again—only this time most diabolically.

"No!" cried Katie, shaking her head vigorously. He was staring down at her, and she realized he was trying to accustom himself to her appearance in Chinese gowns and headdress. "She lied to you! She always lied to have her own way! She knew I was ill; she must have decided to leave me here so the journey would not be delayed—"

"But that would have been criminal," he said gravely. "I think you do not remember what happened, Katie. You must not slander Selina. She has had much to bear."

About to protest again, Katie shut her mouth tightly. So the situation was the same. He would take Selina's part against his own wife.

She turned from him. "Why did you bother to come?" she asked dully. "To see if you could get a divorce here?"

"No, Katie. You must come back home with me. You do not belong here in China. Father was horrified that I had left you here and returned home without you. He scolded me a storm, I must tell you. And Mother urged me often to return to you. When I set out, they sent many loving and anxious messages to you, urging you to return home to them. Your escapade will be forgiven—"

She flung around, her temper rising. "My escapade!" she said indignantly. "That is insulting! I was ill of a fever. I did not know what happened to me until I was on the ship to Peking! And I would have died if they had not taken such good care of me, bathing me in cool water, giving me herbs to drink—"

"Then I must thank them for that," he said wearily. Now that she looked clearly at him, her eyes cleared of the emotion of seeing him for the first time in more than a year and a half, she saw he was much thinner, lines graven in his tanned face, a new maturity in his eyes. "But now you must come with me, Katie. We will remain in the house in Macao until the trading is completed and then return home as soon as we can. I will not rest until you are safely home in London once more."

"And then what?" she flung at him bitterly, all the joy in the reunion gone. "You will divorce me and marry Selina! Is that it? You wish the relationship made legitimate! Does she have your child yet? Does she live in your house with you?"

"Katie! How can you insult us both like this?" His face had flushed, and his eyes were angry. "Of course, she lives in the Llewellyn house, in her own suite. She is unhappy, but she bravely goes out often—"

Katie laughed out loud scornfully. "I'll warrant she does! Has she arranged a duel for you yet? Does she play one suitor against another, as always? Does she reluctantly wear colors and all her jewels and waltz with rakes?"

He bit his lips. She would have wagered that some of her shots had hit home. He said with restraint, "This gets us nowhere, Katie. Get your cloak, and come home with me. We will talk out our problems together."

Behind him the door suddenly opened, and Prince Chen Yee stood in the doorway, tall, formidable, his eyes blazing with wrath. He wore dark robes of blue and silver; his fists were clenched.

"How came you here?" he asked of Rupert. He spoke in English. His accent was heavy, but the words clear.

Katie gasped. "He—he is here at my wish," she said bravely.

"I did not give him permission to come. You will leave now," he said to Rupert, ignoring Katie.

"I will leave and take my wife with me."

One long arm barred him. "No. You do not deserve her. You deserted her when she was ill and almost dying of fever."

Rupert gasped. "Ill, dying?" he asked blankly, turning to Katie for confirmation. She nodded, her lips pressed together. Did he think they both would lie? "But none of that now," said Rupert. "I wish to take my wife home with me."

"And our child? I think not," said Prince Chen Yee. "You will leave now. I have not decided yet what I shall do. I will send you word when you may come and see—your wife," he added, flinging the words.

"I wish her to come with me now!"

"What you wish is of no concern in my household," said the prince grimly. He stood aside from the door. "You will leave as you came, in my wife's carriage!"

So he knew, thought Katie. Of course, he knew all that went on in his household. And he was furious with her.

Rupert hesitated, then nodded. "I will go now. I have much work to do for my father," he said quietly, his head up. Katie was proud of the way he faced the angry Manchu prince. "I must go to Canton for a week. When I return, I would see Katie again and talk to her. There is some misunderstanding between us, and I wish to clear that up."

"I will send word to you when you may come," said the prince. He gestured to the door. Rupert went out where a guard was standing in the hallway. Katie saw the guard gesture toward the front of the palace and indicate to him that he was to follow. Then the door closed after Rupert.

Prince Chen Yee stood gazing at Katie. "You had to go to my wife?" he asked, with ferocious accent. "I told you I would arrange your meeting. Why did you not wait for me to act?" He spoke in Mandarin again.

Katie's gaze fell. She had insulted him deeply. "I am sorry," she whispered.

"This incident shows what you think of me," he said more quietly. "I am grieved that you do not trust me. I ask you again, wait for me to act. Is it too much to require of you?"

"It is not too much. This time I will wait," she murmured.

"Some difficulties must be straightened out," he said. "I knew that an alien environment was hard to endure for a peach tree, and it might not blossom. However, you must wait for the blossoms to come and for the peaches to grow. By the time that they fall, we shall know if the environment was right for them or not right for them."

He bowed and left the room while she was still puzzling out his meaning. She went to the windows that overlooked the Court of the Flowering Peach. The blossoms had not come yet; only yesterday the peach trees had been set in their sheltered court, in the earth, unwrapped from the protective cloth placed around them in Peking for shipment. She had watched from her windows as the trees were carefully planted, and the roof over the court drawn so that the rains would not damage them. Now the roof had been drawn back so that the rainwater might reach them, and they could drink of the fresh waters and grow.

Would they grow or die? They were alien to Macao, as she was to China. Her roots had not taken hold, she thought. And that was what he had meant. Did he still hope that she would adjust, would remain with him, she and her child?

23

Rupert was working hard in Canton, anxious to get the ship loaded, so they could return to London by the end of January if possible. Captain Abraham Potter soothed him, warned him, "They have their own ways of working. Patience, Mr. Rupert. When they get the right goods, they will turn them over. They like you, I think. You have dealt fairly with them."

Rupert sighed, his head in his hands as he sat in the upper apartments over the warehouse on the wharf. "I know, thank you, Captain Potter. But I worry about Katie—"

"Aye, and rightly. But the prince will take good care of her in Macao. He promised, did he not? She is still weak of the fever, you said."

Rupert could not meet the keen eyes of the captain. That was the story he had given out. Whether the English people believed that Katie could be still weak of a fever after a year and a half, almost two years, was another matter. The Shaws had been kind, keeping a room for him, storing his goods as well as Katie's clothes, and they pretended to believe that the Manchu prince was taking care of Katie for friendship's sake.

He returned to Macao every few weeks. It galled him that he had to send word to the prince, requesting permission to see Katie. Permission was gravely sent in return, in a formal note written by Katie, probably dictated by the prince, and he was allowed to see her once on each trip to Macao.

He tried to talk to her earnestly about her duty to return to England and her position as his wife. But there was some deep barrier between them. She was bitterly jealous of Selina and had said some wicked things about her. He had never known kind, sweet Katie to be so fiercely determined to smear someone.

Selina had told Rupert that Katie had gone to the prince because she loved him and could not bear to leave him.

Katie swore she had been ill of a fever when she went to the prince. She swore that Selina had taken her there and left her because Selina feared the fever she had.

And the Manchu prince said Katie was deathly ill of a fever, and they had had a difficult time nursing her back to health.

The question was: Had Katie gone to the prince of her own will? Even feverish and out of her head, had she instinctively gone to him, loving him? Perhaps if she had been well and clear of head, she would not have gone. That made the situation even worse, that she had fled to him when her will was weak, when she was ill and wanting comfort and aid. Rupert paced the floor back and forth, back and forth, unable to resolve the puzzle.

Rupert rarely saw Katie alone. To his dismay, usually the prince Chen Yee sat with them. And now Rupert knew that the Manchu prince spoke English, and quite well, despite a limited vocabulary and accent. He knew what was going on.

And Katie kept turning to him to confirm her

words. Rupert had seen the intimacy between them, the understanding. The prince had frowns for Rupert, smiles for Katie. He touched her hand before Rupert, and it was a caress. And they had had a child—a son. A son whom the prince adored.

Rupert felt wrenched inside. A son—Katie had had a son by the prince. It spoke of intimate nights together in the exotic world of Peking. Katie had told of the way she was treated, given a court and servants of her own, honored with presents of jade, ivory, emeralds, diamonds. He had seen her gowned in elaborate Chinese robes with fur hems and sleeves. As the weather turned hot, she wore magnificent silks of shimmery lightness, so sheer one could see the underrobe of another silk. She had become beautiful, like a bird of paradise, his little Katie, so demure and quiet. She spoke up more; she said things in a spirited fashion and with wit and humor. The prince and she could argue about wisdom and literature before Rupert, and Rupert scarcely knew what they talked about.

In the next days and weeks the work went faster. In January Houqua began turning over to him the products of the porcelain works, some beautiful dishes of white china with gold rims and exquisite design. Rupert had commissioned them by letter a year ago, when the other ship hired by his father had come to Canton.

They were now sending two ships in alternate years, the *China Princess* one year, a hired ship the other. The business was going so well they would be millionaires within another year or two. Yet Rupert had never felt so miserable.

It was Katie, he decided. She made him feel guilty that he had not stayed to search for her. Yet everyone had said it would be impossible to follow her and find her. Selina had wept and urged them to leave.

Selina—He frowned and paced again. She was so lovely, so sweet. Yet Katie had been right; as soon as they returned to London, Selina had taken up her social life again.

His mother had collapsed on learning of Terence's death. In some obscure way she seemed to blame Selina. But it was not Selina's fault that Terence had caught a fever. And he and Katie had nursed Terence as well as they could. He sighed, and paced, and fumed.

Captain Potter watched him over his pipe smoke and finally urged, "Calm down, lad, and get your sleep. Tomorrow will be another day, and we must be fresh to argue with the Chinee," he added humorously.

The next day brought an unexpected turn. The merchant Houqua said through an interpreter, watching Rupert's face, "I understand that your wife remained in China, most unusually, last year."

Rupert flushed. The merchant rarely said anything of personal meaning. "Yes, she did." He repeated his story. "She was ill of a serious fever. The honorable prince Chen Yee and his household took care of her and cured her, taking her to Peking to remain with them. She is now in Macao—waiting for me," he added, hoping it was true.

The merchant nodded. "Thus have I heard," said the interpreter, after Houqua had spoken to him again. "Your talented wife made some patterns and designs for the silk merchants and for the porcelain makers. We have the goods in our warehouses. Samples have been sent to us. We have saved them for you for a year as they are of exquisite and expensive quality."

Houqua added something else quickly. The interpreter said, "We had instruction to save them for the Llewellyn ships. But they cost much."

Rupert stared at the impassive narrow face of the merchant. "I should like very much to have them, these goods of my wife's design. My father sent much gold and silver with me," he added recklessly. "He wished me to buy the best that China would sell to us."

Houqua nodded to a servant waiting at the door. He went out and returned immediately with a black lacquer box embossed with gold and silver patterns of sea horses, waves, and clouds. "From the House of Chen," said the merchant without expression.

Rupert opened the box and gasped. It was about two feet long and a foot wide, and inside were samples of lengths of silk. He lifted one; it clung to his fingers. It was the sheerest fabric he had ever seen, of palest violet with a faint beautiful pattern of seashells. And in the lower right corner was a butterfly. He gazed at it, lifting the corner in his trembling fingers. Yes, there were Katie's initials, *K* and *L*, with the butterfly sketched about it.

He lifted another length, another. The box was floating with color as he drew out the silks. Captain Potter came to take some from him, exclaiming over their beauty. Brocades, sheer silks, raw silks of fine weave—all had Katie's designs on them and the butterfly in the corner. An English primrose in beautiful yellow on a background of almond and a framework of willow leaves. A scene of small children playing with toys. A landscape with fishermen and a river. All had Katie's unmistakable delicate sketching. There must have been more than forty designs, with the samples woven or painted beautifully on the finest silks he had ever seen.

Rupert lifted his gaze to the impassive merchant, Houqua. "May I have all of these?" he asked impetuously, his face alight. "They are all from my wife!"

A faint smile, a nod. Another large black lacquer box was brought in, this one with carefully packed porcelain cups. Each had a different design on it; each was Katie's: one of an English rambling rose, another of lilacs, another of willow leaves, another of peach blossom, each on a most exquisitely designed porcelain cup, with gold or silver rim, beautifully molded feet or rims around the bottom.

"Each is a sample of a full dinner service," said the interpreter. "There are usually forty pieces in a set; four of the sets have eighty pieces. And two sets have two hundred of the plates, dishes, and cups. And then in addition, there are eight sets of dishes for the coffee service and eight others for a tea service."

In all there would be a half a shipload of the most exquisite porcelain he had ever seen. The prices would be a fortune on the London market. But Rupert resolved to keep one of each kind at least of the sets to have in their own home. He asked the price; Houqua waved one delicate hand languidly.

He named the price, amazingly low. Then he added through the linguist, "It is the wish of the prince Chen Yee that these pieces should go to the House of Llewellyn from the House of Chen. He has paid much for them; I take only the go-between price."

Rupert stared down at the boxes and felt a keen revulsion overwhelming him. His first thought was: This is a bribe! A bribe for me to give up Katie! I can have all the fine trade goods practically as gifts from him. And he thought of the thinly veiled contempt on the face of the Manchu prince. The slight smile as Rupert, the Englishman, would eagerly accept the large bribe in return for his wife! Katie would remain with the prince, and Rupert would become wealthy in trade, which the Chinese despised.

Captain Potter was running his big thumb lovingly around the porcelain cup, but not looking at it. He was looking at Rupert. "A fine gift indeed, after all he did for your wife," said the captain. "Saving her life and all."

By the murmurs the linguist was translating this to Houqua. And Rupert regained his senses. "I am overcome," he said. "It is indeed a grand gesture. How kind he is," he said, looking right at Houqua. "Not only does he save my wife's life and care for her in his own household for almost two years while I must return home to England, but he also arranges for her to work on the silk and porcelain designs and has them made up. And now he hands them to us in a gesture of great generosity. How can I thank him?"

This was translated, but Rupert thought: If the prince can speak English but does not do so until he chooses, I bet so can Houqua! Rupert was always very careful what he said in the presence of any Chinese, for he was convinced some of them understood English, though they did not indicate they did.

Then he remembered. "You said the price would be high, Houqua. How is it you name me a low price?"

A half smile and mischief in his dark eyes. "I did

but test your willingness to buy," he said only. Rupert thought more was behind it, but the merchant had relaxed into graciousness. Rupert would ask no questions; the goods were ordered sent to Whampoa for loading on the *China Princess*.

"Well," said Captain Potter expansively that evening. "We could sail for home right now should the winds be right! The ship is not full, but we have a fortune in goods already I never saw such beauties— they'll command top price on the London market."

Rupert nodded slowly, drinking his tea, thinking. He was puzzled over the gift. Was it for him, for a bribe? He could not quite believe it. It would not sway him from demanding that Katie should return home with him. Yet it could be a magnificent gift, offered almost in throwaway contempt, to show how generous the prince could be.

Or was there some other reason beyond Rupert's fathoming? He did not understand the Chinese mind, he realized that. What would Katie say? Perhaps she would understand.

"Well, we have to wait for the other silk we ordered, the porcelain ordered last autumn. I wish we had not ordered it." He grimaced. "It will look poor beside these."

"Aye, but the London merchants will be happy to snatch them up," said Captain Potter. "They looked great—until we saw these. And these will go to the gentry, maybe the royal family! There now, that's an idea. A splendid set for the prince regent, and he might forgive Terence at last."

Rupert's face shadowed, as it did when he thought of the loss of Terence. His gay, brilliant brother, gone so quickly in the dreadful fever. What a senseless loss.

"Yes, it would. I shall suggest that to Father. Thank you, Captain. But I shall keep the best sets for Katie. She deserves them, having designed them with such skill and understanding of the forms. I have never seen lovelier. They are simple, direct, elegant, none of that gaudy bright stuff, and all in the best porcelain. Did you see how the cups were transparent? I held one and could see my thumb behind the porcelain."

"Aye, the finest I ever saw," said the captain. "Well, will ye still be going back to Macao this week?"

"I must—to see Katie. I am anxious about her."

"Still sick, eh? Poor lass."

Rupert nodded. She was not sick in body, but he thought she must be sick in mind. Perhaps having the child had turned her mind. She argued so—sometimes she said he did not love her, and she might prefer to remain in China. She was so different from the girl he had left.

When he thought of her, his wife, lying willingly, eagerly, in the arms of Prince Chen Yee, he had to restrain his fury with great effort. How could she! An Englishwoman! Yet the prince was very handsome, tall, masculine, virile, Rupert admitted, writhing in his bed. Had the prince found more with Katie than he had? More willingness, more eagerness, more ecstasy? Katie had been so sweet, so gentle, so lovable. But what had she found with the prince and he with her? Was this why he would not let her go?

When he returned to Macao, he sent a note eagerly to the prince, indicating he had returned and asking permission to see Katie again. When he had not heard in two days, he became anxious. Mrs. Shaw was clearly wondering why he had not gone there at once. He had to explain lamely that the prince was not always home and he permitted no one to enter unless he was there. That seemed to satisfy her.

She said, "Well, why don't you have Katie come to us now? As you will be going home within the month, you said, she would be most welcome. We shall be quiet as she wishes."

He thanked her but refused, again lamely. He was intensely relieved to have a note from the princess Mei-ling, written in very stiff English evidently by a scribe, inviting him to a banquet the following evening.

As he dressed in his finest white linen suit, linen shirt, emerald cuff links, lace neckerchief, he thought he would have to do a good hard job of persuading Katie to leave. It was late January, and they should sail as soon as the last load was put on board. Captain Potter had remained in Canton to wait for any shipments of silks and porcelains that might come through. With luck they could leave in another two weeks, in mid-February, while the winds were most favorable.

He drove up to the palace in the early dusk and thought how beautiful the buildings and the grounds were. The lawns were exquisitely kept, with hedges of greens and ferns, ponds of water lilies and fish, pots of roses, lilacs, camellias, fragrant magnolias all about and on the marble steps into the palace. Guards came to take the horse and carriage, giving him strange looks.

The prince strode out to meet him almost as soon as Rupert had set foot on the marble stairs. His brow was black and thunderous in a scowl. "Why do you come? I did not send for you!" he said dangerously.

Rupert stared at him in the light of the flares held

by other guards. "Why—why," he stammered, "I had an invitation—to a banquet—from your wife, the princess Mei-ling. She said to come at six o'clock. What is wrong?"

His gaze met that of the prince squarely, though he felt terrible. He must have mistaken the date; he was clearly unwelcome; he turned to leave. "I must have the day wrong," he muttered.

"No, wait. I will inquire. Come in," said the prince, slowly, and gestured for him to come.

They walked together down a long hall, turned into a huge dining room. The table was set for five persons, a beautiful shining cedarwood table, with a long lace scarf down the center, a huge bowl of fragrant roses on it. At each end were huge armchairs of carved dark wood and deep crimson cushions. The prince gazed at it and snapped something at a guard. The guard nodded and pointed toward the hallway.

The prince turned to Rupert. Expressionlessly he said, "It seems I was mistaken; there is a banquet this evening. We shall go to the reception room, where my wife awaits."

They went to the next room, equally large, where the princess Mei-ling waited, arrogantly splendid in black and silver. Her Manchu headdress was wide, a butterfly arrangement of black hair, gold headdress, dangling gold earrings and gold ornaments, gold stick-pins with flowers on the tips. Behind her Moon Blossom stood up. She was dressed in a modest blue gown, with a matching blue robe over it. And Katie stood beside her, in a fragile-looking rose sheer gauze gown over white taffeta.

Conversation was stilted. Katie's anxious gaze kept

going to Rupert. He tried to smile at her. "The ship is almost loaded. And guess what I have on board—all the silks and porcelains you designed! Houqua had kept them for the Llewellyn ship."

He told her about it and thanked the prince formally for the generous gift. The pirnce nodded, accepting the thanks stiffly. He seemed to have other matters on his mind. He wore dark blue tonight, a regal blue gown over a paler blue informal gown. Rupert thought: He did not expect company tonight! He wondered what Princess Mei-ling was up to, perhaps hastening Katie's departure. She was quite evidently not fond of Katie.

"You leave soon?" was her only question of him. Katie translated.

"Tell her I hope to leave in two or three weeks," said Rupert.

The princess only nodded; her giant headdress moved forward at a dangerous angle, then went upright again. She studied her long gold-glittering fingernails.

They went in to dinner. In the usual manner many courses were served, tidbits of delicacies following one after another in separate precious porcelain dishes. Katie sat at the right of the prince, Rupert beside her to the left of the princess Mei-ling, and Moon Blossom across from them. The princess roused herself and offered several toasts, coyly to the handsome Englishman, to friendship, to the relations of their country. The prince drank them in almost total silence.

Desserts were brought, small bowls of custard, tiny delicious raspberries, little cakes. Princess Chen Mei-ling gestured to her own woman, who was helping serve, and obediently the woman went to a sideboard and poured out five glasses of wine in elaborate crystal glasses.

She set them around, one at each place. Mei-ling waited until all were served. She raised her own glass as the woman moved to stand behind her chair. "This is a special delicious wine of the north near Peking," she said with a smile. The wine glowed ruby red, sparkling in the candlelight. "We shall drink to your safe journey to England, Mr. Llewellyn, and your wife, Katie Llewellyn!" She raised her glass.

Rupert raised his to his nose and sniffed politely. He had drunk so much tonight he didn't really want more. "Ah, this smells strange and potent, like almonds," he said.

Prince Chen Yee leaped from his chair so quickly the massive chair fell over with a bang. "Stop!" he cried in a shrill, wild voice in Mandarin. He grabbed Katie's glass from her as she was putting it to her lips. He came around the table, moving like a panther, and snatched Rupert's glass from his hand. He did not spill a drop, so firm was his control.

Moon Blossom sat frozen, the glass halfway to her lips. Slowly she set it down. The Princess Mei-ling sat frozen also, a half smile on her wide lips, a gleam in her narrowed black eyes.

The guards did not move a quiver of a muscle. The prince set the two glasses before Mei-ling. He took the other wineglass from her hand and passed it before his nose; he did not stop staring at her directly. He sniffed it, then set it down.

"My wife," he said in a deadly quiet tone. "You will drink—to our guests!"

"A toast," she said, her smile mocking. "A toast? My prince, gladly will I drink to our guests." The hand moved to the glass he had taken from her. He moved it aside and put toward her hand the glass that had been Katie's.

"This one. Drink," he said.

Her smile faded. She swallowed, gazing up at his blazing black eyes. She reached out slowly for the glass; he put it firmly into her hand.

"Drink with me," she said, her smile returning. "Drink with me, Prince Chen Yee; we shall drink together—to our honored guests!"

"I will drink later," he said grimly. "Drink! Drink!" His voice rose to a roar of fury.

She quivered just slightly. She pushed back her chair and stood; the glass wavered a little in her long slim hand; the fingernails glittered gold against the ruby wine.

"Drink!" he yelled. Not a guard moved.

Uneasily Rupert pushed back his chair and rose. He felt something terrible about to happen. It could not be, it could not—

Katie rose also and gripped Rupert's arm. He drew her protectively toward him into the circle of his left arm. He put his hand to his right hip, but of course, he did not have his sword with him, not even a dagger.

Only Moon Blossom remained as Rupert moved back from the long beautiful table, a little untidy now with the dishes cluttering it. All gazes were on Princess Mei-ling.

At the remorseless gesture from the prince she raised the glass to her lips and sipped at it.

"Drink it all," he said in Mandarin. Rupert did not

know the words, but the tone was sufficient. She lifted the glass further, tipped it back, and the red wine slipped down her throat.

He waited in silence. She was staring down; she quivered, then shook. She began to moan and put her hand over her mouth. The glass fell from her hand, crashed on the tiled floor. Slowly she sank to her knees, moaning, bending over, her head down as though she kowtowed to the tall Manchu prince who stood over her remorselessly.

She wailed, once, then began to writhe on the floor. It was horrible to watch. Katie gave a heartfelt moan of horror, and Rupert turned her so she could hide her face against his shoulder. He could not help watching, in shock, as the woman writhed, crawled over the floor, retched, but could not vomit.

Her legs kicked out spasmodically, and her arms; then she curled up in pain. Scarcely a sound passed her lips; her formidable control kept her still until the last moments. Then she gave a screech which set the hairs up on Rupert's neck, a long scream of sheer terror. Finally she went limp, flung out on the floor, a painted doll in black and gold.

The prince drew a long sigh and gestured to the nearest guards. "Carry her out. Prepare her for burial at once."

They hastened to obey him. He turned to the woman who had waited on them. At his gesture she picked up the glasses of wine that remained near the princess's chair and took them out with the bottle. His eyes blazed at her; her head was bent.

Moon Blossom spoke in a small, shaken voice. "My prince, how did you know—the wine—was poisoned?"

Katie translated quickly for Rupert, who looked to

the prince for his reply. He glanced at Rupert. "The smell of almonds," he said somberly. "It is a very quick poison. She would have given it to Katie and to her husband."

Even as Katie was translating this to Rupert, Moon Blossom spoke again. She lifted her glass and smelled it. "And me—also, my prince," she said, and her face crumpled.

He grabbed at her glass, raised it to his nose, and smelled. "My gods in heaven!" he moaned. "By the gods, the woman was a very fiend in hell! To poison you also—and be rid of my unborn child!"

Katie stiffened as she translated for Rupert. The prince had lifted the weeping Moon Blossom and folded her protectively into his long arms, his robes covering her. As tears rained down her cheeks, Katie whispered, "Did Mei-ling know of this, Prince Chen Yee? Did she know that Moon Blossom was—going to have your child?"

She spoke in English, flatly. He nodded. His face was grimly furious, the black brows drawn together. "I told her myself three days ago," he said, also in English, so Rupert would understand. "I told her Moon Blossom is to have my child. I told her she was not dishonored; she would still be my honored wife, with all position and regard. I thought she took the news well. She smiled and congratulated us."

"And planned to poison us all, all but herself—"

"And me," said the prince quietly. "She did not know what I would do to her—for this. If she had succeeded, I would have had her drawn and quartered, remaining alive as long as the torturers could keep her alive, should it be weeks!" Something savage in him made him bite out the fierce words.

His big hand was stroking Moon Blossom's glossy hair back from her forehead; he soothed the girl as she trembled.

He gestured to a guard, spoke to him, and the guard began to clear away the other glasses, handling them as cautiously as if they were fangs of snakes.

"Come, we will retire to another room and compose ourselves," said the prince. He led the way, still holding Moon Blossom within his arm.

They sat down in still another room, this one full of severe black chairs and sofas and handsome simple tables with prints of calligraphy lining the walls. The view looked out over the city, and the harbor, with ships like toys in the water, tied to their moorings or anchored farther out. A soft blue haze spread over the purpling night. How peaceful, thought Rupert, after the wild storm of the scene. He would never forget the sight of the woman writhing on the floor. If Prince Chen Yee had not moved so quickly, he and Katie and Moon Blossom would have been writhing there instead and probably dead by now. He shuddered and felt Katie shuddering also within his protective arm.

"I must get Katie away from here," Rupert said flatly.

The prince had his handsome head bent. He seemed to be thinking deeply. "You will come again in two days. We must have the ceremony of the funeral of my wife. The service shall be minimal but it must be done," he said wearily.

"Katie does not need to remain for that," urged Rupert. "My God, let me take her away from here!"

"There is no further danger from us," said the prince with quiet dignity. "No one else would harm her. I should have settled the matter long ago. I never dreamed my wife—would do—such. I thought her an honorable woman, though cruel and jealous of nature." He sighed, then straightened. "No, come in two days. I would talk with you and with Katie at that time. A difficult matter still remains undecided. I will have my words ready for you in two days."

He called for Rupert's carriage and walked to the door with him. Rupert turned at the last as he was about to step into the carriage. "I must thank you," said Rupert, "for saving my life and that of my wife, twice over now. I owe you so much I can scarcely think how to repay you."

An ironic smile came to the prince's face. "I shall ponder that very thing," he murmured enigmatically. He bowed and motioned to the driver to leave. The carriage started up, and the carriage rolled down the hill, leaving Rupert to think about what the prince meant.

24

Prince Chen Yee came to Katie's drawing room on the morning of the second day. She and Moon Blossom had remained secluded in their rooms away from the turmoil when the authorities came, matters were discussed, and the princess Chen Mei-ling was buried.

He entered the room, quietly shutting the door after him. It was about ten in the morning. Katie exclaimed in shock on seeing his face.

"Elder Brother, you have not slept or rested!" She rose and set little Prince Chi-chi down on the floor on a blanket to let him scramble about. She came forward and put her hand impulsively on his arm. "You must rest, Elder Brother."

"I must first speak with you, Katie." They sat down across from each other in armchairs. His gaze was strange, she thought, tired, yet resolved, the black eyes calm.

"Your husband comes this afternoon at three. First there is a matter you must consider."

He would tell her now whether or not he would let her go! Her eyes widened; her hands clenched tightly. He noted the gesture and smiled sadly.

She could not speak; she must await his decision.

He began to speak slowly, after a long pause. "I have thought long and spent many nights awake, my dear adored. We had together a beautiful year of much happiness, and together we made a magnificent son." His glance fell tenderly on little Prince Chi-chi cooing over one of his wooden toys.

She bent her head. She felt a little chilled, apprehensive. Did he wish her to remain and live as his concubine forever?

"I think you experienced with me much joy, at least I hope so. You also knew terror, the depths of despair, the heights of pleasure, the wonders of my beautiful country, the fright of being—close to death on two, nay, three occasions." He paused again, as though gathering his thoughts.

She could not speak yet. Her throat was dry.

"Yet your heart still inclines you to your homeland. And you think wisely of your duty to your husband. I cannot fault you for this. You are a wise and loving woman, faithful to your family in England. If you were truly a woman of my family, you would not have this choice. But you are a foreign woman, accustomed to being allowed your own decisions."

Her own decisions! If he knew how funny that was, she thought sadly. It seemed to her she had been swayed this way and that since childhood. Her father had made their decisions. Then Mr. Douglas Llewellyn had decided she was to marry Rupert. And Rupert had ruled her until Selina took it on herself to get rid of her! From then on she had belonged to Prince Chen Yee, to do with as he chose.

"I have watched the sadness in your eyes, heard you weeping over your child, singing English songs to him," he continued quietly, but with a sort of melancholy in his face. "The songbird began to resent her cage, though it was filled with jeweled toys, the finest foods, the softest silks and velvets. So I have come to you to offer you the choice."

She held her breath. What choice?

"You may live with me as an honored concubine. You are the mother of my son, a fine, healthy, intelligent child, my eldest son and heir, no matter how many other children I may have. You know that Moon Blossom is to bear my child—" And his face lightened for a moment; he mused over the pleasure of that thought. "She is a good girl, my third cousin, a delight to me. You get along well together. Now that—that my wife is gone, I shall make Moon Blossom my wife. It is suitable."

More than suitable, thought Katie. The gentle girl was growing more and more important to him. His arms had gone round her before a foreign man; he had held her and soothed her without thinking of protocol or formality.

The prince was gazing at Katie. "You were first in my heart," he said simply. "The joy you gave me was very important to me. And I think it was important to you also. The hours and days and nights in the arms of each other—it was pure delight. You gave yourself completely to me. It could be so again; you will be my honored concubine, my joy, the core of my heart. Whether or not you conceive again, I shall adore you always. Honors shall be heaped on you; my mother shall kowtow to you."

Her heart seemed to leap in her breast. She thought of his strong arms, his warm and naked body against hers, the sheer pleasure of his caresses, the wild ecstasy—it could all be hers again. He loved her still.

But England, and Rupert, and the Llewellyns, and

her homeland, the smell of English flowers, the noisy bustle of London, the raging beauty of a Cornwall storm over the sea, the green and fragrant fields—they all drew her. She was sick for want of her homeland.

"You are gracious to me, a foreign woman," she said blankly. She did not wish to insult him, but she hurried on to ask, "And what is—the other choice, my prince?"

He sighed wearily, and the light seemed to die in his black eyes. He gazed down at Chi-chi, lying on his back, kicking up his strong, sturdy legs.

"You may go home to England with your husband," he said. "You may leave with him when he is ready to go. My gifts go with you; my thoughts bless you; I open my hand and let you fly away. However, I must keep my son."

She stared at him, unwilling to believe he had said those words. "Chi-chi!" she whispered, her hand going to her breast. "Not—Chi-chi—not keep him—no—no—"

"Yes. He is my son, the son of a strong, courageous, and intelligent woman. He bears my mark on him; he is my image, my eldest son, perhaps my only son. I must keep him, to train him, teach him to follow in my steps and one day to be prince of the House of Chen, master of all of Chen, ruler and leader."

Impulsively she slipped to the floor and gathered up Chi-chi in her arms. She held him to her, her face wretched and afraid. "I cannot give him up!" she cried.

She looked pleadingly at the prince. His face had gone impassive, but his gesture was noble. "Do not tear yourself apart. You may stay with him as my concubine or as the honored mother of my son without my disturbing attentions. It is for you to say, Katie. If you wish to remain with him and not suffer my attentions—"

"I did not suffer!" she cried hotly, flushing. "I—I loved you. I—I enjoyed your—attentions, you know that! But I must go home! I must go home!" She bent her head, and her tears began to fall on Chi-chi's bewildered head.

He reached up his small hand and patted her cheek, making soothing sounds, as if distressed for her. His black, alert eyes worried over her. She hugged him closer, feeling the little warm, dependent body, the strength of his small arms about her neck.

"You may go home," said Prince Chen Yee's deep voice. "But you must leave Chi-chi with me. I had to make you understand this before your husband comes. You must think and make your decision by the time his ship sails. Once you sail, there is no turning back."

"And leave Chi-chi?" she whispered. She raised her head. "This was on your mind when we came south, was it not? You knew I would try to find my husband, send word to him—"

He nodded slowly, the lines showing on his dark, handsome face. "It is best to go out and meet one's fate and not cringe in a corner waiting for fate to find one. You must make up your own mind, Katie, make your own decision. You know I want you to return to me, but it must not be unwillingly. You have three choices. You may return as my loved concubine, and I will enjoy you, and you will enjoy me. Or if you do not choose that, you may come as the mother of my son and heir, help to raise and educate him, see him become honored and wise. Or—the third choice—you will leave him to me and return home with your husband to the land for which you are sick in your heart. That is for you to decide."

He ceased speaking and rose to his feet. She could not move, bent over Chi-chi, hugging him to her. Her heart was desolate; she felt frantic. Could she take him with her by stealth? Could she steal away with him, sneak him onto the ship, sailing quickly before the prince could stop them?

No, Prince Chen Yee would have them stopped before they could pull up anchor. He would have sharp guard over his son. And worse, he would never trust Katie again. He would cut her off completely from the child; she would have no word of her baby ever again. She must continue to deal honestly with him, as she always had, no matter what it cost.

She had another thought and grasped for it. "But Moon Blossom is to have your child! It could be a son—he would be your son and heir—"

He was slowly shaking his head. "I cannot count on it," he said definitely. "She is a good girl, but she has not your brilliant mind and courageous heart. She is honest, artistic in nature; she learns quickly. I hope her son or daughter is born healthy and grows sturdily to adulthood. But you can see, I cannot count on anything. One cannot, in this life," he added heavily, half to himself. "One cannot know what the fates will bring to one. I am only grateful to the gods that the fates brought you to me, and we had one year of joy."

"I must—think," she muttered, still on her knees on the floor, holding Chi-chi tightly to her, so that he whimpered. Slowly she put him down to play again, as the prince watched them both.

Finally he turned and went to the door. He paused, his hand on the doorknob. "Your husband comes at three. If you cannot decide now, tell him. I will tell him to come again when the ship is loaded and he is ready to depart."

He went out and closed the door softly behind him.

Katie sat numbly on the floor and tried frantically to think. Her mind went around and around. She changed it a dozen times, twenty times, while Joy worried around her, took care of the baby, brought her lunch and tea, tried to persuade her to lie down.

Katie fed the baby once more and laid him down to sleep. And then she began to weep. Joy was distressed; she sent her away, so that she might weep and try to think.

Three o'clock came; she went out to the drawing room where she was to receive Rupert. He came in with Prince Chen Yee. Rupert's face was eager and open. He stared at her, the signs of tears, the redness around her eyes.

"What is wrong? What is it?" he blurted out. He held out his arms, and she went to them automatically. He held her closely, protectively and glared at the prince. "What have you done to her, said to her?" he asked. "What is wrong?"

"We shall be seated and talk calmly," said the prince. He had rested and changed his robes to ones of crimson silk. He seemed more aloof, a little formidable now.

He waited until Katie had sat down beside Rupert on a sofa and then sat opposite them in a large armchair. His long hands rested calmly on the arms of the chair, motionless. Not a bejeweled finger twitched. He looked very much the aloof, masterful prince Chen Yee, head of the House of Chen, as the bright afternoon sunlight streamed into the room and the fragrance of peaches came through the open windows. His perfume was the heavy jasmine today, the jasmine he favored. Katie remembered how her robes and her body would be scented for days with jasmine after he had been with her.

"I have said to Katie that she has a choice. She may live with me and be honored as the mother of my son and heir. Prince Chi-chi is a strong lad; he will be a magnificent man. He will inherit my lands, my property—and my responsibilities. He will do well," said the prince calmly.

Rupert stared at him. "But—but we wish to take him with us," he said.

The prince stared back at him. "That is impossible," he said in his deep voice. Somehow he seemed years older, much more mature than Rupert, for all they were about the same age. He had so many more duties and weights on him than Rupert, thought Katie. Since he was a boy, he had been given more and more responsibilities, as her son would have. If she could not succeed in taking him from the prince—But did she want to take him from his father, from his positions, his honors, and the duties of the House of Chen? She had seen how hard the prince worked, how anxious he was about his people. If the prince and his brother had no other sons, who would rule the House of Chen? What would happen to them? Would some other house take them over, perhaps with a cruel master? It would be their ruin; they would dissolve into nothing.

"What is the other choice?" asked Rupert in a low tone, and his arm curled protectively closer about Katie, until he was hugging her. The prince observed, his eyes narrowed.

"The other choice is that she shall return home with you and leave her son for me to raise. I shall have the assistance of my concubine, who shall be my wife, Moon Blossom. She already loves the child."

Rupert bent his head to gaze down at Katie's face. His free hand gently stroked her fingers. "I see," he said in a low tone. "This is why you are crying."

She nodded and put her handkerchief to her eyes. "To leave—my baby," she said brokenly.

Rupert sat in silence. The prince studied their faces keenly. Finally he rose, and said, "I will leave you here to discuss the matter. Whatever you decide, it must be settled soon. You leave in two weeks?"

Rupert nodded. "The ship is almost loaded full. I shall return once more to complete the loading, make final payments; then we shall sail from Whampoa to Macao, pass customs, and depart."

"Yes, I see. Talk then to each other. I shall return in two hours."

He left the room and shut the door after him. They were alone. Rupert stood up slowly and began to walk about the room. Katie thought he did not see the precious porcelain vases on the lacquer and sandalwood stands, the valuable tapestry on the wall, the view from the windows of the peach trees.

What could he say? She wondered dully if he had ever loved her. She was homesick, yet the prince had been kinder to her and more loving than Rupert. But Rupert had married her, made love to her, and he had been her first love. She had been so happy when they married—in spite of all the difficulties. She had wanted to belong to Rupert.

He was strong, masculine, hard, firm. He had taken his duties well, as he had as an officer. He had always been so responsible. Was this why he wanted her to return—only because she was his responsibility?

He came to a halt before her, finally sat down opposite her, unconsciously assuming the pose of the prince, hands on the armchair, and his gaze upon her. Both strong men, she thought, both conscious of their duties—

"Does the prince always mean exactly what he says?" asked Rupert thoughtfully. "Is there any chance of begging him to release the boy? Would he listen?"

Katie gave him a grateful look. But she shook her head. "I fear he means it," she said dully. "He loves Chi-chi, and the boy is his only heir. If Moon Blossom has a son, it might be different—yet he says not. He says Chi-chi is his eldest son and heir and will be trained to follow him." She did not add Prince Chen Yee's praise of her and of her heritage to his son.

Rupert was thinking deeply. He was silent for a time. He gazed into space, at the wall behind her, then back at her face, as she mopped up the tears that ran down her face.

"Katie, in China you felt very much a foreign person, did you not?"

She nodded.

"And people treated you differently? Did any mock you? Did any scorn you?"

"Well—the prince protected me from much of that," she said reluctantly. Then she remembered that the dowager had commanded the midwives to save the unborn child, regardless of her, a foreign woman's, fate. "Yes, I felt it," she added. "I would always be foreign here. My face is different, my upbringing. Sometimes I felt they laughed at me or scorned me. That was mostly Mei-ling, however."

He nodded. "And she was jealous of you. Katie, I think you would always feel an outsider here in China. I know I do, yet I cannot speak the language. But even if I spoke it, I know they would look on me as different and mock me."

"But I cannot leave Chi-chi, my son," she said brokenly. She twisted her hands together. "You don't know how a mother feels, Rupert. He has fed at my breast; he is closest to me; he smiled first at me, and said 'ma-ma' to me. And soon he will have his first birthday—When I think I shall never see him again, I think I shall go mad!" she cried out.

He got up, came to her, and sat down to hold her in his arms. "Katie, Katie, don't torment yourself," he said firmly. "We must think rationally. What is best for you, and what is best for Chi-chi. Have you thought about him, Katie?"

"Thought about him? He is first in my thoughts; he is my son!"

She thought he flinched a little. But he persisted.

"Think of him from his own point of view. You know, Katie, if we take him to England, he will be discriminated against. He looks very Chinese—"

"He is Manchu!" she said haughtily, her head up.

"The same to Englishmen. He will be tormented as a boy. He has slanted eyes, a touch of yellow to the skin; he will look more and more Oriental as he grows. What do you think it will do to his spirit to be called Chink and Chinee? You cannot expect any other treatment for him in England. As a sensitive child he will either be crushed or grow up defiant and difficult, a person set apart. And he will know he is not my son."

Katie was silent, in shock and surprise. She had not thought about this, but it was all too true. She knew

what Selina had said about Prince Chen Yee, and he
was a man and very handsome and wealthy. Still, she
had disdained him. To Selina and people like her, any
European was to be preferred to an Oriental. Orientals were not in her class; they were very low in the
social order.

And England was very conscious of class and the
class system. In China Prince Chi-chi would be ruler
of his House of Chen, following in the steps of his
father. He would have honors, wealth beyond avarice,
silk and jewels and lands and women. In England he
would be wealthy, but scorned, perhaps unable to
marry the woman he would choose. Laughed at,
jeered at, lashed by the whips of prejudice.

"You had not thought of this," said Rupert perceptively. "Think about it, Katie. How a sensitive and intelligent child would feel, a yellow child in white
England. Much as we would want to protect him, how
could we after he goes to school, mingles with other
boys his age, hears the comments from them and from
their parents? And as your son and not mine, he
would be known to be illegitimate."

He paused to let his forceful words sink in. She
jerked in protest but could not deny it. Her son was
illegitimate. In China alone it would not matter because he was the son of the House of Chen, and her
own status as a concubine was not considered unusual.

Rupert proceeded slowly, almost delicately. She
thought she could hear his father in him, the slow,
thoughtful, careful words, the logical thinking behind
them.

"Katie, if you remain here with the lad, he will feel
the stigma of your position. The prince will not marry

you; you will be a foreign woman, a concubine always. He will be reminded of his mother's low position, her differentness. If, instead, he is raised by Moon Blossom, people will gradually come to forget he is not her son. People are forgetful if they do not have evidence continuously before them," he added ironically. "It would be best for the boy if you leave him. Then he can grow up as the son of his father and be honored and proud."

She put her hand to her throat. "It would be better for Chi-chi if I gave him up!" she said poignantly.

"Yes, my darling." Rupert hesitated again. "This is probably not the time to speak of this, but I am not noted for my tact." His mouth twisted as he spoke. "In England we shall be together again, and in time I hope you will give a son to me. And a daughter if God wills. The House of Llewellyn is reduced to me, Katie, and to you. I hope we may continue it with our children. I love you, and I had hoped that you love me. I hope you will again when we are able to be together and quiet and to think clearly. And to feel, my dearest."

He held her gently; his hand went up to stroke her hair. He gazed down into her face, and she thought his expression was different from before. How tender, how anxious for her. He put his fingers on her cheek, caressed it slowly.

"I missed you so much," he said softly. "Those two years we were apart—how they dragged! I missed my lovely wife, her sweetness, her charming ways. I lived alone in our apartments, and they echoed with ghostly sounds."

She thought: Did Selina never persuade him to go out with her? How does he feel about her? Has he lived a bachelor existence?

When she did not speak, he went on slowly, "When we married, I thought of you only as a little cousin, a dear friend. However, I soon came to cherish you, Katie. I was so happy; the nights with you were enchanting. Do you know what passion is in you?" He smiled a little at her blush and kissed her cheek swiftly. "And when we were parted those long months, I came to know truly how dear you are to me."

He hesitated, then added, "And one day we also will have a child." He brushed his lips against hers. "Will we not, Katie?"

Katie leaned against him. He smelled not of exotic jasmine and sandalwood, but of English leather and hair tonic. He was garbed not in silk robes, but in linen. He would not write poetry to her, and it embarrassed him to speak of love out of the marriage bed, in daylight.

But he was solid and English and dependable and had a strong sense of duty. And he said he loved her. Her hands clung to his jacket. Could another child comfort her, help ease the pain from the loss of Chi-chi?

She drew away. "It is what is best of all the choices for Chi-chi," she said dully, her hand to her aching head. "The child is the most important, isn't he? He isn't big enough to cope by himself."

"He is important, but so are you and I, Katie. Think of our future together. Think of what we can accomplish together. Think of our marriage, our children, of carrying on what my father has done so well. You can help me. I need you," he urged gently. "My father misses you so much, as he missed your father. You are needed, Katie. Is that enough for now? One day I hope you will come to love me again."

She raised her gaze to his and met it honestly. "I still love you, Rupert, I think more than you ever loved me. That was much of the trouble, for your heart was with Selina."

Rupert flushed and shook his head vigorously in protest. "She is not my wife; you are my wife, Katie. Forget anyone else, as I shall. She is a valued member of our family, and she still mourns Terence. But for now forget her—think only of what you want, what your future will be."

They talked for some time. Rupert urged her to return with him and let Chi-chi be raised as a Chinese prince. He urged that the boy would be much happier here; his father would see to that. "The child would be tormented in England," he told her, and she knew that now.

By the time Prince Chen Yee returned she had made up her mind. It was a terrible decision to make, but she could not remain in China; she was an alien. And Chi-chi could not go to England as her son without many taunts and mockery and hurts.

Prince Chen Yee seemed to read the decision on her face, or he might have known what it would be. He nodded. "You go with your husband," he said.

Katie murmured, "Yes, I must go, and Chi-chi must remain. I am grateful to you for your many kindnesses—"

"We do not part yet," he said kindly. "You shall remain here with your son until the *China Princess* is ready to sail. You shall pack your trunks slowly, putting good memories in to scent them. You shall have good hours with your son and with us. A parting is a wrenching, but we shall make it smooth with the ointment of loving attentions."

Rupert began to protest. "She could remain with the Shaws while we wait for the ship—"

"No," said the prince definitely. "She would be lonely for her boy and wish to see him daily. And the English would pester her with their questions and their side looks. No, you may safely trust her to us."

Rupert nodded. "Yes, I trust you," he said, and the prince gave an ironic half smile.

Rupert left to see to the completion of the ship for sailing. The days sped past, for Katie knew they would be the last she would be with her son. She held him as much as possible, watched him play, wept a little as she fed him, wiped away the tears, determined that his last memories of her would be with smiles and kisses.

Moon Blossom was with her daily, helping care for the boy. A wet nurse was found to nurse him until he was able to eat other foods. Gradually Katie turned Chi-chi over to them.

Prince Chen Yee spoke with her several times, calming her, reassuring her. "I shall write to you of the boy's progress and his growth," he said. "He shall be much loved and taught with loving care by Wu Lung and myself and Prince Chen Lo. He shall hear of his mother that she loved him enough to give him up."

"If I only knew that I was doing the right thing—" she fretted, watching her son on the floor with anxious love.

"The fates would have it so," said the prince. "Remember our arguments about the fates?" he reminded gently. "It seems you came to me to give me a year of joy and the son who will follow me. Think of that if you mourn for him. Before you came, I had learned to have contempt for women and their cruelty, the les-

sons of my wife. I had practically resolved to retire to
a monastery and live a life of contemplation as soon as
my younger brother was able to take over the House
of Chen. See how you have turned my life around,
given me hope and a future in the world of men. I
have a son, and thus I will continue in the life set for
me and my heritage. You taught me also to love, what
it is to love, and so I have love in me to give, for you
gave and received freely."

"You will love—Moon Blossom," she murmured.
"She is a dear good girl—"

He nodded. "I love her already. She shall be my
gentle wife and give me another child, as many as the
fates allow. But she is not you—with your courage,
your intelligence, your spirit. I shall not forget you,
my adored." Gently he drew her to him and set his
lips on her forehead. She thought then he was saying
farewell to her.

"And you will write to me?" she asked desperately.

"I have promised," said the prince Chen Yee.

Her trunks were packed. The *China Princess* arrived, fully laden, and the trunks were sent down to
her at the harbor. Prince Chen Yee had a farewell dinner, with just them, Moon Blossom, and Rupert to eat.
She could scarcely force down the delicate morsels.
The last dinner, the last time to see and kiss Chi-chi,
the last time to hold her son, the last time to see the
handsome, ironic features of the Manchu prince who
had loved her so deeply—for one year.

Was she doing the right thing? Could she endure
the parting?

No time to think, no time to reconsider. The prince
put a small painting in her hands at parting. It was a

painting he had made of their son, playing on the floor, a little grin of satisfaction on his face as he clutched his toy and gazed up at his father.

Tears blurred her eyes. She thanked him, her voice shaking. She said her farewells, to Joy, to the other maids and the guards, to Moon Blossom, weeping. To Prince Chen Yee, who bowed formally, his blue robes crackling. To little Chi-chi, who cooed and put his arms about her neck and clung until the prince lifted him away from her.

Then she and Rupert were in the carriage, leaning out, looking back at the people gathered on the marble steps of the palace of the House of Chen until tears blurred her eyes and the turn in the drive hid them from her.

Katie made it all right to the ship, up the gangway, into her cabin, where the huge trunks filled the room. The English sailors seemed strange to her, the hearty, loud voices as they moved some of the trunks along the hallway into the cabin she had first occupied when sailing from England to China. She and Rupert had the main cabins, where Selina and Terence had slept and fought and laughed in the night. Even now their ghosts haunted those cabins.

The ship sailed slowly out on the tide the next morning, that late February day 1819. And she thought of her son, about to celebrate his belated birthday party without her. And she returned to the cabin, feeling faint and sick.

There was no going back. No going back. Her son was gone from her, and she might never see him again in this world. She fell across the bed and sobbed as though her heart had broken.

25

The *China Princess* sailed southward into the South China Sea, in the company of half a dozen ships from Macao. It was comforting to have their presence—the ships of England, France, and America—as pirates roamed the seas and waited on the horizon for a stray ship traveling alone.

The ships arrived safely at the port in northern Sumatra, and they anchored in the harbor. Rupert was anxious to distract Katie from her silent grief over the loss of her small son. He and Captain Potter took her ashore with several burly sailors as guards to view the port and the markets while they purchased black pepper, nutmeg, mace, cinnamon, allspice.

Katie wandered about the markets with them, enjoying the exotic sights. The trunks in her cabin had been filled with English clothes; the Chinese dresses were in trunks in the storage cabin. It seemed odd to her to be wearing a white muslin dress again and a pale blue pelisse and matching large blue bonnet that sheltered her neck and face from the burning tropical sun. Evidently Mrs. Shaw had given orders for all her dresses to be washed and cleaned; everything was fresh and sweet-smelling, ironed, and in good condition. Katie gave silent thanks to the good woman and resolved to write to her from England. Rupert had given her some lengths of silk and a set of porcelain upon leaving.

There was a farewell party on board the French ship, though three of them would travel in convoy on to the coast of Africa, around the coast, and up to France. The *China Princess* would travel with the other two English ships and try to keep in touch also with the French ones, but they might become separated in the wide Indian Ocean. Any excuse for a party, as the French captain said merrily.

Katie sat in silence but learned to smile again at the parties they held. She danced a little awkwardly with the eager men, women in very much a minority here. She talked with the women but said little of her experiences in China. They knew only that she had been very ill with a fever, a Chinese household had taken care of her, and she had been cured by Chinese herbs.

That was sufficient to arouse their curiosity, but Katie did not mean to satisfy it. She was a woman now, she thought, and had her own dignity. She did not listen to gossip if she could help it, and she had no wish to furnish any.

Rupert was very good to her. His attentions were kind and unvarying. He took her on shore excursions in the port of Sumatra, and later, as they went along the coast of East Africa, he saw to it that she went ashore whenever it was safe for her.

The *China Princess* paused at Zanzibar to make more purchases of spices. Rupert had been given much money by his father this time, and the gold and silver coin was welcomed eagerly by the native dealers in spices. He was able to purchase many barrels of spices, and they would bring good prices in London.

With what they had in porcelain, silks, jade, ivory, and many spices, the cargo would be worth about half a million pounds.

"We might never have to go again," said Rupert thoughtfully as they left Zanzibar, while he leaned on the rail beside Katie, watching the harbor slip away. They waved to the dark-skinned natives in small boats who had come out to see them off and try to make a few more sales of "Spices, missee!" "Bananas, master!" "Buy a little monkey for your missee!"

Katie waved at them a little more boldly than she had felt onshore where she was practically the only white woman, except for the few French- and Englishwomen who had also ventured ashore. She had strolled among the stalls of spices and encountered bold black gazes, and grins showing white teeth stained with red betel. She gazed in her turn at women in floral prints showing long brown arms and legs, other women garbed from head to foot in black or gray robes that showed only brief glimpses of shy eyes.

"Never come again—to China?" asked Katie blankly. Her desolation over her son overcame her, and she put her face in her hands. "Never?"

"Oh, Katie, we may," he said gently, and put his arm about her. "Would you want to risk this rough journey again?"

She nodded. "I would want—to try to see—my son again," she whispered.

No one else knew she had had a son. Captain Potter worried kindly over her ill health, tried to cheer her up and assure her that malaria sometimes went away after a few years. He seemed to have decided that was what she had had since it had lingered so.

"We shall see then," said Rupert. "Do not cry, Katie. You have been much improved in health on this journey, and I am proud of your courage. Brace up, my dear, and smile. Life goes on, and I shall try to make it as sweet for you as I possibly can."

She leaned against him gratefully, and her tears did dry. She even managed a laugh at the antics of one long-legged native who jumped up and down in his small boat threatening to swamp it, as he begged someone to "buy one little more food."

The ships sailed on down to the island of Madagascar, off the lower east coast, and they stopped to take on water. Rupert had still more money and was resolved to take as little coin home as possible.

"I have Prince Chen Yee to thank for this," he said, using the man's name naturally. "He gave us porcelain and silks you designed, Katie, and Houqua took only his commission from me. It was a very generous gift."

He told her about that and went on to talk about the many dealings with the smart and sometimes crafty hong merchant. They talked also of the silks and of more designs to be made when they saw how well these sold.

They went ashore at Madagascar, Rupert and some sailors protecting Katie. She wandered about the markets there, wondering at the wealth of goods and the poverty of the natives. So many seemed to have sores or to limp heavily. The children that ran about seemed healthy and laughing, though, she consoled herself. She thought again of little Chi-chi as she saw the small babies in their mothers' arms. It would always give her a pang, she thought grimly. But perhaps the hurt would grow dim with years. . . . Would it?

She would take out the picture the prince had painted of Chi-chi, study it, and weep for him, his little warm arms about her neck, his cooing, his smiles when she entered the room. How he bounced with eagerness just as she bent to pick him up. How he enjoyed his toys, the singing, and the way Moon Blossom played her lute and the ch'in.

Katie turned twenty-two on the ship home in April 1819. So much had happened to her since she had turned eighteen, she thought. Temporarily she put from her the thoughts of the past and enjoyed the party that Rupert and Captain Potter put on for her as a surprise.

They ate on deck with the sailors serving them, then entertaining her—dancing to hornpipes and other sailors' dances, singing songs and performing comic turns. They laughed at one sailor until their sides ached; he was a natural comic with a rubbery face which he pulled as he told about his imaginary adventures in a port.

It was a warm night, and on deck the torches flared against the purple sky. The stars had all come out in glorious silver abandon, filling the tropical sky, and the moon was brilliant in its light. Not a cloud hid even a small star.

After the party Rupert and Katie leaned on the rail and talked until past midnight. They had so much to say, it seemed. He told her about his mother and her illness, that she had been frail since the word of Terence's death.

His father was very pleased with the shipments, and the store he ran had done very good business. They would be eager to have this load, he declared, beaming. "I'll be very particular who is allowed to buy your designs, Katie!" he said.

He spoke of the servants. "Several of the Irish maids have left us," he said with a frown. "I was amazed when Mother told me. They gave little reason. She offered more wages; they refused. She has had a time hiring more."

"Oh, I am sorry to hear it," said Katie, surprised. "What went wrong?"

"We have no idea. Mrs. Garrison was angry and tried to blame Selina for being too particular. Father refused to become involved; he stamped off to the warehouse."

Katie bit back her own words. She must wait until she arrived home to see what the situation was before she commented. But there was Selina again, souring all. She would not be surprised if the maids had left because Selina was difficult and capricious.

"Milbank surprised me also," said Rupert, after a pause in which he seemed to expect a comment from her.

"Oh, really? How is she?"

"I have no idea. After we arrived home, she went right to Mother and asked for a character. Mother said, 'Why not ask Selina?' and Milbank stuttered something. Mother felt sorry for her, she seemed so upset, so gave her the character and also the name of a friend of hers. The woman's daughter had married and set up housekeeping, and Mother thought Milbank might suit, she was so experienced and quiet. She did get on there. But Selina was furious, raved that Milbank had gone behind her back. It was rather unpleasant," said Rupert thoughtfully. "The daughter removed to the country home and had a child. Mother heard Milbank was doing well, but we have seen nothing of her. Can't help thinking she would miss London and all the balls and such. She always went to them with Selina to chaperon her."

As Rupert spoke, Milbank's words came back to Katie, dimly remembered and barely comprehended in the mists of fever. "It is wicked! It is wicked, Miss Selina!"

Selina had threatened her. What was it? Something about leaving her in Macao, leaving her when they sailed on the *China Princess*. And there was the time that Milbank had whispered that she had wished to help nurse Terence. And Selina had come out in the hallway and asked them what they were talking about.

Rupert was still speaking "Selina has had a succession of maids since then; I think she missed Milbank like fury. The woman was older and responsible and very good with hair, said Mother. Selina said she wasn't that good, and she could train any maid to take care of her."

Katie did not answer. She gazed out over the rolling dark waves with their white caps.

"You know, Katie," Rupert added gently, "When we get home, we will all be living together. It will be difficult if you don't get along with Selina. She is Terence's widow and lives in their apartments, and it is very lonely for her. I could wish she would remarry, but she doesn't seem to fancy any one fellow for long; she says they don't measure up to Terence or to me."

Katie stirred. "I don't think I wish to discuss Selina," she said, forcing herself to sound dispassionate. "When I get home, I will see if she has changed her nature and is kind and loving and gentle. However, I have little hope for that; she never cared for anyone but herself."

He groaned. "A woman will make up her mind and never change it! And I thought women always changed their minds." He tried to tease her into good humor.

"It is my experience," said Katie gravely, "that women have one nature all their lives. I think they do not change it, Rupert. I have known more women now than I had in my sheltered life before. Your mother is always good and firm, doing her duty, putting her husband first and the sons second and everyone else after that. I know she will be that way all her life and never vary or be anything but considerate and fair to everyone in her household. The princess Chen Meiling was cold and selfish and cruel, and no matter how wealthy she became, or how many honors she had, or how nice people were to her, she thought only of herself and her pride. She was quite incapable of being loving and good."

Rupert listened in troubled silence.

Katie finally went on, groping for her thoughts. "And Moon Blossom is a good fine girl. She was ignored and made little of, but she persisted in doing her duty, enjoying her music, doing what little things she could for others. And she blossomed out and learned how to read and write and so on, but her essential nature did not change. She is loving and giving, thinking of others, considerate. I am glad Prince Chen Yee will make her his wife; she will be very good to him and for him."

"And what of Katie?" said Rupert finally after a long pause in which they both gazed out to the rolling seas rather than look at each other. "What of Katie? I think she is not the quiet, demure girl I once knew, so soft of voice and passive. She seems to have gotten a stronger voice and a more passionate nature."

Katie thought about that seriously. "I think I have changed, but not in my true nature," she said with deliberation. "I always hungered for something; I did not know what it was. Now I know—I wanted to be appreciated for what I did. I was kept in seclusion, and I worked hard. I did not mind hard work, but I wanted to play also, to learn to dance well, and go to balls, and have pretty clothes and jewels. I wanted—I wanted love, Rupert. I wanted to be loved and to give love and to be admired for my good qualities and forgiven for my tempers."

He turned slowly and stared down at her. She had amazed even herself with her own outburst. "Katie, I did not realize," he said slowly. "I thought you preferred to remain with your father, to design, I think you said so. You liked drawing and sketching. Why, I remember how you glowed when we took you to the warehouse; it seemed a rare treat for you to see the trade goods."

"It was," said Katie bluntly. "It was one of the few times I was allowed out of the house!"

"Oh, Katie," he said in a low tone. He took her in his arms and held her against him. "Oh, Katie, if you had only said—"

"How could I? I was a clerk in your household," she said without bitterness. "Your father was so good to Father and me. And I—I was a child, without knowledge of the world. I did not know what I wanted or how to ask. I only know I gazed from my window to the world and thought I was not a part of that world, nor ever could be. My part seemed cut out for me, my father's assistant, and I adored him and followed him eagerly."

"And did not have the normal joys of childhood," said Rupert. "And did not have the growing up, the pleasures, the delights of balls and parties. I remember," he added, slowly, "at the wedding of Terence and Selina you were not even allowed to come down to dance! Oh, Katie, how selfish and thoughtless you must have thought us."

She shook her head but did not deny it in words. He had drawn her closer, the first she had been so close to him, and put his lips softly on her forehead. She remained still and quiet in his arms, wondering. He moved his lips down her soft cheek, chilled a little by the night winds stirring, and then down to her lips. Their lips clung together; he kissed her more deeply.

"Oh, Katie—" he whispered in a different tone. "Oh, my little Katie—"

He drew her with him down the little flight of stairs to the cabin floor and to the door of her cabin. He said, in a teasing, intimate tone, "Am I to be allowed to come in tonight, my wife?"

"You know you do not have to ask, Rupert," she said, thinking of Selina with her door locked against Terence.

They went inside, and Rupert shut the door. He helped her undress in the half-light from the porthole and then undressed himself. When he came to the bed, she welcomed him eagerly; it had been so long—

And she was curious, though she would never have told him. Would he make love like her prince, so passionately, because now she knew how to answer? Or would he be careful, loving, kind, because he had affection toward her, but not passion?

He moved into bed, and she lifted her arms. He sank down toward her. "Oh, my darling," he whispered, and began to kiss her eagerly, over her face, her bare throat, his hand seeking her full breasts. "Oh, so silky, so soft and adorable—"

His voice stopped—he was kissing her down to her breasts, drawing aside the muslin nightdress, holding a breast cupped in his palm as he kissed it softly. Her breasts had ached for a time after she had stopped feeding little Chi-chi, and now he seemed to take away the rest of the ache, with his full lips pulling at the nipple, kissing the round whiteness, fondling her passionately with his hands.

His naked body pressed against her limbs, and he pushed up the hem of the nightdress to feel her fully. He was roused to passion at once, and Katie feared he would rush at her and take her before she was ready. She misjudged him.

Rupert lingered over her body, drank at her lips, caressed her throat, her arms, her waist. He flung the nightdress onto the floor at some point in his caresses. His body rubbed against hers. He kept whispering to her of her beauty, her sweetness. It was not poetry, but in his coaxing, singing voice it seemed so. She remembered he was part Welsh, and though he had never showed this side of himself to her, she was delighted with his deep voiced murmuring to her.

"Adored, lovely flower. So warm and fragrant, like the lilacs in springtime. Oh, adored, lovely. Open your lips, let me drink of them—"

He kissed her mouth as though he were sucking life from her and were giving it to her again. Their tongues touched; he started, as though not expecting this caress. But she answered him eagerly; their tongues twined together, pressed, until they both were breathless. Then he moved lower on her body, kissing her all the way down to her feet and up again. Her hands reach over his back and chest, touching him, learning him all over again, after the long absence.

He moved his body on hers as she stroked her hands over his chest and down shyly to his thighs. She dared hold him and felt him swell in her hand. He squirmed with pleasure in her hold.

Rupert moved, then said in a groan, "I have to—oh, love—want you so much—so much—oh, love—"

He came to her then, and she opened wide for him, her rounded hips pressed down to the mattress by his. He pressed to her, came inside, groaned a moment with pleasure.

"It has been so long—so very long. How often I lay awake and thought of you—"

"Rupert, Rupert—" she whispered. "I love you—oh, I do love you—"

He jerked and moved in and out, quickly, more quickly, as she whispered to him. Her hands clutched hard at his shoulders; her breath caught in her throat. She moved her head on the pillow; her long hair fell loose from the soft coil of hair. He buried his head against her, his face in the fragrant tresses of hair, held tightly, high.

"Oh, darling Katie—darling—" He came in a great warm gush of ecstasy, and she felt the quivers in herself. She reacted to him strongly, and he managed to keep hold in her for several moments until they both lay back, gasping, clinging, wetly.

He fell asleep in her arms and slept deeply. She took longer to get to sleep, and her hand stroked his hair tenderly from his damp forehead. He was so dear, so sweet—

They continued to sleep together now and then. He was careful of her, gentle with her, passion overcoming him at times, but very considerate of her. He did not beg to come every night, but on the long voyage home they grew closer, with more understanding of each other.

She missed little Chi-chi dreadfully. Nights she wakened with a start, thinking she heard his voice calling to her. Or his little fretful cry when he had a fever or was too warm or too cold. She would waken, sit up, start to leave the bed only to realize she was on shipboard, and Chi-chi was far away in China. Never to see him again! Oh, it seemed unbearable at times. She would sit and rock herself, arms clenched about her body, striving to keep back the sobs.

She was sitting up so one night when Rupert stirred beside her. "My darling? Katie? What is it?" he asked gently. He sat up and put his arms about her.

"My son," she said. "My son! Oh, I miss Chi-Chi so much—how could I have left him?" She rocked back and forth, her fist against her mouth to hold back more anguished words.

"My dear love," he said gently. He held her against him, and his hand stroked her loose hair soothingly. His voice seemed deeper, more mature. "You did what was best for him, Katie. You must not reproach yourself. But you are a mother, and you will miss him. Do you not think I comprehend your anguish, the sacrifice you made?"

"Perhaps I should have stayed with him," she whispered. "I should have been stronger. I thought of myself—my homesickness, my strangeness—"

"I know, darling, I know," he assured her, and she thought he did comprehend her suffering, how torn she had felt. "Choices are so difficult at times. But Moon Blossom loves him; she will care for him. And his father adores him; one could see that. He will lack for nothing; he will have love surrounding him all his life."

Katie leaned her head on his breast and relaxed a little. "I feel so guilty, leaving him, my dearest son—"

"You must not feel so," said Rupert firmly. "You did what was right for both of you. He must have his inheritance and his birthright, remain in his land. And you must have yours, Katie. You belong in England; you are my wife; your home is with me. We belong to each other. And one day, Katie—"

He hesitated; she asked, "What, Rupert?"

In a low voice he continued, "One day I hope we will have a child, a son or a daughter, and you will find the empty place in your heart filled again. I shall delight in that, will you not also, Katie?"

"Oh, Rupert," she whispered, overcome. "I do wish this—I do. Our child—"

He kissed her forehead gravely, as though pledging himself forever. And she felt comforted and hopeful of their future together.

He showed his growing love for her in his thoughtfulness and understanding. But he also showed it by wishing to make her laugh and be happy. He brought her small interesting presents from trips ashore: a beautiful strange flower for her to sketch, the short branch of an unusual tree, ferns of odd shapes, a fringe of beading and cloth usually worn by native women.

He and the captain arranged for frequent evenings of entertainment by the sailors, who were only too happy to spend hours playing their hornpipes or fiddles, dancing away the hot summer nights of the tropics.

Days they strolled the decks, and Rupert spent many afternoons with her, pointing out the land-masses, the oddities of the sea, searching the horizon with telescope, telling her of his adventures in the army. And the captain would also talk of his times at sea.

So the long, lazy days of the hot tropics continued as they sailed. And the nights were warm and purple, studded with stars. Often, when they stopped to take on water Rupert would take Katie ashore and show her the wonders of Africa, as they traveled down one coast and up the other. He was careful with her, very cautious, always taking several armed sailors with them.

Katie was delighted at seeing all the marvels of this strange dark continent. In the fern jungles she stepped cautiously, fearing snakes but charmed with the monkeys. She loved the exotic bright birds and once caught a glimpse of a leopard in a tree when she stumbled into a clearing where some baboons sat eating bananas, tearing back the peelings as humans would.

Several times they came to ports which had small towns, and they walked among houses set on stilts, pigs and chickens running about among the children in the dirt. They bargained for bright lengths of cloth such as the women wore and fine carved wooden boxes made of mahogany. Katie tried to talk to the women in sign language, but they giggled and ducked their heads, and some of them ran away on their long, graceful dark legs.

They stopped briefly at Dakar and went cautiously into town in a hired carriage, and Katie hid her face behind a bonnet and veil against the stern looks of the Muslims there. Rupert piled the carriage full of fresh fruits and coconuts, some ivory necklaces and boxes, even a huge long tusk of an elephant, perfectly smooth and unmarred. Men ran up to the carriage, seeing a foreign man buying, and bargained briskly to sell more fruit and jewelry, grinning with betel-stained teeth when the white man gave them silver and copper coins.

Women came up shyly, holding out henna-stained palms and fingers, showing locally woven cloth goods with strange designs in black, white, gray, and cream. Katie begged Rupert for some, eagerly, wanting to study the design more closely, and he bought as many as she wanted. More women came up to the carriage in their long gray robes with only their eyes and hands showing, to hold up handmade dolls of husks or wood and intricately carved toys. Katie wanted one of each, and she laughed ruefully at Rupert.

"You will be sorry I came with you! I am very extravagant!"

He smiled at her indulgently. "Mere toys, and costing but pennies. Buy what you wish, Katie. But what will you do with all these?"

She blushed but did not answer. It was obvious she was thinking about the children she hoped to bear in the future. He smiled and did not pursue the question. They drove back to the ship, leaving the crowds behind in the market.

Captain Potter met them at the dock. He laughed aloud when he saw their finds and sent sailors to collect the goods and take them aboard. "Well, Miss Katie, you'll have us fill the ship with your treasures!" he joked.

"I'm sorry, Captain! I do not mean to clutter your ship with all this. Would you rather I did not—"

"No, No! I do but jest! I am happy that shopping and all the riding about have brought the color to your pretty face! Lord, you do look a sight better than when you came aboard! I'll warrant you are about well. England will put the finishing touches on you, and then you'll finally have your health again."

"Thank you, Captain." She smiled, and for once the mention of her health did not sting.

They sailed on past the entrance to the Mediterranean Sea, which was beautifully blue and clear, and up the coast to Portugal. They took on water again, filling the casks with pure water from bright streams.

Ashore in Lisbon, Katie marveled at the blue and green porcelain tiles on the fronts of houses, in courtyards and on bubbling fountains. She and Rupert rode in a carriage much of the day, pausing to see the cathedral, the royal palace, the shops. Rupert bought more, recklessly, buying anything that Katie admired, until she was afraid to speak of liking anything: samples of tile; pretty dolls in Portuguese costume; cute objects made of cork; brilliant glass bottles of port wine.

Rupert only laughed and ordered a number of cases

of the famous port sent to the ship so his father could enjoy the wines also.

Once on shipboard they talked about the next ports. Rupert teased, "We shall sail into Paris and squander the rest of the money!"

Captain Potter laughed aloud, and Katie shook her head at them both. "I know that is not a port. I am not so stupid!" she said firmly, though with a twinkle of joy in her brown eyes. "And what kind of wife would I be to persuade you to buy all of Paris for me?"

"Nevertheless, one day I shall take you to Paris," said Rupert softly. "I shall enjoy strolling with you along the beautiful boulevards and showing off my beautiful wife!"

26

The *China Princess* sailed up the Thames and dropped anchor at the wharf in front of the Llewellyn warehouses on a hot day in August 1819. Katie was leaning on the railing, watching eagerly as the ship pulled into the dock. Then she saw her father-in-law on the dock, Douglas Llewellyn, wildly waving his hat to her!

She screamed out to him, "Oh, Father—there you are! Hello—helloooo!"

His face was one big grin of delight. He waved his hat wildly. As soon as the gangplank was set down, he dashed up it to grab her and kiss her and hug her tightly in his big arms.

Katie was laughing and crying with happiness at his welcome. She clung to him, smelled the tobacco on his coat, felt the burly, fatherly arms about her.

"Oh, I'm so glad to be home, I'm so glad to be home," she said over and over.

Rupert came up to them, his face beaming, and his father turned to wring his hand tightly. "My children," said Douglas Llewellyn. "Home again, home again!"

"How is Mother?" Rupert asked at once.

His father's face shadowed. "She lies in bed much of the time. Her latest grief was that you also would not return home. How she will rejoice to see you!"

They went immediately to the house, leaving Captain Potter to attend to the formalities and to begin unloading the heavily laden *China Princess*. His nephew worked in the Llewellyn warehouses on the docks now. He hoped to go on the next voyage, Mr. Llewellyn said.

Katie was shocked at seeing Mrs. Matilda Llewellyn. Thin and gaunt, she was lying in her bed. When she did arise, it was to dress in rustling black satin or ghostly gray garments, emphasizing her grief. She seemed indifferent to the household. Mrs. Frances Garrison ran everything with only the interference of Selina to bother her.

Katie soon saw how matters ran. Selina rose at noon, ran her maids ragged attending to her, then sallied out to shop or pay calls. She returned at evening to command the foot of the table, to order people about, before changing to another more glamorous gown to go out at night for dinner or dancing.

When Rupert learned that Selina was running about much with a certain Lord Chester, he was horrified.

"Selina, that is Hal Varian! He is a well-known rake; he had a reputation long before he came into the title!" Rupert cried. "You must not be seen with him; it will ruin you!"

"Oh, Rupert," said Selina lightly. "What else could I do? You were gone so long; I missed you sadly. Nobody is so amusing and charming as you!"

Douglas Llewellyn looked with a stern reproach, while Selina pretended not to see him. He finally said, "Rupert's wife is home now, Selina; you cannot expect him to dance attendance upon you!"

"Of course, he must go with me to balls." Selina laughed. "If he does not wish Viscount Chester to attend me, he must come! And I adore his dancing; it is so grand!"

Rupert seemed torn, looking dubiously at Katie, sitting at her father-in-law's right hand instead of the foot of the table. That should have been her place in the absence of Matilda Llewellyn, but Selina kept it firmly.

"Of course, we will attend you when we can," said Katie quickly. "We shall go to balls with you and chaperon you. And since Rupert does not approve of Lord Chester, he may be able to find a more suitable beau for you."

"Good for you, Katie," said Douglas Llewellyn, patting her hand. "That's the thing. You shall all go and look after Selina. She is sadly misled by men, I think."

Selina displayed her fury for one moment only; then smiled prettily, her blue-violet eyes sparkling. "Thank you, Father, you are so considerate. But perhaps Katie will be bored; she does not dance so well, you know."

Douglas Llewellyn looked thoughtful. "Well, she must learn. And also learn to be hostess in Mother's place. We cannot expect to keep Selina forever. She is so attractive I think she will marry again."

"I will teach her, Father," offered Selina quickly. "Poor Katie was not brought up to know the niceties of society. I must teach her many things, such as table manners and how to act at tea parties and so on. After all, I was brought up correctly, and so it comes naturally to me! But dear Katie must learn it all, and it will take some time."

Both men looked approvingly at her, while Katie burned inside. "How very kind of you," she managed to say. "Shall we say, beginning tomorrow morning about ten o'clock?"

Selina kept her smile but looked a blue dagger at Katie. Both women knew that Selina never arose until past eleven, when she drank her hot chocolate and ordered her maid to arrange her hair. After that she went out to shop or pay calls. "An excellent time," said Selina blandly, and Katie knew she had no intention of teaching Katie anything but a lesson in how to lose Rupert.

Katie had a maid of her own, one Molly, a cheerful Irish girl who had been about to leave the household when Katie arrived. She gossiped cheerfully and constantly.

"Sure, I would have walked out the door and shaken the dust from me shoes," she confided, brushing Katie's long dark hair lovingly. "That Mrs. Selina, giving her orders, then changing them and changing them again! No pleasing her, and Mrs. Garrison fair distracted over it. Caused a commotion from the time she came home from China, she did, says as how she is used to good service and wanted us to bow to her. Mrs. Douglas put an end to that, she did, but with her lying in bed much of the time, she don't know half what goes on."

Katie thought for a time carefully. She talked to Mrs. Garrison and found the woman frank—and exasperated. "I cannot endure it much longer. I am tempted to return to Cornwall," said the good woman.

"Wait a bit. And let us talk to Mother," said Katie. "I think she is not so much sick in body as in mind and spirit. We must find a way to get her up and about and taking command of the household again. She is the only one who can control Selina."

"But how? She swears she is ill and frail, I know that. And if she arose from her bed and forced herself to work and died of it—oh, how horrible to contemplate." Mrs. Garrison turned quite pale.

"Pleasant work for one's loved ones, that does not kill," said Katie quietly. "But grief can kill if one does not overcome it and resolve to put it behind one and continue living as best one can."

So they went to Mrs. Llewellyn, lying in a black negligee on her lounge chair, her feet up.

"Dear Mother, how are you today?" asked Katie, sitting down beside her. She looked with concern at the worn face, the gray in her hair much more abundant than before Katie had left two and a half years ago.

"The same as always," said Mrs. Llewellyn wearily. "Dear Katie, how bright you look in that yellow gown. What a pretty odd gown. Is that from China?"

She picked fretfully at the silk gown in the shoulder closing and straight skirt. Katie nodded, "From China, Mother. Someday I must show you the magnificent silks and taffeta robes in my wardrobe. If only I could wear them about London, how people would stare!"

Mrs. Llewellyn sighed and sank back in her chair. Mrs. Garrison nodded at Katie as if to urge her on.

"But I came to ask your advice, Mother," said Katie, deciding on frankness. "You know I do not get along with Selina, but I do not wish to fuss openly. She keeps the foot of the table during your illness; she tries to get Rupert to attend her alone to balls and so on. And of course, I never learned to dance well."

Mrs. Llewellyn blinked at her, and more color came into her cheeks. "Of course, of course! Dance! Katie, you are young and slim, and I declare prettier than ever! Mrs. Garrison, we shall hire a dancing master!"

"A dancing master?" asked Katie hopefully. "What is that?"

"A man—unfortunately most of them are those French persons, but excellent in dancing—a man who teaches ladies to dance well, in the contra dances, polonaise, and even the waltz."

"The waltz, Mother?"

"Exactly. Selina knows it, and I am told she dances it beautifully. She made Rupert take lessons, so he knows. And of course, she makes him partner her. Yes, you shall learn the waltz and do it more beautifully than she does!" The gray head nodded firmly. "Good. Let me see—have him come mornings—"

"No, afternoons," said Mrs. Garrison quickly "We can arrange the ballroom, there is a piano there—and Mrs. Selina will not know! Say, from two to three o'clock. She will be sure to be out then."

The conspirators beamed at each other. "Then, Mother, I want to learn my manners," said Katie. "I want to learn how a table is properly set for luncheon and for dinners, how to gesture to the butler to remove the plates, how to see to the comfort of guests—"

"I shall teach you myself!" said Mrs. Llewellyn. "What else, Katie?" There was a new sparkle in her eyes; she looked younger and brighter already.

Katie thought, her finger on her lip. "Let me see—I shall need to meet more people. I scarcely know anybody in London."

Mrs. Llewellyn nodded. "Of course! I myself shall take you out in the carriage. I have dear friends in London, some in positions of influence. Let me see—I have not seen my friend Jane Harrison for some time, and Mrs. Wicks, and Lady Daphne—dear me, she sent me a note just the other day."

"If you are sure you feel well enough," said Katie gently.

"Oh, I shall rest mornings," said Matilda Llewellyn. "Dear me, I really must go out. It has been such a time—it is September, is it not? The season will be starting up soon, and Katie, you must be launched!"

In the next few weeks Katie felt as though she had been truly launched, a tremulous three-sailed vessel thrust out on the heavy seas of London society. With Matilda Llewellyn pushing, introducing her, and taking her everywhere during the day and Katie tagging on Rupert's coattails at every evening event, she began to get her sea legs quite quickly, even if she was a bit tired out by it all.

She had to give up some of her artwork, the designing she loved so much. Mornings she could still devote to that and to working with Rupert on new designs and supervising the sales of the precious silks and porcelains. Both were determined that prices should be high, and the showrooms of the goods were beautifully arranged with the materials. It took time and patience, for people were accustomed to the gaudy designs of the usual China trade porcelains and the heavier bright silks. But people became aware of the beauty of the delicate fragile silks, the lustrous fabrics. And next to the gaudy porcelains, the exquisite beauty of the good ones shone all the more.

The sales grew brisk, and finally most of the material was sold. Katie and Rupert had kept a set of two hundred pieces for themselves, with Douglas's approval. And they kept two tea sets, one in yellow primroses and the other in willow green.

And Rupert was lavish in keeping silk lengths for Katie. Selina was not consulted, to Katie's pleasure.

She knew she was being very jealous, but she did not want to see her silk designs on Selina's back.

All three of them went out often to dinners, balls, parties as the season progressed. In the carriage one evening Rupert said to Katie, with Selina listening in pretended indifference, "You have given Mother new life, I believe. She is so much brighter. How much she is improved since your return!"

"I am extremely fond of your mother, Rupert. She treats me just like a daughter. No one could have been kinder or more helpful. I love to go calling with her," said Katie demurely.

"Calling? She has been out much? I am delighted to hear it. No wonder she is brighter," said Rupert warmly.

At the home of Lady Daphne Tweed the footmen stood at the entrance and a red carpet covered the steps. Katie was handed out, then Selina, and then Rupert. Selina went on up the stairs, her head up proudly, flashing smiles left and right. Katie lingered a moment, pretending to fasten her bracelet more securely.

When they went up, it was some paces behind Selina. She had entered the upstairs ballroom when they were still on the stairs. Her name had already been called; she had entered alone and was standing beside Lord Chester, splendid in ivory satin suit and black waistcoat with gold and silver embroidery. But *he* was not looking at *her*, he was staring at Katie as she entered, her hand on Rupert's arm. The Chinese gold robe swung about her, the deep hem of mink just above her golden slippers with their small heels. She had removed her golden scarf—it hung from her fingers—and her opened coat revealed the golden gauze dress. Her jewels caught the candle's soft lights. Everyone began to turn and whisper.

Lady Daphne, splendid in purple velvet and amethysts, moved to meet her. "Dear Katie," she cooed, "how lovely to see you again! I am so glad to have you here. How is your dear mother? How much brighter she looks! I marveled at her the other day when you came to tea."

She bent from her lean height and pressed a lavender-scented kiss on Katie's cheek, a concession from this formidable woman; it was almost as good as an invitation to Almack's.

Katie smiled back. "Thank you, Lady Daphne. How beautiful your home is tonight. The lights shone from the windows, and it looked so warm and welcoming as we came along the street."

"Thank you, darling! And dear Rupert—" She gave him her hand to kiss, which he did gallantly. "You are sitting at my table tonight, you know! I must hear the latest about your designs, dearest Katie! You have promised me two lengths of your best silks from next year's ship, you know!"

"I shall not forget. I shall have designs to show you the next time Mother and I come. Or perhaps you could come to tea next week? I think Mother would like to have a select little group—"

Lady Daphne adored being part of a select little group. She glowed with pleasure, and they set a date for the following Tuesday. Then Rupert and Katie went on into the room, having taken up several minutes of the hostess and host's time. He was a silent man, much more at home in the outdoors, but anything Lady Daphne wanted he gave her, even though he suffered at balls.

Katie deliberately removed the long Chinese robe and handed it to an attendant footman. She turned about again to find herself surrounded by half a dozen men of all ages, beaux in brilliant scarlet, in deep blue, in gold, or gray.

Among them was Lord Chester, holding out his arm to her. "My dear lady, the first waltz is mine, I believe?" Behind him Selina was choking with rage, standing quite alone in the center of the floor as the waltz music struck up, the frail violins sounding gay in the suddenly quiet room.

"I am sorry, the first waltz always belongs to my husband," said Katie clearly, with a brilliant smile, turning to Rupert. She lifted her small face in appeal.

"Rupert!" commanded Selina loudly.

He did not seem to hear her. He gazed down at Katie and slowly put his arm about her. As the music swept along the shining floor, they began to waltz, turning and turning in beautiful patterns, the handsome, tall, dark-haired man, the smaller girl in the gilded dress, her jewels sparkling. The older people smiled with pleasure at the sight; the younger girls stared in envy; the men waited their turn to dance with her.

It was definitely Katie's night. Her program was scrawled full of names before three dances were over. She had to protest to save for Rupert the dances before and after the collation. Lord Chester was persistent in his attention, but Katie was cool to him, and in a huff he finally went off with a new girl who was rumored to be a very wealthy heiress.

Katie was next to her host during the collation and fascinated the company and the silent host with her stories of their journey around the African coasts.

Lord Tweed was brightened up considerably by her account of a walk in the jungle and questioned her eagerly about it.

"By Jove, I shall certainly go!" he said, glowing with pleasure. "I never heard such a thing! Houses on stilts, by Jove! Saw baboons, by Jove!"

After the dinner Rupert squeezed her arm. "Katie, you have bloomed beyond imagining! I am proud of you!"

"Thank you, my love," she said deliberately, smiling into his eyes. "I am so proud to be your wife, I want everyone to know how happy I am!"

In the carriage going home, Selina turned on Katie. "I have never seen such a display of country behavior!" she said furiously, her fan tapping on her hand. "To behave so—and flirt with everybody—"

Katie could not speak in her surprise. She knew that Selina had been sullenly furious that Katie had been the center of attention, but Selina had had her share of dances.

Rupert said quietly, "That will do, Selina! Katie has always behaved with perfect propriety," and his hand closed over Katie's hand protectively.

"Oh, has she? And when she ran off with that Chinese prince, I suppose that was also with perfect propriety!" cried Selina in pettish outrage. "If London knew how Katie had acted in Macao, and living two years with a heathen—her lover, no doubt—"

Katie caught her breath; her free hand went to her heart. Did Selina know, guess? And little Chi-chi—if people learned of that—Pain stabbed through her.

Rupert's hand was close and warm. "I wonder at you, Selina, daring to bring up that matter now," he said in a very chilly tone, "when one knows that it was you who took Katie to the home of the prince and dumped her on his doorstep—all because you were so fearful of catching the fever! I would not bring up that topic if I were you!"

Katie's heart almost stood still. Rupert believed her! He must be completely over his infatuation with Selina!

"Who told you such a silly tale?" cried Selina wildly, her violet eyes darting fearfully from one to the other. She was always sulky at having to sit with her back to the horses, and tonight Rupert had simply taken his place beside Katie as they entered the carriage. "Katie! Did you make up the story—to hide your indiscretions?"

"No, it was the truth," said Katie soberly.

"But you were unconscious!" said Selina. "And Milbank—" She stopped, realizing she was damning herself.

"She told you it was wicked," said Katie softly. "I remember that. Milbank kept saying how wicked it was to take me there—"

"She is a silly, foolish woman!" And Selina began to weep into her hands. She took on the high, girlish voice which meant she knew she was in the wrong and was meant to make Rupert sorry for her. "I thought I could trust her, but she turned on me. Everybody is jealous of me because I was—was born pretty! It has been a curse—just because men like me—"

Rupert said no more. Inside the house he turned to Selina and Katie. "Will you come into the study for a few minutes?" he said, and led the way to his father's study. His shoulders seemed wider, and he seemed older, thought Katie. His face was grave; his chin, stern.

In the study he did not sit down. He turned to them, his comprehensive look on Katie's anxious face and Selina's scared one.

But he spoke to Selina. "I regret that I must say this to you, Selina," he said. "However, it is for the best. I cannot continue to allow you to remain in this house. It would be best if you returned to your mother's home and protection."

She gasped at him, her coquettish expression fading. "Return—to Mother's? But it is a small, poor flat—"

"That is one opinion," he said dryly. "I believe it is popularly supposed to be large and luxurious. However, you will be comfortable there. Father and I believe that in time you will marry again, and I wish you well. However, we cannot continue to have you here; you cause too much dissension."

When Selina protested and began to wail, he sent her to her rooms. He ordered the maids next day to pack for her, and she was sent back to her mother. With relief his father supported him in the decision.

Rupert said to Katie in their own apartments, "I am sorry for her. She has always had her own way and so been spoiled. However, I cannot close my eyes to the fact that she causes trouble daily for Mother and for you. She must find her own destiny."

"I am very—relieved." Katie gulped. "She makes me feel—so inferior—at times—"

"My dearest Katie," he said tenderly. "You could never be inferior. Indeed, you are such a superior female that I wonder you condescended to marry me!"

At his smile she flew into his arms. "Oh, Rupert. You are so good, so kind—"

"No, I am selfish also," he said tenderly. "I cannot endure to see my lovely wife unhappy. She must be happy, she must smile on me, and then I am content." His kiss on her lips was so gentle she could have cried.

Instead, she smiled radiantly at him. Her round arms wound about his neck.

"Darling, I have some news—I think you will be more happy still, as I am!"

"What is it? Some new design—some new conquest in the London scene?" His Celtic blue eyes glowed on her. His arms were folded tenderly about her.

She shook her head. Confidently she put her hand on his cheek. "Darling, Rupert—I am to have your child! That is, I am fairly certain—it is but six weeks now—but I think so—"

As he did not speak at once, she gazed up anxiously at him. "Rupert, you are—not pleased?"

"Pleased?" he whispered. "Oh, Katie, I am overwhelmed! It is what I wished very much. For you as well as for me. I know how much you have mourned for your lost son, little Chi-chi. Can my child take his place?"

"Never take his place," she said steadily. "Can one child take the place of another? No. But our child will be loved, wanted, and adored, Rupert. I want your son, and more children, if God wills."

He bent and kissed her forehead tenderly. "My wise Katie! How happy I am!" And he began to glow, his face brightening and his eyes sparkling. "Our child! A son, to carry on one day! Or a lovely, bright, pretty daughter looking like her mother! How—how splendid! Our child—I say, won't Father be pleased? And Mother will be beside herself!"

And so they were.

* * *

Katie settled into her new life joyfully. There were times when she missed Chi-chi unbearably, but the baby growing within her more and more absorbed her thoughts and hopes.

Selina was out of their lives. She coquetted her way about London, but they rarely saw her.

Prince Chen Yee wrote to Katie twice that winter and each time sent miniatures of little Chi-chi for her to cherish, and she did. He told her that Moon Blossom had had a girl child and was a fond mother of Katie's son also.

Katie and Rupert had decided not to tell Rupert's parents about Chi-chi just yet. Not that they were ashamed—both of them had come to accept that their love was born out of unique circumstances—but they respected their elders' world view and knew it would be a hard reality for them to adjust to. Perhaps when their children-to-be had grown older, it would not seem such a shock.

Someday, thought Katie, I will return with Rupert to China to see Chi-chi again. The prince would permit that; he had a generous nature, and he knew she loved her son, the son they had created together.

Sometimes it seemed like a dream, now in London, in her new matronly state, expecting her second child. Rupert loved her, cherished her, and her love was returned in full measure. His parents loved her as their own daughter. Society welcomed her and her husband, and their business prospered also.

Yet—yet when Katie went to the warehouse and sniffed the sharp tang of spices and sandalwood, or when she looked at the miniature of her son in the privacy of her room, or when she fondled a bit of green jade—

Sometimes a dreamy look came into her eyes, and she drifted away from the stately London home, and for a little time, a few minutes only, he lived again the days and nights in the enchanting Court of the Flowering Peach.

THE WILD ONE

by
MARIANNE HARVEY
bestselling author of *The Dark Horseman*
and *The Proud Hunter*

Proud, beautiful Judith —raised by her stern
grandmother on the savage Cornish coast—
boldly abandoned herself to one man and sought
solace in the arms of another. But only one man
could tame her, could match her fiery spirit,
could fulfill the passionate promise of rapturous,
timeless love.

A Dell Book $2.95   (19207-2)

At your local bookstore or use this handy coupon for ordering:

Bestsellers

- **WHEN THE WIND BLOWS** by John Saul $3.25 (19857-7)
- **THY NEIGHBOR'S WIFE** by Gay Talese $3.95 (18689-7)
- **THE CRADLE WILL FALL**
  by Mary Higgins Clark $3.50 (11476-4)
- **RANDOM WINDS** by Belva Plain $3.50 (17158-X)
- **THE TRAITORS** by William Stuart Long $3.50 (18131-3)
- **BLOOD RED WIND** by Laurence Delaney ..$2.95 (10714-8)
- **LITTLE GLORIA . . . HAPPY AT LAST**
  by Barbara Goldsmith $3.50 (15109-0)
- **GYPSY FIRES** by Marianne Harvey $2.95 (12860-9)
- **NUMBER 1**
  by Billy Martin and Peter Golenbock $3.25 (16229-7)
- **FATHER'S DAYS** by Katherine Brady $2.95 (12475-1)
- **RIDE OUT THE STORM** by Aleen Malcolm ..$2.95 (17399-X)
- **A WOMAN OF TEXAS** by R.T. Stevens $2.95 (19555-1)
- **CHANGE OF HEART** by Sally Mandel $2.95 (11355-5)
- **THE WILD ONE** by Marianne Harvey $2.95 (19207-2)
- **THE PROUD HUNTER** by Marianne Harvey..$3.25 (17098-2)
- **SUFFER THE CHILDREN** by John Saul $2.95 (18293-X)
- **CRY FOR THE STRANGERS** by John Saul ..$2.95 (11870-0)
- **COMES THE BLIND FURY** by John Saul $2.75 (11428-4)
- **THE FLOWERS OF THE FIELD**
  by Sarah Harrison $3.50 (12584-7)

At your local bookstore or use this handy coupon for ordering:

Dell **DELL BOOKS**
P.O. BOX 1000, PINE BROOK, N.J. 07058

Please send me the books I have checked above. I am enclosing $_____
including 75¢ for the first book, 25¢ for each additional book up to $1.50 maximum
postage and handling charge.
Please send check or money order—no cash or C.O.D.'s. Please allow up to 8 weeks for
delivery.

Mr./Mrs._____

Address_____

City_____ State/Zip_____